THIS LITTLE WORLD

IMOGEN PARKER

CORGI BOOKS

TRANSWORLD PUBLISHERS
61–63 Uxbridge Road, London W5 5SA
A Random House Group Company
www.rbooks.co.uk

THIS LITTLE WORLD
A CORGI BOOK: 9780552151542

First publication in Great Britain
Corgi edition published 2009

The quotation from *The Art of the Novel* by Milan Kundera
is reproduced by kind permission of Faber and Faber Ltd.

A CIP catalogue record for this book
is available from the British Library.

Addresses for Random House Group Ltd companies outside the UK
can be found at: www.randomhouse.co.uk
The Random House Group Ltd Reg. No. 954009

The Random House Group Limited supports The Forest Stewardship
Council (FSC), the leading international forest certification organisation.
All our titles that are printed on Greenpeace approved FSC certified
paper carry the FSC logo. Our paper procurement policy can be
found at www.rbooks.co.uk/environment

Typeset in 11/12pt Janson by
Kestrel Data, Exeter, Devon.
Printed in the UK by
CPI Cox & Wyman, Reading, RG1 8EX.

2 4 6 8 10 9 7 5 3 1

In loving memory
of my consistently unpredictable father
John Parker
who always believed in me

This royal throne of kings, this sceptred isle,
This earth of majesty, this seat of Mars,
This other Eden, demi-paradise,
This fortress built by nature for herself
Against infection and the hand of war,
This happy breed of men, this little world,
This precious stone, set in the silver sea

William Shakespeare, *Richard II*

Principal characters

In Kingshaven

Michael Quinn, author of two novels published in the
sixties, now owner of The Bookshop on the Quay.
Father of Iris and Anthony by his former wife Sylvia,
and twins Bruno and Fiammetta Dearchild by his lover,
Claudia, who died tragically young.

Liliana King, ancient matriarch at the Palace Hotel.

Ruby Farmer, Liliana's friend since childhood, now in
permanent residence at the Palace.

Libby King, dutiful daughter of Liliana, and currently
manager of the Palace Hotel.

Eddie King, Libby's husband.

Christopher King, their eldest son.

Bertie and Archie, children of Christopher and his wife
Julia.

Sir James Allsop, recent heir to his family's ancestral
home the Castle.

Fiammetta Dearchild, his girlfriend, an artist.

Julia King, sister of James Allsop, just separated from her
husband, Christopher King.

Pearl Snow, Libby's scandal-prone sister.

Millicent Balls, landlady of the Ship Inn and Christopher King's long-term mistress.
Dr Ferry, Kingshaven's GP.

In the outside world

Iris Quinn, Michael Quinn's older daughter, who ran away from Kingshaven as a teenager, now living in self-imposed exile in Rome.
Anthony Quinn, a recently elected New Labour MP.
Bruno Dearchild, young chef at London's Compton Club.
Cat Brown, a recent graduate and bookshop assistant.
Esther Stone, granddaughter of publisher Roman Stone, and Cat's old schoolfriend.
Mr Patel, originally a refugee from Uganda, now millionaire owner of retail chain, Sunny Stores.
Sonny Patel, his older son, a property developer.
Nikhil Patel, his younger son, now a doctor and Bruno's friend since childhood.
Winston Allsop, one of Britain's most successful media entrepreneurs and once teenage soulmate of Iris Quinn.

THIS LITTLE WORLD

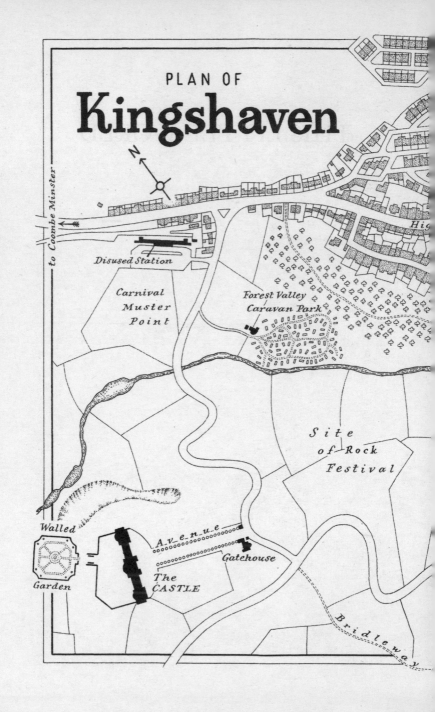

PLAN OF
Kingshaven

N

to Coombe Minster

Disused Station

Carnival Muster Point

Forest Valley Caravan Park

Hig

Site of Rock Festival

Walled Garden

A·v·e·n·u·e

Gatehouse

The CASTLE

Bridleway

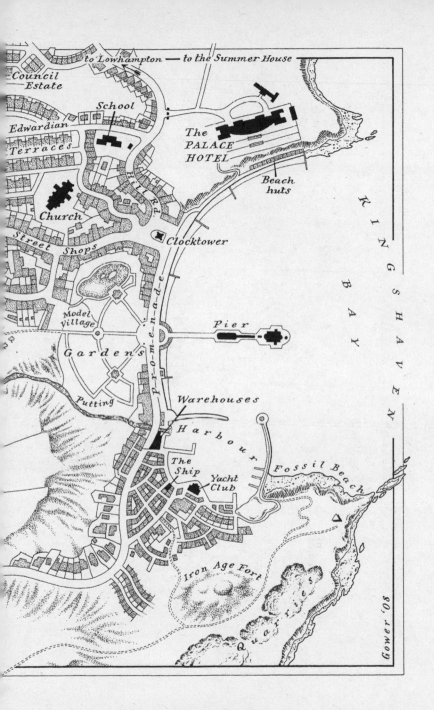

to Lowhampton — to the Summer House

Council Estate

Edwardian Terraces

School

The PALACE HOTEL

Beach huts

Church

Hill Rd.

Street Shops

Clocktower

Model Village

Gardens

Pier

Putting

Promenade

Warehouses

The Ship

Yacht Club

Harbour

Fossil Beach

Iron Age Fort

Quarries

KINGS HAVEN BAY

Gower, 80.

Prologue

February 1993

It was one of those beautiful English seaside days, with sparkling sunshine and a vivid, cloudless sky, the kind of day that made strangers smile at one another as their paths crossed on the promenade, or exchange a few friendly words – 'Nowhere better on a day like this!' – tilting their faces happily heavenwards, as if to thank a beneficent God for shining good fortune upon them.

It was the sort of day recorded on the picture postcards racked in the spinner outside the Beach Stores: a line of white surf separating the deep-blue sea from yellow sand; a couple of fishing boats in the harbour beyond adding bright splashes of red and green. It was still too early for the blur of small yachts that arrived with the summer, bobbing like a flock of seagulls on the surface, or for even the most intrepid of holidaymakers – 'foreigners' as they were known in Kingshaven – to brave the inky water.

February half-term was not a school holiday favoured by visitors, because of the generally poor weather conditions, but this year the faces of those who had elected to make the journey down beamed smiles of satisfaction as they watched their children exploring rock pools, until the cold began to seep up through the boulders they were sitting on into their bones, signalling time for a hot chocolate in the Expresso Café.

13

It was such a family that caught the attention of the photographer who was standing on the harbour wall. A confident, well-to-do middle-class family, the mother and father both in their early forties, her shoulder-length hair blowing round her face as she turned to say something, his hand reaching fondly for hers. Even from a distance of a hundred yards, an observer could tell that they were still interested in each other by the shape their bodies made. Some distance along the beach their three sons ambled – the oldest at that lanky stage between boy and man, the middle one a head shorter, still compact, and, between them, a small determined bundle of toddler exactly mimicking his brothers' actions as they stooped to pick up a ribbon of seaweed, or to skim a smooth oval stone across the flat, silver water. Silhouetted against the pale cliffs, in almost white winter sunshine, the three children were a shining triptych of boyhood, a radiant image of the innocent pleasures of seaside holidays.

It was the image that would link Kingshaven, briefly, with the rest of the world.

The lens of the camera stretched out like a telescope as the photographer zoomed in. The shutter clicked.

Now, the older boy was pointing at something, his brother leaning to get a closer look. Determined not to be left out, the toddler struggled up the bank of shingle. The photographer zoomed in closer, clearly able to see the redness of the little boy's nose and the concentration on his face as he reached a mittened hand towards the object.

'No!'

The photographer opened her mouth to shout, but the air was sucked from her throat as a cloud of darkness suddenly obliterated the sky, a thump of explosion ricocheting round the bay, and shingle rained down like torrential hail.

Through the cloud of dust, the photographer could just see three black shapes on the ground, two juddering, one very still. The parents were running now, their silhouettes all jagged and disharmonious.

*　　*　　*

The publication of Michael Quinn's collection of short stories entitled *Foreigners*, his first book for thirty years, had, as his publisher Roman Stone had warned, passed almost unnoticed, apart from one perceptive review in the *Financial Times*. There had been only brief mentions in the other papers; a particularly galling one in the *Guardian*, under the heading 'Angry Young Man Grows Middle-Aged in Middle England', compared the work unfavourably with his two novels published in the sixties. Although the excitable publicity girl at Portico Books assured Michael there was a lot of interest that she was actively chasing up, the only interview he had been offered so far was with the *Lowhampton Echo*, the newspaper group that owned and supplied editorial content for most of the free local papers along the South Coast, including Kingshaven's own *Chronicle*.

Michael was serving a customer in his second-hand bookshop, The Bookshop on the Quay, when the reporter arrived. He noticed him pick up a battered Wilbur Smith on the 10p table, read the back cover and put it down again. When the shop was empty, Michael put the 'Closed' sign up, showed him upstairs to the living room of the converted warehouse and made them both a cup of tea. The reporter's face was smooth, as if he had yet to start shaving, and his rather large teeth gave him the look of a schoolboy, but, somewhat to Michael's surprise, he had read the book.

'I'm wondering why you chose to set it in a "fictional",' the journalist raised both hands to indicate the intended quotation marks round his choice of word, 'South Coast town.'

Michael thought for a moment. 'There's something

about English seaside resorts that epitomizes the decline of Empire,' he offered.

The reporter started scribbling.

Encouraged, Michael tried to elaborate. 'There's the shabbiness of it all coupled with this misplaced pride . . . you know, every resort has to be best of something – Britain in Bloom Winner, the English Riviera, the Biggest Rollercoaster, Award-Winning Fish and Chips . . . Doesn't matter whether it's Scarborough or Bognor Regis, there's a kind of lingering nostalgia . . . I suppose there was a time when these places were the best in the world—'

'Until people saw the world . . . ?' the reporter interrupted, making Michael feel he had spoken for too long. 'You're originally from the North, but you've lived in Kingshaven since . . . ?'

'Nineteen fifty-two,' Michael replied.

'Are you still a "foreigner"?'

Michael laughed, but it was a slightly more penetrating question than he had been expecting. 'I think a writer is always, to a certain degree, an outsider,' he said, unwilling to get into the specifics of his life.

'The town in the stories is unnamed, but it's clearly somewhere very like Kingshaven . . .'

Michael said nothing.

'There's an intriguing piece about the discovery of an erotic Roman mosaic under the garden of a grand hotel . . . What was your inspiration for that?' asked the journalist.

'I rather liked the idea of a solid Victorian edifice with a seething sexual orgy in its foundations . . .'

'Just another metaphor, then?' the journalist said.

Michael said nothing.

'Several of the stories are set in the war and its after-math,' the journalist went on. 'Does that era particularly interest you?'

Michael winced at the word era, which made it sound

like ancient history, which, he supposed, to the young man, it was.

'I think the character of my generation, if it has one, was to a greater or lesser extent formed by the war,' he offered, standing up and looking out of the window.

It was a lovely day, one of those days when the air was so clear it almost looked blue. There were one or two weekenders strolling along the quay in sleeveless Puffa jackets. Across the water, standing up on the harbour wall, he was startled to see the petite, distinctive silhouette of his daughter Fiammetta. He'd heard she was back in Kingshaven, staying at the Castle, but seeing her unexpectedly, just the distance of the harbour away, seemed to underline their estrangement.

'Are any of the stories autobiographical?' the reporter asked.

Michael sighed. It was the question every writer was asked, sooner or later. He had recently read a sentence in Milan Kundera's *The Art of the Novel* which contained the perfect response. He turned away from the window to face the reporter.

'The novelist destroys the house of his life and uses the stones to build the house of his fiction,' he said.

As the reporter began to write it down, an ear-splitting bang rocked the whole building, as if it had been hit by a demolition ball, or a bomb, Michael thought, rushing to the window again. Fiammetta was still standing there, but beyond her billowed an enormous cloud of dust. For a moment there was silence, then the terrible sound of pebbles thrown up by the explosion falling back to earth.

For some reason, it made Michael think of *Chicken Licken*, which he had read often to his children when they were little.

'The sky is falling down,' he said.

But the reporter had already rushed out to investigate.

* * *

17

'What on earth was that?'

In the breakfast room of the Palace Hotel, Libby King, the proprietor, snapped down her newspaper.

'Sounded like a bomb,' said her husband, Eddie.

'Perhaps it's a landslip,' offered Christopher, Libby's oldest son.

'What possible reason could there be for a landslip?' demanded Liliana King, her ninety-three-year-old mother.

'Granny, they're naturally occurring events, they don't have to have a reason,' Christopher explained.

'I'm perfectly aware of that!' Liliana's fork clattered against her plate.

Libby wasn't sure if it was the slow, loud voice Christopher adopted these days when speaking to Liliana that had so upset her, or mention of the landslip. There were very few moments she could recall her mother flustered, but the landslip of 1956, in which Libby's sister Pearl had almost died, was certainly one of them.

'Landslip!'

Nine-year-old Archie tipped off his chair, dropping his napkin to the floor, and rushed to the French window to get a better view of the exciting event he had heard people talking about.

'There's a cloud of smoke on the beach on the other side of the harbour,' he reported.

'Perhaps it's a barbecue?' his older brother Bertie suggested.

'In February! At breakfast!' Archie screeched with derision. 'Can we go and see, Dad? Dad? Can we go and see?'

Her older grandson, Bertie, noticed Libby, was shaping into a handsome, thoughtful boy, even though he looked so disconcertingly like his mother, Julia, but the younger one, Archie, was beginning to display a few worrying tendencies.

Automatically, Christopher glanced at Libby.

One of the more irritating aspects of the breakdown

of her son's marriage to the boys' mother was his habit of checking with Libby before making any decision. There were only three years to go before her seventieth birthday and she'd had quite enough childrearing for one life, thank you very much. In any case, judging by her own children's complicated lives, she didn't think she'd been much good at it.

'Ring Adrian. See if he knows what's going on,' she advised.

Libby's second son, Adrian – her favourite, although she knew that these days parents were not supposed to have favourites – now lived at the Harbour End, in what had been, in more elegant times, the Yacht Club, where only a certain class of person had been permitted on to the terrace to sip Pimms and watch the regattas, a civilized tradition that, like so many others, had disappeared. Adrian had converted the upstairs room into a flat, and the cavernous boatroom below now housed racks of kayaks and windsurf boards, and a children's area called Jolly Roger's, which reeked of damp wetsuits and cheap hamburgers.

'Probably a bit of unexploded ordnance.' Eddie King was now standing at the window beside his grandson. 'Left over from the war,' he told Archie.

'On the beach?'

'Maybe it was washed up, or maybe it's been lurking there for years, waiting for its moment . . .' said Eddie in his salty sea-dog voice.

For some reason, Libby shivered, even though the room was quite warm with the unusually bright spring sunshine pouring in.

'I'm going to sit with Ruby,' said Liliana King, rising slowly but steadily to her feet.

Unlike her friend and companion Ruby Farmer, Liliana enjoyed a healthy appetite for someone her age, but Libby couldn't help noticing that her mother had left most of her bacon. For some reason, that only added to the insistent feeling of disquiet.

*   *   *

In the gatehouse at the bottom of the drive up to the Castle, where she had been living since her separation from her husband, Julia awoke from her doze with a start. There had been a bang and a rumble that sounded not unlike thunder, but now she thought she must have dreamt it because she could tell from the blade of light falling across the middle of the bed that it was a beautiful day. Without her sons, without a job, without a man, there wasn't much reason to get out of bed in the mornings. Julia pulled the coverlet up over her head and tried to go back to sleep, but however tightly she squeezed her eyelids shut she couldn't persuade her mind to drift away from the room with its extravagant, fussy furnishings.

Since the death of her father the previous year, the Castle, her family's ancestral home, had passed to Julia's brother James. When their father had still been alive, the house had been a hotel, designed and run by their stepmother, Sylvia. Now James, who came down most weekends with his girlfriend, was determined to rid the main building of all traces of Sylvia's influence, but the gatehouse, which had been the honeymoon suite, was still decorated in their stepmother's taste. The curtains were ivory silk damask with coral piping on the swags and tails, as was the canopy suspended over the headboard of the bed. There were heart motifs everywhere. Some were easy enough to get rid of – such as the heart-shaped coral silk scatter cushions Julia had stuffed in the cupboard, and the heart-shaped ashtray, which she'd put in a drawer with the hairdryer – but others, like the heart-shaped back of the padded dressing-table chair, would still suddenly manifest themselves as if to mock her.

Julia became aware of a distant and elusive wail magnifying so quickly she almost felt it was coming into the room. Jumping out of bed, she raced to the window just in time to see three police cars and two ambulances speeding past. There must be an emergency at the Harbour End. Was the bang she had heard earlier the flare going up for the lifeboat? It had sounded louder, more like an explosion. Julia leapt across to her bedside table and picked up her watch. It was after ten o'clock in the morning. Late enough for her boys to be out and about. Little drips of panic became a flood of fear.

She picked up the phone. 'It's Julia!' she said, glad that her mother-in-law, Libby, had answered, rather than her husband. 'I heard sirens. Do you know what's happening?'

'Adrian says there's been a bomb. Some boys were playing on the beach—'

'My boys?' Julia shrieked.

'No.'

'Where are they?'

'They're here,' Libby said crisply.

'Are you sure?'

'Quite sure.'

Now Julia felt foolish. The Kings were always insinuating that it was her erratic temperament as much as her husband's indiscretion that had led to the breakdown of their marriage, and now she'd given them further cause to dismiss her as hysterical.

'Could I just speak to Bertie?' she asked, but Libby King had already put down the phone.

*   *   *

Liliana King's best friend, Ruby Farmer, was fading like a single pink rose in a vase: once proud, pretty and perfumed, now her head was drooping and she was beginning to smell slightly. She'd fallen asleep in the middle of her breakfast, and there was a blob of scrambled egg on her nightgown. Liliana gently removed the fork from Ruby's hand, and gave it a stroke; then, repelled by the bruise-like colour of the veins, which stuck out like bones, she dropped her friend's hand back down on the bedspread.

'What are you going to wear today?' Liliana asked.

Ruby's eyes immediately opened.

It was important to keep up the normal routines. In Liliana's opinion, the helpers who came each morning to give Ruby a wash were far too casual with her. Of course, it was less work for them to pull a dressing gown over her nightie and plonk her in a chair for the day, but Liliana knew that if there was one thing guaranteed to perk Ruby up it was talk of clothes.

'I haven't worn the broderie-anglaise blouse for a while,' Ruby said. 'Is it pressed?'

It had certainly been a while since Ruby wore the broderie-anglaise blouse, Liliana estimated with a slight smirk: at least seventy years. She wondered why Ruby's brain – which Liliana imagined as an old, frayed bath sponge – had selected that particular garment.

The broderie-anglaise blouse had been one of the samples Ruby had most struggled with at the domestic science college she had attended in Lowhampton.

After the Great War and the epidemic of Spanish flu straight after, there was such a shortage of men that girls whose parents weren't wealthy enough to support them had been obliged to learn a trade. Ruby had made the journey to Lowhampton once a week for tailoring classes, but the cutting and sewing of garments had suited her better than the intricate white-on-white embroidery. When Ruby washed the finished article, she'd let the water get too hot and the stitches had shrunk, bunching up the scalloped neckline. How strange, Liliana thought, that a memory so old was still as bright and detailed as the finished garment had been. One of the unexpected benefits of Ruby's decline was her random recall of long-forgotten episodes, which returned both of them briefly to times gone by – happier times, mostly.

'I'm not sure the broderie anglaise would fit you any more,' said Liliana, glancing at her friend's sagging body. Instinctively, Liliana pulled her own tummy in as she stood up and walked stiffly across to Ruby's wardrobe. 'How about a nice blue cardigan with this pleated wool skirt? You don't want to get a draught on your legs.'

Ruby squinted across the room.

'Jaeger,' she said.

There were some faculties that appeared perfectly undiminished, like Ruby's ability to spot a label at fifty paces.

Liliana spread the clothes she selected at the foot of Ruby's bed, then picked up the breakfast tray, carried it across the room and put it on the floor outside the door for collection, then returned to the bedside to sit with her friend.

Ruby's wedding ring was still on her finger, in a deep groove the years had made. Liliana couldn't see how they'd ever get it off when she eventually died. Perhaps undertakers had their methods.

'Did you hear the bomb, Ruby?' Liliana asked.

'They're not going to drop a bomb on Kingshaven – they wouldn't dare!' said Ruby, opening one eye.

The word bomb had taken her back to the war and the senseless mantras that people had relied on to keep their spirits up. Even then, Liliana had found it ridiculously optimistic to believe that the Germans would flinch from bombing Kingshaven. It was luck and German incompetence rather than the deterrent of the town's resolve that had seen the many bombs rain down into the waters of the bay; only one was a direct hit, from a doodlebug, which had damaged the church and shattered a few windows, but caused no injury to the living.

'Apparently, a little boy is dead and two others are fighting for their lives,' Liliana informed her friend.

'Our boys will be all right, won't they?'

Another cheery wartime platitude.

Liliana gazed out of the window of Ruby's bedroom, at the wintry skeletons of trees on the land that stretched back from the hotel. The sky was a particular clear light blue.

'Won't they, Lil?'

The abbreviation of Liliana's name, which she had never encouraged because it sounded so common, brought Liliana's attention back to the bed.

'I'm sure they'll be fine,' Liliana replied, relieved to see her friend's eyelids closing again.

*   *   *

'Kingshaven? Didn't we go to Kingshaven once?' Cat's father asked, as they sat watching the news in the front room.

'Nineteen seventy-six. When we had the caravan,' said Cat's mother. 'We didn't stay. There was no water at the site. Would anyone like a cup of tea?'

Without waiting for a response, she got up and left the room to put the kettle on. It was the usual nightly ritual. Cat's parents would wait dutifully for the evening news, then almost before the headlines were read her mother would go to make the tea. If Cat ever went to help, she would find her mother wiping surfaces that were already spotless, or arranging a flower shape of Rich Tea finger biscuits on a plate, as if she was trying to keep a distance from the contagion of the outside world.

'There's never any good news, is there?' she would say.

In contrast, Cat's father always seemed to want to try to find a connection with events.

'Wasn't that where Torvill and Dean won their gold medal?' he had asked, when harrowing scenes from the siege of Sarajevo were relayed to their screen in suburban North Harrow.

'I expect you can see that from the M4,' he'd commented, when Windsor Castle was ablaze.

In the hall of the semi-detached house, the phone began to ring. Cat and her father continued to concentrate on the screen.

A reporter was standing in front of police tape on a dark and blustery beach.

'. . . It's a quiet spot, the sort of place you'd come to get away from it all, but that peacefulness was shattered this morning . . .'

The caption beneath him said 'Live from Kingshaven'.

'It was a pretty little place,' Cat's father was remembering.

Cat had no memory of it.

'But there was no water, so we moved on to the Chesil Beach.'

Chesil Beach was a name Cat did recall because the golden beach had stretched as far as the eye could see, with delicious blue sea on one side and a lagoon behind. But, close up, it had turned out to be pebbles not sand, and there had been red notices forbidding bathing, because of dangerous currents.

On the television screen, the reporter was now talking to an eyewitness, and then a photograph of three children silhouetted in the sunshine flashed up on the screen.

'Just this morning, they were playing on the beach. Now . . .'

Cat's mother put her head round the door, the telephone receiver in her hand. 'It's Esther Stone for you,' she said, with a frown. Cat's mother had never approved of Esther.

Cat leapt up. The last time she'd heard from Esther was a postcard from New York, where she was staying with one of her many relations on what she referred to as her 'world tour'.

25

By the time they'd got through catching up, the news was long over, and Cat never did find out what had happened to the boys on the beach.

* * *

News from England rarely made the Italian news bulletins, but the story of the *bambini inglesi* featured several times, not just on the day it happened, but also at the funeral of the toddler, and then again when the two surviving brothers left hospital on crutches. Italians adored children, but children died every day. Perhaps it was simply the photo that had lodged itself in the popular consciousness. The soft-focus, black-and-white image of children on a beach, apparently taken just before the explosion, appeared again and again, a portrait of innocence about to be lost that spoke to everyone, whatever their nationality.

Each time Iris heard the newsreaders struggling with the word 'Kingshaven' it felt almost as if the town where she had grown up was calling her back. She'd run away from Kingshaven as a rebellious teenager when her parents, Michael and Sylvia, split up, and she'd run away again as a young woman in her twenties, to seek a career for herself in London. Six years ago, she'd run away from London to start a new life in Italy, but it didn't seem as far away now as it had then.

Nobody took the train any more. There had been something magical about falling asleep in a chilly, dark couchette compartment, with the snowy Alps outside, then waking up and seeing the Mediterranean out of one window, palm trees and terracotta roofs out of the other, and feeling the soft, warm kiss of foreign heat on her skin.

Now, a cheap two-hour flight meant people could come for weekends, like Iris's friend Josie, who'd visited recently. It had been good to talk to someone in proper English, and yet the familiarity had been bittersweet, as Josie had relentlessly probed Iris's life choices, making her feel anxious about things she had not questioned, like what she was doing drifting along teaching English as a Foreign Language, and why she was in a relationship with a man half her age. Iris had always tried to keep the different areas of her life separate, but as she grew older it seemed to be increasingly difficult to stop one bit from running into another. Since Josie's visit, she hadn't been able to stop asking herself whether this life was really making her happy.

Sometimes Iris thought she should run away again and do something worthwhile, such as work for Amnesty International, or train to be a nurse. At nearly forty-three she was probably too old, she thought. Too old and way too bolshy. She wouldn't be able to tolerate doctors ordering her about. She wouldn't last five minutes.

Perhaps she should travel for a while – maybe go to India, learn yoga, as Josie advocated? Or perhaps America would suit her better now that the Democrats were back in power? What was to stop her getting a convertible and driving down Route 66, or whichever road it was, like in the film *Thelma and Louise*, except with a different ending? But, of course, she couldn't drive, thought Iris, and if she was Thelma who would be Louise? Her sister Fiammetta was now hooked up with James Allsop, of all people! Her brother Bruno was the best travelling companion, but he had a job in London now. Not Josie. With Josie's constant interrogation, anyone would want to drive straight over the edge of a canyon.

Was this what people called a mid-life crisis, Iris wondered, as she gathered up a pile of books to take to her next lesson.

Chapter One

Spring 1993

'I took that photograph!' said Fiammetta, pointing at the front page of the newspaper James was sitting up in bed reading.

'What?' James looked over the top of the paper with bleary eyes.

Strangely, Fiammetta didn't feel like repeating what she'd just said, some sixth sense telling her that she'd just created a problem by mentioning it.

'Nothing,' she said.

'You took this photograph?' he asked. 'And that one?' He pointed at the front page of the *Guardian* that was lying on top of the duvet.

'It's the same photo,' she said.

'And you syndicated it to all the newspapers?'

She couldn't be sure whether James's reaction was admiring or annoyed.

'I think the reporter must have done that,' she said.

'What reporter?'

Reporter was a dirty word in the Allsop household after the one who'd tricked James's sister Julia into revealing the intimate secrets of her marriage.

'I was down at the Harbour End when the bomb went off, and a reporter from the *Echo* rushed up and asked if he could borrow my camera.'

29

'Where's your camera now?'

'I suppose he still has it.' Fiammetta shrugged. In the scheme of things the whereabouts of her camera didn't seem very important.

'But it's your copyright. The money's due to you!'

'It's not really about money, is it?' she said, throwing back the covers and getting out of bed.

There were so many crocuses in the overgrown lawns at the back of the Castle that Fiammetta had to walk on tiptoe to avoid trampling their fragile purple flutes. The sun was up, but there was still a shallow fog of frost suspended over the town. Beyond, the sea was a pale iridescent blue. It looked so beautiful, it was difficult to believe that anything bad could happen here.

There was a faint whiff of chlorine round the empty turquoise basin of the swimming pool, but if she closed her eyes she could almost imagine the scent of lavender and roses. Even though the walled garden had been razed, she still felt at peace in this place, as if she had travelled back in time.

Fiammetta was distantly aware of her name being called from the house, and then James was bounding towards her, like an enthusiastic golden Labrador, with no thought for the crocuses.

'I'm sorry,' he said, putting his arms round her waist and resting his chin on the top of her head. She could feel his long lean body pressing against her back, and when she turned into his embrace he kissed her face and her hair, murmuring tenderly. 'Come back to bed.'

When they were together, when they were *really* together, skin on skin, flesh inside flesh, breathing each other's breath, it felt right. Yet as soon as there was any distance, even the distance of a bed, Fiammetta found herself looking at him and thinking *why?*

James was a businessman, with a crowd of loud friends in the City; she was an artist, a solitary person. This land and house had been passed down the male line of his aristocratic family for generations. Fiammetta was the illegitimate daughter of a bohemian couple who had squatted there in the sixties. The only thing they had in common was this place.

If someone had asked her to describe her idea of love, Fiammetta would have talked about trust, shared values and a feeling that you were in some way part of your lover, that you made each other better people. And yet she felt none of this with James, and she suspected that, if she confessed that to him, he wouldn't be bothered, but would probably say something like, 'You think too much!' Which is what her brother, Bruno, always used to tell her.

James was a man's man, driven by sport, money and sex, not necessarily in that order. Sometimes Fiammetta wondered how a family background that had left his sister Julia so insecure and eager to please had made James so self-confident and resilient, but then it occurred to her that the same upbringing had made her twin brother Bruno an extrovert and herself an introvert. Was it that women absorbed the damage, while men seemed somehow to repel it? But there were sensitive men with artistic souls. She had fallen in love with one, given herself totally in a way she could never give herself to James. Perhaps that was why she felt safe with him?

Fiammetta was suddenly aware that James was staring at her across the pillow.

'Marry me,' he said.

Fiammetta smiled, assuming he was joking.

'If you marry me, you can live here all the time!' he offered, as if he'd been reading her thoughts. He rolled on top of her again. 'Marry me?' he demanded, kissing her roughly.

She wanted to be kissed again, and again, so that all her thoughts were obliterated by physical sensation.

'Yes,' she murmured. 'Yes, yes, yes . . .'

* * *

Cat guessed immediately that Esther's house would be the bright pink one in the early Victorian terrace, and she had to suppress a familiar feeling of envy as she climbed the steps that led up to the front door. Esther's family, the Stones, were rich and stylish and it was entirely to be expected that they would buy Esther a *bijou* terraced house in Islington when she returned to London from her travels. Cat couldn't help wishing, as she had from the first time they met at Lady Collingburn School for Girls, that she came from an interesting family like Esther's, even though, as Esther always pointed out, her life was very complicated.

That Esther's parents were divorced was one of the first things Cat had learnt about her when they'd met as eleven-year-olds. There had been a competitive atmosphere in the cloakroom at Lady Collingburn School, with girls asking one another what they wanted to be when they grew up. Cat was one of two scholarship girls in her class. At her primary school, everyone had wanted to be a hairdresser. Here, one lofty individual called Miranda said film star, another called Chloë said fashion designer, and the one with unruly dark hair called Esther declared that she wanted to be a producer.

'What does a producer do?' Cat – Cathy, as she'd been then – had asked Esther, when they'd found themselves side by side in the line waiting outside their appointed classroom.

'Don't know really, but my dad's one,' Esther had told her, adding, 'My parents are divorced.'

Cat didn't know how she was supposed to react to that. 'I'm sorry,' she offered.

Esther laughed. 'It was absolutely ages ago! I've had one stepfather and stepboyfriend, if that's the right word, because Mum absolutely wasn't going to make the same mistake three times since then . . . And a stepmother, of course. And I've got seven brothers and sisters. It's all terribly civilized!'

Cat had immediately been in awe, not just for her great big family, but for the sophisticated way she talked.

'Here goes!' Esther whispered as the rest of the class fell silent as they filed in and the teacher told them they were to sit at the single desks in alphabetical order.

Catherine Brown was the fourth girl to be called and Cat went and stood by her desk. Esther followed, taking the fifth desk in the row at the back of the classroom.

'Name?' the teacher enquired.

'Esther Brown-Stone,' said Esther.

The teacher checked the register. 'I don't have a Brown Stone . . .'

'It's probably under Stone,' Esther told her. 'People always get it wrong. Brown is my mother's name and she is my legal guardian since the divorce. The irony is that she works for the Equal Opportunities Commission.'

The teacher looked at the register again. 'Very well,' she said, a little dubiously.

Cat was later to discover that Esther's mother's name wasn't Brown at all, and nor did she work in Equal Opportunities.

'It's the principle, though,' Esther had insisted hotly.

Cat was so thrilled that this naughty, funny girl had chosen to sit behind her she hadn't wanted to spoil it by asking, 'What principle, exactly?'

'Well, what do you think?' Esther asked, as she showed Cat round the house, which was still in the process of being converted from a basement flat and maisonette into one dwelling.

There were two empty rooms in the basement, the one at the front rather dark; the one at the back was a kitchen-diner with French windows out on to a tiny courtyard garden with terracotta pots containing the straggly remains of last summer's geraniums. There were two bedrooms on the upper floor of the house. The large room at the front had a huge bed with a white duvet and pillows, a clothes rail on wheels, and a floor strewn with underwear, empty wineglasses, blister packs of paracetamol and contraceptive pills. The back bedroom was empty. On the raised ground floor, two rooms had been knocked through to make one long room. The ugly seventies wallpaper had brush strokes of bright emulsion paint where Esther was trying to decide what colour looked best.

'It's fab,' said Cat.

'Can I offer you a drink?' said Esther archly, clearly enjoying playing hostess. 'There's white wine.'

'I'd love a glass of white wine,' said Cat, laughing.

'Make yourself at home,' Esther called as she rattled around in the kitchen in search of a corkscrew.

The living room was about as far from home as Cat could imagine. In fact, Cat's mother, Joyce, would probably be ill if she saw it. Their front room at home was determinedly colourless, the walls magnolia, the curtains and soft furnishings pinkish beige. A glass vase of ivory silk poppies stood on the occasional table in the bay window. The only other decorative element was her mother's collection of Lladro on the sideboard. Cat had always detested the pale, bleached-out colours and smooth, eyeless faces. At home, the floor was covered in a cream carpet that necessitated the removal of outdoor shoes in the hall; and if tea or coffee were offered, Joyce would stare as cup was raised to lip, alert for drops.

Esther's living room had a huge mirror in an ornate gold frame above the tiled fireplace, and a large sofa upholstered in black-and-white zebra-print fabric. The only other item of furniture was a wide-screen television. The stripped-wood floor was covered with magazines, unlabelled video tapes and shiny new hardback books courtesy of Esther's grandfather, Roman Stone, the publisher who had founded Portico Books after the war and steered its course all the way to the multi-million-pound international corporation it was now.

Cat was attracted by a cover that looked a bit like a 1950s railway poster of a seaside town, the title *Foreigners* written in large white letters. The blurb on the back announced it as a collection of short stories by the acclaimed writer Michael Quinn. Cat had never heard of him.

'He's some old bloke my grandfather used to publish yonks ago,' said Esther, putting a large glass of white wine down on the floor beside her. Instead of feeling lucky or privileged to have spent her life in the company of books and authors, Esther affected boredom with it all.

'Have you read it?' Cat wanted to know. Books had been the companions, saviours even, of her own life.

'Not personally, no,' said Esther. Then, seeing Cat's disapproving look, she added: 'Why don't you read it yourself if you're so bothered?'

It was such an absurd thing to say that they were suddenly both laughing.

'Shall we go out to eat?' Esther asked. 'There's lots of places round here. It's one of the advantages . . .'

Cat had been slightly surprised when Esther had invited her to supper, home economics never having been her friend's strongest subject. On Upper Street in Islington, they wavered outside Café Rouge, before choosing a new Italian restaurant.

Cat glanced at the price column before making her decision.

'Butternut-squash risotto,' she told the waiter.

'That's what I was thinking of having!' Esther exclaimed, as if Cat's choice had denied her the opportunity.

'It's really good,' the waiter affirmed.

'But it's probably about a thousand calories.' Esther sighed, pausing to allow one or other of them to contradict her. 'I suppose I'd better have the Chicken Caesar salad, with the dressing on the side,' she said, handing the menu back to the waiter. 'You're so lucky to be able to sit there stuffing risotto into your face all day,' she told Cat.

It was a typically unfair exaggeration, especially when the food had yet to arrive, but Cat was used to it. Even though they hadn't seen each other for several years, they had fallen instantly back to their old relationship. Sometimes Cat wondered if the combination of love and irritation they felt towards each other was what it was like to have a sibling, although they'd never been mistaken for sisters. Cat was tall and skinny. It wasn't that Esther was fat, but being quite short and curvy meant that extra pounds showed more. Esther's life had always been a rollercoaster of crash diets and failures of willpower.

Esther lit a cigarette. She still blew the smoke out of her nostrils as she had demonstrated when they were thirteen and had started meeting up regularly on Saturday mornings in the coffee shops of Swiss Cottage. Cat's parents hadn't liked the idea of her going all the way into London to meet her friend, but Swiss Cottage had a safe sound to it, and it was on a direct line from North Harrow, although the Continental ambience was as far from the suburbs as Switzerland itself. Cat had developed a liking for the strong, dark taste of proper coffee, having only tasted Nescafé before, but she had never really got the hang of smoking.

'Are you working?' Cat asked.

'Sort of. Dad got me a job at an independent television production company . . . Don't look so impressed, I'm only a gofer – do you know what that is?'

Cat shook her head.

'When my boss fancies sushi for lunch, I have to gofer it . . . No, really! Today I had to go for publicity stills from a photographer in Hackney, a bag of cat litter and a smoked-salmon-and-cream-cheese bagel. But I'm learning about the business. Dad says it's the only way.' Esther's father, Tim Stone, was something very high up in the BBC. 'What about you?' Esther asked.

'I'm working in Brook's,' Cat told her.

'The bookshop? I thought you were going to be a writer!'

Not for the first time, Cat regretted revealing her eleven-year-old ambition in the cloakroom of Lady Collingburn School. It was typical of Esther to have forgotten Cat's modified ambition to become a librarian, which had itself proved unachievable in the midst of recession at the beginning of the nineties when she graduated. A degree in English Literature was not an automatic passport to a career, but the bookshop where Cat had worked during her vacations had offered her a full-time job. The pay wasn't great, which meant having to live at home, but she enjoyed spending her days surrounded by books, sometimes making suggestions to customers who asked for her advice.

'You did the whole university *schtick*, but you still ended up with a crap job,' said Esther.

Esther had flunked out of her own degree in media studies after the first year, and set off with a backpack round the world. It was easier to drop out when you had siblings in Hong Kong, New York and Los Angeles, cousins in Paris, Cape Town and Sydney, even an eccentric aunt in Cuba, and could roam secure in the knowledge that you could return to a pink house in Islington.

'Actually, I don't think I could stand it if you were much more successful than me. I'm quite relieved,' Esther went on. 'Are you going out with anyone?' she demanded, with her usual directness.

'Not really,' Cat equivocated.

'What's that supposed to mean?'

What did it mean? Cat asked herself. Sometimes Roy

called. He had been her tutor at college. He was funny and brilliant and she'd believed all the stories about his marriage being over, gone along with his insistence on secrecy because of his job, been grateful for the hours they had managed to sneak together. It had all been a lie, but sometimes Cat still agreed to spend the weekend with him; sometimes she even believed him when, after a bottle of wine or two, in some anonymous conference-hotel room, he said that he would try to get a job in London, he would leave his wife, and they would find a flat together.

'I suppose it means no,' she told Esther.

'Good!' said Esther. 'Because I absolutely couldn't live with a couple. You are up for sharing with me, aren't you?' Suddenly she was the one sounding a little nervous. 'It has to be better than living at home, doesn't it?' she pressed, when Cat didn't immediately agree.

'But . . . have you asked your parents?' Cat heard herself sounding just like the awestruck eleven-year-old on the first day at Lady Collingburn.

'For heaven's sake! Inviting you was practically a condition of my getting the keys. You're my only friend they think is sensible,' Esther told her. 'Anyway, I can't possibly pay the bills on my own.'

*   *   *

Everyone at the Palace Hotel dated Ruby Farmer's sudden deterioration to the explosion that had cast a dark cloud over the whole town. When she kept asking about the boys, the Kings assumed that she was talking about her great-grandsons Bertie and Archie, so they were brought home from their boarding school for the weekend, and told to sit on either side of the bed, each holding a hand. When Ruby opened her eyes and found Bertie's concerned face only a foot or so away from hers, she screamed, making Archie almost wet himself trying to contain his laughter.

'Are the boys all right, Lil?' shouted Ruby.

'Perhaps she means the children on the beach?' suggested Christopher as they all trooped out again.

'My boy, Lil?' the renewed cry went up, not entirely muffled by the closing of the door.

'It's lucky that the hotel's out of operation,' Christopher remarked.

'Could Dr Ferry give her something to calm her down?' suggested Bertie.

'What a good idea!' said Liliana, wondering why no one had thought of it before. She smiled approvingly at her great-grandson. He was only twelve but he already seemed to have a great deal more sense than his own father did.

'Or perhaps a camomile tea?' Christopher suggested.

Dr Ferry had been Kingshaven's GP for twenty years but Liliana, who had always been blessed with good health, hadn't needed to see him for as long as she could remember. She was pleasantly surprised that his beard had gone grey, giving him a greater air of authority than when he had arrived in the town as a young man.

'Such a shame to see her like this,' she said, when he had administered a syringe of something that seemed to get a hold of Ruby almost immediately, shutting her up and driving the alarm from her features.

'Have you known each other a long time?' asked the doctor, eyes full of concern behind his pebble glasses.

'More than eighty years!' said Liliana, adding proudly: 'I will be ninety-three in two weeks' time!'

'I'd never have thought it,' said Dr Ferry.

It was what everyone said, but it somehow sounded truer coming from a medical person.

'Can I offer you tea, doctor?' Liliana asked.

The doctor glanced at his watch. 'Perhaps a quick cup,' he said.

'A sandwich, perhaps . . . or some shortbread?' Liliana offered, picking up the phone and dialling the number for room service, completely forgetting, in her bid to impress, that the hotel kitchen, like most of the main building, had been destroyed in the recent fire. She listened for a few seconds to a dead line before realizing her mistake and putting down the phone quickly.

'No one answers!' she said, with a brittle laugh, as if to imply that non-existent staff were somehow at fault, and hoping the doctor didn't know her well enough to notice the flush of embarrassment she could feel creeping over her face. 'Let me ring my daughter . . .'

'No, really!' said the doctor. 'I'd better be on my way. Better for my waistline, in any case!'

On the bed, Ruby Farmer issued a fart that was so loud and prolonged it was impossible to politely ignore. The doctor and Liliana exchanged sympathetic looks.

'It may be time to consider alternative arrangements . . .' said the doctor.

'Such as?' Liliana asked.

'Specialist nursing, residential care . . .'

'I couldn't put Ruby in a home,' said Liliana categorically. It was one of the vows they'd made each other. One of the many vows, Liliana thought, with slight bitterness, that she was now the one left having to keep. 'We promised each other, you see,' she told the doctor.

'It's easy to promise. Harder when you're the one doing the caring,' Dr Ferry remarked, picking Ruby's wrist off the bed to take her pulse.

How very understanding he was, thought Liliana.

'Something you should think about anyway . . .' he told her. As he shut his case, 'Now, I think she'll have a peaceful night. Make sure you call me if there are any problems at all,' he added reassuringly.

'You're very kind,' said Liliana.

'It's a pleasure to meet you again,' said the doctor, extending his hand.

He really was a most charming man, thought Liliana, feeling another blush suffusing her features, a decent, civilized sort of person.

'And there aren't a great many of them left in Kingshaven, are there?' she asked Ruby when he'd gone.

No response.

'The doctor was suggesting a nursing home,' Liliana said, in an attempt to shock her friend into consciousness.

Not a flicker.

Liliana stared at Ruby, trying to conjure up feelings of fondness and loyalty. They had been through so much together – marriage, children and two world wars – but Liliana could barely recognize the frail being that lay on the bed.

'I'd rather die than get like that,' both of them had declared cheerfully when they'd seen their peers descend into senility, like poor old Mr Makepeace wandering around the town in his pyjamas. But you never really believed it would happen to you. Human beings possessed the most remarkable capacity to imagine that they'd be the exception, that they'd be the ones to get away with it.

'Just get a gun and shoot me!' Liliana could almost hear Ruby saying it.

'Easier said than done,' Liliana told her friend now.

Perhaps a home was the only answer?

No.

Apart from anything else, thought Liliana, it might set a precedent.

*   *   *

'And how is poor Mrs Farmer?' Sylvia asked Julia, as they squeezed in beside each other on a low, squashy leather sofa in a crowded corner of a coffee shop, one of a proliferation

41

of similar establishments that had recently opened in the newly pedestrianized centre of Lowhampton.

Julia knew that her stepmother's concern was approximately as sincere as her own. Julia would never forgive Granny Ruby for encouraging her to marry Christopher King knowing full well that Christopher was in love with someone else, but, for the moment, she couldn't remember the reason for Sylvia's grudge. When Sylvia had married Julia's father, she seemed to remember Granny Ruby calling her a gold-digger, though at the time Sylvia Quinn had been a rich woman in her own right. Everyone hated Sylvia, except for Daddy. Daddy had loved Sylvia, and Sylvia had made him happy, and Julia had to keep reminding herself of that in her stepmother's company.

'I haven't really seen my grandmother since . . . the fire.' Julia found it easier to cite the fire rather than the irretrievable breakdown of her marriage as the reason for her moving out of the Palace Hotel. Both events had happened in quick succession.

'Oh, it must have been terrible,' Sylvia breathed. 'When I saw it on the telly, I thought, poor Julia!'

Julia wondered whether there was anyone who had *not* seen the bulletin that fateful evening with its dramatic pictures of the main part of the building collapsing in flames, and, behind the reporter, the unmistakable image of Christopher's mistress being carried down an extendable ladder in her lingerie. So humiliating, but at least people now realized what she'd had to put up with. Poor Julia indeed!

'Are they rebuilding the hotel?' Sylvia enquired. 'They'll never keep it going. That place is nothing without you.'

Julia felt a flutter of pleasure at the compliment, but though privately agreeing with Sylvia's assessment she felt it would be unseemly to admit it.

'The recession's supposed to be over,' she said, evenly. 'And the Kings are survivors. If I've learnt anything, I've learnt that.'

'What about your hospice?' asked Sylvia.

One of Julia's proudest achievements during her reign at the Palace Hotel had been the project to convert the Summer House at the far end of the Palace land, where she had spent her own childhood, into a hospice where terminally ill children could have a seaside holiday. The hospice had opened the very day of the fire, and closed almost immediately after as the Kings redirected the funding into the rebuilding of the hotel.

'I'm hoping to raise enough money to get alternative premises,' Julia told Sylvia, with more optimism than she felt. Now that she was just a nobody again, she'd carry no clout as a fundraiser. Whenever she thought about the hospice, Julia's eyes welled with tears, not just for those poor sick children, but because its closure seemed to symbolize the failure of her own life.

Once a week, Julia came to Lowhampton to talk to a therapist recommended by Sheila Silver, her friend who owned the Crystal Circle, but it only seemed to make her cry even more, and afterwards she always felt drained and had to wander round the shops for a while before she felt capable of driving home, which was how she'd bumped into Sylvia looking extremely businesslike in a slim navy trouser suit.

'What are you up to anyway?' Julia asked her stepmother, keen to change the subject.

'I'm working with Mr Patel,' Sylvia replied.

'Mr Patel?' Julia echoed, surprised.

Twenty years ago, Mr Patel had arrived with his family as refugees from Uganda, and had risen from taking over the Post Office on Kingshaven's High Street to owning a successful chain of 7/11 supermarkets called Sunny Stores.

'Such a kind man . . .' said Sylvia.

In her mind, Julia substituted the word 'rich' for 'kind'. Sylvia had never set much store by kindness.

'And so polite,' Sylvia went on. 'Mr Patel is more British than most people who like to think they are,' she said, with a look Julia couldn't quite read but instinctively felt referred to the Kings.

'What kind of work are you doing?' Julia asked politely. Although Sylvia was a resourceful woman, she couldn't picture her working in a supermarket.

'I don't think I'd be giving away any trade secrets if I said that Mr Patel has plans for expansion,' said Sylvia, importantly. 'Three out-of-town mega-stores already in the region and more in the pipeline. What's our most precious asset these days?' she suddenly asked.

Julia froze, afraid of offering the wrong answer. 'Health?' she ventured.

'Time!' said Sylvia. 'Time's our most precious asset.'

'Yes, of course!' said Julia, with a light laugh as if she'd thought that all along.

'Wouldn't it be marvellous if we could do all our shopping under one roof?' Sylvia swept on with her marketing pitch. 'That's where I come in . . .' She beckoned to Julia, as if to let her in on a confidence. 'Mr Patel asked me to design a signature range for Sunny Stores!'

'A signature range?'

'My first summer collection is about to go into his out-of-town flagship store. If that's successful we'll be rolling out the autumn collection across the other two.'

'Clothes?' Julia finally cottoned on.

'Marks & Spencer's sells food, so why shouldn't Sunny Stores sell fashions?' asked Sylvia. 'I'll send you an invitation to the launch, shall I?'

'Well, yes, that would be lovely,' said Julia, unable to think of an immediate excuse.

'Well,' said Sylvia, looking at her watch, 'I'd better be

on my way. Important to keep moving on,' she said, giving Julia another significant look.

'Quite!' said Julia, watching her stepmother strutting off down the street, suddenly feeling rather lonely without her.

Sylvia's words repeated in Julia's head as she wandered down the pedestrianized High Street, making her wonder why she didn't seem to be able to pick herself up and brush herself down like Sylvia had.

'Important to keep moving on.'

Perhaps Julia should move out of Kingshaven, move to Lowhampton? It wasn't so easy when you had children. As a child of an acrimonious divorce herself, Julia had spent her life on trains travelling from Mummy to Daddy, putting on a happy face at each destination, always trying to pretend that she preferred the one she was with to the other one. Julia couldn't bear the idea of her boys having to travel to see her in their school holidays, or, worse, thinking that the Palace was their only real home.

Julia stopped to look in the window of the travel agent's. The upcoming holidays were supposed to be Christopher's turn, but Christopher would hardly be able to object with the Palace in the state it was in and Granny Ruby not even recognizing the boys any more. Julia pictured herself lying in sunshine beside one of the large blue swimming pools displayed in the window, and the boys splashing and larking about in the water. A holiday was what they all needed, she decided. Things might become clearer, given a little distance.

* * *

Iris stood scanning the passengers as they came through the Arrivals gate. There were quite a few tourists, families with children blinking, bewildered, at the directions for the Metro and struggling to take off their jackets in the sudden change of temperature; more nuns than usual, probably because it was Easter, Iris thought. No one who looked remotely like Vic, who had called out of the blue to say he was coming to see her. She hadn't set eyes on him since leaving England six years before, and was beginning to think, as the surge of arrivals became a straggle, that perhaps he'd changed or she'd changed so much that they'd missed each other. Then she heard him calling out, but she recognized his voice before his face. She'd been looking at eye level. Nothing could have prepared her for the emaciated skeletal figure in a wheelchair being pushed by one of the airline staff.

Aids, Iris thought immediately. Why had he not told her?

'My nurse said he should come with me,' Vic said, trying to reassure her with a brittle joke. 'But I told him three's a crowd. Still, I thought we'd need a driver.'

He'd organized a chauffeur, whose name was Mauro, who pushed him to a black limousine parked illegally just outside the concourse. Vic was just strong enough to stand up and get into the car, while Mauro folded the wheelchair and put it with his suitcase in the capacious boot. The limousine had tinted windows and air-conditioning that made it so cold it was like getting into a fridge. Murmuring the theme tune to the *Godfather*, Vic played with all the buttons, making the windows go up and down, the fan go on and off.

'Champagne?' he asked, opening a little fridge as they drove into the city. 'Better than the number 38 bus, eh?'

He was exactly the same Vic, talking as if he'd seen her the day before, and yet the scenario was so different from anything Iris had imagined, her brain scrabbled to work out what to say, or what to do now that everything she had planned for his visit was redundant. Even though she knew it was completely the wrong emotion, her predominant feeling was crossness.

Trying to recall telephone conversations they'd had,

Iris knew she must have asked him how he was, and he must have told her he was fine. Why hadn't he told her the truth?

'Where's nice for lunch?' Vic asked.

Iris directed Mauro to the Trevi Fountain, where she had planned to take him on foot. The limousine could barely squeeze down the narrow streets and tourists had to squash into doorways. Iris took Vic's arm to help him over the cobbles to the trattoria. He was as frail and bony as a bird, but his grip was desperately strong.

'Just like Audrey Hepburn and Gregory Peck in *Roman Holiday*,' he said, pointing at the tourists by the fountain.

'If you throw in a coin, you'll come back to Rome,' Iris told him, then couldn't bear to look him in the eye, knowing that the superstition wasn't going to work for him.

Iris ordered a Negroni as an aperitif. With equal measures of gin, Campari and red vermouth, the first gulp was as close as she could get to mainlining alcohol.

'Why didn't you tell me?' she asked sharply, unable to contain herself any longer.

Vic shrugged. 'Didn't want you to think you had to come back to look after me,' he said.

'I would've.' It was only when Iris heard herself saying it that she realized, with relief, that it was true.

'I know you would've,' said Vic.

How could she be cross with him, thought Iris. They'd been mates since she was fourteen when he'd arrived in Kingshaven with a gang of Mods. She'd run away from Kingshaven on the back of his Lambretta and shared his council flat with him and his brother during the swinging sixties.

'The thing is,' Iris told him, more gently, 'my flat's in the roof. There are stairs . . .'

'No problem,' said Vic. 'Life is easy when you've got money. Course, it's better if you've got life too,' he added.

Iris spluttered with black laughter.

'I've got all the money in the world,' Vic told her, his loud, camp voice attracting curious glances. 'I could live the rest of my life – the rest of your life, even – at the Ritz if I wanted, and I'd still have more money tomorrow than I have today.'

Accustomed to living on an English teacher's salary, Iris found it quite difficult getting into the mindset of taking espresso at expensive pavement tables, ordering every single flavour of ice cream she'd ever fancied at Gioliti, buying a handbag from a street vendor and leaving him disappointed that she hadn't haggled over the price, or shopping for a Pucci silk top that cost what she earned in a month, then horrifying the snooty assistant by walking out on to the Via Condotti wearing it with jeans. But no amount of money could get Vic's wheelchair up to the Palatine to see the view, nor lift him on to the number 26 tram that trundled all the way round the city.

'You know what I'd really like to do?' Vic said, as they sat in a café on the Piazza di Spagna, gazing at the flower-decked Spanish Steps, but unable to climb them.

'What?' Iris asked.

'Do you remember the back wall of the Luna Caprese?' Vic asked her.

The Luna Caprese was the little Italian restaurant in Soho where Iris had worked as a waitress when she first arrived in London. On the back wall, there'd been a garish mural of the Bay of Naples.

The travel agent booked them into the most expensive hotel in Sorrento. The drive down was only a few hours. When they arrived, Mauro carried Vic into the cool marble reception like a pietà, and laid him on a vast leather chesterfield as Iris checked them in. When they opened the shutters of their suite on to a vast terrace, the view of the bay was so exactly like the mural on the back wall of the Luna Caprese, with Vesuvius looming darkly mauve in the background and the sea garishly turquoise, Iris felt like crying.

'See Naples and die!' said Vic brightly.

*   *   *

The taxi was waiting outside and Julia was all ready to go – suitcase, passports, tickets – when the postman arrived.

There was an official-looking envelope, franked with the Sunny Stores logo. Inside was a typed letter from Mr Patel, which Julia quickly scanned.

After a formal expression of sympathy regarding her separation, Mr Patel went on to say that he had been impressed with her charity work in recent years, and in particular the Summer House Hospice. The purpose of the letter was to enquire whether she might be interested in discussing ways in which Sunny Stores plc might make an ongoing contribution to further charitable endeavours. With a little leap of excitement, Julia put the heavy cream sheet of paper back in its envelope and stuffed it into her handbag to read properly on the plane.

'Good news?'

Sid Farthing had been the night porter and general factotum at the Palace Hotel, but was now driving a taxi, since there was no job for him after the fire. Julia was fizzing with the need to share Mr Patel's letter with someone, but she'd never really trusted Mr Farthing, who was a particular favourite of Granny Liliana's.

'Possibly,' she said, closing the door of the taxi.

Mr Farthing drove too fast, and she could feel him watching her in the rearview mirror, almost as if he knew she was slightly scared, and he was enjoying it. Julia decided not to give him the satisfaction of asking him to slow down.

The boys were waiting with their suitcases on the gravel drive, so she didn't have to get out of the cab.

'Mummy!' Archie shouted, throwing himself along the back seat to hug her.

'Have you been having a nice time?' Julia asked, as the taxi pulled away.

'Yes, thank you,' said Bertie politely.

Nearly twelve, and on the cusp of puberty, Bertie had grown tall in recent months, and Julia recognized the awkwardness that accompanies the beginning of adulthood.

'It was *boring*!' shouted Archie.

'Well, we're going to have a lovely time! Are you excited about going on a plane?' said Julia, putting her arm round both boys, who automatically snuggled against her chest. Buoyed up by their love, she stared defiantly in the rearview mirror at Mr Farthing, wishing he would keep his eyes on the road.

The swimming pool looked even better than it had in the brochure, cut into the sheer rock and with a perfect picture-postcard view of the bay of Naples, but it wasn't customary in Italy to heat the water. The waiter who brought a coffee to Julia's sunlounger seemed mystified as to why anyone would want to swim before the summer months.

The boys dived in and swore manfully that it wasn't a bit cold once you got used to it, but were very quickly out, with teeth chattering, demanding to know what they were going to do next.

'Let's go for a walk round the town,' Julia suggested.

The shops were rather disappointing. Instead of Gucci and Pucci, they found windows full of painted ceramics, musical boxes shaped like mandolins, and miniature bottles of the local liqueur, Limoncello. Julia bought the boys football shirts with the names of Italian national stars printed on the back and they went to check out the times of boat trips they might take. Then they sat outside an ice-cream parlour eating tiny scoops of twenty different flavours served in oversized brandy glasses, and shivering a little in the wind. She had expected Italy to be warmer. It was a steep climb back up to the hotel, and Archie said he was bored. A break in the sun with the chance to spend endless ages with her two darlings was beginning to feel more of a chore than staying at home.

Julia turned on the television in their room, hoping to find a movie or a football match, but there only seemed to be loud game shows, and when they went down to dinner Archie took one look at the gloriously kitsch dining room, with its marble palm trees supporting a baroquely frescoed ceiling, and said, loudly, 'Oh, no! Not proper food!'

'What do you mean, darling?' Julia's sweet smile begged indulgence from the nearby diners who'd looked round sharply. The inlaid marble floor seemed to magnify the noise.

'I want pizza,' said Archie. 'Not proper food.'

'Perhaps they will have pizza, darling,' Julia said quietly.

'Bet they won't,' the nine-year-old replied sulkily.

'We'll get pizza tomorrow. I saw several places in town.'

'I don't want pizza tomorrow, I want pizza now!'

Julia looked round the room for help, as if by wishing it enough she could conjure a pizza-bearing waiter, but instead, on the far side of the room right next to the window, she caught the eye of someone she thought she knew, and when Iris Quinn looked away quickly, Julia was even more certain that it was her. She waved and Iris waved back half-heartedly. Julia could see that Iris would prefer to be left alone with the man she was with, but if they were staying in the same hotel, one of them was now going to have to say hello at some stage.

'Small world!' Julia said brightly, approaching Iris's table with her boys behind her.

'Isn't it?' said Iris.

The man she was with was terribly thin.

'This is Vic,' Iris said.

Julia's brain made a rapid series of connections. Bruno had talked about Iris's gay friend Vic. Wait a minute, hadn't Vic been the boyfriend of Robbie Pluto? Julia looked at the emaciated figure. Aids. He was stretching out a bony hand for her to shake. Julia grasped it over-enthusiastically, determined to look absolutely cool about it.

'So pleased to meet you,' she said. 'These are my sons, Bertie and Archie.'

She was proud of Bertie following her lead, giving Archie no option but to shake Vic's hand too, even though she could see in his eyes that he was scared of this frail man with a head like a skull.

'We always like to eat with this view!' said Vic, exchanging a glance with Iris. They both giggled. It was obviously a private joke.

Outside, darkness was beginning to fall, the bright-blue sky fading to grey, the lights of the distant city twinkling weakly.

'It's beautiful, isn't it?' said Julia wistfully.

'Why don't you join us?' Vic suggested.

Julia could sense Iris's objection without looking at her face, but, selfishly, the prospect of talking to adults (especially someone who'd known Robbie Pluto!) after an afternoon of Archie was too attractive to turn down.

'Are you quite sure?' said Julia, pulling out a chair.

'What brings you to this part of the world?' Vic asked Julia.

'It's the boys' holidays,' she told him. 'Technically, it was their father's turn, but it's all rebuilding work, so I was granted leave to take them away on a suitably educational trip. Archie's doing the Romans at school . . .'

'We're going to Pompeii!' Archie suddenly perked up. 'There's real dead bodies. They got caught in the ash and died, just like that!'

'Some of us are not quite so keen on trailing round a dusty old ruin!' said Julia, feeling a little uncomfortable that he'd brought up the subject of mortality. 'I've never been very keen on all that mosaic stuff.'

'Me neither!' said Vic, pulling a face.

Even though he looked so ill, Vic seemed full of life.

'I'll take them tomorrow, if you like,' Iris volunteered. 'If you keep an eye on this one?'

'Don't worry,' Vic put his hand over Julia's and gave it a little squeeze, 'I am house-trained.'

Which made everyone at the table laugh.

*   *   *

After a few hours with Bertie and Archie, Iris realized that she'd escaped the background noise of fear that drummed in her head when she was with Vic, and the constant clatter of camp jokes that made her think he was trying to trick death by not letting it get a word in edgeways.

Despite their posh accents, Julia's boys were normal enough kids, not very bright, but perfectly happy charging up and down the raked seats of the amphitheatre while she read the guidebook. Since living in Rome she'd become interested in Ancient Roman civilization, although she found it curious to think that the vain and lazily beautiful young men she taught at the language school could have come from the same stock as soldiers who'd conquered most of the known world.

Bertie and Archie weren't very interested in anything apart from the casts of dead bodies that had been found in the ash. But when Iris pointed out the mosaic of a dog with *Cave canem* written underneath, they suddenly seemed to engage. At first, they didn't believe Iris when she said that the words meant 'Beware of the dog!' but when she showed them proof in the guidebook their behaviour changed subtly. Instead of wandering through the ruins looking at the ground, they were now taking in their surroundings, making the connection that these had been homes that real people with dogs had lived in, and their eyes lit up when Iris told them that the Circus Maximus was the Roman equivalent to a football stadium. Bertie began to regale her with long and detailed accounts of famous goals he had scored for the school team, which reminded Iris a lot of her half-brother Bruno's accounts at the same age. People said that girls were chatterboxes, but, in Iris's experience, if you got boys on to the subject of sport there was no stopping them.

'Which do you prefer, football or cricket?' she asked on the train back to Sorrento, trying to eke out the undemanding conversation for as long as possible before having to think about the evening ahead.

'Football in winter, cricket in summer,' said Bertie, his tone of voice suggesting it was a silly question, because you didn't actually have to choose between the two.

'What about football or rugby?' she asked.

'Archie prefers rugby, only because he's useless at football,' said Bertie.

'I'm not!' Archie protested, giving his older brother a not very friendly punch.

'Which do you prefer?' Bertie asked Iris politely.

'I don't know,' Iris said. 'My brother Bruno preferred football . . .'

'Is that the same as Chef Bruno?' Bertie asked.

She had forgotten that they must know Bruno. He'd worked at the Palace as a chef for a couple of years. And had an affair with their mother.

'Yes. Chef Bruno,' said Iris, smiling to herself.

'Chef Bruno actually taught us to play football,' Bertie told her.

'We're not supposed to talk about Chef Bruno,' Archie admonished him. 'Daddy says.'

'I like him anyway,' Bertie told Iris.

For a King, he was a most charming boy, Iris thought.

'So do I!' she said.

Vic and Julia had spent the day lying on sunloungers, wrapped up in blankets because of the chilly wind.

'A bit like *Death in Venice*,' Vic said. 'Without the adolescent pretty boy in a bathing costume, sadly, but you can't have it all.'

He was slurring his words and Iris wondered how much they'd had to drink while they gossiped. In the bar, she downed two Negronis before dinner to catch up.

As a treat because she hadn't seen them all day, Julia took the boys down into the town for a pizza, and so Iris and Vic were alone for dinner.

'Julia wanted to know all about Robbie,' Vic told her, making Iris feel as if she hadn't talked enough about his boyfriend.

'She was his biggest fan . . .' Vic went on. 'And she's been telling me all about her hospice for sick children, and now she's thinking about making a place by the sea for people with Aids too. I'm going to leave her some money.'

For a moment, Iris found herself wishing that Julia and the boys were there, so he couldn't be so mawkish. And then she reminded herself that he was dying, it wasn't self-indulgence. She ordered another bottle of red wine, the first having disappeared very quickly.

'Julia's going to get me some crystals,' Vic was saying. 'Apparently they have healing properties.'

'Honestly!' said Iris.

'It can't do any harm, can it?' Vic said.

Iris could hardly bear the hurt in his eyes. What was wrong with her? Why couldn't she be soothing, like Julia, and offer him hope? It was ridiculous to be jealous of a stupid Sloane Ranger spouting some half-baked, New Age gobbledegook and yet Julia seemed to be better at being a friend to Vic than Iris who'd known him thirty years.

'I think she's an angel!' said Vic.

'Oh, for God's sake!' said Iris.

'The whole point about angels is that they appear in human form,' Vic was saying. 'They don't have to have wings – that's what Julia says. Apparently, there are guardian angels all around us. She knows someone who can see them and give you a reading . . .'

Iris drained another glass, and another, as Vic droned on, his face swimming in and out of focus. Suddenly, she couldn't remember leaving the table, but they were in the lift going up to their suite. The moon made it look light outside. There was a silver path over the water. Iris sat down on a lounger on the terrace, then got up again. She needed more alcohol.

The piano lounge was even more kitschly ornate than the dining room, with huge chandeliers of multicoloured flowers, gilded rococo furniture, a ceiling painted with cherubs festooning ribbons. Iris spotted Julia sitting alone at a table on the other side of the dance floor. To turn round would be rude, to sit at another table even ruder.

'Safely tucked up?' asked Julia brightly.

Iris nodded.

'I expect you could do without me barging in on your holiday . . .' said Julia.

'Not at all,' Iris felt obliged to say.

'You must be terrified.'

The steam of crossness that had been building up in Iris's head all week suddenly seemed to condense just behind her eyes, and she had to look out of the window and stare at the moon's path on the water, the lights of Naples twinkling in the blackness. Terror was exactly what she felt. She'd been terrified ever since she set eyes on Vic. And now she was even more terrified that she was going to ruin this last time together with her crossness. And that made her even crosser, and it just seemed to be an inexorable cycle that could only have one ending.

'I'm sorry,' she said, blinking away a single tear. 'I'm sorry, I never cry.'

'Don't you? I cry all the time,' said Julia.

'But you seem so . . .' Iris searched for the right word, 'brave?' she tried.

'I've always been good at putting on a brave face,' said Julia.

'I've always been good at putting on a cross face,' said Iris.

The tension between them seemed to bubble away and suddenly they were both laughing.

'You and I have quite a lot in common, don't we?' Julia said.

Iris couldn't think of a single thing. Perhaps she was drunk?

'Sylvia!' she exclaimed suddenly. 'My mother. Your step-mother!'

'I saw Sylvia recently,' said Julia.

'Poor you!' said Iris.

Their laughter echoed round the lounge.

'When I was little, I always wished I had a big sister like you,' Julia confessed.

'Did you?' Iris was beginning to see why Vic liked Julia so much. She was guileless and refreshingly open.

'Bruno was always talking about you . . .' Julia blushed.

Another person they had in common.

'Was he?' Iris felt a little swell of pride.

'Are you with anyone?' Julia asked, pushing the intimacy a little further.

An image of Fabio, her young lover back in Rome, sprang to Iris's mind.

'Not really,' she said.

'Bruno always said that you should be with Winston,' Julia told her.

Once Iris's soulmate when she was growing up in Kingshaven, Winston Allsop was now an enormously successful businessman, who'd had a string of glamorous wives, each new one younger than the last.

'I'm far too old for Winston,' Iris scoffed. 'You're even too old for Winston!'

'The boys really enjoyed their day with you. You're very good with them,' said Julia. 'It's a pity you didn't have children yourself.'

Iris froze for a second. Then, 'I didn't want to make a child unhappy like I was,' she replied.

'My therapist says there are two reactions to broken families,' Julia told her. 'Some people like me spend their lives trying to repair the damage. They have children and try to make their lives perfect . . .'

'What about the others?' Iris wanted to know.

'Oh, they spend their lives running away from any situation that feels remotely like a family,' said Julia.

Normally Iris had no time for psychobabble, but Julia had uncannily struck a chord.

Now a tenor had joined the piano-player. He was singing the tune that had been used on that TV commercial. Iris could only think of the words as 'Just one Cornetto'. It was gloriously unreal, sitting in this camp room high up on a cliff, looking at the lights of a distant city twinkling like stars, being serenaded with Italian love songs.

'I did have a child,' Iris heard herself saying. Suddenly it seemed incredibly easy in this alien place to tell a secret to somebody she would probably never see again. 'People think the sixties was all about the Pill and liberal values, but women still got pregnant by accident, and being a single mother was still unacceptable then, especially if the father was in jail . . .' She looked at Julia, caught her disbelieving expression. 'You think I'm making it up? Sometimes I wonder myself.'

'But the baby . . . ?' Julia stuttered.

Iris was aware of Julia leaning across the table, taking her hand, the heavenly smell of her perfume, and suddenly Iris saw that there was something sticking out of her back: a pair of stiff white feathery wings . . .

Iris woke up, fully clothed, on the lounger on the terrace. It was chilly now but her clothes had stuck to her body with a clammy sweat and her head was pulsing with palpitations. She got to the bathroom only just in time to be horribly sick, and the next thing she knew she woke up again curled up on its cold tiled floor in the grey light of dawn.

The sweet smell of patisserie that was one of the things she loved about mornings in Italy drifted up from the kitchens, sending shudders of nausea through her body. She couldn't face breakfast. Couldn't face Julia. Inside her skull, her brain felt sore and swollen, almost feverish, unable to fit the pieces of her dream – if it was a dream – together, yet unable to stop them jumping to the forefront of her consciousness even when she lay down on her bed and closed her eyes.

Why now? Since that first night in the couchette all those years ago, she had always slept peacefully in Italy. Her past couldn't touch her here. Why had it come back to haunt her now when she was at her most vulnerable?

She woke up again to find Vic sitting next to the bed, watching over her.

'Suffering?' he asked, stroking a lock of her hair away from her face.

She smiled at him, quite liking the feeling of being the looked-after one for a moment.

'How much did I drink last night?'

'Most of three bottles . . .'

'Three? Jesus!'

'You were thirsty when you came in from Pompeii. You probably should have started with water instead of Negroni. Sorry,' he said.

'For what?' Iris asked him blearily.

'For dying on you,' said Vic, and for the first time she glimpsed the anguish behind the face he was putting on.

'Not your fault,' Iris said, clasping his hand hard,

determined to get a grip of herself. She couldn't spoil this time they had together. Mustn't.

'Julia's gone,' Vic told her.

'Gone?'

'She got a message from home that her grandmother's died.'

'Oh dear!' Iris tried to get the appropriate sympathy into her voice, but privately she was relieved. For the time being, her past had been forced into retreat, allowing her the chance to build up her defences again, enjoy a few last hedonistic days with Vic, before she had to think about what happened next.

*　　*　　*

Bruno was sitting at a table outside a pub on the corner of a square in central London waiting for his friend Nikhil Patel. They both wore white for work, he thought, as he spotted Nikhil across the crowded forecourt, but their jobs couldn't have been more different. He was sure that Nikhil wasn't supposed to wear his doctor's coat outside the hospital building, let alone the stethoscope that still hung round his neck. It wasn't that Nikhil was absent-minded; rather, that he was so focused on more important things it wouldn't have occurred to him to look in the mirror. Nikhil clearly wasn't aware of the glances he was attracting from the usual loud Friday evening crowd of office girls sitting in groups at the tables on the pavement and quaffing the pub's cheap, over-oaked Australian Chardonnay. It was funny seeing someone you knew really well in a different setting. Nikhil was really good-looking, Bruno realized with some surprise. With his sad dark eyes, he bore more than a passing resemblance to the guy who played Dr Zhivago in that movie they always showed on telly at Christmas. The moustache made him look older. Bruno was sure Nikhil didn't realize it was only gay men who wore moustaches these days.

'What can I get you?' Bruno asked, extending his hand to his old friend.

It was only since they'd lived in London that they'd adopted the practice of shaking hands when they met. It seemed oddly formal on this sunny evening, but Bruno wasn't about to publicly embrace a man with a moustache.

'Er, just some water,' said Nikhil.

'Fizzy?'

'Why not?' Nikhil said.

'Can't tempt you with something a little stronger. Lime cordial perhaps?' Bruno teased.

'Lime cordial?' Nikhil considered the suggestion. 'Yes, that would probably be refreshing, wouldn't it?'

It was the first warm evening of the year. Friday nights in the city were very different from Friday nights by the sea, Bruno thought, as he waited at the bar. In Kingshaven, a pint at the Ship meant cold cider and a waft of sea breeze drying the sweat tightly, saltily, on your skin. In London, no amount of draught lager could cool you down and the sweat remained like a fine coating of oil. The more you drank, the more it felt as if you were melting into the warm gloop of humid humanity. He took a long gulp of his second pint of lager before picking up both glasses and taking them out to their table.

Bruno had been working daytime shifts all week, which meant being at the market at five in the morning and rarely leaving the kitchen before six in the evening, exhausted.

'How long have you got?' asked Bruno, as he deposited Nikhil's pint of lime and soda water in front of him.

'About half an hour,' said Nikhil, checking his watch.

Bruno was a little disappointed. They'd finally managed to find a time when their schedules coincided, and he'd assumed that meant a couple of hours.

'I'm on call tonight,' Nikhil explained.

Nikhil was the only person Bruno knew who worked longer hours than he did, which seemed crazy because he knew how tired he got himself, and his job didn't involve responsibility like Nikhil's. The closest Bruno got to a life-or-death decision was being scrupulous about cleaning the surfaces that had had contact with raw poultry. Nikhil was working as a houseman in the A and E department of one of London's busiest hospitals.

'How can they expect you to make accurate diagnoses with no sleep?' Bruno asked.

'In the quieter periods, you can sometimes get your head down for an hour or two,' Nikhil said. 'Anyway, it's not long to go now.' He had always had an extraordinarily equable temperament.

'Do you know where you're going next?' Bruno asked, finishing his pint, impatient for another.

'I've applied for a registrar post in the oncology department at Lowhampton General.'

'You're going home?'

'It will be good to be near my father. He's quite lonely now . . .'

Nikhil's mother had died the previous year. The Patels had always been a very close-knit family.

'Oncology?' Bruno asked, not absolutely sure what branch of medicine that was.

'Cancer,' said Nikhil.

'Because of your mother?'

'It's always been a field that interests me,' said Nikhil evenly. 'What about you?' he asked. 'Do you ever think of going home?'

'Not really,' said Bruno. 'I'm head chef at the Compton Club now. The next step has to be my own restaurant. I'm hoping that won't be too long now that the economy's on the move again and people are looking to invest. It's got to be London – it's the only place to get reviewed, make a name for yourself.'

'So when can we expect to see your first Michelin star?' Nikhil poked gentle fun at Bruno's unashamed ambition.

'Not my style.' Bruno shook his head. 'I'm not interested in fancy linen napkins or waiters looking down their nose at you. I want people to come in hungry, go out happy. Rustic Italian cooking isn't going to get you recognition from Michelin, but it's what I'm good at. What I really want to do is get a pub like this and get all these people eating.' He waved his hands at the frontage of the quintessentially London pub with its Victorian embellishments and engraved-glass windows. 'Imagine how much nicer it would be on an evening like this to have the smell of garlic and rosemary wafting on to the street. I'd keep one half of the bar exactly the same as it is, but with better wine. I'd turn the other side into an open kitchen . . .'

Obligingly, Nikhil turned round to look, as if to watch Bruno's plans materialize before him.

'Yes,' he said. 'It's a very good idea.'

'It won't be the first gastropub,' Bruno said. 'There are a couple in the City and they're coining it in.'

There was a part of Bruno that wished Nikhil was the sort of person who would go home and pitch the idea to his father, Mr Patel, who could probably provide the investment Bruno needed from the change in his pocket. But he resisted the temptation to suggest it to him. Over the years, he'd been sickened to witness the way people had changed from ignoring Mr Patel when he was a simple shopkeeper to sucking up to him as his fortunes rose and he became one of the country's leading businessmen. He didn't want Nikhil to think he was trying to use him.

'How's Sonny getting on?' Bruno enquired. The last time he'd heard, Nikhil's older brother Sonny had been studying Architecture at university.

'He gave up his degree,' said Nikhil. 'It was a very long course. Seven years,' he added, as if to excuse him. 'He's helping my father with a property portfolio now.'

'Tell him to buy me a pub, if he finds one!' Bruno couldn't resist hinting.

'I will.' Nikhil took a gulp of his drink. 'Do you see Fiammetta much these days?' he asked, his brown eyes determinedly looking at something in the middle distance.

Nikhil had always held a candle for Bruno's twin sister. For a brief moment, Bruno wondered whether he shouldn't tell him about her engagement, because he didn't want to see the pain on his friend's face, but he knew that he had to. It would be unthinkable for Nikhil to hear the news from someone else. For a moment, Bruno was annoyed with his sister for impinging on his life. Her engagement was awkward enough because James was Bruno's boss. Now she'd put him in a situation with his best friend. Bruno couldn't understand how anyone could find Fiammetta remotely attractive. He didn't know what was going on in her head half the time, but some men appeared to find this irresistible, rather than plain weird.

'She's engaged to James Allsop,' Bruno said bluntly.

'Please send her my sincere good wishes,' Nikhil said, draining the last of his drink, leaving an oily slick of lime cordial at the bottom of the glass. He put it down carefully on the wooden slatted table.

'I will,' said Bruno.

It was an awkward moment. What Bruno wanted to say was, I'm really sorry, mate. With anyone else, he would have made a joke about there being no accounting for taste, but Nikhil was proud, and he didn't want to insult him. They both sat staring into the middle distance, and then Nikhil sighed and looked at his watch. 'Better be getting back.'

'Yeah. Why don't we try and have a game of squash next time?' Bruno asked.

'Good idea,' said Nikhil, but as Bruno watched him hurrying away, his white coat flapping, he wondered whether there would even be a next time. If Nikhil got the post in Lowhampton, as he was bound to, then the opportunity to meet up wouldn't arise without one or other of them making a big effort. They'd never had a great deal in common. Nikhil had always been the studious, conscientious one; Bruno, the one who winged it. Nikhil was shy; Bruno was confident. When they were growing up, it was sport that had played the major role in their friendship. Bruno had been captain of the football team; Nikhil a reliable defender; Nikhil had been captain of the cricket team; Bruno a creditable fast bowler. Nikhil usually beat him at tennis; Bruno, at athletics. Neither of them had time for sport now, and as Bruno finished his third pint of lager he wondered whether they even liked each other very much any more. Nikhil wasn't a judgemental person, but Bruno sometimes thought that his friend couldn't possibly approve of what he did. They both wore white to work, but Nikhil was a teetotal vegetarian who saved people's lives, whereas Bruno was a chef who stuffed the faces of the rich élite with unnecessary food and drink. Compared with Nikhil's, his job was embarrassingly shallow. Was it possible to be deeply shallow, Bruno asked himself, debating whether to have another pint. One of the office girls at the next table kept catching his eye, then looking away. It would be easy enough to hold her gaze, buy her a drink, take it from there. Too easy.

It was a bit early for his appointment in Islington, but he decided to make his way there and check out the area. The advertisement for the house share hadn't given much away, but the girl who'd answered the phone had sounded fun.

*   *   *

The third member of the household had to be a man, Esther declared, because otherwise it would all be far too menstrual.

The house in Islington was now more or less decorated. After sleeping in her childhood single bed ever since she returned home from university, Cat's new double divan felt gloriously roomy. She had chosen the back room upstairs for her bedroom and made curtains from a length of 1950s-style toile, with scenes from Paris sketched in blue on a cream background, that she'd found in a fabric shop near Brick Lane.

The man would have the dark bedroom in the basement. She and Esther had discussed the profile of the housemate they were looking for, with Esther favouring somebody boring who worked in IT and stayed in his room playing computer games.

'An axe murderer, in other words,' said Cat.

'God, I hadn't thought of that aspect,' said Esther seriously.

Because of the proximity to the City, most of the candidates who turned up were overgrown public school-boys in loud navy-blue pinstripe suits, bankers or lawyers, who took over the room as soon as they walked in.

'We can't have anyone who calls us "ladies",' said Esther, inventing new restrictions after every interview.

'Or "girls",' added Cat.

'No pets at all,' Esther said, after a well-mannered foreign-exchange dealer called Dirk seemed perfect until he asked if they would object to his snake.

'I thought he meant something else at first,' said Esther, giggling as she closed the door behind him. 'Either way, too weird.'

'Nobody who thinks they're funny,' said Cat, after the part-time stand-up's jokes became tedious within five minutes.

'No estate agents,' said Esther, after an eager young man in a cheap suit made the mistake of telling her that the value of the property would be enhanced by painting the exterior in a neutral colour.

'I only bought it because it's pink – so he's wrong on both counts.'

'Who's next?' Cat asked.

'A chef,' said Esther, looking at her list.

'Could be useful . . .' Cat suggested.

'Not as useful as a plumber or a carpenter,' said Esther. 'Why don't men do proper things these days?'

'Perhaps we should have put "practical skill required" in the ad?' Cat joked.

The chef was tall and slim and he was wearing clean jeans and a white T-shirt. His smile sparkled with an engaging blend of curiosity and confidence. Long, dark curls flopped over his large brown eyes. Determined to be unmoved by someone who was so clearly aware of his own good looks, Cat found herself wondering whether he tied his hair back when he was cooking. She could almost hear her mother's voice saying 'rather unhygienic'.

'This is Bruno,' said Esther, following him into the living room.

Her face was almost as bright a pink as the house, and her eyes contained an I-saw-him-first warning that Cat remembered from the days when they'd gone to joint school discos with the boys from Haberdashers' Aske's.

'I'll show you round, shall I?' Esther volunteered.

As the two of them toured the house, Cat could hear Esther laughing at everything he said.

When they returned to the living room, the chef sat down at one end of the zebra-print sofa, Esther at the other, leaving Cat to sit on the hard kitchen chair that had been designated for the interviewees.

'Bruno works at the Compton Club!' Esther told her. 'Which is weird, because I was thinking of joining.'

'What's the Compton Club?' Cat asked.

Esther's eyes rolled to the heavens. 'You know the Groucho? Well, it's like that, but cooler, more meejah!' she said, smiling conspiratorially at Bruno.

'Can I ask where you're living now?' said Cat, determined that one of them would pose the sensible questions.

'In a flat in Soho,' said Bruno. 'Unfortunately, the person I was subletting from died recently, so I'm having to move. Wouldn't otherwise. Love it there.'

'Does that mean you couldn't supply a reference?' asked Cat suspiciously, aware that Esther was glaring furiously at her.

'It's no problem to get one from my boss,' Bruno replied evenly.

'James Allsop,' said Esther knowingly, as if the name would mean something to Cat.

'Do you have a girlfriend?' Esther suddenly blurted.

'No one special at the moment. Are there rules about that?' Bruno gave her a slow smile.

Cat said 'Yes' and Esther 'No' simultaneously.

'It's just that neither of us particularly wants to live with a couple,' Cat was left to explain.

Esther nodded.

'Understood,' said Bruno.

'Is there anything you'd like to ask?' said Cat, sticking to the list of questions they'd agreed beforehand, although she was aware that Esther was determined to let the room to Bruno whatever he said.

'There is something that comes with me . . .'

A moment of anxiety flashed across Esther's adoring face, but Cat suspected that if Bruno had asked permission to bring a pet rat or a whole tank of reptiles she would happily agree.

'It's a range cooker,' said Bruno. 'It's pretty big, but I think it would fit in your kitchen if you took out what's there now. I'd cook you brunch on Sundays . . .'

'Deal!' said Esther immediately.

*   *   *

Liliana didn't know the exact moment that Ruby had ceased to be Ruby, but her own grieving for the loss of her best friend had been stretched over such a period of time it was already over before Ruby finally took leave of the world.

Now, as she listened to the young vicar's funeral address, Liliana couldn't honestly say that she felt anything at all except a vague kind of irritation. The callow young man hadn't met Ruby until almost the end, and his string of platitudes, chosen for their universality, failed to hit the mark.

No one who had known Ruby Farmer, even at her best, would truthfully have called her kind, thought Liliana. Which wasn't to say that she hadn't had many sterling qualities. Ruby had been a strong and surprising woman. Canny rather than intelligent, but it had been quite something in their day to run a business on her own for more than twenty-five years. The young vicar knew nothing of that.

Ruby's husband – Liliana couldn't for the life of her now remember if she'd ever known his Christian name because Ruby had always referred to him as Mr Farmer – had lost his life at Dunkerque. Whether the attempt to sail a leaky little dinghy across the Channel had been an act of bravery or foolhardiness, there was no doubting his desire to serve having missed out in the First World War because of a defective heart valve.

Was it Bill? Liliana wondered, or Will? She seemed to think there was 'ill' in it somewhere.

Widowed at just forty, and with a young child in tow, most women of their generation would have gone to pieces, but Ruby had soldiered on, getting to grips with double-entry bookkeeping, clothing coupons, all the new regulations, as well as volunteering as an air-raid warden and learning to drive. Whereas Mr Farmer had always looked a touch uncomfortable in the draper's shop, implicitly acknowledging that shopkeeping wasn't quite a proper profession for a man, Ruby had been in her element.

When Kingshaven's only bomb shattered most of the shop windows on the High Street, Ruby had jumped at the chance to get new lettering engraved on the replacement glass and 'Farmer's Gentlemen's Outfitters' became 'Farmer's Famously First for Fashion'. Some people had thought it disrespectful.

The young vicar was now claiming that Ruby's family meant more to her than anything. The absence of her daughter, Jennifer, at the funeral should have given him a clue. There were those who thought that Ruby should have learnt a lesson from the failure of her daughter's marriage, and not been so very keen to push her granddaughter at the town's most eligible bachelor. Liliana cast a glance across to the Allsop pew. Julia was wearing a hat with a rather showy veil that Ruby would have approved of. Underneath the lace mantilla, her big blue eyes shone with a look of wronged self-pity that seemed to have become her natural expression.

The trouble was, thought Liliana, girls had such different expectations nowadays. When she and Ruby had been young women, you took what you could get. Love was the icing on the cake, not one of the necessary ingredients. In their day, he was the flour, you were the eggs, a bit of sugar helped leave a nice taste in the mouth, fruit and a judicious measure of alcohol made it last longer. Liliana found herself smiling at the metaphor.

'. . . One thing we can be sure of is that Ruby leaves us all with happy memories,' the vicar concluded, smiling back at her.

The impertinence of it! Liliana turned her face to steel.

Apart from the plots owned by the town's two principal families, the Kings and the Allsops, there had been no new interments in the churchyard for many years.

It had fallen to Liliana to prevail on the authorities to

grant permission to open the grave of Mr Farmer – what was his first name? Maddeningly, the undertaker must have removed the stone so that Ruby's name could be added.

As Liliana watched the coffin being lowered into the trench, she suddenly recalled Ruby's girlish voice, as clear as a bell, asking in astonishment: 'The man lies on top of the woman?'

They couldn't have been more than ten years old, but living in a hotel Liliana had known about these things.

'Well, animals do it standing up,' Ruby had informed her. Living on a farm, Ruby had seen those things. 'I don't want any man lying on top of me!' she'd added indignantly.

Now Liliana was aware that everyone was staring at her. Julia, James, even her grandson Christopher. Had she laughed out loud?

*　　*　　*

There was a general feeling in the Kings' private lounge that almost everyone would rather be somewhere else. It wasn't a very big gathering, as Ruby had survived most of her own generation. Julia's brother, James, was standing over by the buffet table talking to his old friend Edwin King. Julia's own boys, Bertie and Archie, were the only children present. They looked rather angelic in their suits with their hair parted and combed, Julia thought, but it was a pity that they'd been called back from their holiday in Italy just when they were beginning to enjoy themselves.

Libby King was making small talk with the young vicar, who kept surreptitiously checking his watch. Eddie was talking boats with his son Adrian. Everyone was speaking in quiet, respectful tones, interrupted by occasional hearty bursts of laughter from Granny Liliana, on her second large glass of gin and Dubonnet, and the GP, Dr Ferry, who was on at least his fifth sausage roll. There was a pale shard of

71

flaky pastry clinging to his beard; another stuck like a tiny piece of litter to the grey hedge of his moustache.

Julia wasn't sure whether she was imagining it or whether it was the case that, every time she tried to move towards joining a conversation, the parties shifted the angle of their shoulders subtly to deny her access. It felt as though everyone was deliberately not looking at her. She'd chosen to wear black patent-leather heels because they looked good with her black suit, but now she almost wished she'd stuck to the flatties she used to wear so that she didn't appear a giant beside her husband. The only other person in the room not engaged with someone else was Christopher, who was standing awkwardly beside the table of refreshments, intermittently trying to get involved by picking up a plate of sandwiches and walking round the room with the enthusiasm of a badly paid waiter.

It was inevitable that they would speak, Julia decided, even though he was deliberately avoiding wandering her way. As host, it was really his call, but she thought she'd better get it over with. Taking a deep breath, she strode over to the table. The high heels gave her a good three inches.

'Ah, Julia!' he said, as if he hadn't noticed her before.

'Christopher,' said Julia.

She could feel her face burning up, and all the things she had rehearsed in her mind to say to him if they ever met danced around her brain, stumbling and bumping into each other.

'How's Millicent?' she asked, trying to sound nonchalant, but as it was the first time she had ever spoken his mistress's name the syllables went up and down in a most peculiar way. Even though she had her back to her mother-in-law, Julia immediately felt Libby's glare falling between her shoulders like the blade of a knife.

Christopher visibly cowered, and said nothing.

Emboldened by the feeling that she had got the upper

hand, Julia pushed her luck a little further. 'It's rather an exciting time for me. I've just landed a new job . . .'

Christopher raised an eyebrow.

'A job?' asked Julia's brother James behind her.

Had he come over to protect her? She hadn't been aware of his approach, and she felt slightly aggrieved that he should feel she needed a chaperone through any unpleasantness. It was also much trickier to exaggerate when James's sharp ears were listening. Her brother knew her far better than Christopher ever had.

'What sort of job?' Christopher asked, with little interest.

'Charitable work,' Julia mumbled, her confidence draining away.

'In the cancer shop?' asked Christopher.

Several of the shops on the High Street had closed as a result of the recession and what had been Green's the Confectioners had been rented on a short lease to the Imperial Cancer Trust.

Julia was outraged at the suggestion that she would be spending her days sitting in a shop surrounded by bric-a-brac and dog-eared paperback books. 'As a matter of fact, I am going to be working with Mr Patel to assure the future of the hospice,' she improvised.

That wiped the smile off Christopher's face.

'In more suitable premises, obviously,' she added.

Now, Christopher looked relieved. He didn't care a jot for the welfare of the children, Julia thought, only that he had a shag pad for him and his mistress.

'Shall I give you a lift back to the Castle?' asked James.

Sometimes it was good to be tall, thought Julia, as she and her brother swept out of the room. In the car, she waited for James to congratulate her, but she sensed he was not happy.

'How did I do?' she asked, anxious now that it seemed her performance hadn't been quite as triumphant as she'd felt it to be.

'I expect you'll be moving to Lowhampton, then?' James enquired.

'I hadn't really thought . . . The arrangements aren't exactly finalized . . .' she stuttered.

'I've been intending to redecorate the gatehouse,' he said.

Had he guessed that the job had come from her meeting Sylvia? Was this her punishment?

'You're chucking me out?' she asked, dismayed.

Julia thought perhaps she should be crying, but, oddly, no tears came. The big house that had dominated so much of her life had never once felt like home.

What was it that her therapist was always saying? Every ending is also a beginning.

Chapter Two

Summer 1994

On the Friday before the fiftieth anniversary of the D-Day landings, the headline on the front page of the *Chronicle* read: **OVER HERE AGAIN! Kingshaven prepares for invasion of D-Day Vets!**

Under it was a grainy old black-and-white photograph of some cheerful-looking GIs standing in a jeep. In the driver's seat was a woman whose smiling face Michael Quinn felt he recognized, but couldn't put a name to.

Michael handed over the money for the local paper along with his usual copy of the *Guardian*.

'Is there anything else today?' asked Raj, the manager of Kingshaven's Sunny Stores, as he did every day.

'No, thank you,' said Michael.

'A beautiful morning!'

'It is indeed.'

They always exchanged the same few words, with appropriate variations for the weather.

The sun was already blindingly bright as Michael began to walk back along the promenade to the Harbour End. Since living alone, he had developed routines to mark out the day, otherwise time seemed to take so long to pass. He was always up at six and had completed two hours' writing before going along to pick up his newspaper, which took forty minutes for the round trip. On Fridays, because of some deeply rooted notion from his childhood that on Friday you were allowed a treat, he would be the first customer in the Expresso Café. The taste of the coffee was never quite as delicious as the anticipation created by the aroma, but the whoosh of the Gaggia machine returned him to the days when real coffee had been a modern, almost subversive, luxury.

Joe Rocco said '*Buon giorno!*' when Michael came in. Michael suspected it was one of a handful of Italian words the proprietor of the café knew, having been born and brought up in Kingshaven. Occasionally Joe asked how Michael's daughter was getting along in Italy, but since Michael rarely heard from Iris there wasn't much mileage in the conversation. Most days, Michael would pay for his coffee and discuss AFC Lowhampton's prospects that weekend. With the English football season over, and England's failure to qualify for the World Cup tournament in America, Joe's allegiance had switched to the Italian national team. A large Italian flag bearing the legend *Forza Italia* was strung up on the wall behind the counter and he was wearing a blue replica shirt.

Michael ordered a coffee, chose a Danish pastry and walked over to a window table with his newspapers.

There was speculation in the *Guardian* that, following the unexpected death of John Smith, Gordon Brown, the shadow chancellor and obvious choice for the leadership of the Labour Party, was going to support Tony Blair's candidacy instead. If true, that would mean the Tory Party was led by someone with far better working-class credentials than the Labour Party. Michael was instinctively suspicious of anyone who spoke with a public-school accent, as Mr Blair did, while calling himself Tony. Michael's own son Anthony had recently taken to abbreviating his name in the same way. Perhaps there had been a directive from Labour Party headquarters?

Anthony's Christmas card had been printed with the

greeting 'With best wishes for a peaceful Christmas and a prosperous New Year! Tony and Marie'.

Even though Michael wasn't the slightest bit interested in Christmas or greetings cards, it had irked him that his son had not signed the card and there was something he found almost comic about the carefully crafted image of a perfectly symmetrical middle-class family in front of a tasteful Christmas tree that must have been decorated especially for the photo shoot long before the season of advent.

'One *espresso macchiato*, one Danish,' Joe Rocco announced, as Michael shifted the papers to allow space to put the cup and plate down on the table. 'Good for business, eh?' Joe pointed at the *Chronicle*'s headline.

'I doubt there'll be a run on second-hand books,' said Michael laconically; then, seeing the uneasy expression on Joe's face, wished he was the sort of person who was able to make small talk.

Michael thought that the locals probably saw him as a recluse. Occasionally, someone in a position of authority – Dr Ferry the GP, or the spotty young vicar – would come into his bookshop to browse the shelves and pass the time of day. Checking up on him, Michael suspected, but whether out of curiosity or simple kindness, he was never sure. After forty years living in Kingshaven, he felt his foreignness had become more acceptable. Political views that were once seen as subversive were now dismissed as eccentricity after Thatcher's virtual eradication of a credible Left. With one of his sons now an MP, it occurred to Michael that he might even be considered, if only by association, part of the Establishment. The thought made him smile. Even though he was alone, he was probably as happy as he'd ever been, or as content, happiness implying a more active engagement than he was capable of. He had no wish to start another relationship. He had lived with three very beautiful, very different women and he had damaged them all: Sylvia, his childhood sweetheart and mother of his first two children; Claudia, the love of his life and mother of the twins, with whom he would have been happy for ever had she not died at the age of only thirty-two; and Pascale, who had appeared like a blessing he did not deserve. Michael sometimes comforted himself with the thought that at least his betrayal of Sylvia had given wings to her ambition, and Pascale had left him in time to make a good life for herself.

All Michael's children were grown up now and he had little to do with any of them. Iris telephoned infrequently. He had no idea what her life was like, and sensed that she would not welcome any attempt to find out. Anthony kept in touch dutifully and visited once a year with his family. The twins, Bruno and Fiammetta, were in their twenties. He had promised Claudia that he would try to give them wonderful lives, but he always felt he had let her down. Occasionally, Bruno came down from London for a weekend. He was the only one of the children who had ever taken advantage of Kingshaven's attractions. A keen sportsman, Bruno kept a windsurf board in the storage area at the back of Michael's converted warehouse. He was the most obviously gifted of the children, endowed with a compelling combination of good looks, intelligence and charm, and yet he had elected to pursue a career as a chef, a decision Michael couldn't pretend to understand. Fiammetta was apparently engaged to be married to the local toff, James Allsop. The vicar had imparted the news as he handed over 20p for a frayed volume of G. K. Chesterton, clearly having no idea that the young woman was Michael's daughter.

Michael folded his newspapers.

'*Arrivederci!*' Joe Rocco called, as Michael stepped back out into the glare of the sunny promenade.

With very few visitors around on weekdays, except during the summer holidays, it was barely worth opening up The Bookshop on the Quay, but Michael found it pleasant enough to sit in the shop reading, surrounded by floor-to-ceiling bookshelves, the silence and slightly musty smell reminding him of the Public Library in the days before they'd taken out the stacks and replaced the reference section with miniature chairs and a dinosaur-themed area for children.

Michael opened the *Chronicle* to read the 'full story' of the town's D-Day commemorations. The next day there was to be a parade along the promenade and a visit from the Red Arrows. Later, there would be a barbecue on the Quay and fireworks. That evening, the Palace Hotel was officially reopening with a forties-theme dance in the newly refurbished ballroom. In recognition of the sacrifice American troops had made in the war, the Palace Hotel was extending a free welcome to fifty former GIs from the Third Army.

You had to hand it to the Kings. Less than two years ago, the hotel had been a smouldering heap of rubble and the town's exemplary family torn apart by scandal, and yet they had bounced back. How typical of them to cash in on a patriotic event, gaining disproportionate publicity and goodwill from a gesture that had probably cost them very little!

Michael found himself wondering which one of them had come up with the idea. The stunt bore all the hallmarks of the matriarch Liliana, whose supposed largesse during the war was still remembered with near reverence by the town. It was Liliana whom Michael's brother Frank must have been referring to as the lady of the house when he'd written from the Palace during the war. The hotel had been requisitioned by the RAF and, in the run up to D-Day, Frank's squadron had been billeted there.

'You'll never guess what the owners of this place are called,' Frank had written. 'The Kings. The Kings in the Palace. How about that? . . . There's this huge fancy clock, so big they can't get it down to the cellars, a porcelain tree with birds and flowers stuck all over it. The lady of the

house sucks in her breath whenever one of us walks past
. . . Oh, the temptation to lose your footing and bring the
bugger down! If we're bombed, God help me, at least I'll
go to hell knowing that thing's shattered in a thousand
pieces . . .'

But the clock had survived intact. Michael had seen it
for himself each time he had visited the Palace during the
fifties when he had played the piano for their tea dances. It
had been a gaudy reminder that worthless things survived
and his brother had not.

Michael returned to the newspaper, trying to distract
himself from the rawness of the pain that still engulfed
him whenever he thought about Frank.

Unlike the comrades of the D-Day vets who were
returning to Kingshaven this weekend, Frank had not been
killed in action. Michael wondered if he would still feel the
same sting of bereavement if Frank had died a hero's death.
Although he'd tried all these years, Michael had never been
able to understand how Frank could have arrived at the
decision to take his own life, and his failure of imagination
sometimes made him wonder if he had known his brother
at all. Had Frank planned to jump off the cliff, or was it
a spur-of-the-moment decision? And why Kingshaven?
He had been billeted at the Palace Hotel in the build-up
to D-Day, but after that his squadron had been stationed
several miles away at Coombe Minster.

The last communication Michael had received from
Frank had been a postcard.

'Can't wait to see you!' he had written on the back of a
postcard. 'I'll be there as soon as I've sorted a few bits and
pieces . . .'

But he had never returned.

An accident, Michael's aunt, his only remaining relative,
had told him. Michael was fifteen years old, and he hadn't
put two and two together until much later. By the time
Michael had come to Kingshaven himself, any tentative

enquiries had drawn blank shrugs from the locals. A lot of things had happened in the war that were best forgotten.

The romantic side of Michael's nature imagined the answers he sought might come to him if he walked the paths his brother had walked and gazed at the same perspectives. But he had come no closer to understanding what had been going on in Frank's head.

Occasionally, Michael had felt a glimmer of his brother's presence in his children. Iris's colouring was so much like Frank's, and so was the candid way she looked at him. When Fiammetta arrived years later with the same red curls, Michael had felt it was almost as if Frank were trying to send a message, as if the first hadn't got through, but when you had a baby, lack of sleep could make you think all sorts of weird things.

Many years later, there had been a flash of déjà vu when Michael happened to see his son Bruno chatting up a girl on the promenade. With his dark lashes and deep brown eyes, Bruno looked nothing like Frank, but as he leant forward and licked the trickle of ice cream from the girl's forearm, Michael had shuddered, because he had seen Frank make the very same gesture with a girl in a milk bar in Scarborough. And when Bruno winked at him with roguish male complicity, just as Frank had that time, Michael had felt as if Frank were somehow reaffirming their relationship.

Which was completely ridiculous, thought Michael, because he didn't believe in an afterlife, let alone messages from the dead.

*   *   *

Esther's presence was always felt. It was impossible for her to slip into a room unnoticed, or go about her business quietly. Cat knew that Esther was home, not just because of the running commentary as Esther hauled her pushbike up the steps outside and into the hall, and the crash of the heavy front door behind her, but because she shouted, 'Anyone home?'

'Up here!' Cat called.

Esther clattered up the stairs.

'What are you up to?' she asked.

'Reading,' said Cat.

'You're always reading!' said Esther.

'It's for the book group tomorrow evening,' said Cat. One of the innovations she'd introduced since becoming assistant manager at the bookshop was a reading group for some of the regular customers.

Esther pulled a face.

'Can I run an idea past you?'

'Sure,' said Cat.

'One word: Bruno.'

Esther's crush on Bruno showed no signs of fading, even though he had so far demonstrated no interest in taking the friendship to another level.

Cat had to admit that he was the ideal person to share a house with. For one thing, he was rarely there, because he worked long hours, leaving before she or Esther came back from work, and returning in the early hours of the morning, and once a month, on the Sunday he wasn't working, he fulfilled his promise to cook them brunch. The food was delicious, and, unlike the male students Cat had shared a house with in her final year at University who'd used every saucepan and surface in the kitchen, leaving it all for the lucky recipient of their culinary efforts to clean up afterwards, Bruno was scrupulously organized and tidy. He was also much better than either she or Esther at cleaning the house, a virtue Esther attributed to his mother having died when he was two, giving an additional tragic gloss to his appeal.

In fact, Bruno was so funny and charming and good-looking that Esther had initially feared he must be gay.

When she was fifteen, she'd loved George Michael with the same passion, insisting she and Cat spend many Saturdays hanging round the suburban village of Bushey, a couple of stops up the line from Cat's home, in the hope of bumping into George if he popped out in his white suit for a pint of milk or a newspaper.

Bruno's heterosexuality had been affirmed by the presence of an attractive waitress from the Compton Club one Sunday brunch, which put Esther off her food but hadn't shaken her belief that Bruno would one day realize that the only woman for him was living right under his nose. The waitress was clearly a one-night stand. Bruno just wasn't ready to settle down yet.

Cat was continually amazed by Esther's ability to turn non-existent signs into reasons for hope.

'Bruno cooking on television,' said Esther. 'Brilliant, yes?'

Esther's imagination worked very well in her job, where she now enjoyed the title Producer, Development. Her flair for a popular format had started with her own experiences dealing with plumbers, carpenters and decorators in the renovation of the Islington house.

'Why can't there be teams of people who come round and just do it all in a day?' she'd moaned, exasperated, one evening.

Less than a year later, *What a Difference a Day Makes*, in which a team of experts changed the interior of a house in twenty-four hours, was one of the most successful lifestyle programmes on terrestrial television.

Sew Good, an idea that had stemmed from Cat's hobby of recycling second-hand clothes she bought in charity shops into wearable outfits, was in development, with Esther trying to find a hip young presenter to front it.

'But nobody knows who he is!' said Cat.

'Did anyone know who Keith Floyd was before he was spotted and given his own series?' Esther countered.

'He did have his own restaurant, didn't he?'

'You'd be hopeless in television,' Esther told her. 'Who wouldn't want to watch Bruno?'

Cat knew she had to be tactful. If she said anything negative about mixing professional and personal behaviour, Esther was bound to ask how come she was suddenly the expert on relationships. But if she was too positive, Esther might be equally sharp. There was a fine line between approving of Esther's object of desire, and appearing to set yourself up as competition. Cat still remembered wearily agreeing that George Michael was without doubt the most gorgeous man in the universe, only to have Esther immediately snap at her, 'Well, you're far too tall for him.'

'What if your bosses don't like him?' Cat tentatively suggested. 'Won't that be a bit awkward . . . at work . . . and at home too?'

Esther's face fell momentarily. This clearly hadn't occurred to her as a possibility. 'Oh, God, listen to you!' she said. 'What's not to like?'

*   *   *

In the vast hall of the Castle, Kingshaven, Fiammetta was standing on a stepladder with her paintbrush on the canvas when the phone rang. Reluctant to break the thin horizontal line of pink acrylic paint she was making, she left the answerphone to pick up.

'Winston's coming down for the weekend.'

The background noise made it sound as if James was speaking from the inside of a washing machine. He was probably calling on the new mobile phone he was so proud of.

'Can you get something decent in for supper?' the voice barked impatiently out of the machine, which made an extended whining sound before clicking off.

Was it oversensitive to feel offended at the word decent,

Fiammetta asked herself, with its implication that the food she usually provided was somehow lacking? When you spent a great deal of time on your own with no one to talk to, you could sometimes read more into remarks than was intended. On Thursday evenings, she always made a point of driving to the big Sunny Stores on the outskirts of Lowhampton to pick up supplies for James, choosing simple fare, such as a packet of fresh pasta, or a carton of soup and a baguette from the bakery section, because James was always complaining about the amount of rich food he ate in London. She had interpreted a couple of comments he had made recently about not marrying her for her prowess in the kitchen as backhanded compliments, but perhaps that was not what he'd intended.

James appeared to be serious about getting married. He'd gone as far as arranging an appointment to see the vicar, a man so young his face was still dotted with yellow pinheads of acne. It was inconceivable to Fiammetta that such a person would officiate over her life, but, strangely, neither the vicar nor anyone else seemed to find the engagement as peculiar as she did.

When Fiammetta asked her twin brother, 'You don't really think I should marry James, do you?' Bruno had replied, 'Why not?'

And she hadn't been able to think of a specific reason.

'You're happy, aren't you?' Bruno had asked.

'I'm very happy,' said Fiammetta.

Her paintings had a joyous quality her work had never contained before. She found herself using the exuberant colours she saw in nature, like the luminous lime green of the first beech leaves, the vibrant purple of wild rhododendrons, or the almost crude dapple of turquoise and pink in a mackerel sunset. The difference between painting the country and the city was that the principal axis of vision was horizontal rather than vertical and the shapes she made gradually simplified until they were nothing more than lines of differing depth and colour across the canvas. When James suggested that she exhibit them in the gallery bar of the Compton Club, they all sold within a week. Now she was able to afford larger canvases, the size of her paintings grew with her confidence.

Fiammetta backed gingerly down the stepladder and played the message back again, this time registering happily that Winston was coming down. It had been ages since she'd seen him, but she was confident that he wouldn't mind at all what they had for supper. Nevertheless, she'd better go shopping, Fiammetta thought.

As she wandered up and down the supermarket aisles, she tried to picture one of Bruno's Sunday lunches and bought a leg of lamb, a small bottle of anchovy fillets, a head of new-season garlic, an aubergine, some capsicum peppers and a box of couscous. The couscous label said 'instant', and she knew there was a trick with clingfilm for the peppers. How difficult could it be to roast a leg of lamb? A wedge of ripe Brie from the deli counter and a punnet of strawberries would do for dessert.

James and Winston were standing looking at her unfinished canvas when she arrived back at the Castle.

'We wondered where you'd got to,' James said, striding across, kissing her cheek and putting a proprietorial arm round her.

A blush spread across Fiammetta's face as she realized it was probably the first time Winston had ever seen her with a boyfriend.

'I didn't expect you so soon!' she flustered.

'Winston had his helicopter drop us off,' said James.

She was suddenly conscious of her grubby old T-shirt, and the kerchief on her head she always wore to stop the paint spattering in her curly hair. She knew that Winston wouldn't care one way or the other, but James's relationship with Winston was more nuanced than hers, and he would expect her to put on a good show.

'What's for supper?' James wanted to know.

'Roast lamb,' Fiammetta replied.

'Wonderful. Would you like to take a quick look at the plans before?' he asked Winston.

It suddenly dawned on Fiammetta that Winston's visit was not social. There was some form of negotiation going on between the two men. James was probably trying to get money out of Winston, hence the eagerness to impress. Winston was deliberately keeping a cool distance.

'How long will it be?' James wanted to know.

'At least a couple of hours, I should think,' she replied.

'It's half past eight now!'

'God. Is it?'

Fiammetta felt herself colouring, embarrassed that Winston should witness what was beginning to feel like a domestic tiff. It was outrageous of James to turn up like this virtually unannounced and expect her to rush around making dinner like a . . . like a wife, Fiammetta suddenly thought.

'I'm really not very hungry,' Winston came to the rescue.

'There's some cheese and some strawberries . . .' Fiammetta looked directly at their guest, ignoring James's sigh of exasperation.

'Perfect!' said Winston.

There was a slightly awkward silence.

'Welcome!' said Fiammetta, stretching out her arms belatedly to embrace Winston, then wondering whether it was the right thing to say.

The Castle had been Winston's home too. Sir John Allsop, James's eccentric grandfather, had found a mixed-race baby in a basket on VE night. Fiammetta wasn't sure whether Winston had ever been officially adopted by Sir John, but he had spent his childhood at the Castle under Sir John's guardianship until he went off to Oxford in the sixties. Winston was generally assumed to be the product of a local girl's liaison with one of the black GIs who were billeted in Kingshaven during the build-up to D-Day, although there was also speculation that his father could have been the popular cabaret singer Leslie 'Hutch' Hutchinson, who had entertained the troops at Weymouth, just down the coast, and had been a notorious ladies' man.

While Fiammetta prepared the cold food, James discussed his proposal with Winston. It appeared that he was planning to turn the Castle into a country-house version of the Compton Club, using the same style of interior decoration with its attractive combination of shabby antiques and cutting-edge modernity.

'What's the main problem with booking a weekend in an English hotel?' James asked.

'The weather?' Winston volunteered.

'Apart from the weather,' said James, a touch impatiently.

'I'm sure you're going to tell me,' said Winston, shooting a conspiratorial smile at Fiammetta as she slipped on to the chair beside him.

'Other people,' said James. 'What I mean is, you never know who's going to be sitting next to you at breakfast.'

Winston listened impassively, and for the first time Fiammetta saw what an awesome presence he could be, and began to have some understanding of how this calm, languid man she'd known all her life had become one of Britain's most successful entrepreneurs.

'At a Compton Country House—' James continued.

'You're planning more than one?' Winston interrupted.

'Obviously, if the Castle works as I am sure it will . . .' James hesitated, trying, Fiammetta thought, to gauge whether Winston thought this was a good or bad idea. '. . . At a Compton House,' he continued, 'you will know you're among people like you – members of the Club who've been elected, staff chosen for their discretion and their easiness on the eye . . .' He smiled.

Most of the waitresses at the Compton Club were aspiring actresses or models.

'Are you saying your income stream would be entirely dependent on members?' Winston interjected. 'I should have thought that a good number of your members would have their own country retreat.'

'Not with a billiard room, a cinema, a decent restaurant offering round-the-clock room service. It will be a perfect venue for exclusive functions, launches, parties, and the new civil licences mean we can use the Castle as a wedding venue combining ceremony, reception and accommodation on the premises.'

'How many of your members get married each year?' asked Winston.

'I'm not sure there are any figures . . .' James mumbled, before starting on another tack. 'We would also of course promote to selected non-members – the sort of people who appreciate exclusivity and discretion – film stars, rock artists . . .'

'Hotels outside London – and in London, as a matter of fact – are generally dreadful,' Winston conceded. 'All shortbread and chintz.'

'Exactly,' said James, brightening instantly in the chink of light Winston had allowed into the conversation.

'And what's your view on all this?' Winston turned to Fiammetta.

Did he know, she wondered, that it was the first time she'd heard anything about it?

'It's really nothing to do with me,' she said.

'Keen to have film stars swanning around your home?' asked Winston light-heartedly.

'We're going to keep the private wing private,' James offered reassurance. 'And we would show Fiammetta's art . . .' He looked across the table at her. It sounded almost like a bribe.

'We could restore the walled garden,' Fiammetta suggested.

'Wonderful idea!' said Winston. 'You could grow fresh herbs and vegetables for the restaurant. The kind of people you're talking about demand organic. Fresh flowers too . . . The walled garden used to smell so good . . .'

'Roses and lavender and love-in-a-mist,' Fiammetta said.

The two of them smiled shared memories at each other.

Did Winston ever resent the way he had been passed over by the next generation of Allsop family after Sir John's death, she wondered. Had his meteoric rise as a businessman been in part an attempt to prove himself? Did he feel affronted by James's request, or was this situation deliciously ironic for him? It was impossible to tell from the serene expression on Winston's face.

'I'm going to leave you to it,' she said, pretending to yawn.

'Off to bed?' James asked.

'I thought I'd take a stroll in the garden,' she said. 'It's such a lovely evening.'

'Do you mind if I join you?' Winston asked, pushing back his chair.

Fiammetta could feel James glaring at her back as they left the room.

The air was close, but occasional warm gusts of breeze indicated there was a thunderstorm on the way. Even though it was nearly ten o'clock at night, there was still some light in the sky. Fiammetta loved long summer evenings when it never seemed to get completely dark. It reminded her of the long hot summer of 1976, when their father had rented a caravan in the Forest Valley Caravan Park after they'd had to move out of the Castle because James and his family were moving in.

She and Bruno must have been about eight, she calculated, and they had thought it the most exciting thing ever. Though they were used to having the run of a huge, dilapidated house with corridors and stairs and endless gardens, living in a caravan – with a dining table that turned into a bed, and a Calor Gas hob hidden under the draining board, and having to fetch heavy buckets of water from a standpipe – seemed like a huge adventure. Iris had come down from London and they'd all been so cramped up together in the caravan that if you woke up in the night you could hear the others breathing. As the drought continued, the sea had become their bath. It had been too hot to sleep, and she remembered lying in her bunk, listening to the strumming of a guitar, and the murmur of adult conversation, and smelling the sweet aroma of the spliff they passed round. The heat had gone on so long, nobody had ever thought it would end. And then it did, quite suddenly, with a massive thunderstorm that had changed everything.

'How do you feel about James's plans?' Winston asked.

She had quite forgotten he was standing next to her.

The truth was she didn't know. Fiammetta often felt as if her emotions had been wrapped up into a parcel and stored somewhere else. When she was painting, she was subsumed in the work. When she was not, she felt almost as if she was floating across the surface of life.

On the other side of town, a necklace of pearly white lights had been strung round the terrace of the Palace Hotel. Occasional snatches from vaguely familiar songs drifted across the valley from the Kings' D-Day ball.

'You would let me know if you ever needed anything, wouldn't you?' Winston said softly.

He had known her all her life, always remembered birthdays, had always been there for the best treats. It felt good to be reminded of his permanence.

She turned to face him. 'I probably wouldn't,' she said, never able to tell a lie. 'But thank you for the offer.'

*   *   *

'Americans always did have big bums,' said Libby's sister, Pearl, as they watched a group of the vets and their wives attempting a jitterbug to the strains of the swing band playing 'In the Mood'.

In their youth the men had looked so dashing in their pale uniforms compared with the unflattering greenish khaki of the British army. Now they wore a different kind of uniform. The American idea of smart appeared to involve beige trousers and navy blazers that came off at the first sign of sweat, to reveal short-sleeve polyester shirts straining across ample girths.

Pearl drained another glass of the New Zealand bubbly that Eddie had unearthed in a wine warehouse in Lowhampton for a quarter the price of real champagne. Any doubts Libby had about offering a New World label had been assuaged by Eddie pointing out that the Aussies had been a great deal more use in the war than the French ever had, and after a couple of glasses nobody would be able to tell the difference anyway. Certainly not Pearl, thought Libby. Her sister had downed several glasses already, perhaps confirming the rumours that she had a bit of a drink problem. Since her divorce from her long-suffering husband Tom Snow, Pearl had become something of an embarrassment to the family, just as she had been before the marriage. When Pearl was young, the problem had been men who were much too old for her; now it seemed it was men who were far too young. It must be difficult for someone who had been such a renowned beauty to look in the mirror each morning and see the ravage of the years, Libby thought, although of course Pearl's chain-smoking only made the decline more rapid.

It crossed Libby's mind that if a stranger were to look at the two of them now standing side by side at the edge of the dance floor, they might well judge Libby the younger and better preserved of the two sisters, possibly even the prettier. Pearl had become very jowly of late, and the attempt to squeeze into clothes a size too small, and many years too young, somehow exaggerated the blotchiness of her skin tone and the loss of her wasp waist.

'Well, I'll be darned!'

For a moment, all Libby could see was gleaming teeth. A large black man standing a fraction too close for comfort beamed down at her.

It had been something of a shock when he'd climbed down from the coach that had brought the American vets from the airport. During the war the coloured GIs had been billeted in separate accommodation from the white ones, and it hadn't occurred to Libby that there would be any of them among the commemorating guests. Some of the vets had brought their wives with them, but the lone black man was without a partner and that made him stand out even more. Libby sensed that her mother, from whose window they had been watching the arrivals, had also been shocked. Liliana had yet to appear at the dance, which was a shame because there was nothing her mother liked more than a brisk military two-step.

'How're you doing?'

'Very well, thank you. And you?' said Libby, extending her hand formally in the hope of pushing the black man back a little.

'You don't look a day older!' he said cheerily.

It was an absurd compliment for any number of reasons, but Libby felt herself blushing nonetheless.

'Perhaps he thinks you're Mummy,' Pearl suggested. 'You're looking awfully like her these days.'

Pearl's really losing it, Libby thought, to imply that Mummy would have known a black GI! Liliana had never associated with anyone lower than the rank of squadron leader. One of Libby's principal memories of the war was her mother standing in front of the porcelain clock in the hall, defending it from the lower ranks as they clattered past to mess.

'Would either of you fine ladies care to dance?'

'I thought you'd never ask!' said Pearl, immediately linking with the arm the black man offered.

Even though she'd had no intention of accepting the invitation herself, Libby was slightly irked that Pearl had stolen a march on her. Not for the first time that evening, she wished she had resisted the impulse to invite her sister to the dance. Pearl had always been good at making people feel sorry for her, but after seventy years of taking pity and receiving scant reward for her trouble Libby should have known better.

'I'm so sorry, ma'am, but I don't believe we've met,' Libby heard the black man say as he guided her sister firmly towards the dance floor.

Which was something of a relief, Libby thought. Pearl had been preposterously advanced with the RAF boys who'd stayed at the Palace, but Libby was sure that even she would have drawn the limit at a black man. In those days, at least.

*   *   *

When Michael Quinn returned home on Saturday after his morning walk for a newspaper, he had a visitor. The shape of the man standing outside The Bookshop on the Quay was instantly recognizable from a distance. Winston Allsop must be almost fifty, Michael realized, but he still had the long, lean body of a young man.

'What brings you down to these parts?' Michael asked.

'I'm visiting at the Castle,' Winston told him. 'Thought I'd drop by.'

'Come in, come in,' Michael said, unlocking the door and showing Winston up the steep staircase to the living accommodation above the bookshop.

It was rare for him to have guests, and, seeing the big open-plan living and kitchen area through a visitor's eyes, Michael was suddenly acutely aware of the mess he had grown accustomed to living in. There were several precarious stacks of newspapers he kept meaning to take up to the recycling bins near the caravan park; books were piled on most of the surfaces, others left open and face down on the floor; there were at least half a dozen mugs containing varying levels of tea dotted round the room and a washing-up bowl full of dirty crockery in the sink. Fortunately, Michael had taken out the rubbish for collection by the dustmen the previous morning, but a faint odour of rotting vegetables remained.

'I'll put the kettle on,' Michael said. 'Unless you'd prefer to go for a coffee at the Expresso?'

'No, no,' said Winston.

His plain white shirt seemed to emphasize the general grubbiness of the room, but Winston's expression betrayed no trace of distaste as he cleared a space on the dilapidated sofa and sat down with a bump rather closer to the floor than he was anticipating.

'I'm on my own now,' Michael offered, as if in explanation.

'Yes, I heard,' said Winston. 'So am I,' he added.

'How many marriages is that?' Michael asked.

'Three,' Winston admitted.

Michael found it slightly odd talking man-to-man with Winston, whom he had first encountered in the fifties as a schoolboy. Winston hadn't changed fundamentally. He had been an exceptionally courteous child, with a distinctive, relaxed confidence in his own intelligence. Even at eight years old, in spite of all the challenges he faced in life – being abandoned, illegitimate and black

95

wasn't easy for any child in the fifties, let alone in an insular little place like Kingshaven – Winston had been a leader. Michael was sure he must have encountered bullying, but his natural superiority had allowed him to rise above it.

Michael had become better acquainted with Winston during the idyllic period he'd spent with Claudia at the Castle. At the time, Winston had been a young man in his twenties, embarking on his brilliant career, first at Oxford, then at the Bar, but he had occasionally returned to Kingshaven to visit his guardian, Sir John Allsop. And later on, after Claudia died and Iris had come to help out with the twins, Winston had been a regular visitor. Michael was never quite sure whether Winston's relationship with Iris had been anything more than platonic. Sometimes he had found himself entertaining the hope that the two of them would get together, but Iris wasn't the settling-down type, and nor, it seemed, with three failed marriages under his belt, was Winston.

Michael bulldozed a space on the low pine coffee table to put down a mug of tea in front of Winston.

'So you're at the Castle this weekend,' he said. 'How is Fiammetta?'

'She seems very well. She's painting some huge canvases,' Winston told him.

'She's happy, then,' said Michael.

'I think so.'

Michael thought he detected slight uncertainty in Winston's voice.

'Actually, my invitation to the Castle is more business than pleasure,' Winston revealed.

'Oh?'

'James wants to turn the place into an exclusive country-house hotel.'

'I thought Sylvia had already done that.'

'James's vision is rather different,' said Winston.

'Yes,' said Michael, remembering his ex-wife's very feminine taste. 'I'm sure it is.'

'James's vision is quite costly,' Winston elaborated. 'Which is where he hopes I will come in . . .'

Michael couldn't quite work out what Winston was telling him, but he thought he detected the hint of a question Winston had yet to ask.

'You know that Fiammetta doesn't speak to me any more?' Michael felt obliged to inform him. The words were difficult to say and tasted bitter in his mouth.

'Yes,' said Winston.

Did Winston know why as well? Michael couldn't bring himself to ask.

'I also know that you'd want what's right for her.' Winston sat forward. 'What do you make of this marriage business with James?'

'I've never pretended to understand what goes on in my daughter's mind,' Michael said. 'Not Fiammetta anyway. With Iris I have more of an idea.'

'Iris normally tells you what's on her mind!' Winston said fondly.

'Yes. Yes, she does.' Michael felt a little wistful. Of all his children, the only one he truly ached to see was Iris.

'The fact is, I'd always be delighted to invest in Fiammetta's happiness,' said Winston.

Another unspoken question. Michael could only assume that Winston suspected that James would make Fiammetta unhappy.

'They are planning to restore the walled garden,' Winston said.

A memory of another bright summer's day, long ago, fluttered across Michael's brain like a butterfly. The walled garden was so sheltered it had felt almost steamy the day he had scattered Claudia's ashes there, and the air had smelt faintly of roses and lavender where bees murmured lazily.

'It would be good to restore the walled garden,' Michael said.

'Yes,' said Winston. 'Yes. I thought so too.'

Michael felt as if a whole conversation had taken place in the subtext of their exchange, but he wasn't quite sure what had been agreed.

'Are you going to watch the parade?' Winston suddenly rose from the sofa and walked over to the window that overlooked the quayside.

'I thought I might as well,' said Michael.

'Shall we go and reserve ourselves a position outside the Ship?'

The landlady of the Ship Inn, Millicent Balls, who had continued running the pub on her own after her recent divorce, had made significant improvements. The partition between the old saloon and public bars had been knocked down, creating a brighter airy space. The forecourt outside had been fenced and decked. The old menu of sandwiches and basket meals had been replaced by crusty baguettes, grilled steaks, garden salads and a children's selection. What had been a smoky, beery, predominantly male preserve was now an attractive place for families to lunch. The old fishermen who'd effectively been ousted muttered their complaints in the public bar of the Anchor, and amused one another with innuendo about Millicent's 'skills in the hospitality business'. Her clandestine affair with Christopher King, the heir apparent to the Palace Hotel, had become very public on the night of the hotel fire, when Millicent had been caught by television cameras being carried down a fireman's ladder wearing only scarlet-and-black camiknickers. The town's disbelief that any man could prefer the distinctly middle-aged body of Millicent to the lithe and decorous figure of Christopher's young wife Julia had been superseded by speculation about whether the matriarchs of the Palace would allow Christopher to install Millicent as his mistress. The more mean-spirited of Kingshaven's opinion-formers believed that Millicent's 'tarting up' of the Ship was a blatant attempt to prove her credentials as a proprietor.

Winston and Michael chose a small table with an umbrella outside, and Michael went inside to order drinks.

'All right, sir?' Millicent said, putting two brimming glasses down on the mat on the bar. She had been in Michael's class three or four years after Winston, and had never been able to bring herself to use her teacher's first name, even though they'd been neighbours for nearly twenty years. Milly Bland, as she had been in those days, had always been a vibrant personality, although Michael struggled to find vestiges of the girl in the woman's face. Today, in honour of the D-Day commemoration, she'd had her hair fashioned in a forties style and her lips were a bright-red cupid's bow, rather like Betty Grable's. Unlike the majority of Kingshaven's male population, Michael could quite see that her voluptuousness would be very attractive to the scion of the disapproving, buttoned-up Kings.

'How much do I owe you?' he asked.

'On the house today,' said Millicent. 'It's a small price to pay for our freedom, isn't it?'

The townsfolk of Kingshaven were in a peculiarly generous frame of mind, Michael thought, as he brought the drinks back to the table.

It was fairly blowy outside, and they could hear distant snatches of the brass band as it made its way through the town. Winston seemed if not preoccupied then perfectly content not to talk, whereas Michael, who rarely spoke to anyone from the outside world, felt positively expansive.

'Terrible shame about John Smith,' he said.

Winston nodded.

'I see they're talking about Blair for the leadership. Is that likely?' Michael asked, taking a sip of cold cider.

'More than likely,' said Winston, which Michael took to mean yes.

Having dismayed Iris by publicly supporting Thatcher in 1979, Winston had returned fairly rapidly to his natural political roots in the mid eighties, and had been a major donor to the Labour Party during the 1992 election campaign.

'Blair has charisma,' said Winston.

'"Tough on crime, tough on the causes of crime",' Michael quoted. 'The words sound good, but does it actually mean anything?'

'It's a commitment to put public money into health, education and social services, couched in terms *Daily Mail* readers can identify with.'

'Do we have to dress everything up to make it acceptable to *Daily Mail* readers, then?' Michael asked.

'If you want power, yes, you do,' said Winston.

Michael's son Anthony had said much the same thing when he last saw him. It was almost as if a line had been agreed among the new, besuited managerial Labour Party that anyone who questioned the means to power must be dismissed for not wanting power. But how far would they be prepared to abandon their principles and their own supporters in their bid to attract the Conservative vote, Michael wondered. Wasn't it a slippery slope?

'Anthony seems to rate Blair very highly,' Michael acknowledged.

'Anthony is Blair's kind of man,' said Winston. 'Do you see much of him these days?'

'They come down once a year,' said Michael. 'The kids sleep on the floor in the living room. They seem to quite like slumming it.'

Anthony and Marie had three children to date. Michael was particularly fond of the oldest boy, Jack, who sometimes accompanied him on mooches along the shoreline. There was something timeless about the pleasure of finding the perfect flat round stone, skimming it across the water and seeing how many times it would bounce. The positioning of fingers round the pebble was a skill passed down from boy to boy. Michael could remember his brother Frank showing him how to do it, and he had heard himself using just the same words as Frank had when he in turn showed Jack. But the last time they'd visited, Marie had banned them from going on Fossil Beach because of the bomb, and the boys had spent days machine-gunning video enemies on the games machines in the amusement arcade, an activity Michael considered far more dangerous than the minuscule risk of treading on any further unexploded ordnance.

The chink, chink, of yachts in the harbour punctuated the companionable silence between him and Winston. He was startled when Winston asked, 'Would you mind my asking why you and Fiammetta have fallen out?'

Michael's inclination was to say that he would prefer not to talk about it, but he guessed that Winston's interest was not prurient. His companion was looking for something more – an explanation, perhaps, for Fiammetta's curious behaviour.

Should he explain? It wasn't something Michael had spoken about with anyone except Iris and Bruno, and his brain filled with chaos as he tried to order the few salient facts.

'Quite early on in my marriage to Sylvia, when we still lived in the North, I had an affair with a married woman – the wife of my boss, as it happens. It was one of the reasons Sylvia and I came down here. We were trying to start a new life . . .'

He took another draught of cider. Winston was listening carefully.

'I wasn't aware that I had fathered a child, who grew up and became a lecturer at Etherington Art College . . .'

'. . . Where he met Fiammetta?' Winston finished the staccato sentence.

Michael nodded. 'I had no idea,' he said, although that wasn't quite true. The reason Fiammetta now hated him was that he had become aware of his other son but had decided not to effect a meeting, not wanting to cause the boy any problems. For Fiammetta, his failure to disclose the existence of an illegitimate half-brother, and all the trauma it eventually caused, was an unforgivable act of cowardice and dishonesty.

'So *that's* why she's chosen someone so completely different from her!' Winston exclaimed, his quick brain working out the clue to the puzzle of Fiammetta's engagement.

'I thought I was doing the right thing . . .' Michael faltered. 'I mean, would you . . . ?'

Would you want another father turning up in your life when you already had a perfectly fine one, he was about to say, but stopped himself, remembering that Winston had not known even one father.

The parade was getting closer. The tune of 'When The Saints Come Marching In' was now clearly audible. Winston suddenly leapt up and leant over the balustrade of the decking, like a child determined to be the first to see the procession as it turned off the promenade on to the quayside.

The band came first, followed by a contingent of high-kicking drum majorettes trained by Cynthia Clark's Dance Academy wearing skimpy stars-and-stripes dresses; then came the American vets, walking in lines six across, and happily waving small stars-and-stripes flags. They were followed by a boy scout in uniform holding a maple-leaf flag heralding a line of well-preserved Canadians. Behind them, marching properly, instead of walking in the amiably haphazard manner of the Americans, were six straight rows of veteran British servicemen wearing the uniforms of the Army, RAF and Navy, followed by an equally well-disciplined outfit of cadets. The children of Kingshaven's Primary School followed, dressed in coats and hats with labels round their necks to represent evacuees. Some of the mothers had gone to some lengths to dress themselves in forties-style frocks. Bringing up the rear was an army jeep bedecked in Union Jacks and driven stutteringly by Eddie King in his naval uniform. In the back sat his wife, Libby, and her mother, Liliana, waving regally at the crowd.

As the Americans marched past the decking, Winston's eyes scanned the ranks of veterans intently, and Michael suddenly understood why he had wanted to watch the parade. He had come to see whether his father had returned, but the only black face was that of a British army cadet young enough to be Winston's son.

Was Winston disappointed, Michael wondered. Or relieved?

'I wonder if any of them knew my brother,' Michael said, trying to offer Winston the opportunity to talk about it.

'I didn't know you had a brother.'

'He was billeted here. He died just after the war.'

'I'm sorry,' Winston said politely, but Michael could tell that his mind was elsewhere.

There was a shriek of feedback from a loudspeaker, as the editor-in-chief of the group of newspapers that owned the Kingshaven *Chronicle*, Robert Murphy, climbed up on to the small stage that had been erected beside the Yacht Club, and spoke into the mic.

'On behalf of the *Echo* group, I'd like to thank you all for coming back to Kingshaven. It's still a beautiful, quiet little town, where people live happily, and visitors come to refresh their spirits. That's in no small part due to you brave boys who congregated here fifty years ago, not knowing what fate lay in store across the Channel.'

Robert Murphy waved at the sea, and all heads turned, as if miraculously they would be able to see the coastline of France instead of the blue horizon.

'It was your courage, facing the enemy, that protected all of us, and granted Kingshaven the freedom to remain the peaceful little place it is. We owe it to you, we're grateful to you, and we all want you to enjoy your time here. Now, I'm sure you're all ready for a drink, so that's enough speeches. Enjoy the party!'

*　　*　　*

It had all gone as well as could be expected, thought Libby King, as she stood at her mother's window, watching the coach pull away from the front entrance of the hotel.

There had been an alarming moment when the jeep, which they'd borrowed from the Army Transportation Museum at Coombe Minster, had stalled on the hill up from the Harbour End. Liliana had made the situation a great deal worse by wishing out loud that Ruby Farmer were driving instead of Eddie. Libby's momentary anxiety that her mother had forgotten that Ruby was dead was swiftly allayed when she saw the triumphant smirk on Liliana's face. Her mother had always relished the opportunity to wind Eddie up, almost literally, Libby thought, as she'd watched her husband struggling with the crank handle at the front of the jeep. There had been no harm done apart from some oil smears on Eddie's white uniform jacket, but his more than usually red and sweaty face had given Libby brief cause for concern because they certainly didn't want another heart attack at the Palace.

It was difficult to resist the temptation to blame Pearl for the one major flaw of the commemoration weekend, although, to be fair, the black veteran should have known better. Having thrown herself into the jive in a manner more appropriate to someone far younger and more athletic, Pearl had leapt at her dance partner, wrapped her legs round his waist and commanded him to spin. A less chivalrous soul would have let her drop, but instead the black man twirled manfully, until he lost his footing and toppled to the floor with Pearl on top of him. General hilarity and

104

applause had rapidly turned into an emergency when, after Pearl had been helped to her feet, her partner remained writhing on the floor, clutching his chest. Suspecting that her overweight sister had cracked the poor man's ribs, Libby sought the advice of Dr Ferry, whom her mother had invited to the dance. Had it not been for the GP's quick intervention, a PR disaster might well have ensued because the man suffered a heart attack in the ambulance on the way to Lowhampton General and had to be resuscitated four times.

'Did the coloured fellow die?' Liliana now asked, as if she was reading her daughter's thoughts.

Libby was chilled by the bright expression on her mother's face. One could only assume that as one approached death oneself, it lost some of its fear.

'No. Apparently he's in a stable condition,' she told her.

'He's not coming back here, is he?'

'Of course not!' Libby reassured her mother. 'The tour operator has contacted his family. His daughter is flying over to accompany him home when he's well enough to travel.'

'They all look the same,' said Liliana.

Libby was glad that she was the only other person present. She knew her mother didn't mean anything by it, but these days you really couldn't say that sort of thing.

'The funny thing is that they think we all look the same too,' Liliana mused. 'One of them told Ruby Farmer she looked like Ingrid Bergman.' She smiled mischievously.

It *was* an amusing thought, Libby conceded. Even in her heyday, nobody could have called Ruby Farmer a great beauty.

'He can't stay here,' Liliana suddenly declared. 'Say we're full. Send him back to the Albion.'

Not for the first time, Libby wondered whether the D-Day celebrations had been too much for her mother.

All the upheaval, after a long quiet period when the hotel had been closed for rebuilding, seemed to have disturbed Liliana's equilibrium. There had been several occasions now – Libby was sure she wasn't imagining it – when Liliana seemed momentarily to have forgotten what time frame she was in. The Albion was the coaching inn on Kingshaven's High Street where Liliana had grown up. It had never reopened as a hotel after the war. Some people put it down to the fact that the black GIs had been billeted there. Now, only the public and saloon bars remained and the upstairs rooms were solicitors' offices.

'Thank God that's over,' said Liliana as they watched the coach turn out on to Hill Road.

'Quite,' agreed Libby.

Although it had been quite jolly having the hotel full of guests again, Libby had forgotten quite how relentless the daily grind of being nice to people could be. There was a part of her that wished that she and Eddie had decided to throw in the towel after the fire and retire like any normal couple of their age. Annoyingly, at the time, the value of land had been at its lowest for many years, and they couldn't bring themselves to give it away after everything they'd put into it. Neither of them set much store by Christopher's promise to run the hotel properly if only they would allow him the chance. And of course there was always the question of what to do with Liliana. At the hotel, her mother could feel she was leading an independent life in her own suite of rooms, with her mind kept alive by looking out of the window at the new arrivals. It made it easy to keep an eye on her, and, to be fair, it was often useful to have the benefit of Liliana's experience, although that of course would diminish if she continued to go doolally.

*   *   *

THANKS FOR THE MEMORIES!

The front page of the *Chronicle* was given over to a selection of photographs from the previous Saturday's D-Day celebrations. Julia was flicking through the newspaper as she waited in the reception area of Mr Patel's business headquarters.

'You can go in now,' said Mr Patel's PA.

Julia snapped the newspaper closed and put it back alongside *Business Week* on the glass table, then smoothed her short pencil skirt over her hips.

Mr Patel's boardroom was very much in the style of the man himself – extremely businesslike, but with a touch of the exotic. On one wall was a shimmering representation of the Taj Mahal. Julia could never work out whether the brightness of the colours and the illusion of three dimensions was a product of the materials used to make the picture, or whether it was some sort of lightbox with no visible wires.

There was a long glass table, at which Mr Patel, his accountant, his lawyer and various other board members were seated, along with Sonny, his older son, who gave her a broad smile.

'Ah, Julia!' Mr Patel looked up, as though Julia's appearance was a delightful surprise.

Mr Patel no longer stood up to shake Julia's hand as he had done on their first meeting, partly, she suspected, because it put him at such a disadvantage in terms of height, but partly because she worked for him now, even though he treated her more like a favoured niece.

Julia was now publicity director of Mr Patel's charitable trust, and he also provided premises and invaluable practical advice for her hospice project. Much to her surprise, Iris's friend Vic had left a substantial bequest in his will. Julia had thought of their conversation over *limoncello* in Sorrento in much the same way as people talked about what they would do if they won the lottery, and when Vic's brother had challenged the bequest Julia would readily have given in had it not been for the help of Mr Patel's lawyers.

Julia had always been hopeless at maths at school, and she hadn't improved much since. Now, as the accountant took them through the Trust's end-of-year figures, she found it difficult to stop her mind wandering. The boardroom was on the top floor of the Sunny Stores Tower and had a magnificent view of the harbour, with container ships unloading and a couple of little pilot boats guiding a towering cruise ship into berth.

Feeling an almost imperceptible nudge against her left arm, Julia turned sharply and saw that Sonny Patel, who was sitting next to her, had written a note on his copy of the agenda.

'I'm taking delivery of a Sunseeker this summer.'

Julia scribbled a reply in the margin of her agenda. 'Lucky you!'

'G & Ts on deck?' Sonny scribbled. He was a terrible flirt.

'You bet!' Julia wrote back, then quickly covered her agenda with her elbow as Mr Patel looked in their direction.

'Will someone propose approval of the accounts?' he asked.

Sonny raised his hand.

'And a seconder?'

Julia obediently raised her hand. She had never understood why you had to approve the accounts – wasn't that the whole point of paying a professional? – but the time to ask the question had passed.

'Thank you,' said Mr Patel. 'Item two on the agenda is the proposed development of our first Sunnyside Care Home for the Elderly in Kingshaven. Sonny?'

Sonny Patel stood up self-importantly, even though he

was addressing only the six people in the room.

'Offers on the properties have been accepted. I've engaged an architect to work with a chartered surveyor who specializes in the regulations surrounding care homes to draw up a specification.' Sonny handed a sheaf of photocopies to Julia, who took one for herself and passed the others up the table. 'If we can approve that at this meeting, the next step is to move towards a planning application.'

'But first we need Nikhil's comments,' Mr Patel interrupted.

'Nikhil doesn't seem particularly interested,' said Sonny.

There was a hint of petulance in his voice that made Julia wonder whether Nikhil was their father's favourite, or whether his opinion was valued more because he had completed his studies and was now a doctor. For some reason, she didn't think Mr Patel held property development in the same regard.

'It's important to have a medical opinion,' said Mr Patel.

He was a very wise man, Julia always thought, and made his pronouncements like a sage. She'd never seen him ruffled. These were clearly not qualities his older son had inherited.

'Nikhil's speciality is oncology, not geriatrics,' Sonny declared, throwing his papers back down on the table. 'The chap I've employed is a proper expert in the field.'

'Nevertheless . . .' said Mr Patel patiently.

Julia exchanged awkward glances with other non-family members in the room.

'Well, if you're prepared to wait,' said Sonny, 'bearing in mind that the esteemed doctor hasn't turned up for the last five board meetings . . .' He sat down, folded his arms across his chest and rocked back on his chair, balancing on the two back legs.

Julia felt a terrible urge to giggle, as she often did during family rows, but she bit down hard on her tongue to suppress it.

'Nikhil said he would be here,' said Mr Patel.

There was a moment's silence, and then, as if by magic, Mr Patel's phone rang. He picked it up, listened, smiled, and said: 'Send him in!'

'I apologize to you all for my late arrival,' Nikhil said, looking at each person round the table in turn. 'I was giving a patient a diagnosis. It wasn't something that could be hurried.'

Wasn't oncology the medical name for cancer? How awful! thought Julia. Perhaps it was terminal? Poor thing! Mr Patel's second son looked too young to be informing people of their own mortality, although she thought he would do it with calmness and empathy beyond his years. He was a leaner, taller version of his older brother, but their eyes betrayed very distinct characters. Sonny's shone with cocky confidence; Nikhil's were deep pools of compassion.

He pulled out a chair and sat down opposite Julia.

'We are looking forward to hearing your opinion about our proposals for the Sunnyside Care Home,' Mr Patel announced.

As Nikhil stretched his legs under the table, he accidentally kicked one of Julia's ankles. His expression changed in an instant from surprise to concern, then relief as his eyes met hers and she half-smiled reassurance at him. The exchange couldn't have taken more than a second, and wasn't apparent to anyone else at the table, and yet Julia felt a pink blush creeping up her chest and blossoming on her face at the secret intimacy of it.

Sonny pushed a copy of the plans across the table to Nikhil, who flicked through and looked up.

'I'm really not sure how much use I can be to you, Daddy,' he said. 'I should imagine the principal issues for old people centre around access and convenience . . .' Nikhil was trawling for something sensible to say.

'The plans show several bedrooms on the ground floor for the more infirm,' Sonny explained. 'We've put the kitchen in the basement, because the people using that will be able-bodied. And the staff bedrooms are in the attic. There's a lift to the first and second floors . . .'

'Very good,' said Mr Patel, nodding at Nikhil as if he, not Sonny, had put in the thinking. 'Julia's hospice is the next item on our agenda.'

Julia cleared her throat and shuffled her papers together nervously. She seemed to know instinctively how to deal with Sonny's flirtations, but, as Nikhil Patel looked at her now, she felt stripped of all her defences by the penetration of his gaze. It was as if he was staring into her soul, and she suddenly, desperately, wanted him to like what he saw.

'As I think you're all aware,' she began, 'the Summer House project, our children's hospice, is now up and running in larger, more suitable premises in Havenbourne. Fundraising activities are ongoing, but the principal income stream is from Sunny Stores, and we couldn't exist without it, so we do thank you very much, and we try to mention your support in all our publicity.'

She looked across the table, and Nikhil Patel rewarded her with such a wonderful smile that Julia had to remind herself of the advice of her old friend Bee: 'Don't shit where you eat.'

It was never a good idea to fall in love with someone you worked with, and she'd vowed she would never do it again. It had never been a problem so far because, she realized, she hadn't fancied anyone since Bruno. Until now.

*   *   *

Esther had instructed Bruno to wear a white T-shirt and the bandanna he wore at work to keep his hair off his face. 'It's a question of your image,' she'd said. 'Young sexy chef cooks new, sexy food . . .'

The T-shirt was fine, but Bruno wasn't about to wear a bandanna in the street. Instead he'd put it in the bag of shopping he'd brought with him.

Esther greeted him with a kiss on both cheeks in the reception area of the state-of-the-art offices in Camden. Bruno suspected that Esther wasn't nearly as important as she claimed to be, but he liked her confidence. She was one of the most in-your-face women he'd ever come across, but he often got the feeling that she was very adept at remembering phrases she'd heard her seniors using and repeating them as if they were her own. As he followed her shapely little body up the cast-iron staircase in the middle of the open-plan space, breathing the trail of perfume she left behind her, and sensing the gaze of many eyes on his back, he was glad of her encouraging face as she introduced him to Brian, whose name Bruno recognized as a serious documentary-maker, and Venetia, the co-director of the company.

Esther had suggested that he surprise her bosses by magically producing a signature dish in five minutes from shopping bag to table, but as he was introduced to Venetia, Bruno wasn't sure that strategy was going to work. She was one of those anorexically thin, slightly faded English roses with permanently hostile expressions on their faces, who, when they lunched at the club, chose roasted cod and baby vegetables, but spent the whole meal smoking.

They all sat down in a conference room that was like a glass box in the middle of the first floor. Brian asked him what television programmes he liked and Bruno replied that he didn't get a lot of time to watch.

'Do you have a favourite television chef, at least?' asked Venetia, already looking bored.

As Bruno tried to work out what would be the clever thing to say, Esther stepped in.

'As I see it, the point of Bruno is that he's a chef for a

different demographic,' she said. 'He's cool, he's sexy and he rides a motorbike . . .'

Bruno wasn't sure where she'd got that bit from, but he supposed it would be simple enough to learn if necessary.

'Clearly, I haven't done any extensive research,' Brian interrupted, 'but my instinct is that people who watch cookery programmes are middle-aged housewives rather like Delia Smith herself.'

'You're right,' said Esther. 'But the thing is that they'll fancy Bruno. He'll be their guilty secret. But he'll also bring a whole new audience to cookery.'

Unused to being talked about in the third person, Bruno suddenly stood up, took a saucepan from his shopping bag and banged it on the table.

'Boil us a kettle, would you, darling?' he asked Esther.

'Certainly,' said Esther, smiling at him, relieved that he'd finally come to life.

Bruno fitted together a single-burner camping stove, then produced a wooden chopping board, a handful of cherry tomatoes still on the vine, and a bunch of fresh basil.

'Hungry?' he asked, thrusting the herbs under Venetia's nose.

She looked taken aback.

'Don't worry, it's only five minutes till lunch,' Bruno said, striking a match and lighting the Calor Gas burner as Esther returned with a kettle of boiling water. He poured the water into the saucepan and sprinkled in some salt. 'In Italy,' he said, 'they say the water for your pasta should be as salty as the sea.'

Bruno poured in a packet of orecchiette, then, as it bubbled on the stove, set about halving the tomatoes and draining a jar of sun-dried tomatoes, talking all the time about the simplicity of the ingredients. When the pasta was tender and drained, he threw in the tomatoes with a heavy slug of olive oil, shook the mixture about, then tipped four portions into white plastic bowls.

'Some freshly grated parmesan all over!' he said, shaving soft curls from a hard wedge of cheese. 'And some torn basil! *E basta!*' He pushed the plates across the table.

'Six minutes,' said Esther, looking at her watch.

'This is good,' said Brian, tasting the food. 'The sauce is lovely and peppery.'

'It's the quality of the olive oil,' Bruno told him. 'My philosophy is simple: fresh ingredients used well. Doesn't have to be complicated to taste good; doesn't have to be difficult to impress . . .'

'Yes, all right,' said Venetia. 'I think we get the point.' She turned to Brian. 'He's definitely got something,' she said. 'But it's a question of finding the right place to put it. I don't think you'd work in a straightforward kitchen,' she told Bruno.

'We'll have to put our thinking caps on,' said Brian, and then both of them left for other meetings, leaving Bruno feeling deflated.

'I'm sure they completely loved you,' said Esther, as she helped him to pack up his gear. 'It's just a question of finding where to put you,' she echoed Venetia's words. 'Somewhere different. Somewhere that's unique to you.'

Bruno looked down into her eager face. A tomato pip had stuck to her cheek as a result of eating enthusiastically and talking at the same time. His natural instinct was to kiss it away, but he resisted. The transparency of her enthusiasm was girlish, almost childlike, and made her curiously vulnerable, and sometimes he wanted to pick her up and cuddle her hard, but he resisted, because he was pretty sure he knew what she felt about him, and it wouldn't be fair.

114

Chapter Three

Summer 1995

Iris had a fear of flying. She had waited until the last minute, hoping that she would be able to say, in all honesty, that she couldn't get a flight, but the travel agent was delighted to inform her there was a remaining seat on the Friday evening flight to London, Heathrow.

Staring at the ceiling of her one-bedroom apartment in Trastevere, with Fabio breathing evenly beside her, Iris wished women had a little of whatever it was in their bloodstream that made men sleep after sex. In her head she tested 'I dozed off and missed the plane' as an excuse, but in her heart she knew she could never bring herself to say anything so feeble.

She swung her legs out of bed. It was time to go, otherwise all the excuses she had toyed with and rejected might really come to pass: the Metro might genuinely get stuck in the tunnel; there might really be a traffic jam all the way to the airport; she might actually have her bag snatched – and then she would never forgive herself.

In the kitchen, Iris poured hot water on to a Lipton's tea bag, and absently corrected the homework Fabio had been working on, making several underlinings and omission marks in red pen on the paper before it occurred to her that it was not homework, but one of his poems:

When you gone, I wish you here with me
Instead with your family
Your sister engage her man
I engage you

The words were all the more touching for the uncharacteristic effort Fabio had put in. Iris guessed engage
must have involved looking up *fidanzata* in a dictionary.
She loved the way the poem ended so simply and wondered
whether this was an artistic decision or whether he just ran
out of ideas. She folded the piece of paper and slipped it
into her wallet, checking she had her passport and ticket,
then picked up her rucksack, not daring to go back and
kiss him goodbye in case he opened his eyes and pulled
her back down on top of him. But after closing the door
she wished she had, because in the coolness of the stairwell
she had a sudden shiver of presentiment that she would not
see him again. Iris told herself not to be so melodramatic:
she had a return flight booked in less than forty-eight
hours.

The plane took an age to taxi to its starting position and
stopped several times, allowing the tantalizing opportunity
for Iris to throw such a wobbler they'd have to let her off.

Was there something wrong? Out of the window, Iris
could see bits attached to the wings that looked flappy. Had
anyone checked that they were properly attached? A blur
of petrol vapour swirled round the engine. Could that be
right? Iris read the safety information on the card and the
advice, in Italian and English, on the sick bag in the pocket
on the seat in front of hers. Having stowed her book in the
overhead locker and become desperate for distraction, she
took her diary out of the soft brown leather shoulder bag Vic
had bought her in Sorrento, and concentrated on the page
of notable dates and religious festivals. The letters blurred
as the plane began its race to take off. There was a judder
of throttle, the ghastly sensation of nothing holding them

up, then, after a few seconds of miraculously not plummeting like a stone, Iris felt as if she could finally breathe again because there was absolutely nothing she could do now to change her fate. As the plane soared out over the sea, she craned her neck to catch her last glimpse of Rome, then, facing forwards, wondered whether she should get a gin and tonic to calm her misgivings about what lay ahead. The unassailable hurdle of getting on a plane had temporarily taken her mind off the fact she was returning to England, something she said she would never do. When Iris had left, Yuppies ruled, Mrs Thatcher was invincible, and the first evidence of mad-cow disease felt like a metaphor for the way the country was going. She'd vowed never to return. Sipping her drink, it occurred to Iris that she hadn't *vowed* anything for ages and she wondered whether this dulling of extremes was a good or a bad side effect of middle age.

'We're now beginning our descent.'

The pilot's voice woke Iris up and she looked out of the window.

Below, a line of twinkling resorts marked the English coast and Iris began to feel almost excited as she tried to pick out recognizable features. Was that Lowhampton below with its long harbour inlet? How far away was Kingshaven? If someone were standing on the promenade looking up at the sky, would they be able to see the lights on the wing-tips flashing? Would they wonder for a fleeting second, as Iris always did when she saw a plane, if there was someone they knew up there on board?

As the plane began to drop towards London, bumping through a layer of cloud, Iris's heart started to race again as her hearing muffled. She swallowed and yawned and, when the cloud parted, the bright grid of suburbia was unexpectedly close and rapidly getting closer. She stared at the lines of street lights, and the dashing headlights of cars on the motorway, thinking about all the lives and stories those houses and vehicles contained. Apparently, there were only six degrees of separation between any two people on the planet, which must mean any one of the stories down there might at any time coincide with hers. It was a strangely humbling thought, but as the plane thumped down on the runway Iris realized it was completely irrelevant, because they were certainly going too fast to stop. The pilot applied the brakes, but it was no use! Iris closed her eyes, bracing herself for inevitable impact, explosion, flames!

The plane slowed almost to a standstill and began its wander round the maze of runways to the terminal.

'Welcome to London,' said the pilot.

Iris was the only person in the cabin clapping.

She expected the temperature in England to be cooler than in Rome, but, if anything, it was closer and hotter. At the rail information desk, Iris discovered that it was too late to get to Woking in time to catch the last train to Lowhampton.

Faced with the alternative of hiring a cab to take her all the way to Kingshaven, which would cost a fortune and probably involve telling her life story to the cabbie, there was something perversely appealing about the anodyne anonymity of an airport hotel, a kind of staging post between the present and a past that felt so much closer now that she was back.

Iris finally managed to open the door of her hotel room with the plastic card the desk clerk programmed at reception. It closed behind her with a squelch of suction, as if it had been sealed. The room was as cool as a fridge and the lights came on automatically. It was so impersonal and soundproofed from the world outside that Iris felt a little as if she was unwittingly participating in an experiment to see how human beings behaved in isolation. She looked at the telephone beside the double bed, wondering whether she should ring Kingshaven, but she knew that one of them would probably offer to drive up to get her. Anyway, she'd prefer to surprise Fiammetta in the morning, rather than land on her late at night when she was getting her beauty sleep or ironing her dress, or doing whatever it was that brides did the night before their wedding.

'Why are you getting married?' Iris had asked when Fiammetta rang to tell her.

'Because we're in love,' Fiammetta replied cautiously, as if suspecting a trick in the question.

'Why can't you just live together?' Iris wanted to know. 'What difference does it make?'

It should make no difference logically, Iris supposed, because she didn't believe in marriage, just as taking vows in church shouldn't mean anything to an atheist, but a church wedding was emblematic of everything Iris had rejected in her life. For a moment, with the international connection yawning between them, Iris had been at a loss; it was a bit like talking to some of her intermediate students, who could tell you in near-perfect English what colour their hair and eyes were, and how many brothers and sisters they had, but struggled to a standstill when you tried to engage them in meaningful conversation.

Inexplicably, she'd felt a surge of anger with Fiammetta for expecting her to spout the usual thrilled congratulation.

'Aren't you happy for me?' Fiammetta had asked.

'I suppose, if *you're* happy.'

'Well, nobody's making me get married, are they?' Fiammetta had sounded quite spiky, and there had been a bit of an awkward pause, before she continued, a little timidly, 'You will come, won't you?'

'I'll try,' Iris had replied, feeling rotten as soon as she put down the phone, wishing they could just start the conversation all over again, so that she could act overjoyed like any normal person.

Iris took her outfit out of her rucksack and hung it up,

hoping that the creases would fall out by the morning. The navy-blue sleeveless shift with narrow white belt was definitely classy, with a touch of Jackie O about the straight-across neckline. Freckles with too much tan was never a good look, and though Iris had been thin all her life, with none of the usual sagging of upper arms and thighs she'd noticed among her peers, the bit between her neck and boobs had recently gone a bit baggy. The white linen jacket was smart, although she couldn't help thinking that Fabio, whom she had taken shopping with her, based his choice on what his bourgeois mother might deem appropriate attire for a wedding. She took his poem from her wallet and read it again, thinking how silly it was. A forty-five-year-old woman in reasonable shape was allowed to have fabulous sex with a twenty-four-year-old man, nothing more.

Iris couldn't face the idea of eating alone in the restaurant, so she raided the minibar for a packet of salted cashew nuts and poured herself another gin and tonic.

*   *   *

WELCOME TO KINGSHAVEN. The sign was defaced with indecipherable graffiti.

'Look out for the Palace Hotel,' Esther instructed.

'I thought it was the Castle,' said Cat.

'That's where the wedding is, but it's full, obviously. This was the only other place I could find,' Esther told her.

Not for the first time, Cat wondered whether it had been wise to take Bruno at his word when Esther had asked him what he was doing at the weekend, and he'd told them, adding, 'Why don't you both come down?'

Esther insisted it was important, as his future producer, that she see him in his home environment. The seaside town where he'd grown up might even provide the setting for his proposed series. Anyway, who could resist a freebie weekend on expenses, she'd asked, insisting Cat tag along as well.

The reception hall of the Palace Hotel reminded Cat of the foyer of one of London's grand theatres after the audience has left – plush, gilded, and so profoundly empty she could almost hear an echo of busier times.

Esther smiled at the middle-aged man at the reception desk in the expectation of some pleasantry or weather cliché, but he neither smiled nor spoke. There was a claret-coloured plastic badge on the lapel of his suit with a crest and the words 'Here to serve you' printed in gold.

'Esther Stone. I have a reservation . . .'

The man checked in the large leatherbound reservations book. 'Credit card, please.'

'The room's already paid for,' said Esther.

'For any personal charges you might incur.' He looked at them as if they seemed like the kind of people who might do a runner before settling the bill for the minibar.

'Any chance of dinner?' Esther enquired with determined brightness.

'We've had to close the restaurant due to staffing problems. Second floor.' He handed her a key with a plastic fob with the same design as his badge in gold.

The room they had been allocated overlooked the drive, not the sea.

Esther had had enough.

'C-c-c-can I help?' asked the man on reception, now smiling nervously as if he could detect her complaint in the air.

'We've just driven all the way down from London. There's nothing to eat and you've put us in a horrid little room!'

The man's expression twitched. 'I see no reason, since we're not c-c-c-completely full this weekend, not to up-grade you to one of our luxury twins.'

Esther said nothing.

'With a s-s-s-sea view?' he went on.

'Fine,' Esther finally agreed, cutting short his worsening stutter.

'I can only apologize about d-d-d-dinner. There are tea- and coffee-making facilities in the room of course. I could send up additional supplies of shortbread . . . ?'

'If you would,' said Esther, adding audibly under her breath: 'Jesus! What a dump!'

The room had a smell of newness, although the furnishings were claret and navy, and very 1980s. On the desk, there was some writing paper with the hotel's crest and a claret leatherette folder with polypockets containing hotel information with meal times, useful telephone numbers, and flyers for local businesses: KAC Watersport; The Crystal Circle – Well-Being and Tarot; Sid's Taxis. At the back of the folder under a criss-cross of claret elastic was a crested notice printed on thick cream paper.

Cat began to read out loud.

Jewel of the South Coast

The Palace has been owned by the King Family since it was built in 1850. Originally a Seaside Villa, the Palace became a Hotel in 1882 and, except for a short period during World War II when hospitality was offered to the Royal Air Force, has been Open to Guests ever since. Described by novelist Daphne W. Smythe (a regular visitor in the 1930s and 1940s) as the 'Jewel of the South Coast' . . .

'Who's Daphne W. Smythe?' Esther wanted to know. 'I've never heard of her,' Cat admitted.

. . . The Palace Hotel has welcomed many Renowned Guests throughout its Long History. Since 1952, the Hotel has been under the Management of Eddie and Libby King and their Family, who have overseen the modernization of facilities required by Today's Discerning Guest, while making every

effort to retain the Hotel's Traditional Character. Each room is fully En-suite, with telephone, television, trouser press, hairdryer, and tea- and coffee-making facilities. The Ballroom is equipped for Conferences of up to 80 people. The Spa facilities include a Steam room and Jacuzzi.

The steam room and jacuzzi were temporarily closed, the man on reception told them.

'What about the bar?' Esther demanded.

'The bar is open, madam.'

'Well, thank God for that!' said Esther. 'Because Today's Discerning Guest is in urgent need of a drink.'

*   *   *

A heady scent of lilies pervaded the Castle and the grand staircase was garlanded with white ribbons and ivy. All the advance preparations had been made: tables were laid; champagne was cooling in the rented fridges; the party organizers had departed for the evening to return early the next morning.

In the kitchen, Bruno was wondering why he had suggested a tower of profiteroles instead of a traditional wedding cake, because he could no longer remember a time in his life when he hadn't been making choux buns. As he took the final batch out of the oven, he ran through a checklist in his head. The crème pâtissière was made. One of his assistants could pipe it into the buns the following morning. All he would need to do was supervise the chocolate sauce and assembly of the tower. He counted through the courses, now wishing he hadn't decided on such labour-intensive canapés – parma ham and melon had to be assembled right at the last minute or else the ham went wet, the mixed *bruschette* needed different times in the oven, but he thought he could probably trust the staff to get them ready while he was at the church. Once they

123

were out of the way, it was simply a matter of doling out the antipasta, and timing the wild-mushroom risotto. He was serving the *porchetta* with green salad on the table. An Eton Mess of meringues with local raspberries and cream, which had been requested by James for dessert, couldn't be simpler.

Bruno told himself he just had to keep calm as he wiped his hands on a tea towel to answer his mobile phone.

'It's Esther. You'll never guess where we are . . .'

'Surprise me,' said Bruno.

'At the Palace Hotel, Kingshaven.'

'Who?' Fiammetta mouthed, walking into the kitchen halfway through his conversation.

Bruno pressed the end-call button.

'My flatmate and would-be producer,' he said. 'I've asked her to the reception – hope that's OK?' he said.

'Of course! Where is she?'

'At the Palace.' Bruno pulled a face. There had been no reason to mention his history at the Palace to Esther, but it was typical of her to put her foot right in it.

'Maybe she'll get together with James and Winny?' Fiammetta suggested with a little giggle.

James had decreed that he and Fiammetta should spend their wedding eve apart and, since there was no question of Fiammetta going to stay with her father, James had volunteered to spend the night at the Palace with his childhood friend and best man Edwin King, the youngest of the King boys, leaving the twins together in the empty Castle that felt almost sepulchral with the trailing ivy and pervasive scent of flowers.

For supper, Bruno made cheese on toast because it was simple 'comfort food'. The kitchen was now a very different place from when he'd first cooked the dish they used to call Welsh Rabbit. Amid the industrial stainless-steel units he could barely visualize the kitchen as it had been when they were children, with its old butler's sink and ancient electric hob with grill underneath, where forgotten toast frequently used to catch fire.

The kitchen door was open to the garden, but there was no movement of the stifling air. For dessert, Bruno cut up slices of apple, just as their father used to do in autumn when they brought windfalls in from the orchard.

'They say it's the hottest summer since nineteen seventy-six,' said Fiammetta.

Bruno thought that on the night before her wedding they should probably be talking about something more profound than the weather, but he found it difficult to fathom what his sister was feeling. Fiammetta had always been a bit odd, but sometimes he felt as if she had been sleepwalking through her life for the past few years.

'Excited?' he asked her.

'To be honest, it all feels a bit surreal,' Fiammetta replied.

'Living here?'

'I've always felt at home in this place. I was never happy after we moved.'

'No,' said Bruno. He didn't think her unhappiness had stemmed from moving house, but he didn't want to go there. Fiammetta had such a different way of looking at things, it sometimes felt as if they had experienced completely different childhoods.

'I don't know how I'll feel when the guests start arriving. I've told James I'm having nothing to do with it . . .' said Fiammetta.

'Tomorrow?' Bruno asked, not understanding.

'I meant when we open the house to guests.' Fiammetta laughed. 'But as a matter of fact, tomorrow as well. I'll hardly know a soul, except you and Winston.'

'And Iris,' said Bruno.

'Do you think Iris will come?' Fiammetta asked anxiously.

'I think she will,' Bruno said, with more confidence than

he felt. 'Is Julia coming, by the way?' he asked, trying to make the question sound casual.

'No,' said Fiammetta. 'She and James have fallen out. Are you relieved or disappointed?' she asked, as ever, straight to the point.

It had been nearly five years since Bruno had last seen Julia in person although he had spotted her photograph once or twice in the *Lowhampton Echo* when he was down for weekends. She looked good. Better, almost, than she had in the days when she was his boss, and his lover, at the Palace. Liberation from the Kings suited her. Her hair was shorter, her dresses were shorter, as if she'd finally realized how sexy she was. It was probably a good thing that she wasn't coming, he thought.

*   *   *

Iris decided that it would be sensible to have breakfast before putting on her wedding outfit. It wasn't that she was a messy eater, but she had noticed that the only time she ever spilled sauce down her front was when she was wearing a pale colour, and, by the same logic, she was almost bound to drip milk on her navy linen dress. The restaurant was divided into sections with fake terracotta roofs and crude murals to give the impression of views even though there were no windows. Iris chose Sugar Puffs. She never ate breakfast cereals in Italy, but the smell of Sugar Puffs – like the warm sweet smell of hay – conjured an almost Proustian memory of wellbeing. She seemed to remember the jingle, 'Pour out the sunshine', but thought, on reflection, that might have been about cornflakes.

The wedding was scheduled for two o'clock and Iris reckoned that if she was at Woking by ten she should be at Lowhampton by eleven. The bus to Kingshaven took about an hour and if there was no bus she would have to get a cab, but, either way, there was plenty of time. After eating and

126

reading a broadsheet newspaper, something she had missed after years of the *Guardian International*, she was back in her room by nine o'clock. Wearing just her underwear, she cleaned her teeth, packed her rucksack and finally slipped on her outfit.

The woman in the mirror looked sophisticated and discreetly rich. Her hair was short, her dress elegant. Even her mother, Sylvia, would be pressed to find fault. Almost before the thought had flown through her mind, Iris looked down at her bare feet. Frowning, she picked up her rucksack and tipped the contents out on to the bed. Her spongebag, jeans, vest, book and yesterday's underwear were all there, but there was no pair of white leather court shoes with navy toes and heels and Iris knew why, because now she remembered putting them right by the door of her bedroom in Trastevere so that she wouldn't forget them. A moment of grim triumph – she clearly remembered telling Fabio in the shop that they were not the sort of shoes she would ever wear – was followed by a judder of panic: how on earth was she going to fit shoe-buying into her suddenly hurried schedule?

*   *   *

The sea was a sheet of silver and the solidly azure sky scratched by the vapour trail of a plane too high up to see. The weather was going to be kind, Michael thought, feeling a throb of pleasure as he stopped for a moment to incline his face to the sun on his morning walk.

And Iris was coming!

'Fiammetta asked me to give her away!' she'd told him on the phone. 'I suppose I should be pleased she hasn't been entirely subsumed by sexist convention, but I haven't got the first idea what to do in church. I've bought them a Parmesan cheese,' she'd added. 'Do you think that'll be all right?'

'You're bringing it with you?' However would one carry such an object through an airport, he wondered. Perhaps roll it?

'Have you any idea what a Parmesan cheese weighs?' Iris laughed. 'Or how bad it smells? I'm having it sent. If they don't want it, I'm sure Bruno will.'

'Good idea,' said Michael, unable, for some reason, to get the idea out of his head of Iris sitting on a plane with a Parmesan cheese on the seat beside her.

Now, as he straightened up and continued his morning walk home, it occurred to him that perhaps he should have got Fiammetta and James a wedding present and felt ashamed that he hadn't thought of it. It suddenly occurred to him that he had the perfect gift in his possession, if only he could think where to find it.

Michael began to hurry along the promenade. He locked the door to the shop behind him when he went in, and left the sign saying CLOSED, then made his way to the back of the shop, where another padlocked door led to the storage area, which had once been the yard at the back of the warehouse but was now enclosed by the first-storey floor. As well as Bruno's windsurf board and sail, which were almost as wide as the space, there were a couple of children's bikes with punctures that had waited years to be repaired and a small tower of faded plastic buckets and spades bought by Anthony and his family over the years. The concrete floor was slightly gritty with sand, and the room smelt of the sea, but it was dry. Michael edged his way through the piles of junk, squeezing between stacks of banana boxes containing books he had acquired in house clearances but not yet sorted.

In the far corner there was an old trunk, one of many from the attics of the Castle. After Sir John's death, Michael had catalogued most of the old folios and documents and persuaded the county museum to house them, but there was one ancient wooden tube that he had never been able to part with containing the original plan for the walled garden. The tube was fastened with a crumbling leather strap with a rusty buckle that Michael now prised open. The plan inside, still dry and intact, was a yard or so wide when unfurled.

As he looked at the meticulously inked and labelled grid, with its tiny, perfect illustrations of box hedges and topiary, Michael's eyes swam with memories.

The walled garden had been Claudia's place. Standing there beside her in the sunshine that first morning they'd come to visit, he'd felt a kind of peace settle on his shoulders.

'It's magical, isn't it?' she'd whispered and he could feel her breath on his cheek as he inclined his head towards hers.

They had repaired it as much as they were able with no money – digging over the beds, patching the broken panes of the glasshouse with polythene to protect seedlings they planted; weeding, watering, watching the fruit of their efforts grow.

Michael could still see Claudia in a flimsy summer dress, as fragile and fleetingly beautiful as a rose in full bloom, picking her way along the broken brick path with a heavy mug of tea in her small hands as he dug the potatoes.

When she died, he'd scattered her ashes in the walled garden, and their two-year-old daughter Fiammetta, who couldn't have known what he was doing, had suddenly demanded to be lifted up to smell one of the roses that rambled across the walls. She'd inhaled deeply, just as she had seen adults do, then spoken one word. 'Heaven.'

*   *   *

Michael rolled the scroll back up, then, with the tube under his arm, he locked the door to the shop and started walking purposefully up the road to the Castle.

The stone frontage of the Castle had been cleaned at some point during the twenty years since Michael had last approached the building from the beech avenue. Otherwise, it was much the same as it had always been, unlike the rear of the property – often seen from his walks along the ridge – which had changed beyond recognition during Sylvia's tenure. A swimming pool had replaced the walled garden, the orchard chopped down in favour of a mini golf course.

Today, several vans were parked on the crescent of gravel in front of the house: a florist's, a greengrocer's, a butcher's. The front door looked wet with the shine of new black paint and was standing slightly ajar. Inside Michael could see staff dressed in black with long white aprons busying themselves with preparations. For a moment, it felt like glimpsing back to a time when there would have been servants at the Castle. As Michael raised his hand to knock, the door swung open.

The waitress looked him up and down. He didn't think she was a local girl, and she clearly had no idea who he was: not a guest, not the postman . . .

'Could you give this to Fiammetta, please?' Michael asked.

'What is it?' She took the large, heavy tube gingerly, holding it away from her body to avoid soiling her apron.

'It's a gift,' he said.

What did I expect? Michael asked himself as he walked back down the avenue under the canopy of beech trees. Was there some romantic part of his brain that had envisaged if not reconciliation, then at least, acknowledgement, or his daughter running after him to say thank you?

What was important, he told himself, fighting the sudden debilitating crush of humiliation, was that he had done the right thing. A small gesture, in the scheme of things, but at least Fiammetta could now return the garden to its former glory. Claudia would approve of that. If Fiammetta wouldn't forgive him for the mistakes he had made in his life, perhaps Claudia would.

It was ridiculous to find comfort in the thought, he told himself, pausing to look out over the glittering bay, because neither of them had believed in an afterlife, and there was nothing logical about his need to know what Claudia would have felt if she were alive. But somehow he did. Not knowing what she would think made him feel as if he had lost connection with her.

*   *   *

When she was a child, the room Fiammetta was standing in had been known as the Chinese room because of the handpainted wallpaper – a pattern of delicate pink lotus flowers on a turquoise background – that had been replaced with wipe-clean peach damask during James's stepmother's tenure. In Fiammetta's childhood, there had been a suite of large black and gold lacquer furniture. Now the space was mostly empty except for her canvases and materials. The walls were white and the floorboards stripped of Sylvia's deep-pile carpet. The room faced east and was very light and quite cold because of the tall sash windows on the front elevation of the Castle.

As she watched her father walking despondently away from the house, Fiammetta found herself thinking that he was wearing old man's trousers that made his legs look frail. There was only a finite amount of time left for them to be reconciled but, whenever she began to incline towards forgiveness, anger frothed up inside her body like a chemical reaction that she couldn't control.

One of the waitresses brought the object up to her, holding it away from her body, as if it might contain explosive. Fiammetta slid the plan out and, seeing what it was, smiled. Her father had brought her the walled garden on her wedding day, knowing it was a special place for her.

Her eyes clouding with tears, Fiammetta rushed back to the window, just as he was disappearing from view. Would he have accepted an invitation to the wedding if she'd asked? He had always been disparaging about the institution of marriage, and, as an atheist, he probably would have refused to come to the church. Anyway, it was too late now. She and James had agreed no parents at the wedding. James's mother's presence at his sister Julia's wedding had apparently been such an unmitigated disaster, James had not been prepared to risk having her at his own. It had crossed Fiammetta's mind to wonder whether it was a good idea to marry into such a quarrelsome family, but her own was just as dysfunctional.

James had never read *Anna Karenina*, and when she quoted Tolstoy's famous words about happy families being all the same and unhappy families being different, he said, 'Well, I'd rather be straightforward than complicated any day.'

It was one of the things that had made her decision to marry him amazingly simple: Fiammetta had had enough complicated to last a lifetime.

*   *   *

'Why did you let me drink so much?' Esther grumbled, pulling the cover up over her head and turning over.

Cat filled the glass of water beside her friend's bed and left the room as quietly as she could.

In the entrance hall of the Palace Hotel there was a life-size porcelain tree covered with flowers and birds. The clock face in the hollow of the trunk showed the time as nine o'clock, although when Cat sat down for breakfast a waiter told her that they had finished serving hot food at nine thirty, but reluctantly agreed to bring her tea or coffee.

'Coffee, please. A cappuccino.'

'There's only filter.'

When the coffee arrived it tasted bitter, as if it had been so long in an urn that the metal had corroded into the liquid.

If Esther had come down, Cat was sure that she would have called the waiter back to inform him that Today's Discerning Guest required fresh fruit salad, not a bowl of sad-looking prunes. Today's Discerning Guest would like wholemeal bread, not flaccid triangles of cold white toast, but, like the few other guests, Cat simply pretended to read her paper, irritated but resigned, and very English.

This morning, the man on reception was Edwin King. Cat and Esther had discovered this when he and his friend James plied them with drinks in the bar the previous evening. It had been great fun until Esther, having consumed three large glasses of poor quality white wine very quickly, asked, 'What are you two doing in this dump anyway?'

'Lovely day,' said Edwin now.

'Yes,' Cat agreed. 'Think I'll explore.'

The High Street had a shabby timelessness that reminded Cat of every holiday she had been on as a child. There was the usual selection of souvenir shops with postcard racks and spinning windmills on sticks, a 7/11 Sunny Stores, with its bright sunrise logo. There was a Chinese takeaway and an Indian restaurant, Taj Mahal Tandoori, whose menu included English dishes with chips and peas for the unadventurous; the Crystal Circle had chunks of jagged amethyst and various sizes of smooth onyx egg in the window, as well as a selection of dangly jewellery and several notices advertising yoga classes and a Psychic Fayre. Further up the hill was a library and a bank (both closed at the weekend), and a charity shop displaying assorted cream jugs and mismatched porcelain tea plates, with a rack of old paperback books outside, their pages spotted with translucent patches of sun oil.

The best hope of a decent coffee seemed to be a Rombout filter in the empty saloon bar of the Albion pub. The room was dark, with net curtains ochre from years of nicotine absorption, the bar made of dark wood, with horse brasses nailed along it. It looked and smelt so much like an old-fashioned pub that in London, where all pubs now had a theme, it might have been described as an 'authentic Victorian-style establishment'. It was empty, apart from the barman polishing glasses and exchanging an occasional word with a grumpy man concealed behind a frosted-glass screen with the words Public Bar engraved on it.

'It'll be a busy day for you, will it?' asked the barman.

'They've all got their own cars,' replied the surly, disembodied voice. 'You can't get up to the Castle for Porsches.'

By the time the coffee had dripped through, it was luke warm. Cat took a sip and abandoned it.

'Can you tell me where the caravan park is?' she asked.

'Turn right, up the hill and left by the station,' the bartender informed her unsmilingly, and, as she left, she was sure she heard the word 'foreigner'.

There was a steam train standing in the station and a banner advertising that Thomas the Tank Engine was coming the following weekend. It was only when Cat walked into the Forest Valley Caravan Park that she finally recognized the place as somewhere she'd been before. The view of the bay from this aspect seemed familiar, with the sea shimmering beyond tall pine trees.

They hadn't stayed long at the site, Cat remembered her mother saying, because it was the long, hot summer of 1976 and there had been no water. Now, standing on stubbly grass baked brown by another unusually hot summer, Cat had a sudden distinct memory of two children about her age filling buckets from a standpipe, the boy mischievously pressing his thumb on the tap, causing a rainbow spray of droplets in the bright sunlight, the girl squealing as she got a soaking, and Cat yearning to play with them, but not knowing how to ask.

The path down through the trees to the seafront gardens stirred no further memories and the promenade was like many others along the South Coast, with rainshelters and a dilapidated pier that had a sign nailed on the gate saying 'Danger'. Cat paused outside the amusement arcade, gripped by the flashing neon and the fruit machines clattering invitingly. The bleeping, bewitching interiors of amusement arcades had been forbidden territory when she was a child, to be hurried past as if danger lurked inside.

'Can't we just look?' Cat would ask.

'It's not a suitable place,' her mother would reply.

'Why?'

'It's not meant for our sort of person.'

'What is our sort of person?'

'Don't be cheeky.'

The area round the harbour had a few pubs, and a café with the appetizing smell of fish and chips wafting out. The window of the Shell Shop featured an illuminated shell sculpture of the Last Supper, reduced from £79.99 to £49.99. Cat suspected that if you were the sort of person who wanted such a thing you would be prepared to pay the higher price; and if you weren't, fifty quid would seem like a lot of money. The careful division of her pocket money to buy presents for her schoolfriends had always been an important end-of-holiday ritual. Her mother always used to suggest letter racks, or those fabric badges embroidered with a single distinctive feature and the name of the resort, but Cat knew that nobody ever used letter racks or sewed badges on. She would insist on purchasing tiny glass swans or ceramic woodland animals that had to be wrapped in her vests to ensure their safety on the journey home.

The Bookshop on the Quay was a three-storey stone building that looked as if it had once been a warehouse.

The windows at street level were stuffed with rows of orange Penguin paperbacks. Cat pushed open the door. Inside, there were books from floor to ceiling, rows and rows of bookshelves with narrow aisles between.

A man with a shock of white hair swept back from his face was sitting at a wooden desk, reading. He looked up.

'Good morning.'

Cat had a peculiar feeling she recognized him.

'I was wondering,' she asked, 'do you have anything by Daphne W. Smythe?'

He looked perplexed. 'Why is that name familiar?' he asked.

'Apparently she used to stay at the Palace Hotel,' Cat elaborated.

'You could try under S.'

He pointed towards the back of the shop. His voice had a northern accent, not the local burr.

Cat's eyes scanned the spines, which were arranged in strict alphabetical order.

'Any luck?' he called.

'No,' she said. 'It's not important. I just wondered what sort of novels she wrote,' she said, walking back to the desk.

'I seem to think a kind of lesser Agatha Christie,' said the man. 'I doubt you're missing anything.'

He went back to the book he was reading. Cat liked the smell of the shop. She didn't feel quite ready to leave.

'Isn't there a children's book called *The Bookshop on the Quay*?' she asked.

The man looked up sharply, but his smile was like the bestowal of a blessing. 'You're the only person who's ever remarked!' he exclaimed.

'I can remember the cover,' Cat said. 'It had a bookshop with a striped awning and the windows seemed to be glowing with invitation.'

'A Puffin. I was reading it to my children around the time we came here.'

Cat suddenly realized where she had seen the man's face before. On the back flap of a shiny new hardback book.

'Are you Michael Quinn?' she asked.

He looked taken aback. 'Why?'

It wasn't the answer she was expecting.

'I read your book, *Foreigners*,' she said. 'I loved it.'

That smile again, making her glad she'd dared to say it.

'You're the only person I've met who's read it,' he said.

'I loved the story called "Romans in Britain". I love the way you write about the betrayals and deceits going on just beneath the genteel surface of things . . .'

'I thought it was a story about censorship,' he said.

'So there are no erotic mosaics lurking under Kingshaven?' said Cat, laughing.

'I don't think they'd put such a thing on public view, do you?' Michael smiled enigmatically. 'Are you a writer yourself?' he asked.

'I work in a bookshop in London,' Cat replied, a little flustered.

'Here for the weekend?'

'Yes.'

'For the wedding?'

'Not really,' said Cat. It was too complicated to explain.

*　　*　　*

Iris was sitting on the train at Woking station. The train had come in on time but now refused to leave the station because of a signalling failure further down the line near Micheldever. The excuse had been made several times over the PA system, as if informing passengers of the precise location of the problem was going to make them more forgiving. As minutes on the station clock ticked by, Iris knew that if she had nipped out and bought herself a pair of suitable shoes, she could have been back on the train by now. As it was, she was going to have to keep on her pink Converse trainers, the only shoes she had with her, and if the train didn't move within ten minutes she wasn't even going to make it to Kingshaven in time for the service.

The irony did not escape her that she was fuming with impatience to get to an event she had been dreading. It was almost the same feeling of tense fidgety anxiety she'd experienced on this same train journey twenty-five years before, when she'd been called back to Kingshaven to meet Bruno and Fiammetta for the first time. Then, as now, her head was full of questions. Would she know what to do? Would she cope? Would she be found wanting and let everyone down?

Iris could remember the conversation with Winston as if it were yesterday because it had changed the course of her life.

'Look, Iris, I think you should come down. Claudia's very ill and I don't know what's going to happen to the twins . . .'

Winston's normally smooth voice had been clipped, staccato. It had frightened her.

'But they don't know me!' Iris protested.

'Who else is there?' Winston asked.

How typically sexist of Winston it had been to think that the children needed a woman to look after them, and how unenlightened she had been to accept it without question. But she'd always been glad he did call, because she couldn't imagine what life would have been like without knowing Bruno and Fiammetta.

*   *   *

It wasn't putting on the original ivory silk Dior dress, nor the specially made shoes that went with it, nor the wide-brimmed, saucer-like hat which completed the outfit

138

that jump-started Fiammetta's nerves, but the sound of Winston's helicopter landing on the lawn. Whether it was the whirr of the helicopter blade resonating with the rhythm of her heart, or simply the realization that guests were arriving and her wedding was no longer some distant event she didn't really have to think about, her pulse suddenly started to race and her legs turned to jelly.

She stared out of the window as Winston got into the waiting taxi and sped away towards the church.

'Are you ready?' Bruno called up the stairs.

There was no saliva in Fiammetta's mouth and yet she thought that if she opened it, a loud scream would come out.

'Iris isn't here yet,' she said, in a voice that sounded disembodied, as if it wasn't coming from her.

'The service is supposed to start in ten minutes,' Bruno called, uncharacteristically impatient. 'We can't all wait until Iris decides to show, if she *is* going to show.'

Fiammetta could hear him coming up the stairs. All she wanted to do was find a place to hide and stay there until the fuss had gone away, just like she used to when they played hide-and-seek at their Christmas party when they were children. Able to keep quiet and still so long, she'd always been the last to be found.

'Are you coming or what?' Bruno was standing in the door.

Fiammetta turned round and watched her brother's features softening from strict to soppily sentimental.

'You look sensational,' he told her, his eyes welling with improbable tears.

'I don't know if I want to do this,' Fiammetta whispered hoarsely, unable to move from her position by the window.

'All brides feel like that, don't they?' Bruno tried to soothe.

'I'm not a bride!' Fiammetta exclaimed.

139

What she meant was that she hadn't stopped being a rational human being just because she'd put on a white dress. But perhaps she had? The outburst made her feel a little calmer.

'What do you want to do, then?' Bruno asked.

'Don't keep looking at your watch! It's the most important decision I've ever made, and I won't be hurried.' She glared at him.

'There are at least a hundred people waiting in the church for you,' Bruno reminded her. 'And I've got a thousand canapés to get ready.'

'All of a sudden, it seems like such a big deal,' Fiammetta said.

The words hung in the space between them for several seconds before Bruno said, 'You can always get divorced . . .'

'All right, then,' Fiammetta finally decided. 'I'll come.'

Now it was Bruno who looked uncertain. 'You're not doing it because of the canapés?' he asked, with a worried look.

Then, she didn't know who started it, but they were both laughing.

He offered his arm as she picked her way down the staircase, careful not to catch her small heels in the layers of net underskirt. Bruno's arm felt strong and steady. He held the door of the convertible white Rolls-Royce open for her, making sure all her skirt was in, and she felt suddenly proud of her brother for being such a gentleman.

'Here goes,' he said.

As the car rolled through the profoundly cool shade of the beech-tree avenue, then emerged into blisteringly hot sunshine, Fiammetta held on to her hat, wishing she'd thought to pin it. Her hair was scraped back into a tight chignon and she didn't dare take out any of the pins in case the whole lot tumbled down. The outfit required smoothness. The chauffeur kept at a steady speed down the hill, past hedgerows lacy with cow parsley, over the humpback bridge, and down towards the recently reopened station with its banner announcing that Thomas the Tank Engine was coming soon.

'All this,' Bruno waved at the rolling fields, 'will soon be yours.'

'Oh, do stop!' Fiammetta laughed. 'Hang on, which way are we going?' she asked, alarmed, as the chauffeur missed the fork to the church and changed to a lower gear for the incline of the High Street.

'We've got to go the long way round,' Bruno told her. 'Everyone wants to see you. There's nothing Kingshaven folk like better than a wedding.'

Fiammetta laughed, hoping that he was joking. But, as he'd intimated, there were people lining the streets who cheered and applauded as the white car drove past. The lights were red at the bottom of the hill and, as the car stopped, several people she didn't know wished her luck, and a little girl handed her a silver plastic horseshoe with a white ribbon handle. Suddenly, Fiammetta spotted someone she did recognize running towards the car.

'Don't move off just yet!' she instructed the driver

Nikhil Patel puffed up and grabbed the top of the car door.

'Hey! Nikhil!' Bruno leant across to greet his friend. 'What are you doing here?'

'Checking out a property for my father,' Nikhil explained breathlessly.

'I thought Sonny was the property expert.'

'My father wanted a medical opinion,' Nikhil said.

'Why don't you come to my wedding?' Fiammetta asked him, wondering why she hadn't thought to invite him. 'I'm sorry I—'

'No.' Nikhil stopped her mid excuse. 'No. Thank you. I couldn't . . .' His limpid dark eyes held hers for several seconds. 'You look beautiful,' he said finally.

Even though he was a grown man now, who shaved and wore a smart suit on a hot day, he couldn't disguise his anguish, and Fiammetta thought that he might be about to cry, just as he had when she had informed him, many years ago, that she had fallen in love with someone else but still wanted to be friends.

'Oh, Nikhil,' she said, clutching his hand.

'We'd better get a move on,' Bruno said, seemingly oblivious to the poignant little drama going on between them. 'We're holding up the traffic.'

As the car moved off, Nikhil ran along beside it, keeping his grasp of Fiammetta's hand, until they were going too fast for him to hold on any longer.

'Don't marry James Allsop!' he suddenly shouted. 'Marry me!'

Fiammetta turned round in her seat to wave at him.

'Marry me!' he called desperately, looking incongruous, standing in the middle of the road, the jacket of his smart suit open.

The cry echoed in her head all the way to the church.

'Wait here a moment.' Bruno quickly helped her out of the car, then ran up the path and into the church to announce their arrival.

Standing alone in the sunshine, Fiammetta could still hear Nikhil's voice in her head, but she was suddenly distracted by the sight of a familiar figure standing on the church steps, looking as alone and anxious as she herself felt.

'Iris!' Fiammetta hurtled up the path to hug her big sister so enthusiastically that her saucer hat was pushed off her head.

'Oh my God!' Iris cried. 'Look at you!' She held her at arm's length, then indicated that Fiammetta should do a twirl. 'Now I understand,' Iris said finally.

'What?' asked Fiammetta.

'You had to have an excuse to wear this dress!' said Iris, bending down to pick up the hat.

'Is it OK?' Fiammetta asked.

'You look like a perfect mixture of Audrey Hepburn and Katharine Hepburn,' Iris told her, which was about the nicest compliment Fiammetta had ever been paid. 'There is, however, a slight problem with my own costume,' Iris confessed.

Fiammetta smiled at the word 'costume', as if it was a fancy-dress party. 'But you look lovely,' she assured Iris. 'So . . .'

'So unlike me?' Iris finished the sentence.

'So smart!' said Fiammetta.

'Apart from . . .'

Fiammetta followed Iris's gaze down to her bare feet.

'It's this or pink baseball boots,' said Iris. 'What do you think?'

For a moment, Fiammetta was tempted to lobby for the baseball boots, just to see the look on James's face.

'Hate to rush you,' said Bruno, emerging from the church, 'but the organist is nearing the end of his repertoire, and it's becoming rather unfashionably late . . .'

Fiammetta and Iris looked at each other.

'Come on, then,' said Iris, as if she was eager to get it over with. 'What do I have to do? I won't have to kneel, will I?'

'You don't have to do anything,' Fiammetta told her. 'Just be beside me. Oh, I'm *so* glad you're here!'

As she gave her tall half-sister another quick hug, Bruno held the door open for them, and Fiammetta felt the congregation turn as one to look at her.

As the organist struck the first familiar notes of Handel's Arrival of the Queen of Sheba, she took a deep breath, and held out her hand to Iris, just like when she was a little girl about to cross a busy road. Automatically, Iris grasped it and together they walked down the aisle.

*　　*　　*

'Wasn't there a film called *The Barefoot Contessa*?' asked a familiar voice behind Iris, as she stood in the churchyard, watching the bride and groom having their photographs taken on the steps.

Winston's smile was so disarmingly frank, Iris couldn't immediately remember the reason she was meant to be cross with him.

'It's a hot day, you should try it,' she said, looking at his immaculately polished black shoes, which had probably been hand-made somewhere posh like Savile Row, as no doubt had his slightly shiny grey suit, his gleaming white shirt and his narrow pale-grey silk tie.

His hairline had receded a little, but otherwise Winston hadn't aged much since she'd last seen him.

'Almost ten years . . .' he said, as if reading her thoughts. 'Live Aid.'

It was mad to hold a grudge for ten years, but Iris still felt herself flushing with the memory of that day. Swept away on a tide of goodwill and cold lager, she'd allowed herself to fancy Winston – which was completely absurd after knowing him all her life – and then he'd introduced her to his new girlfriend, who was about nineteen, and Iris had felt totally humiliated.

'I never knew what had happened to you,' said Winston.

'I went home,' she said, adding pointedly, 'I felt a bit old for it.'

'You look just the same!' he said, with a delighted smile. 'That's a very elegant dress, by the way.'

'My toy boy chose it for me,' Iris told him, unable to resist the temptation to shock.

'Clever toy boy,' Winston replied equably.

'And how is Jazz?' Iris needled.

'What a good memory!' said Winston, making Iris immediately regret that she remembered the Live Aid girlfriend's name. 'I believe she's a children's TV presenter now. I've been married since then. Not to her . . .'

'Oh?' said Iris, feigning disinterest.

'And divorced,' Winston added.

'How many's that?'

'Three.'

'Do you think you're an optimist, or simply a bad judge of character?' Iris asked.

It was as if the last ten years had fallen away and they'd gone straight back to their old banter.

'Maybe I just haven't found the right woman?' said Winston, holding her eyes for a second. 'Perhaps that makes me an optimist.'

'How long do you give this?' Iris said, nodding in the direction of the scene on the church steps. The photographer was ordering some of the guests to throw confetti on a count of three, in spite of the pimply vicar's rather unromantic decree against confetti in his opening words to the congregation.

'In my experience,' said Winston, in a low voice so that people around wouldn't hear, 'the time a marriage lasts is inversely proportional to the expense of the wedding. If the nuptials involve lavish preparations, particularly in a foreign country, guests flown in, designer dress and cake, then it'll last a couple of years at most. This, I'd say, is a medium-sized event, not too flashy, only one maid of honour . . .' He winked at Iris.

'Is that what I'm called?' Iris pulled a face.

'No press,' Winston continued with his calculation. 'I'd say this has an average chance.'

'Meaning?'

'Five years?'

'Not such an optimist, then,' said Iris.

'Perhaps we should be talking about something else,' said Winston, conscious that their irreverent conversation was attracting attention. 'How is Italy?'

'It's fine,' Iris replied.

Less than twelve hours since she'd left, Rome seemed

very far away now, and Iris felt as if the time since she'd last been in Kingshaven had simply melted to nothing. It was the smell of a place that you forgot, she thought – the slight tang of seaweed on the air, an occasional fatty waft of fish and chips – and it made her feel oddly nostalgic.

'However often I try to run away from Kingshaven, there's always something that seems to draw me back,' she remarked.

Winston raised his eyebrows at the wistful tone.

'Maybe I should accept that rather than fighting it?' Iris suggested.

Now that she was here, she didn't know why she had been dreading it so much. It was really good to see Fiammetta, and Bruno, and Winston too, although she didn't want him to know that. He was quite sleek and smug enough already.

'You've changed,' Winston said.

'Have I?'

'Mellower,' he said.

'You've changed too,' she told him.

He looked at her expectantly, as if she was about to return the compliment.

'Balder,' she said.

Winston laughed heartily.

The photographer finally allowed the bride and groom to walk down the path to the waiting car and the chauffeur drove them away in a flurry of more confetti thrown by Bruno and a vivacious-looking brunette. The guests began to disperse from the churchyard, but Winston seemed in no hurry.

'How are you getting up to the Castle?' he asked Iris.

'Don't you have a car?'

'I came down by helicopter,' Winston told her.

'As you do,' said Iris. 'So where is it?' She glanced round the little churchyard.

'It dropped me at the Castle,' he said.

'Yes. I imagine it's tricky landing between tombstones,' said Iris.

'Why don't we walk back together?' Winston asked.

'All right, then,' Iris agreed, glad of the opportunity to acclimatize gradually, rather than being flung into the midst of a wedding reception where she didn't know anyone. 'Let me just retrieve my bag.'

She'd left her rucksack in the cool porch of the church. When she emerged into the bright sunshine again, she had put her pink baseball boots back on.

'Don't even think about saying anything,' she warned Winston, as he took her bag and slung it over his shoulder.

*   *   *

The walk back to the hotel from the seafront was much steeper than Cat expected, and the midday sun felt intense enough to burn her bare arms. As the church bells began to ring, Cat quickened her pace. She'd lost track of the time, and she was a little worried that Esther might still be in bed, expecting Cat to wake her up for the wedding. When she saw the key to their suite hanging on its hook behind the reception desk she breathed a sigh of relief, and as there was no one manning reception she slipped round the back of the desk and took the key herself.

The heavy curtains were still drawn, but the French doors were slightly open, allowing a draught of sea air to waft in, occasionally sucking the curtains against the glass, then releasing them. Cat flopped down on the bed. The church bells had stopped now and there was no sound apart from the occasional distant shriek of children jumping waves, and the faraway jingle of an ice-cream van. She reached for her watch on the bedside table. It was three thirty. No wonder she felt hungry, but she couldn't be bothered to go back down into town to get something to eat.

Cat opened one of the four tartan portions of Highland shortbread piled beside the kettle on the tea tray. The taste of the biscuit was just the same as when she used to make it with her mother, and it returned her instantly to the gritty sensation of sugar and butter sticking to her fingers as she tried to master the art of rubbing in, occasionally looking up from her bowl to see miraculously amalgamated golden crumbs falling from her mother's hands. The mixture was pressed into a round tin, pricked with a fork and baked in the oven. The best bit was not the eating (because, by the time it was cooked, Cat's infant tummy was already full of raw dough she had sneaked into her mouth during preparation) but the presentation of a crumbly triangle to Daddy with his cup of tea when he came home from work.

'Did you make this all by yourself?' he used to say.

'No.'

'Yes, you did!' her mother would correct.

Which had always confused Cat because the normal rule was that you mustn't lie.

The sound of a nearby door banging returned Cat to the present. The slight reverberation of her headboard against the adjoining wall made her think that someone had just entered the room next door. The light coming in round the curtains was warmer, less piercing. Cat was about to step out on to the balcony, when a man's voice instructed: 'Please don't stand out there!'

Automatically, Cat stepped back inside, before realizing that the instruction was not directed at her.

'Why shouldn't I?' The voice of the woman on the next-door balcony sounded defiant.

'You might be seen!' said the man.

'Oh, for God's sake. I'm sick of sneaking around.' Nevertheless, the woman's voice retreated inside.

'Just until the b-b-b-boys are a little older . . .' The man's voice became more soothing.

'The boys aren't even here!' she snapped back.

'Just until the divorce comes through,' he pleaded. 'Or Granny Lily . . . It would kill her!'

'Of course it wouldn't kill her! Some people say your granny knows only too well what men get up to – especially men who are separated from their wives.'

Cat wished that she had managed to get a glimpse out on the balcony. She couldn't picture the woman, but she was certain that the man was the reluctant receptionist on the desk when they arrived.

'I b-b-beg your p-p-pardon. What on earth do you m-m-m-mean?' he stuttered.

'You're very innocent all of a sudden.'

'You're very naughty.'

Torn between guilt at eavesdropping and fascination with the unfolding scenario, Cat strained to hear as the voices became lower.

'When the cat's away . . .' said the woman.

'The mice will p-p-play,' replied the man's voice, with a nervous giggle.

'Are you a man or a mouse?'

'Hickory dickory dock . . .'

'The mouse ran up the—'

His thin squeal of pleasure was profoundly intimate, not something anyone else should hear. Cat froze, unable to make any sound or movement in case they realized someone was listening.

The headboard banged against the wall.

'Ahhh!'

There were a few moments of quiet. Then the man's voice said, 'If I were a mouse, I'd live inside your knickers.'

Cat noticed the stutter had gone.

Still, she didn't dare to move. It was rather like playing an unwitting role in a bedroom farce, she thought, or perhaps a Daphne W. Smythe detective novel.

*   *   *

'I'm Esther,' said the young woman seated beside Iris.

Iris noticed that the arrangement round the table was boy, girl, boy, girl, until it got to Winston, and then it went Esther, Iris, James, Fiammetta and Edwin, a drippy-looking chap, with the distinctive narrow-eyed features of a King, who was best man. The person she was particularly dreading seeing, James's sister Julia, didn't appear to be there, which was a relief. Iris had never been quite sure whether their confessional exchange in the lounge of a Sorrento hotel had been real, or a product of alcohol-fuelled paranoia, but it wasn't something she wanted to revisit on this, or any other, occasion.

'Which one are you a friend of?' Iris gave Esther her full attention.

'Bruno, actually,' said Esther. 'He's the bride's brother.'

'I'm Bruno's half-sister.'

'You're Iris?'

'Yes,' Iris admitted.

'Bruno's always talking about you,' said Esther.

The look of expectation on the girl's face made Iris wonder whether she should respond that Bruno was always talking about Esther too, but since she was sure he'd never mentioned her she thought she'd better not.

'I haven't seen him for seven years,' Iris said.

The waiter refilled her glass of very cold white wine, which was deliciously thirst-quenching after the hot walk up from town.

'You live somewhere exotic, don't you?' Esther asked.

'Rome.' Iris didn't think that really qualified as exotic.

The starter was a salad of tender broad beans and *pecorino*.

Iris hadn't realized how hungry she was before the dish was placed in front of her.

A waiter poured more wine.

'Bruno said you introduced him to Italian food,' Esther tried again.

'Did he?' Iris said, thinking, for some reason, of the menu at the Luna Caprese restaurant in Soho, with its endless pasta sauces and twenty different ways with a breaded veal cutlet. She had sometimes taken the twins when they came to visit her in London in the seventies. Italian food in England had come a long way since then, she thought, as the starter plates were cleared away and replaced with small portions of intensely flavoured wild-mushroom risotto, a small blob of *mascarpone* cheese melting into the middle under a sprinkling of flat-leaf parsley.

'This is my favourite,' said Esther. 'Although it's about a million calories. Not that you have to worry, obviously,' she added.

The wine being served was now red, its depth and warmth a perfect compliment to the dark, earthy taste of the *porcini*. Iris realized belatedly that she had failed to reciprocate or acknowledge Esther's compliment. Iris had always been beanpole thin and flat-chested. Esther was short and curvy. She was wearing a dress that showed quite a lot of cleavage. Iris couldn't think of the appropriate response.

'Bruno said you went on a gastronomic tour of Tuscany together,' Esther persisted.

'In a Cinquecento,' said Iris.

Was it because she was so unused to speaking English that she found the small talk so difficult?

'What's a Cinquecento?' Esther asked.

'It's one of those tiny little Italian cars,' Iris told her. 'Ours was yellow. It was so cramped inside, I had to put my feet up on the dashboard, and, of course, that meant we had to stop, frequently, at every little town, to stretch our legs and taste the local food and wine . . .'

The main course had now arrived: *porchetta* roasted with a crisp crackling on the outside, the melting centre stuffed with herbs and fennel seeds. Bowls of green salad and tiny potatoes roasted with salt and rosemary were placed on the table.

'Bruno has this sixth sense for sniffing things out,' she told Esther. 'I remember once he suddenly swerved off the road we were on and we bumped all the way down a track, and at the end was a kind of castle with an aristocratic family who'd been making Chianti since the time of the Medici. They invited us to dinner.'

'How exciting!' Esther enthused.

'And of course, all the mamas fell in love with Bruno, and wanted to adopt him.'

'Everyone falls in love with Bruno,' said Esther a little wistfully, and then, as if suddenly bored with Iris's answers, she turned to Winston on her right.

'I'm Esther,' she said.

'Winston.' He shook her hand.

'Winston, do you know Iris, Bruno's sister?'

Esther was very confident socially. She reminded Iris of the well-bred young women who used to work in publishing.

'We go back a long way,' Winston replied, smiling across Esther at Iris. 'In fact, in our teens we were the founder members of the Kingshaven Liberation Front, weren't we, Iris?'

'The Kingshaven Civil Rights Movement,' Iris corrected him, immediately realizing that sounded ridiculous.

'We were best friends, but then I did a terrible thing . . .' Winston informed Esther confidentially, as if he were telling a child a story.

Esther was listening eagerly. 'What was that?' she asked.

'The worst possible betrayal of an idealistic young woman in the seventies . . .' Winston looked directly at Iris and she wondered exactly what he was going to say. She frowned at him. '. . . Was to vote for Margaret Thatcher,' he said. 'And Iris has never quite forgiven me, have you, Iris?'

'Clearly, you're the one who's still feeling guilty,' Iris shot back.

'I'm a reformed man nowadays,' said Winston.

Esther looked suspiciously from one to the other, as if there was a joke she wasn't party to. From what Iris had read, British politics was now so much a battle for the middle ground that someone of Esther's age would find it virtually inconceivable that friends could fall out over who they voted for.

'And what do you do?' Winston asked Esther the question Iris realized she should have asked long ago. She was so out of practice.

'I work in television. Actually, I'm developing a series with Bruno.'

Esther turned away from Iris, leaving her without anyone to talk to. As Iris watched them, she found herself mesmerized by Winston. Every mannerism was startlingly familiar – the slight incline of his head when someone else was speaking; the way he always listened with his mouth closed and his eyes lowered, taking in the other person's opinion in its entirety while giving away nothing of what he was thinking; the habit he had of brushing the tip of his nose with his finger before saying something serious – and yet they were details she did not remember when she thought about him.

'Are you through with that?' the waiter asked, making Iris aware that she hadn't eaten most of the food she had piled on her plate. She would have liked to finish it, but it was too late now because as she looked around she saw hers was the last remaining plate on the table. She indicated that the waiter could take it away, and told herself not to drink any more. Then James Allsop addressed her.

'Eyes bigger than your stomach?'

It was an odd phrase for him to use, Iris thought, because it had been a favourite of her mother's. Had James unconsciously picked it up from his hated stepmother, or had he chosen the phrase deliberately to irritate Iris?

'It was delicious,' she said neutrally.

'He's quite talented, your little brother, is he not?' said James.

As a boy James had displayed a sense of mischief that had appealed to Iris, but he had grown up into a man with an arrogant aura about him, and Iris felt constrained from saying what she would have liked because he was now, incredibly, Fiammetta's husband. She said nothing.

The waiter deposited plates with stacks of meringue, cream and raspberries in front of them. James immediately set about smashing his with a spoon.

'Fiammetta is so pleased you managed to come,' James informed Iris.

It was an innocuous enough thing to say, but it riled Iris that he should speak on Fiammetta's behalf to her, of all people! Was the inclination to patronize something that you were born with as an aristocrat, or was it bred into you at public school, she wondered. Was James a successful entrepreneur because he made people feel inferior? Winston's trick was to appear laid-back and inclusive, even though he was presumably just as ruthless.

'I hear you're planning to open again as a hotel?' she said. Winston had filled her in on the state of play on their walk up from town.

James flinched at the word 'hotel'. 'We're striving for the atmosphere of a country-house weekend. I think you'll find it rather different from the old regime,' he said.

'I never came here during my mother's tenure,' Iris informed him. 'We don't like each other.'

A glimmer of something – surprise, possibly, or approval – flashed across James's blue eyes. 'I'll have to show you round,' he said with a little more warmth in his voice.

There was a tinkling sound that made everyone in the room turn towards Edwin King, who was standing, tapping a glass with a fork.

'Ladies and gentlemen . . .' he began, reading from a piece of paper. 'As best man, it behoves me to say a few words about our esteemed host, the bridegroom . . .'

Raucous cheers went up around the room from a group Iris had privately identified as the Hooray Henrys, well-to-do men in their late twenties, who she imagined must have been James's contemporaries at Oxford, who probably worked in the City and drove the fast cars that were parked all the way up the road to the Castle. Some of them had emaciated girlfriends with them, who had stood in clusters, smoking, in the churchyard, and were smoking again now.

'I was delighted when James told me that he was marrying Fiammetta, because all his other girlfriends had been such complete slags . . . although may I say how lovely it is that so many of them are able to be here today!'

Everyone in the room laughed uproariously, except Iris, who couldn't believe what she'd just heard.

'It's from *Four Weddings and a Funeral*,' Esther whispered, seeing her incomprehension.

Iris hadn't been to see the film when it was on in Rome, knowing from experience that Italian dubbing was bound to kill the comedy.

'James and I were born in the same year, nineteen sixty-four . . .' Edwin continued. Having started out with a good joke, not his own, he soon lost the audience in an incoherent ramble and by the end of the speech the Hoorays were openly talking to one another, knocking back champagne that had been poured for the toasts, and loudly demanding more.

'. . . The bride and groom!' Edwin finished.

Everyone in the room scraped back their chairs.

'The bride and groom!'

There was a smattering of applause, then James stood up. Even though he looked every bit the lord of the manor in his morning suit, his body was so tense with nerves that Iris could feel her own muscles stiffening in sympathy as he prepared to speak.

'Welcome, everyone, to the Castle!' he said. There was an obliging cheer. 'As Winny has already explained, at some length . . .' James paused for the mocking laughter, '. . . my family spent a long time waiting to move into our rightful home. When I was a boy, my life seemed to be on hold until we got here. It felt a bit like being in a fairy story – one day the Castle would be mine, and only then would we be able to live happily ever after . . . But occasionally we visited my grandfather, and one of my first memories of the place – I suppose I must have been about six – was walking into the hall and seeing an extraordinarily beautiful little face peeping out from behind the banister on the staircase. When I looked again, the face had gone, and I remember wondering whether I had really seen her, or whether she was a sprite. Fiammetta eluded me for many years, but when I finally managed to catch her and hold her in my arms I knew instantly that I had to bring her back to the Castle, where she belongs. Ladies and gentlemen, I ask you, please, to raise your glasses to my beautiful wife . . . the bride.'

'The bride,' echoed the room.

Iris wasn't sure what to make of it. The speech contained more insight than she would have expected – there had always been a kind of changeling quality about Fiammetta, as if she wasn't quite of this world – and yet there was something alarming about the idea of her being captured and returned.

As the applause was dying down, she caught Fiammetta's eye, and couldn't tell whether she was looking anxious because she had felt the same slight shiver of foreboding, or whether she was expecting Iris to get up and say something.

A moment of panic was stilled by the sound of Winston's chair scraping back two down from her.

The sweep of his glance somehow managed to take in each individual, and the room fell instantly silent. For the first time in her life, Iris had a real sense of Winston's power. He commanded respect and, curiously, she felt tears of pride in her eyes.

'If this is a fairy tale, then I cast myself in the role of Godfather,' Winston began.

One of the Hoorays obligingly hummed the theme tune of the film.

'I've known Fiammetta all her life. She is as strong as she is delicate, as intelligent as she is stylish, and she is also a very fine artist. My hope is that in James she has found someone who will cherish and nurture all these qualities. I'm sure she has . . .'

Was there an element of warning in his voice, Iris wondered. Had he chosen the word 'godfather', with all its connotations of protection, for a reason? If so, she was glad that he would be watching over her little sister.

'James and Fiammetta have asked me to thank you all for being here to witness their union, particularly those who have come a long way, and especially Iris Quinn, who has travelled from Rome.'

Winston turned to Iris. He had a way of making it seem as if he was granting a favour, and even though she knew he was an operator, his charm was still difficult to resist, and she couldn't help blushing in the spotlight of his attention.

'Can we also have a round of applause for the chef who cooked this delicious lunch,' Winston said. 'Bruno? Where are you?'

On cue, Bruno emerged from the kitchen, looking very different in his chef's whites with a long white apron and a bandanna round his forehead. Glancing to her side, Iris saw, from the look in Esther's eyes, that the girl was in love with him.

Two waiters followed Bruno in, carefully pushing a trolley with a cloud of profiteroles and white chocolate on it. There was a collective gasp, and Iris felt more proud tears.

The photographer, who'd been snapping randomly all the way through the meal, now zoomed in on the spectacular cake.

Winston raised his champagne flute. 'May I ask you now to drink a toast, to a long and happy future together for Fiammetta and James.'

'Fiammetta and James,' murmured the guests.

As Winston sat down, Iris stretched her hand out behind Esther's chair to catch his, and mouthed 'Well done!' at him. Gripping her hand, he gave her a questioning look she didn't understand, that made him appear for a moment oddly vulnerable.

'There's dancing in the garden,' James announced as outside, on cue, a jazz band started playing.

Some guests made their way out into the garden, while others stayed at their tables, chatting. Esther stood up and excused herself, and Winston took the opportunity to shift one along so that he was sitting next to Iris. He picked up a half-full bottle of champagne and refilled her glass and his.

'Well done,' Iris congratulated him.

'I think it went OK, don't you?'

'Everything was perfect,' said Iris. 'The food, the wine, the speeches . . .'

'But?' Winston picked up on her hesitation.

'Nobody mentioned the L word,' Iris said. 'Love,' she added. 'Nobody said anything about love.'

'Don't tell me you're becoming a romantic in your old age?' said Winston.

*   *   *

Fiammetta had gone upstairs for a moment by herself. Standing in front of the mirror, looking at herself in her beautiful wedding gown, she was almost surprised to see that she didn't look any different now that she was a wife.

'Problems?'

James was standing in the door. With his golden hair smoothed back and his smart grey suit, he looked even more imposing than usual. Fiammetta's body twitched with lust. Holding his eyes in the mirror, Fiammetta tried to communicate her yearning for him to push her down to the floor and make love to her in her virginal dress, his breath hot and damp in her ear.

'Didn't you like the dress?' she asked his reflection coquettishly, realizing that he was about the only person who hadn't complimented her.

'Isn't it traditional to wear a floor-length gown?'

It was not the reply she'd expected.

'Oh, I hate those. They make me look like a doll with no legs,' she said.

James's eyebrows arched disapprovingly and Fiammetta began to wish she hadn't asked.

'The unconventional length drew attention to your sister's lack of footwear,' he continued.

'It was either that or trainers,' Fiammetta explained.

'She wasn't even wearing nail polish!' said James.

'How odd that you noticed!'

'Everyone noticed,' he said.

'For heaven's sake!' said Fiammetta, quite crossly. 'Iris was there. That's all that mattered to me.'

But clearly not to him. There was no trace of a smile on her husband's reflected face.

'Better not keep everyone waiting too long,' he said.

*   *   *

159

'So, tell me about this lover . . .' Winston said.

Iris couldn't remember mentioning a lover, but thought she must have because how would he know otherwise? How much had she had to drink? There was a half-full bottle of champagne on the table in front of them, but was it the first or the second? The hall was empty now, apart from the two of them. A disco had taken over from the jazz band and the fast dancing numbers were slowing down into smooches.

'He's twenty-four years old and he's my zipless fuck,' she heard herself saying.

'Zipless fuck?'

'Every woman's ambition,' said Iris. 'Pure, unadulterated sex, no ties.'

'I had no idea that was every woman's ambition,' said Winston.

'You never were much of a feminist,' said Iris.

'How long has this been going on, then?' Winston asked, sounding very grown-up, as if he were a doctor asking about symptoms.

'Feminism?' she asked childishly.

'Zipless fucking,' said Winston calmly.

'A couple of years, I suppose.'

Iris felt slightly sheepish. She wasn't sure that a zipless fuck was technically allowed to last that long. When she got back to Rome, she really must end it with Fabio. They'd got into a silly routine of her telling him to go, and him looking hurt, and her putting her arms round him and then it all starting again.

But she didn't have to think about all that now.

'Do you want to dance?' Winston asked Iris.

The song playing was 'Love can build a bridge'. It was far too slow and smoochy.

'Not really,' she said. 'You go ahead if you want to.'

'I'm happy talking with you,' he said.

'What about all the other people?' Iris felt a bit guilty

160

monopolizing the star guest. She'd noticed a couple of people hovering in the doorway in case Winston decided to break away, but he seemed to be either unaware of their presence or deliberately ignoring them.

'I can see them any time,' he said.

Since she didn't know anyone else, Iris was reluctant to push him away. 'I think I probably need some fresh air,' she said. 'Shall we go for a walk?'

'Good idea,' said Winston.

They slipped, unnoticed in the darkness, over the lawns towards the fence that marked the back of the garden. Winston held the wires apart for her to clamber through, just as they'd done as teenagers when they'd been for long walks together, earnestly discussing world peace, concept albums and other pressing concerns.

'I've got the shoes for it,' said Iris, scrambling over the hillocky field towards the ridge as Winston's leather-soled shoes kept slipping.

It was steep and she was out of condition, but she was suddenly crazily determined to get to the top before him.

A full moon was rising over the bay. The vast expanse of sea looked floodlit.

'You forget all this,' Iris said, as he finally arrived and they stood beside each other, gazing out. 'I miss the sea,' she added, turning to face him, and finding him closer than she expected. In the moonlight, his eyes looked very white.

Winston was staring at her.

'Race you to the Fort?' Iris suddenly challenged.

She'd beaten him only once before, when she was thirteen and Winston was about to leave Kingshaven for Oxford University, but she'd always suspected that he'd let her win, because he'd run for both his school and the county. Now, she thought the baseball boots might give her the advantage.

Without waiting for him to accept the challenge, she

hitched up the straight skirt of her dress and set off at a lick. Speed blew a welcome breeze on to her face. They'd never raced from so far away – it was surely a mile at least – and Winston was a sprinter, so the likelihood was that he would be fast for the first few hundred metres up to the bendy tree where the cliff path met the bridleway that led to the Iron Age Fort. If she could keep in front of him until then, Iris calculated, spurring herself on, she might just be in with a chance. She could feel the heat of her unpractised lungs burning in her chest, and her legs screaming in protest, but she kept running, her mind focusing only on her goal. She had forgotten how steep the rise of the bridleway was up to the Fort, but she couldn't stop now! Her heart began to race as she sensed him closing on her. The moonlight made the rocks and potholes negotiable, but she knew not to turn in case she tripped. For a moment she was gripped by panic as the grassy ramparts rose in front of her. She knew she would never manage to run up and down all the ramparts to get to the top. Hadn't there been a gap where the gate would have been in Iron Age times? Yes! There it was!

Winston was right behind her now and her legs were wobbly with exertion, but still she ran, bending forwards as the path got steeper and her knees began to give way. Finally the path flattened out. The top of the Iron Age Fort was a flat oval, the grass nibbled short by sheep who had grazed there since time immemorial. There were a few large stones in the centre where some said a Roman temple had once stood.

'I won!' Iris screamed, collapsing on to the springy turf.

A second later, Winston fell down beside her, and they both lay looking up at the sky, their chests heaving.

Tendrils of hair were sticking to Iris's wet forehead, and she could feel trickles of sweat under her breasts and down her spine. As her heart rate began to slow, she became aware of the turf prickling through the fabric of her dress, the smell of sheep droppings, and she knew she should get up, but she didn't want to. Next to her, Winston propped himself up on his elbow and looked down at her. She stared back at him, her breathing calmer now. Suddenly he was kissing her, and she was kissing him back with the fervour of teenagers, and it felt wondrous, elemental, and somehow inevitable, as if their lives had come full circle. They had always been part of each other, and this was what it had all been for: their bodies fusing together on a bed of history.

Chapter Four

Spring 1996

DYING RESORT?

Libby King stared at the typically tasteless and provocative headline on the front page of the *Chronicle*.

With the previous year's record-breaking summer, the town had just about recovered from the negative publicity following the bomb. About the last thing it needed before the start of the new season was an article about the whole place being turned into old people's homes.

An image flew through Libby's mind of one of those lovely old posters they used to have for the railway – when there was a proper railway. Then a present-day version sprang to mind: **Visit Kingshaven, where toddlers are blown up and old people come to die!**

Planning permission had finally been approved for three guesthouses – the Riviera, the Bella Vista and Sunnyside – to be turned into the Sunnyside Care Home for the Elderly. In principle, Libby believed it was a good thing to open the whole business of social care up to the private sector. When an establishment was run for profit, it certainly cut out a lot of the waste and sloppy habits that were bound to develop in a publicly funded institution. In practice, she wished it didn't have to happen in Kingshaven.

'It'll be nice for the old dears to look out at the sea,'

suggested her husband Eddie. 'It's good that they've found a use for some of those lovely Edwardian houses.'

Libby was slightly surprised at her husband's uncharacteristically positive take on things, until she looked up from the paper to see that he was half addressing his comments at her mother, Liliana.

In the past, the sharp exchanges between Eddie and Liliana that had punctuated most family meals had set Libby's nerves on edge. Now she found herself rather missing them. Though physically present, and still capable of feeding herself, Liliana had retreated to some distant place where nobody had a clue how to reach her. For almost two years she had not spoken, except, very occasionally, to whisper the word 'oyster'.

Everyone in the family had a theory about what it was she wanted, but Liliana had turned her nose up at six freshly shucked oysters quivering on their silvery shells, and when Eddie had mixed her a prairie oyster, a hangover cure involving a raw egg, Liliana had spat it out. Libby's sister, Pearl, who was increasingly unstable herself these days, felt it must be something to do with her.

'Pearls come from oysters, don't they? Mother of Pearl!' she'd added triumphantly.

Liliana said nothing, but occasionally Libby suspected that she was tuning in and out at will, playing a game that only she knew the rules to.

*   *   *

Liliana remembered the game she and Ruby used to play as they whiled away the hours looking out to sea in the bay window of her father's hotel, the Albion.

'If you could have any house, which one would you have?'

'A house with a balcony in that new terrace would be nice,' Ruby would volunteer.

'I'd have the Palace!'

Liliana, plain Lilian as she had been then, was always the more ambitious; Ruby conscious of her own limitations.

'Who would you marry?' Lilian asked.

'I don't care as long as he's rich and handsome!' said Ruby.

'And healthy,' suggested Lilian.

Ruby pulled a face. 'If he died, he'd leave me all his money.'

They'd laughed at that.

Little did they know at the age of thirteen that nearly all the eligible men of their generation would die before they had a chance to marry them, if not in some rat-infested trench or on the battlefield, then afterwards, from the Spanish flu that followed the Great War.

By the time Liliana and Ruby had reached a suitable age, there was barely anyone left.

'Beggars can't be choosers,' as Ruby had put it, when her engagement to Mr Farmer was announced in 1920. He was her senior by at least ten years, and looked even older, because of the valvular heart disease that had prevented his conscription. He certainly wasn't handsome, but he did own the freehold of the outfitters' shop on the High Street, where Ruby had a job as a seamstress.

The marriage was a blow to Lilian, because Ruby had been her constant companion since childhood. It was even more galling when Ruby took to prefacing all her sentences with phrases such as 'when you're married' and 'as a wife', as if to point up the difference between them. Gone were the days when they could confess to confusing thoughts or peculiar stirrings. Ruby's attitude became so insufferable, Lilian couldn't even bring herself to ask what 'it' was like, and whether 'it' was as they had imagined.

For a time, Lilian had felt bereft. There was little for her to do at her father's hotel except sit in the bay window, playing solitaire, looking out at the sound of a carriage arriving, or, very occasionally, a car chugging cautiously down the steep hill.

'In a way, it's a pity you can't work,' Ruby Farmer remarked one day when Lilian went in to buy knicker elastic. 'It would take your mind off things,' she added sympathetically.

Lilian's twenty-first birthday came and went.

'At what age are you officially a spinster?' Ruby wondered.

But Liliana's luck turned when her mother caught scarlet fever and was unable to accompany Lilian's father to the bridge circle they attended once a month at the Palace Hotel. Although a good deal younger than most of the guests, Lilian was a skilled player. When she and her father found themselves in a four with Rex King and his partner, an American woman he called Reggie, she played out the hand, making their contract on a bid of five clubs.

'Who'd have thought that pretty little head would contain such a sharp brain!' Rex complimented her. 'I'm sorry, I've forgotten your name.'

'Liliana Bow,' she heard herself saying, as she'd practised in front of the mirror. The extra 'a' gave the name a whole new dimension, making it sound so much more sophisticated.

'Delightful!' Much to her surprise, Rex King took her hand and kissed it. '*Enchanté!*' he said.

Reggie tittered.

'You must come again,' Rex said, ignoring his partner, his slightly puffy blue eyes looking deep into Liliana's.

'They do say he's a bit of a one,' Ruby opined the following day, when Liliana relayed the conversation complete with all Rex's highfalutin mannerisms. 'Not married either,' Ruby added, tapping the side of her nose.

Liliana blushed. 'I'm sure that's the last thing on his mind,' she said hurriedly.

'You may well be right,' said Ruby.

At the time, of course, Liliana had had no idea what Ruby meant. At the time, she felt as if a fairy godmother had waved a magic wand and granted her a new life with constant parties that required a new wardrobe. It gave Liliana enormous pleasure to order several dresses from Ruby Farmer, re-establishing the hierarchy of Ruby measuring up and sewing, while Liliana boasted about her new friends.

There were three King brothers: Rex, Basil and Alex. Rex and Alex were the racy ones, Basil a much slower soul, with a terrible stutter. Unlike the snootier girls in the set, who had a marvellous ability to ignore anything they found tiresome, Liliana was often the one who found herself listening patiently to Basil as he attempted to make conversation.

'It was so embarrassing,' she recounted one day, as Ruby sewed tiny black bugle beads on to a midnight-blue ballgown in the latest drop-waisted style. 'I was out on the terrace, having a breather, when Basil came and sat down next to me. "I, I, I, I, I w-w-w-w-was w-w-w-w-wondering . . ." he says,' Liliana imitated his stutter, '"w-w-w-w . . ." He tries again. "W-w-w-w-w . . ." Would? Right? I've got that bit, I say, thinking this could go on all night. Would I like to dance? He shakes his head. Would I like a drink? He shakes his head. "W-w-w-w-w . . ." Would? I say. He nods. Would I? He nods. Would I what? "W-w-w-would . . ."'

Ruby's peals of laughter shrieked through the flat above the shop where she lived with her husband.

Liliana continued: 'I'm telling you, Ruby, it was like a game of charades. Eventually we got to "Would I consider", and then he says, just like this: "marrying me?"'

'He asked you to marry him?' Ruby was so surprised she dropped her sewing, scattering the beads all over the floor.

'Eventually,' said Liliana.

'And you said?'

'I said I was sorry, but I couldn't.'

'You turned him down?'

'My heart belongs to another,' Liliana confessed melo-dramatically.

'Don't be so soft!'

'It's true! I can't tell you who it is.'

'You don't need to. You go all dewy-eyed whenever you talk about him. If you want my opinion, you'll wait for ever if you wait for him.'

Liliana wasn't sure she did want Ruby's opinion, nor anyone else's, but when she next went to the Palace, she found herself having to confront the subject sooner than she expected.

Rex King was showing her how to eat shellfish. There was a shallow silver bowl filled with crushed ice on a stand between them, and on it an array of crustaceans and bivalves. Despite living all her life in a town renowned for its seafood, Liliana had never really enjoyed the delicacy. It wasn't so much the taste as the anatomical look of the things, and the repulsive combination of textures: sea water, grit and softness that tasted like rot.

'But you absolutely mustn't chew!' exclaimed Rex, watching her trying to masticate the oyster he had just tipped into her mouth. 'You must learn to swallow!' He winked at Reggie across the room. 'Darling little Lily,' continued Rex, putting his thumb under her chin and drawing her face towards his. 'You really mustn't break my poor brother's heart.' He lowered his voice, his mouth so close to her cheek she could smell the masculine tang of his cigarettes and feel his breath warm and damp in her ear.

'I'm fond of him,' she murmured back.

'Excellent!'

Liliana realized with dismay that she had made a hash of

it. Rex habitually interrupted people's sentences, and now she'd given completely the wrong impression. Covered in confusion, she confessed, 'But I love another!'

Rex drew back his handsome face as if shocked, ran an impatient hand back through his corn-coloured hair.

'Dear little Lily,' he said, softly, 'I very much doubt this "other" would make you happy. I'm sure you're far too good for him. Really I am, quite sure.' His pouchy blue eyes looked deep into hers as they had done the first time they met. 'Now do have another oyster!'

*　　*　　*

In the front room of Cat's parents' house, a new piece of grey Lladro – a woman with a swan – had been given pride of place at the front of the collection. It had been Cat's Christmas present to her mother, but she had handed over her credit card in the Regent Street china shop with a heavy heart and would have much preferred to buy her mother something vivid from Liberty – a luscious devoré velvet scarf in stained-glass colours, or a necklace of amber beads – but at least she knew the gift had given her mother pleasure, and something to show off at one of her WI coffee mornings.

Cat noticed that she was mirroring her mother's posture, sitting on the edge of the cushion rather than relaxing back into the comfort of the armchair. She was conscious that her mother was looking at her clothes, a cinch-waisted dress from the fifties in fine black wool she'd found in an Oxfam shop, with only a couple of tiny moth holes, near the side seam, that no one, apart from Joyce, would spot. Although Cat had thought it suitably smart for Sunday lunch with her parents, she now realized her mother would find it difficult looking at something that she would classify as 'second-hand' as opposed to 'vintage'.

'Your father's trying a new recipe,' said her mother.

As if to confirm the unfamiliarity, clanking noises emanated from the kitchen and Cat and her mother exchanged complicit little smiles. Since his retirement, her father had taken up cookery with the same methodical approach as he lent to his gardening and his golf, reading books thoroughly, as if to make up in research any deficiencies of natural flair.

As a child, Cat had found it hard to believe that her father led such a boring life. When, as a teenager, she had discovered the books of Graham Greene in the library, she had been taken with the idea that Vernon Brown must be a spy. The job he went off to each morning was in the civil service, and his slightly shambling bearing and greyness of demeanour was very Greene-ian. Sometimes, when he came into her room at night thinking that she was asleep, he would spend quite a long time sitting on her bed, holding her hand in the darkness and staring at her, and the air would be full of unspoken thoughts, as if he was about to go away on some secret assignment that he couldn't tell her about, from which he might never return.

Once, during half-term, Cat had followed him to work and watched him enter the Ministry of Transport with many similarly besuited men, and emerge at lunchtime with the Tupperware box her mother prepared each morning. In St James's Park, Cat had hidden among the shrubs to observe him eating his sandwich, but no other person had approached him from the shadows, and his only communication had been with a duck who waddled up to his feet in the hope of crumbs. Watching her father breaking off a piece of crust and offering it to the bird with a gentle smile, Cat had felt ashamed of herself for spying on a moment that felt so intensely innocent.

She hadn't stayed to watch him coming out of work, having abandoned hope of seeing him loosen his tie, or bowl along the pavement with a beery group of colleagues.

Cat had never been able to imagine a secret life for Joyce,

because the most minor unforeseen circumstance made her mother so anxious that Cat knew she couldn't possibly have coped with any sustained deception. A late delivery of milk, or men repairing the gas main, even an unexpected knock on the door, were cause enough for concern. When a bird had got into the attic, she had locked herself in the downstairs toilet until Cat's father returned home from work. During Cat's teenage years, her mother had gone back to work part-time as a receptionist in a solicitor's office in Pinner. She had just about coped with the arrival of a fax machine in place of the telex, but had recently decided to retire early, in order to avoid training to use the new computer. Only minor variations were permitted to occasional coffee mornings she held with her WI friends – coffee cake with buttercream icing and a sprinkling of crushed walnuts might, on occasion, replace the usual shortbread. It was best to stick with what you knew. Once when the chairwoman, Prue Denby, had offered carrot cake with icing that involved yoghurt, it had been a subject of conversation for days.

'Passion cake, she called it!' her mother had reported, covering her mouth as if she'd said something rude.

'Esther and Bruno are making a cookery series for television,' Cat told her now.

An almost imperceptible flinch crossed her mother's face. She had always considered 'that Esther Stone' a bad influence, and thought it odd that they had a single man living in the basement.

'They're in Italy at the moment,' Cat went on.

'Does she speak Italian?'

Esther had rung the previous evening with a hilarious story about having to deal with an Italian used-car salesman. For some reason, they'd been filming in a lay-by when a car had veered off the road straight into Bruno's Cinquecento, writing it off. Luckily, Bruno had been buying fruit from a stall at the time, and nobody had been hurt, but it sounded like a considerable drama all the same.

'She seems to get by,' Cat told her mother, unwilling to worry her with the details. 'You know Esther.'

There was a disapproving silence, interrupted only when her father put his head round the door to say that lunch was served, and they followed him into the dining room at the back of the house.

He had cooked a chicken-and-leek pie with an impressively puffed-up golden pastry crust, but, underneath, the gravy was thin, the leek slightly underdone.

'The mashed potato is very good,' Cat told him.

'That was the work of my helpers,' her father said with a wry smile. 'Mr Marks and Mr Spencer.'

If it had just been the two of them, Cat thought they would have allowed themselves to laugh, but somehow that wasn't possible with her mother there.

Dessert was a rather dry bread-and-butter pudding, followed by coffee and the packet of Elizabeth Shaw after-dinner mints Cat had bought at the newsagent's beside the Tube station.

Her parents relayed news of a change in venue for the Rotary Club quiz night. More excitingly, the next-door neighbours, the Downings, were moving to Spain. Her father showed Cat the brochure for the development with houses painted ochre and terracotta against a bright-blue sky and balconies spilling over with red geraniums. The golf-course greens were vivid, and swimming pools sparkled azure in the sunshine. Cat couldn't tell whether the photographs were real, or computer-generated images. Cat's mother became quite animated in her disapproval of the venture, but her father's reluctance to criticize made Cat think that perhaps he would like to join the Downings sipping lurid cocktails on a terrace with a balustrade against a backdrop of the setting sun.

'I've got some news,' she said.

When her father's eyebrows shot up and her mother put down her cup, Cat immediately felt that she'd raised their expectations unnecessarily.

'It's nothing really,' she said. 'They're opening a new shop in the City and my boss has encouraged me to apply to be manager.'

Cat could see that her mother, while trying to look pleased, would have preferred news of a boyfriend.

'Do you think you'll get it?' her mother asked.

'Of course she will!' said her father.

The responses were so typical. Her mother was always anxious about the idea of anything new; her father unquestioningly over-confident in her abilities. Cat stared at the row of framed photos on the mantelpiece above the gas fire that was never lit, that told the story of a nice middle-class girl's progress from baby in a Silver Cross pram to university degree. The frozen smile under the mortar-board and gown was the only thing she had ever given them to be proud of, she thought, with the creeping sense of failure that always seemed to descend on her when she came home.

*   *   *

Lowhampton General Hospital was always very busy in the early evenings as an influx of after-work visitors arrived bearing fruit and flowers, and trying to compose anxious faces into suitably cheerful expressions. It was the time of day when the night shift of nurses arrived, and the day shift filtered out, dishevelled but gaining a new lease of life as they emerged from the disinfected air into sunlight, loudly shouting plans for evenings in or out across the car park.

From her frequent visits to the children's ward on behalf of the hospice, Julia knew that the doctors changed shift at that time too, and she sometimes hung around longer than was strictly necessary by the lifts, but she had not yet bumped into Nikhil Patel. Now, as the doors opened, he was there, his limpid dark eyes accentuated by a coat so pristine and white that for a moment Julia wondered who washed and ironed it for him, and felt an instant stab of jealousy for a woman she didn't even know existed. Nikhil Patel walked straight past her without a glance. The sensible part of Julia's brain cautioned against running after him – what on earth would she say?

'Excuse me! Excuse me! Dr Patel!'

Finally, he turned round, his serious face morphing from surprise to recognition.

'I'm sorry, I didn't see you!' he said, walking back towards her, and clasping her hand. His palm was dry, his handshake firm. He looked so apologetic, Julia reassured him.

'I'm sure you have lots of important things on your mind.'

Nikhil considered the statement for a few moments, being still too young to have developed the aura of impatience that most hospital doctors carry around them.

'Yes,' he said. 'And you?'

'Visiting,' Julia explained quickly.

'Coming or going?' asked Nikhil.

The story Julia had planned in her head suddenly began to fall apart. To get the maximum time with him, she ought to say 'going', and then they could walk down the long glass corridor towards the exit together. But if she was on her way out, she suddenly thought, wouldn't he wonder why she had been standing waiting for the lift?

'Well, coming really,' she said, trying to leave as many options open as possible. 'What about you?' she asked.

'I was just going to grab some lunch, if there's anything left,' he said, looking at his watch with a resigned smile. He'd obviously been doing something too important to think of eating at the proper lunch, or even tea, time. 'Do you have time for a coffee?'

There was a God!

Julia looked at her watch. 'Well, yes, I suppose,' she said. 'A quick one,' she added, for authenticity.

There were just two filled rolls left in the chilled section of the café, one cheese and tomato, the other containing ham that had gone rather grey.

'Can I tempt you?' Nikhil asked, lifting the glass flap.

Julia's tray bumped up against his on the stainless-steel ledge. She took her hand off, convinced that he would see that she was shaking. He was standing so close she could smell the starch on his white coat. Another shot of jealousy coursed through her limbs.

'No, thanks,' she said.

'Good!' Nikhil awarded her a smile that made her legs go liquid.

'Why?'

'Because I'm vegetarian,' he told her.

He was such a gentleman, he would have let her have the cheese and tomato, she thought. Even though he hadn't eaten all day, he would have given up his lunch for her!

'Me too,' she heard herself saying. Why not? The only meat she ate these days was chicken, apart from an occasional hamburger when she was with the boys. It wasn't much of a sacrifice to make. 'I do eat fish,' she blurted, unwilling to consign herself for ever to a diet of pulses and tofu. Surely even a vegan couldn't object to fish? But Nikhil couldn't be a vegan, she reasoned, because he was eating cheese. That was a relief!

'I thought so,' said Nikhil.

Why? Did she look like a fish-eater? Surely she didn't smell like one?

'Coming from where we do . . .' he said.

She looked perplexed.

'Kingshaven?' he said.

'Of course,' she said, thinking what an idiot she was.

Somehow she never thought of the Patels as Kingshaven people.

Nikhil ate quickly, swallowing each mouthful with a gulp of tea that he had stirred three teaspoons of sugar into.

'Better be getting back!' he said, looking at his watch again.

'Quite!' said Julia, picking up her bag.

'A pleasure to meet you again,' Nikhil said, offering his hand.

'I often visit the children's ward . . . for the hospice,' she volunteered.

Nikhil frowned. 'They'll be closed to visitors now,' he said.

'Yes, well, I'm visiting someone else this time,' said Julia, thinking on her feet. It was too risky to say she was visiting another ward in the main building because then she'd have to go back up in the lift with him and slip out again.

'Maternity!' she suddenly remembered. The maternity ward was in a separate building as you came into the hospital. 'A friend of mine . . .' She let her voice trail away, hating to start a relationship with out-and-out lies. 'Anyway, I mustn't keep you any longer,' she said, looking at her own watch. 'It's been so fascinating to see you in situ, as it were.'

'A pleasure,' said Nikhil, holding out his hand again.

She watched him walking away down the glass corridor until, as if conscious of her eyes on his back, he turned and gave a little wave, which made her realize she was staring and quickly turn away.

The evening air felt pleasantly cool on her face as she left the main hospital building and her footsteps felt light and skippy, although when she went over the encounter she couldn't honestly say there'd been much progress, except perhaps the establishment of a certain bond of caring. This was not a crush, after all, but a deep respect for a kind and

177

sensitive man, who would in time, she hoped, recognize similar virtuous qualities in her.

'All good things come to those who wait.' Was it Daddy who'd told her that, or maybe Granny Ruby? Some grown-up, anyway. It was the sort of thing Granny Ruby used to make her embroider in cross-stitch on a sampler. Not that it always turned out to be true, because sometimes Sylvia's motto, 'Be careful what you wish for', happened instead, although Julia didn't know what reason Sylvia had to be so circumspect, since she always seemed to fall on her feet.

As designer of the Signature label for Sunny Stores, Sylvia had wangled an invitation to Paris Fashion Week, where she had met and rapidly married a French businessman. Her clothing line had not been a success, but Sylvia had found herself another castle, this time with a moat. She'd sent a framed print of her new home to Mr Patel, although nobody seemed sure of the exact location. It was quite clear that Sylvia would not be encouraging visitors. Perhaps she had lied about her age, Julia thought, or perhaps she simply wanted to leave the past behind and start anew. She could sympathize with that.

As Julia walked out of the hospital building, it suddenly occurred to her that Nikhil might be looking down from a high hospital window and wonder why she was walking past the door of the maternity building when she had implied she was visiting it, so she stepped inside.

*   *   *

The pain was like a terrible instrument of torture clamping down on Iris's belly, compressing her insides with a relent-less grip so that she couldn't move, breathe or even think, but only cry out in agony. Then it receded so quickly she opened her eyes, wondering if she had imagined it.

Somewhere in the distance there was a television on.

England were playing Germany at Wembley. She couldn't hear the words, but she could tell from the excited pitch of the commentary that England were winning. She wondered how many baby boys born that night would be called Gazza.

The woman in the next bed had just gone down to theatre, leaving Iris temporarily alone in the ward.

It started again. Iris calculated that ten minutes must have passed since the last one. She tried to remember the breathing exercise they'd all practised in the antenatal class that she'd stopped going to when she realized she was the oldest person in the room, including one of the pregnant girls' mothers. Short little breaths out.

It didn't do anything except make her feel a bit of a fool, panting like an overheating dog. Perhaps they only told you to do it to stop you screaming?

'He-e-e-e-e-l-p!' Iris cried.

A midwife came this time. 'What's the matter?' she asked impatiently.

Iris gripped her arm, unable to speak until the contraction had passed.

'Any chance of some pain relief?' she asked. 'The breathing doesn't seem to help.'

'The breathing is for when you're pushing. You're nowhere near that point yet,' the midwife informed her. 'Try walking around, or having a nice hot bath.'

The bath had a brownish line about two thirds up the side and a dozen or so coils of black pubic hair scattered randomly like a Jackson Pollock canvas. There was a tin of Ajax and a sponge on the shelf beside, but as Iris shook a quantity of it into the bath, enjoying the clean, gritty smell, the clamp started tightening again, causing her to kneel on the floor, her face raised in supplication, like a penitent waiting for the lash.

Italians said 'Ayyyy!' instead of 'Owwww!' but it didn't seem to make any difference what sound roared out of Iris's mouth. When the pain subsided, she grabbed the side of the bath and hauled herself to her feet as quickly as she could, fearing that the next time might be the last, and she would give birth alone on the crusty red lino floor, or perhaps even die there.

The midwife was right about the walking. It was better than lying on a bed staring at the Fire Escape notice, which was just too far away to read. The corridor was slightly cooler than the ward. Iris read all the posters about the benefits of breast-feeding and warning signs for meningitis. Then she positioned herself just inside the automatic doors that led to the outside world and, when the strict-looking nurse on reception was looking the other way, stretched her foot out in front of the sensor, so that the doors slid open and a welcome chill of early evening blew in.

Hospitals had their own system of time that seemed to pass much slower than it did in the rest of the world. From the fading light beyond the doors, Iris estimated it must be nearly nine o'clock. The general hum of traffic was occasionally punctuated by the scream of an approaching ambulance, the cycle of siren growing faster as it came closer to the hospital.

The contractions must have started after five thirty, Iris estimated, because the shops had just closed and she had been standing with a Moses basket in a large plastic carrier bag, waiting for the bus back to Kingshaven. The first one hadn't been much worse than a period pain, and she'd smiled, thinking how sensible her baby was to choose such a convenient time and place. She had simply caught a different bus to take her to the hospital.

The midwives obviously found it peculiar that Iris was by herself, but she was glad it had worked out that way. Her father had gamely volunteered to accompany her to the hospital, but she'd seen the relief on his face when she'd declined. Fiammetta had offered to drive her from Kingshaven and act as birth partner, but Fiammetta's driving skills were erratic at the best of times and Iris had always thought she'd prefer to go through it alone with no one fussing around her.

'Just the two of us,' she murmured, holding her hands against the bumpy outline of her baby as the grip of pain began to tighten again. Iris closed her eyes and tried to visualize other sensations, like swimming in a warm sea or lying on stubbly grass, gazing up at the stars . . .

As the wave of pain ebbed away, she found herself on her knees, staring at a black rubber skid mark on the floor, aware that the automatic doors kept opening then closing, like a very slow hand clap. Someone wearing a pair of expensive-looking red patent shoes was trying to help her to her feet. At exactly the same time as she recognized the familiar waft of scent, Iris looked up into the woman's large blue eyes.

'Iris Quinn?' said Julia King. 'What on earth are you doing here?'

'I'm having a baby,' Iris panted.

'For heaven's sake!' exclaimed Julia. 'Isn't anyone going to attend to this woman?'

It was dismaying to witness how much difference a posh accent still counted for in England at the end of the twentieth century, thought Iris, but she was grateful nevertheless for someone taking charge. The contractions were getting faster and she suddenly felt panicky.

'Who's with you?' Julia asked gently.

'Nobody,' Iris just about managed.

'You can't be all by yourself! Nurse!'

It was such a relief not to be the bossy one.

An auxiliary nurse brought a wheelchair for Iris, and Julia helped her in.

'Shall I stay with you?' she was asking.

Iris's automatic reaction was to say no, she'd be fine, but her head nodded mutely.

'What we need is some lovely gas and air,' Julia ordered,

her high heels tapping along the corridor. 'It's absolutely the best thing,' she bent to whisper to Iris.

'More!' Iris demanded, holding out her hand again for the mask.

She took another long, delicious breath, then handed it back to Julia, who glanced over her shoulder to make sure the midwife wasn't looking, then sneaked a little sniff herself, making them both giggle.

There was almost no gap between contractions now. It wasn't that the pain had gone, but Iris felt oddly as if they were happening somewhere else. She was as light-headed as if she'd drunk too much champagne and was lying on the stubbly turf, gazing up at the stars . . .

Iris was vaguely aware that the midwife was asking something.

What position did she want to be in?

How was she supposed to know? Wasn't that why you came to hospital, where they were supposed to be experts?

Iris realized too late that she was shouting.

'I found it easiest kneeling and holding on to the end of the bed,' Julia suggested tactfully, helping her up.

And then everyone was screaming at her to push. So Iris bore down as hard as she could, twisting her neck back to try and see what was going on, and suddenly, after a gigantic, prolonged effort, she felt the baby whoosh out of her body, and all the pain was gone. There was a long moment of expectant silence, in which Iris held her breath, then came the most wonderful sound in the world: a lusty roar of life.

'A boy!' said the midwife, holding out a sticky, slithery creature. For a moment Iris didn't know what to do, as she was still kneeling up, holding the bars at the end of the bed, but she felt Julia's arm go firmly round her waist, and, supported by her, reached out to take her baby.

'Hello!' Iris said, amazed at the vigour of this small, but very human, being.

Her baby looked up at her with such curiosity, she was sure that if he could have spoken he would have said, 'Who are you?'

'I'm Iris,' she heard herself saying. 'I'm your mother.'

'You got away with it easily for a first baby,' the midwife said, as if she felt Iris should have suffered more.

Iris glanced at Julia. She'd never been quite certain whether she had told her, in that kitsch piano lounge in Sorrento, about her first baby or simply dreamt that she had. Told her, Iris saw immediately, amazed that of all the people in the world it was this woman who had come to help her in her time of need.

'I think she's an angel,' Iris recalled Vic's words. 'The whole point about angels is that they appear in human form. They don't have to have wings.'

*   *   *

'Do you want me to ring anyone?' Julia asked, folding the white gown she'd worn in the delivery room and leaving it on a chair beside the bed. She felt a bit of a gooseberry now that the baby was checked, weighed and washed, and Iris had been stitched up, wheeled back to the ward and was now sitting up with him at her breast.

'Sorry?' Iris looked up, as if she hadn't heard the question, and then said, 'What's the time?'

'Nearly four in the morning,' said Julia. 'I've got my mobile phone, but you're not supposed to use it inside the hospital . . .'

'Could you maybe ring my dad? He might be wondering where I've got to.'

Julia tapped in the number. Then, seeing that Iris was completely absorbed in her baby, 'I'll leave you two in peace,' she said, backing towards the door.

Iris suddenly looked up. 'Would you mind telling Fiammetta too?'

'Won't your father want to tell her?' Julia asked.

'They're not really on speaking terms, but don't worry, I'm sure there must be a phone I can use . . .'

'No. I'll do it,' Julia offered brightly.

Iris looked back into her baby's face, and then, just as Julia was turning to go, she suddenly said, 'I don't know what I would have done without you!'

They smiled at each other, not knowing each other at all, yet close because of what they had shared. It was a special feeling.

Outside, the air was chilly and Julia's bare arms went instantly goosebumpy. She rang Iris's father, Michael Quinn, and explained. He was all for calling a taxi immediately, but she told him that Iris was fine and the hospital would probably be happier to have visitors in the morning. Then she took a deep breath and dialled the number of the Castle, where her brother James answered, as she knew he would. He had always been a light sleeper.

'Can I speak to Fiammetta, please?'

'Julia?'

'Yes.'

'What time do you call this?'

'Can you tell Fiammetta that Iris has just given birth to a little boy? Mother and baby both doing well in Lowhampton General,' Julia told him evenly, as if she were reading words on a telegram.

As she pressed the off button, she thought she heard him saying, 'How come . . . ?'

Dawn was beginning to break, and there was a slight mist blurring the hard edges of the hospital's main building. The yellow lights on all the floors began to pale as the rising sun turned the windows into mirrors of rosy light. There was no traffic, and no sound apart from the hum of the hospital generators. As Julia stood watching

184

an unexceptional vista made beautiful by the dawn, all the emotion that had been welling inside her spilled out in tears of exhaustion, envy and sheer happiness at witnessing the miracle of a new life.

*　　*　　*

Michael Quinn had clearly shoved his feet into the first pair of shoes he came across – a pair of old navy espadrilles with the backs trodden down – and left the house as soon as he'd heard the news. He hadn't shaved and the stubble on his chin was white, which made him look older. His pale eyes frowned, searching from bed to bed, and then lit up when he spotted Iris.

'Are you all right?' he asked, walking quickly towards her.

'I'm fine!' she told him.

'My brave girl!' he said, leaning over to plant a kiss on her forehead.

Iris was forty-six years old, but his praise made her feel as proud and loved as a child. She didn't know why she kept wanting to cry. Perhaps it was the hormones?

'There's someone I'd like you to meet,' she said coyly, pointing at the transparent pod in which her baby was sleeping beside the bed. When she picked him up, he opened his eyes and looked at her. 'This is your grandfather, Michael,' Iris told him, handing him into her father's waiting arms.

He took the baby competently, holding him and rocking him with more confidence than she'd expected.

'He has blue eyes!' said Michael Quinn.

'Yes,' said Iris.

'How extraordinary!'

'Don't all babies have blue eyes to start with?' Iris asked.

'Isn't that kittens?'

It was a strange conversation to be having as they

negotiated their way round the question that the baby's appearance had answered.

Iris herself had not known for certain who the baby's father was but there could be no doubt now. Her son's head was covered in a fuzz of soft little charcoal curls and his skin was the colour of milky coffee. Except for the incongruous blue eyes, the baby was a miniature version of his father.

'I didn't know that you and—' said Michael.

'Why should you?' Iris interrupted, to stop the name being mentioned, wanting the non-identification to go on for a bit longer. It had been just herself and the baby throughout the pregnancy. She didn't even want to think about the other parent right now.

'Have you told him?' Michael persisted.

'Of course not,' Iris said, feeling a sudden shrinking of the joy that had settled over her since giving birth. 'I haven't had time.'

'You *are* going to?' her father urged anxiously.

'When I'm ready,' she replied tightly.

'He'll be . . .'

'What? What will he be?' Iris demanded, a sudden spike of crossness pushing through the mushy haze of post-partum sweetness.

She hadn't seen him since the night the baby had been conceived, that wondrous night when their bodies were drawn together by a force as elemental as gravity, then flung apart, shocked, breathless, gazing up at the stars . . .

'Was that zipless enough for you?' Winston had asked.

The great harmonious dome of the universe suddenly collapsed into a stubbly field covered in sheep droppings, where Iris lay with her smart linen dress rucked up round her waist, knickers at her knees, her mouth sour with the taste of stale champagne.

She'd run away from him as fast as the blisters inside her baseball boots would allow, until his shouts 'Iris! Come back!' were finally inaudible. He had made no attempt to follow her as she charged all the way down to the beach and ran straight into the sea, feeling the cold, cathartic bite of salt water seeping through the most expensive garment she'd ever owned.

When she finally emerged from the water, she'd walked, dripping, to her father's house on the Quay, and later woken in the midday heat to the sound of a helicopter taking off.

Later that day, her head still shivering with the unpleasant sparkle of a hangover, she'd flown back to Italy, taken a taxi from the airport, and stayed in her flat with the shutters closed, trying to work out what to do, knowing in her soul that her life had fundamentally changed. The time had come to run away again, and, not knowing where else to go, she had returned to her father's house in Kingshaven, where nothing she could do would scandalize anyone. She had slept in Fiammetta's old room, surrounded by the paintings of a tormented teenager, and taken turns to look after the bookshop. On sunny days, Iris and Michael had gone out for walks just as they used to when they first came to Kingshaven. Her father had never asked, and she had never told him, who the baby's father was.

'He'll be overjoyed,' Michael was saying now.

'I doubt whether he'll even be interested,' Iris contradicted.

'Look, I don't know what happened between you two,' Michael began, 'but I do know Winston's a decent fellow. He'll—'

'Take care of me?' Iris spat out the words. 'I don't need taking care of, thank you very much.' She held Michael's eyes like a challenge, as if she was fourteen again and pushing the boundaries of her father's tolerance.

'It's none of my business—' he began again.

'You're right. It's none of your business,' she snapped, holding out her arms to take her baby back.

Michael let out an exasperated sigh that infuriated her

even more, and then she felt guilty because her baby began to cry, bewildered by the change of mood. Iris had promised herself that she would never do anything to fuck up her child, and yet here she was already, on the first day . . .

'It's OK,' she whispered, concentrating on getting the baby locked on to her breast as the midwife had taught her, a much less natural, and more painful, act than she had anticipated, hoping that Michael would leave, but when she looked up, there was another complication.

Fiammetta was standing at the entrance with a bunch of royal-blue delphiniums, staring at Michael, as if frozen to the spot.

'I'll leave you to it,' Michael said.

It was only when he had walked past her that Fiammetta seemed to come to life and ran over to Iris's bed.

'Let me see! Let me see! Oh, Iris! He's gorgeous! My God! He looks just like—'

Iris gave her a warning look.

Fiammetta put the flowers down on the bed. 'May I hold him?'

Iris made sure Fiammetta bent over the bed to take him, showing her little sister how to cup her hand under the baby's head, and when she looked up again her father had gone.

*   *   *

There was a public phone in the reception area with a half dome of Perspex round it. *It's none of your business.* Iris's words were in Michael's head. He looked the other way, trying to resist the temptation to pick up the receiver. The phone probably wasn't working anyway.

It was none of his business, but he couldn't forget the image of Winston leaning over the balustrade outside the Ship with childlike eagerness to see his father in the parade of D-Day veterans.

It was none of his business.

Michael picked up the receiver, half hoping that the message '999 calls only' would appear on the liquid-crystal display. Instead, the dialling tone rang in his ear. He put the receiver down again.

It was none of his business.

Michael stared at the phone. To do nothing would make him complicit in another lie, another injustice.

'You *knew*!' Fiammetta had screamed at him when she had discovered the truth about her half-brother.

His sin had been the not telling.

Iris would tell Winston in her own time, Michael told himself. And Winston would do the right thing, whatever that was. But how long would she wait? Long enough for Winston to find out from someone else?

It was none of his business.

Michael's hand trembled as he picked up the phone and put a twenty-pence coin into the slot.

'Winston? It's Michael Quinn.'

'Michael. How are you doing?'

'Fine, thanks.' Michael took a deep breath. There was an expectant silence at the other end of the phone.

'Look, Winston, Iris is in hospital.'

'Hospital?'

The instant concern in Winston's voice gave Michael confidence.

'Lowhampton General.'

'Is she OK?'

The pips were going.

'I just think you ought to come and see her . . .'

'I'm on my way,' said Winston.

Michael stared at the phone for a few moments, still not knowing whether he should have done it and feeling the terrible responsibility of being unable to undo it now. When he finally ducked out from under the canopy, Fiammetta was walking towards him.

189

This time, she did not avert her eyes.

'That was quick!' he ventured.

'I told her she had to tell Winston, and she told me to go!' said Fiammetta, in a state of disbelief.

Iris had made them comrades, Michael thought, if only for a few seconds.

'I've just told him.' He pointed at the phone.

Fiammetta's eyes widened.

'Not about the baby,' Michael added quickly. 'Just that he should come . . .'

For a moment Fiammetta assessed what he'd just said, as if balancing the consequences up in her mind.

'Good!' she said, eventually.

'No more secrets,' Michael added, then immediately wished that he had not as the door that had just opened seemed to slam shut in front of him.

*   *   *

The stark words announcing that her marriage was officially over blurred with tears. Julia didn't know why a piece of paper should make so much difference. She and Christopher King had been separated for four years and they'd stopped loving each other long before that, if indeed he'd ever loved her in the first place. The vicar had called it a fairytale wedding, but when she'd once asked her husband, 'You do actually love me?' he'd replied, 'Whatever love means,' as if it were a question only an ignoramus would ask. Terrified that she had revealed herself as far too stupid for him, she had tried to back-pedal, saying, 'Quite!' As if she'd been joking in the first place.

Whenever she remembered it, she experienced exactly the same agony of embarrassment.

How different she was now, Julia thought, glancing at herself in the mirror before leaving for work. In those days, she'd been naïve and fat. 'Curvy' was the word people had used. By the time the wedding came, several stones had fallen off, and then people had started going on at her for being too thin. Now, daily visits to the gym had toned her muscles, and a sunbed once a week had given her skin a properly healthy glow. In those days, her mousy hair had taken hours with curling tongs to make it look anything, but now she wore it short, with sunkissed highlights, requiring nothing but a ruffle after her shower. In those days, she'd been an invisible virgin in a Laura Ashley frock; nowadays, she could feel men looking at her as she walked down the street. If Christopher had met her now, he couldn't have behaved as he did, she thought. But would he have loved her? And why did it still seem to matter so much?

It wasn't that she wanted it back, Julia tried to reason with the irrational emotion; it wasn't that she had particularly enjoyed it, except for having the children; it was just the terrible sense of failure. She remembered the shame of her own parents' divorce, how she had been constantly teased at school, and how she had promised God, or whoever it was that little girls made solemn promises to, that she would never, ever, get divorced. And now here she was, at the age of thirty-six, a divorcée.

Julia wished she'd had more sleep, because lack of it was making her more than usually teary. There was a part of her that wanted to climb back into her nice warm bed and hide under the duvet, but she knew that would make it worse as the day went on. Work would take her mind off things. It was ridiculous to feel sorry for herself when there were people so much less fortunate. At lunchtime, perhaps she would visit the hospital again. Better to face the world, Julia told the person in the short ice-blue dress who didn't look at all like the person she felt.

The phone was ringing on her desk when she got in. Mr Patel's PA. Julia sometimes wondered whether Mr

Patel had the doorman inform him when his employees were late, because he had the uncanny habit of ringing down whenever she was. As she waited for Margaret to connect him, Julia's heart beat slightly faster than usual, and she wondered why it was she always felt she had done something wrong when Mr Patel was on the line, because she couldn't remember a single occasion on which he had been anything other than courteous to her.

'There you are!' said Mr Patel. 'Do you have any slots in your diary today?'

Julia looked at the blank page, toying with the idea of inventing an appointment, feeling that she probably ought to look busier than she was, and unable to face the level of concentration that meetings with Mr Patel usually demanded. It was probably safer not to lie in case he had had someone check her diary before he asked.

'I'm free this morning,' she said, wanting to keep her lunchtime for herself and leave the afternoon open.

'Splendid!' said Mr Patel, putting down the phone, by which she gathered that she was summoned straight away.

In the lift on the way up, Julia regretted the sandals, which were the highest heels she had, and the fact that she had left the matching ice-blue jacket at home. The narrow straps made the top half of the dress as revealing as a swimsuit, and she felt it wasn't quite respectful to step into Mr Patel's air-conditioned inner sanctum with so much skin on display.

It was just the two of them.

Mr Patel indicated she should take a seat on the sofa, then he followed her over and sat down opposite. The sofa was low and, however nicely she tried to arrange herself, the short, tight dress displayed rather too much of her long legs. Mr Patel made a point of looking only at Julia's face, and yet she could sense his slight discomfort.

'I have been thinking about another property in Kingshaven . . .' he began.

Not another old people's home, Julia thought. The Sunnyside project was going to be lovely, but if Mr Patel went on like this, then the sign just outside Kingshaven was going to have to change from 'Britain in Bloom Runner-Up' to 'Geriatric Capital of the South Coast'.

Stifling a yawn, she wished she'd had more than four hours' sleep.

'I'm sure it's not necessary,' said Mr Patel, looking directly at her, 'but I would like to have your reassurance that anything I say today will remain completely confidential.'

'Of course,' said Julia, sitting up a little straighter.

As Mr Patel began to explain his plan, she concentrated as hard as she could, wishing that she had not inhaled quite so much gas and air, hardly able to believe what she was hearing, because it sounded so much like a dream come true.

'Only one other person knows the details of my proposal,' Mr Patel concluded, 'and it is my hope that you and my son will work very closely together.'

'Nikhil!' Julia exclaimed.

A glimmer of surprise flickered across Mr Patel's impassive features, then his eyes hardened, as if he had understood something, and Julia realized that in her excitement she had revealed her feelings.

In the silence that followed, she could feel everything slipping away from her.

'Nikhil is still a very young man,' Mr Patel finally spoke, putting unnatural emphasis on the word 'young'.

She was thirty-six, he was saying, and wearing a skimpy dress that made her look like mutton dressed as lamb.

'Nikhil has a brilliant career and a future to build.' Mr Patel measured each word, his black eyes as inscrutable as marbles.

She was thick and divorced. Damaged goods.

'Nothing . . .' Mr Patel paused.

Julia felt her bare arms puckering to goosebumps under the penetration of his gaze.

'Nothing,' he repeated, 'must distract him from that.'

There was another moment of ominous silence then Mr Patel suddenly smiled, as if he had decided to let her off with a warning. 'I think you and Sonny will make an excellent team,' he said. 'Sonny can be a little hot-headed, but he knows about business. You have the talent at public relations and marketing, and, I hope, the drive to see through a project that you have started?'

It took Julia a couple of seconds to realize that he was asking her a question.

'Oh, yes. Absolutely,' she agreed, with fervour.

'And what is your opinion of my plan?' Mr Patel had returned to his usual avuncular style.

'I think it's . . .' Her mind still bleary, the only word she could think of was one that her sons Bertie and Archie used these days to express wholehearted approval: 'Wicked!' she said.

*   *   *

Sometimes Cat thought she was actually a much smaller person who'd been put inside a tall body. When she first shot up, her mother had been sensitive enough to stop using one of her favourite phrases about tall poppies being cut down to size, but the idea that you shouldn't stick out of a crowd had imprinted itself on Cat's subconscious by then. Two things had helped. One was the phenomenon of Lady Diana, because until she arrived on the scene it had been impossible to get nice flat shoes; the other was being approached by a modelling agent in Top Shop on Oxford Street when she and Esther were on a shopping expedition. Cat had never been brave enough to ring the number on the card, fearing it was some kind of scam – surely a proper agent would hang out in Bond Street, or Selfridges at the very least, Esther had said – but the approach had made Cat look at herself differently in the mirror. Whereas she'd previously seen her face as ugly, now she thought the word 'striking' might be appropriate. She'd often been told that her dark hair, cut in a bob, and wide-apart blue eyes, made her look like a Siamese cat, and so, at fifteen, she had started calling herself Cat instead of Cathy. But the excruciating shyness had remained. Now, as she stood with her back pressed against a wall and her feet stretched out at an angle, she was aware of using a technique perfected at school to make herself appear to be the same height as the crowd.

Once a year, the Stone family congregated at the Belsize Park home of the patriarch, Roman Stone, for the Treasure Hunt. Cat had been thirteen when she was first invited, and she and Esther the youngest in their team of six who drove round North London against the clock, gathering answers to the enormously complicated clues that Roman Stone devised. When all the teams returned, there was a buffet lunch in the enormous glass room at the back of the house, and Roman announced the results from the gallery at the top of the staircase. Their team had won and each member was awarded a bottle of champagne, which Cat deliberately forgot to take home with her when she left, knowing that her mother would never allow her to go to the Stones again if she had any idea how liberal they were.

The Treasure Hunt became an annual fixture in her life and was still something she anticipated with excitement as well as a certain dread. It was the closest she'd ever got to being good at competitive sport, but she still felt intimidated by the Stones and dreaded one of them asking, as one of them always did, in that slightly distracted way they all had, 'How's the writing going?'

Cat felt as if the Stones had stuck an invisible label on her that read: 'Bright girl, comes from nowhere, but good influence on Esther, so be kind.'

Team leaders on the Treasure Hunt were selected by

virtue of having a car, and they were allowed first pick of the remaining guests. A television executive called George remembered Cat from previous years, so she didn't have an agonizing wait in line like in the school playground. Esther automatically fell in behind her. The other members of the team were a chain-smoking model called Phlox, apparently a distant cousin of Esther's, who insisted on sitting in the front seat because of the length of her legs – even though, as Esther pointed out loudly, Cat's were just as long – and Finn, a serious-looking Irish journalist with light-brown curly hair and glasses, who squashed into the back seat of the BMW on the other side of Esther from Cat.

George read the first clue: 'Go south on street where Nabokov heroine seduced.'

'Didn't he write *Lolita*?' said Esther.

'Ada,' Cat offered tentatively. 'Ada seduced. Ada loved . . .'

'Ada laid,' said Finn.

'That's it!' said Cat. 'Adelaide Road. It's down the bottom of this road, then turn left,' she instructed.

'How come you're always so clever at this stuff?' Esther asked, a smile of reflected glory teetering precariously towards a frown of resentment.

'A misspent childhood doing the *Telegraph* crossword with my father,' Cat replied.

'Crosswords?' said Phlox, blowing a dismissive stream of smoke out of the window. 'How boring!'

'Useful on occasions like this, though,' Finn said, smiling across Esther at Cat.

As well as using directions to determine answers to clues that might be found on blue plaques, pub names, ads in bus shelters, or even current bits of graffiti, Roman's rules demanded the collection of certain items of treasure that teams were, on pain of disqualification, forbidden to buy. This year, the items included a rose, something Victorian, an animal, a playing card, a drink, a religious object, something over six feet long and an Easter egg.

Esther, who had never been very good at concentrating, soon lost interest and started exchanging television gossip with George. Phlox found a woodlouse under an ornamental urn on a doorstep on King Henry's Road, put it into her cigarette packet and, having volunteered herself as the something over six feet long, sat in the car, smoking. The rest was left to Cat and Finn.

They found both a cracked ceiling rose and Victorian bricks in a skip outside a house that was being converted. In an Irish pub in Camden, Finn managed to beg half a pint of lager from a pub on condition that he brought the glass back. Outside, he picked a wilted Jack of Diamonds out of the gutter. Cat went into a newsagent's to cadge a Creme Egg, but the proprietor had given five away already to other teams who had got there first and Cat came out empty-handed, so Finn went in, bought a newspaper and came out with an egg in his pocket.

'You stole it!' Cat was shocked.

Nobody could think of anything religious except singing a hymn, which might or might not earn a point depending on how generous Roman was feeling, and they had made the decision to return to the house to avoid time penalties, when suddenly Finn shouted, 'Stop the car!'

George's brakes screamed, Finn handed Cat the glass of beer, jumped out of the car and ran into a church. He returned with his hands cupped.

'What's that?' asked Esther.

'Holy water,' he told her.

'How will they know the difference?' asked Cat.

'Because I will swear a sacred oath,' he said solemnly.

She liked the way his eyes sparkled with gentle mischief.

Their team scored equal points with another team on the quiz questions, and the winners were decided by the treasure. The rival team had brought back a beautiful long-haired cat they had picked up in the neighbourhood, which scored much higher than the woodlouse (although there were heated protests about the ethics of kidnapping, and the team had to promise to return the cat to where they found it). Finn put up a vociferous argument for the holy water but by the time Roman made his decision, the only evidence was his damp hands, and the rival team won the day with a stolen hymn book.

Cat looked across the crowded room, exchanging a disappointed look with Finn. All around him the Stones were talking in loud, confident voices. She'd forgotten what it was like to witness them en masse.

'Ah, Cat!'

Every quality the Stones possessed was present in undiluted concentration in Roman Stone – he was the most intelligent, most charming, most powerful of the lot of them, a man who naturally demanded that you impress him.

'How's your writing coming along?' he asked her.

'Slowly,' Cat told him.

Working in a shop, even a bookshop, simply wasn't a job people like the Stones would understand. The irony was that none of them knew about the notebooks she had kept since her first Treasure Hunt, volumes that contained agonizingly pretentious teenage analyses of novels alongside melancholy poems and a haiku about the ticking clock in the living room at home, but, mostly, accounts of times spent with the Stone family. Sometimes Cat felt almost like Charles Ryder, the narrator of one of her favourite novels, *Brideshead Revisited*, an impossibly lower-middle-class outsider to this exotic clan, who had somehow gained entry into their midst and half-longed to be absorbed by them, half-wanted to remain detached.

Cat looked across the room to the place where Finn had been standing, but found herself smiling at someone she didn't know. Tracking round the room, she saw that he was halfway up the steps to the gallery with his back to her. In front of him a very pretty woman with tumbling dark hair was bidding farewell to Roman's wife Pippa. Behind her and on the step above Finn, a small child was protesting at the wait. Cat watched, disappointed, as Finn scooped the child into his arms and put him over his shoulder.

*   *   *

Iris had always wondered why so many television dramas were set in hospitals, but now she realized it was because all of life was there. Not just the patients on life support, the admissions to Accident and Emergency, the births and deaths, but all the visitors too, each with their own story.

From the vantage point of her bed just opposite the door of the ward, she watched the comings and goings. It didn't matter whether you were a bodybuilder whose arms were black with tattoos, a salesman in a suit with a wilting bouquet purchased from a bucket outside a petrol station, or a grumpy sibling carrying a teddy bear and a pink helium balloon, you still looked around anxiously as you came into the ward, your face lighting up as you recognized family that belonged to you, softening as you held the baby for the first time.

When she saw Winston standing at the door, Iris's first thought was to pull the sheet up over her head so that he wouldn't see her as he looked around. She was furious with her father, or Fiammetta, or whoever it was for telling him.

'Knock, knock!' Winston said to the sheet.

'Who told you?' Iris growled.

'I thought you were meant to say "Who's there?"'

'I know who's there, don't I?' said Iris, letting the sheet drop from her hands.

'I've been so worried,' said Winston, bending to kiss her cheek.

Iris averted her face.

'I was told you were in hospital, but I wasn't told why.'

'How did you find me, then?' Iris asked.

'They have a register of patients,' Winston explained.

In all the conversations Iris had ever imagined them having, none was as banal as this one.

'You've had a baby!' said Winston, sitting down uninvited on the chair beside the bed.

'Yes.'

'Congratulations!' he said.

'Don't you want to see him?' Iris asked.

She noticed that Winston hadn't even looked for the baby, who was sleeping in his pod a couple of yards away from the bed in a pool of sunlight because the midwife said it would help with his slight jaundice, which, she had assured Iris, was perfectly normal.

Iris swung her legs out of bed.

'Are you allowed to get up?' Winston asked anxiously.

'I'm not an invalid,' Iris told him, walking two steps to the pod and picking up the baby. There was a little suck blister on his upper lip that was so sweet it made her want to cry.

'What's the matter?' Winston's voice was just behind her.

If she didn't stop shaking, would he think her mad, or unfit to be a mother? She was suddenly terrified that they would take the baby away from her.

'Shall I get a nurse?' Winston was behind her, his hand touching her elbow very gently.

'No,' she said, breathing deeply to control herself.

It was Winston. He wouldn't do that to her.

She turned to show him his son, but he wasn't looking at the baby but directly at her. Then the baby made a funny little sighing sound, and Winston saw him and Iris witnessed his expression changing, and she realized that the most intuitive and intelligent man she had ever known hadn't put two and two together until that moment.

'Oh my God!' he said.

She'd only seen his face like this once before, looking down at her, with the starry sky behind his head. He looked . . . in love.

'He's beautiful, isn't he?' she whispered.

'The most beautiful little person I've ever seen,' Winston said.

Iris liked it that he said person.

For a moment it felt as if there were only the three of them in the whole world, a shining aura of happiness and pride descending as they gazed at their child.

'Why didn't you tell me?' Winston asked.

Iris bristled. 'I didn't think you'd want to know,' she said crisply, returning, too soon, to their old adversarial roles.

'How could I not want to know?' he asked gently.

'You didn't even try to talk to me after we'd . . .' Iris reminded him.

'You ran away!'

'But . . .' Now she felt confused. Had she misread the situation?

Winston was staring at the baby in wonder.

'Do you want to hold him?' Iris offered.

He took the baby in his big hands, more tentative than she had ever seen him before. The baby snuffled and stirred as if he was having a bad dream. Winston quickly tried to hand him back.

'No,' said Iris. 'Just talk to him. He senses you're nervous. It's OK,' she told the baby. 'This is your father. He's a bit rubbish at holding you, but he means well.'

Winston was staring at her in a way she'd never seen before.

'Marry me?' he whispered.

'I'm the one who's meant to have gone soft in the head . . .'

'Please?' said Winston. He looked so big and the baby so small, and she felt a rush of love for both of them.

'It's a bit sudden, isn't it?' Iris said suspiciously.

'How long have we known each other?' he asked.

'Thirty-odd years, I suppose,' said Iris.

'I've loved you all that time,' he declared.

'I was only eleven when we met.'

'Well, I didn't love you in that way then, obviously,' said Winston, exasperated with her pedantry.

'When did you, then?' she wanted to know.

Winston thought about that. 'I think it must have been 1968, the demo in Grosvenor Square. You had blood all over your head and I thought you were so brave. Braver than I was.'

Iris remembered. He'd taken her back to his squat. They'd smoked a little grass and he'd kissed her.

'But you ran away then too.' Winston remembered.

'I was with Clive,' Iris said. 'He was my first proper boyfriend and I knew he'd kill me if I kissed someone else.'

'Nice,' said Winston sarcastically.

'You can talk! How many wives have you had? Or have you lost count?'

'I thought each time that I'd found what I wanted,' he protested.

'Maybe that's what you're thinking now.'

'No. I know this is what I want. I knew last summer.'

'On the Iron Age Fort?'

'Before that – when I saw you walking down the aisle with no shoes on.'

'Because I looked an idiot?'

'Because you were strong and brave and you had no idea what to do, and you disapproved of weddings, and

202

yet you were prepared to go through it because you loved Fiammetta and felt responsible for her.'

'So, why did you say what you did, then?' Iris challenged.

'What?'

'About it being a zipless fuck.' Iris lowered her voice, realizing suddenly that their conversation was being listened into by the whole ward.

'It was a joke. I was trying to save face after what you said.'

'What did I say?'

'Your exact words were "This was such a mistake".'

'Oh . . .' Her memory had conveniently erased that bit.

'You ran away,' Winston repeated.

'You could have run after me!' The flaw in his excuse was suddenly obvious to her.

The ward was silent as people strained to hear the next twist of their exchange.

'No, I couldn't! Really, I couldn't,' Winston protested. 'I caught my foot in a rabbit burrow and broke my ankle!'

'Oh, *please*!' Iris began, and yet, somewhere in the back of her mind, she had a vague memory of Fiammetta saying something about Winston breaking his leg and at the time she'd thought, meanly, Serves you right!

Now the thought of Winston, cool, elegant Winston, with one of his handmade shoes stuck down a rabbit burrow, made her suddenly helpless with laughter.

How strange and wonderful it was that the baby's first glimpse of his father was of him laughing. Because Winston often smiled, or smirked, but she'd rarely seen him laugh, and never before with such uncontrolled joy and abandon.

'Marry me?' Winston whispered in her ear.

Iris looked at him sharply. 'Don't be ridiculous,' she said.

'Please,' he whispered again.

'Are you mad?'

He looked gratifyingly perturbed.

'If we don't get married, there may be a slight chance we'll stick together.'

Chapter Five

2 May 1997

'A new dawn has broken, has it not?'

The sun was rising, and the air had a gentle, balmy warmth, as if a blessing had been cast upon the new Prime Minister. As Cat looked at the sea of smiling faces around her, she wondered if they would all look as happy and hopeful if it had been raining. The campaign song, 'Things can only get better', heralding Tony Blair's arrival on the South Bank was, for the first time, a statement of truth and not just wishful thinking.

Still scarred by unexpected defeat five years earlier, Labour Party supporters at election parties all over London had been reluctant to claim victory before it was beyond doubt, but as the night wore on, and one extraordinary event followed another – Hamilton gone, Rifkind gone, Portillo humiliated – the champagne began to flow. But there had still been stutterings of anxiety amid the whoops of joy – was it too good to be true? – and it was the need for confirmation as much as celebration that had brought them en masse down to the South Bank in the small hours.

Cat had never thought of herself as a political person. She'd only qualified to vote in two previous elections, 1987 and 1992, and she'd put her cross beside Labour each time knowing that it wouldn't make the slightest difference in the true-blue suburban constituency where she'd been brought up. Cat assumed her parents voted Conservative. When she had once asked as a child 'Are we Labour or Conservative?' her mother had warned, 'Nobody's allowed to tell anyone what they vote,' making it sound like a crime.

Now Cat lived in Esther's house in a constituency where there had always been a Labour MP, so she still didn't feel as if her vote had changed anything, but even the most cynical person would have found it impossible not to be buoyed up by the wave of optimism. It was one of those historic moments, Cat thought, that people would look back on in future times, and remember exactly what it was like to be alive on 2 May 1997.

'Are you coming in, or what?' Esther stretched a hand back to Cat as she and Bruno pushed through the crowds, conga-style, in the wake of her grandfather, Roman Stone, whose election party they had all come from.

Cat caught the eye of the Irish journalist, Finn, who had bounded up to her earlier and complimented her on her dress, a full-skirted fifties cotton dress with a bold print of oversized red roses, which was perfect for the moment, even though the belt buckle was a little rusty, the duck-egg-blue background unevenly faded. Now, Finn smiled encouragingly.

'I think I'll stay outside.' Cat held back. 'Might as well walk to work.'

'Nobody's going to work today!' shouted Esther, as the tide of revellers sucked her away.

Looking up, Cat saw that the sky had lightened without her noticing. It was going to be a beautiful day. Weaving her way along the riverbank, through the cohorts of Labour Party pilgrims, Cat felt almost guilty for going in the opposite direction, but by Blackfriars Bridge the crowd had thinned out, and once Cat had crossed the river the City was like an empty film set. Without the usual rumble of traffic, noises one didn't normally notice – the bleeping of a pedestrian crossing when the lights were red; the shunt and grumble of a refuse truck – were the title soundtrack of a movie that had yet to start. The sky was a deeper, more intense blue now, and the buildings gleamed in the sunlight.

Cat thought that Esther had probably been right about everyone taking the day off, because there were few people about, and those who were looked as if they'd been up all night. The bleary-eyed young man in a creased navy pin-striped suit was probably a Tory who'd been drowning his sorrows and missed the last train back to his Essex home; a couple languishing against each other in an alleyway, who jumped apart as Cat passed, had perhaps got off with each other the night before but hadn't yet worked out how they were going to behave at the office. Cat wondered whether people made up a story to explain her in her fifties frock.

Opening up was one of the best things about being manager of the bookshop. With nobody else in, the space felt like her domain, and she was proud of the layout, the displays in the window and, particularly, the coffee shop at the back of the store, an idea of hers that was now a feature of several Brook's Books shops in the metropolis, providing a comfortable setting for book-group meetings and occasional author talks, as well as being profitable space where booklovers could sample books over coffee and muffins.

Cat liked to change the tables at the front of the shop each month to reflect current cultural interests. In March, she had featured *The English Patient* and other books that had become Oscar-winning films; in April, when the election had been called, she had gathered together the current crop of political biographies. Now, as she boxed up the biographies of John Major for return to the publishers, she decided to showcase the latest first novels by young British authors. New Voices for the New Politics, Cat thought, or perhaps she could call it 'Cool Britannia'.

* * *

When Iris Quinn was living in Italy, and people asked why she left England, she usually replied that she gave up on her country the day that Margaret Thatcher was elected for a third term. It was true that both events had happened in the summer of 1987, and it was true that Iris had felt that she no longer recognized, nor much liked, her compatriots, nor even herself, in those greedy, selfish years, but her departure had in fact been precipitated by the personal rather than the political. Ironically, the real reason for her exile, Roman Stone, was now standing only feet away from her at the New Labour victory party on the South Bank.

Unnerved by the presence of her former lover, Iris stood on tiptoe to look for Winston, her spirits lifting when she caught sight of his calm, handsome face on the other side of the room, listening to one of the new intake of young female MPs. Winston was a powerful, wealthy man and he and Iris had arrived at the South Bank party in a limousine, but he was also still the boy she had met on the school bus over thirty years ago who had earnestly plotted with her to change the world. She couldn't imagine Roman Stone ever being a boy at all.

Iris watched from a distance as Roman acknowledged the obeisance of the Party apparatchiks, the confidence of wealth radiating from him and making him appear taller than he was. For a moment, she remembered exactly what it felt like to be anointed with Roman's particular attention.

The mood of the party was not just of victory but of joyous liberation, a bit like Iris had always imagined VE night at the end of the war. However much she worried about the quasi-military organization of the campaign and deletion of the word socialism from the Party lexicon, it did feel somehow miraculous that the nation had finally said no to Tory sleaze and yes to education, education, education. Iris didn't believe that change was going to happen by putting New in front of Labour or adopting Conservative limits on public spending, but after a year of living with Winston, she had grown to accept that, in the absence of revolution, which the British weren't very good at, the only way to do anything was by being in power. Even a cynic had to admit that it immediately felt like a better world for a child to grow up in.

Iris and Winston had named their son John. When he was awake, he was a vigorous presence, and had just started walking. When he was asleep, as he was now, in her arms, because when they'd arrived at the party they'd realized it would be impossible to bring the buggy into this crush of people, he still looked as vulnerable as he had as a small baby. Iris kissed the top of his head.

If someone had told Iris in her youth that she would find the identity she was searching for in motherhood, she would have considered it an insult, but now that she was a mother she felt more comfortable in her own skin than ever before. Media parties had always made Iris feel self-conscious and inadequate, but with John sleeping on her shoulder she felt no compulsion to glug several glasses of wine to get up the courage to socialize. It was purpose enough to be there looking after him.

Roman Stone was now shaking hands with one of Blair's spin doctors and Iris wondered whether he would eventually look in her direction, whether he would even notice her. There was a part of her that wanted him to know she had survived in spite of him, but Roman was at his most devastating if he picked up the slightest hint of need. Deciding that the true measure of being over Roman was not caring what he thought, Iris began to edge away. Then her brother Anthony blew discretion out of the water.

'Iris! Iris!' He bounded towards her making everyone around, including Roman, look in her direction.

Anthony kissed Iris on both cheeks and ruffled the baby's hair, a gesture that irritated Iris. John's hair was deliciously soft and curly, but she found it intrusive that so many people, even strangers, gave themselves permission to touch it. She was sure that they wouldn't have done the same to a white child.

'A new dawn, eh?' said Anthony.

'Congratulations,' said Iris.

She had never quite understood how her brother, who had grown up without expressing a political opinion in his life, could have become a Labour MP in the previous election in 1992. According to Winston, who knew about these things, Tony, as her brother now styled himself, was tipped for a job in government. Iris had seen him only occasionally over the years since she'd run away from home as a teenager, but now that she lived in London with Winston, Anthony seemed to pop up everywhere. She was under no illusion that his public displays of affection were due to her closeness to Winston, rather than brotherly love. The truculent-older-sister part of Iris's DNA, undiluted by age, always had to fight the temptation to sing the 'Red Flag' or loudly say the word 'socialist' in his company.

'Come and meet some people.'

Anthony took her firmly by the elbow.

'Roman, do you know my sister Iris?'

She should have known that Roman would not react as she expected. Instead of the surprise, or even pain, she yearned to see, Roman's eyes smiled with amusement as he took in the scenario, detected her embarrassment, understood instantly what she was thinking.

'We certainly do know each other,' Roman informed Anthony smoothly. 'How delightful to see you, Iris.'

There had been a time when Iris had spent every other hour planning what she would say to Roman if she ever saw him again, but now no words came. As her former lover clasped her hand, she had a sudden memory of him touching her, the unexpected delicacy of those slightly rough fingertips, and she hated herself for it.

'There is clearly an attraction between our two families!' Roman said, smiling devilishly at her confusion. 'It appears my granddaughter Esther is professionally involved with your brother Bruno.'

He nodded at the young couple. Bruno was standing behind Esther, with his hands on her shoulders. Iris had known, of course, that Esther was a Stone, but tried not to judge her because of it. She had been very good for Bruno's career. Just as Roman had once been for hers.

'This is my nephew John,' said Anthony, touching the baby's hair again, and adding, just so there was no doubt, 'Winston Allsop's son.'

'Yes,' said Roman. 'Yes, I've heard about John. You must be very happy, Iris.'

'I am,' she told him, holding his level gaze. 'Very.'

'You have what you wanted,' said Roman, the slight inflection at the end of the sentence making it sound like a question.

'Yes, I do,' said Iris. 'Everything,' she added, with fervour.

'You've been lucky, then,' said Roman.

Was there a hint of regret in his resigned tone?

Iris wanted so much to say, 'No thanks to you, you bastard!' but Winston was approaching, his expression asking if she was OK, did she need rescuing? Iris felt the tension in her body melt away.

Around the time she'd first met Winston, in her first year at Lowhampton Girls' Grammar School, there'd been a craze for silly pink stationery with cartoon cupids bearing the message 'Love is . . .' For a fortnight or so, the girls on the school bus had vied to make up the cutest motto. 'Love is . . . giving someone your last biscuit'; 'Love is . . . holding hands in the rain'. Iris had never offered her own motto up for public ridicule, but in her head it had always been 'Love is . . . Winston Allsop's smile'.

How peculiar to remember such adolescent silliness

now, after all those years, and to have to gulp back sentimental tears! She'd spent so much of her life thinking that love had to be dangerous. Now, as Winston put a protective arm round her, she thought, Love is . . . feeling safe.

*   *   *

Esther was in her element here, thought Bruno, as he watched her working the room. The sheer energy of Esther's personality made people do what she wanted them to, whether it was forcing an Italian mechanic to do a cheap re-spray job, or television executives to commission a second series. When they were alone together, she was much more hesitant, as if because she didn't dare to ask him what she wanted, she didn't dare ask him anything at all. He kind of wished she would be confident all the time.

It was no good trying to blame her, Bruno told himself. Esther knew what she wanted. He was the one who wasn't sure. Sleeping together was surely the next logical step. He and Esther were a successful team. There was a lot of respect between them, as well as physical attraction. Wasn't that what a relationship was all about?

Esther prised herself away from the rich businessman she was chatting to.

'Had enough?' she asked.

'Yup!' said Bruno. There was only so much champagne and self-congratulation he could stomach.

Esther looked at her watch. 'There's something I want to show you,' she said, grabbing his hand, pulling him through the increasingly drunken crowd into fresh morning air. The grey concrete of Waterloo Bridge looked almost white in the sun's glare. Taking his hand, Esther pulled Bruno towards a bus stop, which was a bit odd because Esther didn't do buses. She always took cabs. As the red double-decker approached, her grip became tighter, but when the bus stopped she made no attempt to get on. 'Look!' she said.

It was only then that Bruno registered the banner advertisement running down the side of the bus with its photograph of him leaning on the Cinquecento, the rolling hills of Tuscany behind him, and the words *Benvenuto Bruno!* in jazzy writing the same yellow as the car.

He was suddenly aware that his own hand was squeezing Esther's really hard. As the bus pulled away, he stared after it.

'Look!'

Another bus with the same advertisement went past in the opposite direction.

It was weird that after all the months of preparation and filming, and meetings with executives and publicity photo shoots, it was a strip of paper on a bus that made the television series seem real for the first time. And it was all due to Esther, Bruno thought, and her crazy belief in him. He looked down into a face that was beaming with childlike excitement, and wanted to give something equally exciting back to her.

Their first kiss was brief, and when he pulled his head away, her hand went to her lips as if she had to touch them to believe what had happened. Then suddenly her arms were round his neck, kissing him back, and he could feel her happiness pressing into his body.

'Let's go home,' he whispered into her ear. 'Let's go home, and I'll cook you breakfast.'

*   *   *

Julia awoke early, her senses taking a moment or two to realign and remember where she was. The sea was calm, but there was an almost imperceptible rocking motion that made her feel slightly nauseous. She tucked her arm back under the duvet, surprised by the coldness of her skin against her warm belly. Beside her, Sonny Patel snuffled and turned over. She waited for his dream to settle, then slid her body to the edge of the bed and swung her legs out. The carpet felt deep and dry under her toes. In the bathroom, Julia pulled a fluffy white robe, with *Principessa* embroidered on the pocket, from the heated towel ladder, and felt her goosebumps soften under its warm embrace. Out on deck, the air was hazy and the sea so still, Julia could hear herself breathing. The only other sound was the random chink, chink, of yachts in the harbour, like a soothing wind chime.

She had pictured her return to Kingshaven differently. A balmy evening; drinks on deck against a backdrop of sunset; people on the promenade speculating who might be on board the ninety-foot motor yacht that was moored in the bay. But, unfortunately, due to a last-minute meeting with the lawyers, they hadn't set sail until after dark, so no one would have seen them arrive. Sonny had wanted to know the results of the General Election, so they'd just watched television in bed as if they were in any normal room.

As the sun began to burn off the morning mist, the red-brick frontage of the Palace Hotel emerged from the North Cliff. Julia wondered which room her boys were in, and imagined their sleeping faces as untroubled as babies', even though Archie was taller than she was now, and Bertie had reached that awkward height where their heads didn't know which way to go when they hugged.

Only another day until she could tell them her secret!

She thought they liked Sonny. When they'd met him, he'd joined in their football game so enthusiastically he'd suffered a stress fracture of the metatarsal. She'd seen the boys exchanging glances, as if agreeing to discuss him later. Sonny was not like any other man they'd known. Julia guessed that any doubts her sons might have would be mitigated by the two new jet skis sitting invitingly on the flybridge deck with their very own crane to lower them into the water.

In her dressing room, Julia stepped into a simple linen shift dress, geranium-red with a narrow belt, which looked sufficiently summery, she thought, as well as sufficiently smart. It was never a good idea to wear black when visiting people who were elderly or sick. She was suddenly aware of Sonny standing right behind her. As he kissed the back of her neck, she wasn't sure whether his proprietorial closeness made her feel safe or a tiny bit scared.

'Good morning,' she said, with a shivery giggle.

'Class,' he said as she turned round, which was exactly the compliment she wanted.

Red could never be prim, exactly, but sharply cut linen was not a look he was compelled to ravage. She was still feeling slightly battered after last night's energetic bout. The relationship was still new enough for them both to want sex at least twice a day.

Though they'd worked closely together on Mr Patel's secret project, Julia had only succumbed to Sonny when the deal was done, unable to think of a reason not to go out to dinner with him to celebrate, half hoping that Nikhil would hear about it and be madly jealous. Sonny had whisked her to the South of France for their first date, a weekend in New York for their second. He'd wooed her with roses, and gifts from Tiffany, vintage champagne and extravagant compliments. When she'd finally given up resisting his charm, she'd been deliciously rewarded, realizing, as she lay in his arms after the first night of passion, what had been missing all these years. Not inner balance, nor self-esteem nor whatever it was the therapist said, just sheer steamy sex.

The aroma of fresh coffee mingled with the buttery sweet smell of warm croissants. Julia didn't know how the crew managed to create delicious meals in the cramped galley below, or keep the boat spotlessly clean and tidy while remaining virtually invisible.

'What's the plan for today?' Sonny asked as they sat down to breakfast, his mouth already full of croissant.

Sonny's manners were the one thing Julia had found it difficult to get used to. He was a man of appetites, someone at ease with his physicality, and that was what made him attractive, she told herself. It didn't matter about the gobbets of pastry landing on the smooth cherrywood table-top.

'I've got to be at Sunnyside by eleven thirty. Do you want to come along?' she said.

'They'd rather see you than me.'

Julia couldn't deny that this was true. The old people lucky enough to have their needs catered for by the generosity of Sonny's father at what had become the Sunnyside Retirement Home, which she was officially opening today, came from the generation who thought it was polite to refer to Asians as 'coloureds'.

The Patels had been the first dark-skinned people to live in Kingshaven, apart from the black GIs during the war, one of whom was generally thought to be responsible for Winston Allsop. The Patels had arrived in the early seventies, and the first time Julia had become aware of them was at the funeral of Christopher King's great uncle Rex, when she was a little girl.

A peculiar-looking woman had accompanied Uncle Rex's body home. Regina, Julia had afterwards discovered, was in fact a transsexual called Reginald, whose elopement with Rex in the nineteen thirties had caused a great scandal. With truly English propriety, the people of the town who turned out to watch the coffin pass by on its way to the church had pretended not to notice the size of her feet, or the five o'clock shadow, until a little Indian boy standing in the churchyard with his father had pointed and said, in a voice as clear as a bell, 'Look, Daddy, it's a man lady!'

The memory still induced a blurt of laughter in Julia.

'What's so funny?' Sonny frowned across the table.

'I was just thinking about the man lady!' Julia explained.

'The whole town laughing at me, you mean?' For someone who was such fun to be with, Sonny could be a bit prickly in the sense-of-humour department.

'Not *at* you,' Julia soothed. 'You were just expressing what everyone else was thinking but didn't dare say. A bit like the "Emperor's New Clothes".'

'The emperor's what?'

Sometimes it startled Julia how the stories she listened to as a child, which had shaped her life, meant nothing to Sonny. He had a different set of stories from his father's culture. It was one of the things that made her feel that they would never fully know each other.

'Oh, you must know,' she said: 'it's a fairy tale. Two tailors pretend they have made a fine suit for the Emperor—'

'Which emperor?'

'That doesn't matter . . .' Now Julia wished she'd never brought it up. '. . . Anyway, the fact is, they've made nothing at all, but nobody dares say, because the Emperor is so powerful, but then a little boy in the crowd asks why the Emperor is naked . . .' Julia tried to explain.

'And what happens to him?'

Julia thought about it.

'Do you know, I'm not sure. The moral of the story is that children tell the truth, I suppose . . . or perhaps it's that powerful people get away with things because nobody dares to question them,' she mused.

'I didn't know the right word!' Sonny was defensive.

'But that wasn't what people were laughing at! It was that everyone was going along with the pretence . . .'

'Why?' Sonny asked.

'Things were different then,' she said. 'It was a huge scandal that Rex King eloped with an American woman.

217

Even worse, that she turned out to be a man . . . do you see?'

Finally, Sonny laughed and Julia breathed a sigh of relief. At least Sonny's moods were quickly forgotten, unlike her former husband Christopher's. Sonny had better things to do than wear her down.

'Is the *Chronicle* going to be at the opening?' Sonny returned to the subject of the old folks' home.

'Of course!' said Julia.

'Aren't you clever?'

'Do you think so? Nobody's ever thought I was clever,' she said bashfully.

'You're extremely clever and extremely sexy,' he told her, reaching across the table to take her hand and kiss it with slightly sticky lips.

*   *   *

'There's a bloody stink boat in the bay!' shouted Eddie King as he helped himself to scrambled eggs at the serving table by the window of the Kings' private dining room.

Libby didn't know whether her husband was getting more irascible with age, or more deaf, or whether he simply didn't care any more whether the guests heard him ranting. Although it made little difference one way or the other now, Libby still found it difficult to alter the habits based on the premise that hoteliers should be seen and heard only as required by the guests. In Libby's experience, allowing one's private life to become public could lead to all sorts of problems.

'The bloody thing must be ninety foot if it's an inch.'

Eddie was now looking through the pair of binoculars he kept by the window. As a lifelong sailor, he was affronted by the showy gin palaces that had pushed up the mooring fees so much that it had become too expensive to keep his precious yacht, the *Brittany Anna*, in the water.

'*Principessa!*' he scoffed, zooming in on the name of the boat. 'Some bloody foreigner, no doubt!' Eddie turned round with his plate of eggs and glared at the breakfast table.

'It's probably Mummy,' said Archie, the younger of their two grandsons.

Bertie shot him a furious glance.

'Don't be ridiculous,' said their father, Christopher. 'What would Julia be doing on a thing like that?'

'She's got a new friend. Ow!' Archie cried, as Bertie kicked him hard under the table. 'He's a very rich businessman and his name is Sonny. He's got a boat, and we're going on it, so there!'

Most fathers would have rebuked their son for such rudeness, but Christopher's reaction was to throw his own napkin down and leave the room. Sometimes Libby despaired of him.

'Do you know anything about this?' Libby addressed Bertie, keeping her voice calm and trustworthy.

'Mummy's coming to open the old people's home,' Bertie revealed. 'She's picking us up tomorrow anyway,' he reminded her. 'It's her weekend.'

'Of course it is.'

Libby decided to leave it at that for the time being, but something Archie said continued to niggle as she watched the boys wolfing down their cereal, then gave them permission to leave the table.

'Did you notice anything?' she asked Eddie, once it was just the two of them, and Liliana.

'What?' her husband asked over the top of his newspaper, which had a one-word headline: **Landslide!**

'Archie said, "A very rich businessman". Does that sound at all familiar?'

'What?' Eddie repeated.

'Did you not hear?' Libby hissed, exasperated with him. She nodded her head in the direction of her mother.

Liliana's eyes were closed, but Libby wasn't about to run the risk of alerting her to the sale of the hotel at this late stage.

Libby told herself that if her mother were in her right mind she would surely see the inevitability of selling up. The place needed investment, but, with the numbers of guests, it was difficult enough even to keep it ticking over. The simple fact was that there was no future in traditional English hotels like the Palace, certainly not for their family. Christopher was utterly useless as a manager, Adrian and Angela had enough on their plates with their own businesses, and Edwin wasn't much good at anything. Even though everyone told her she looked good for her age, Libby was beginning to feel too weary to keep up with all the new rules and regulations.

Despite all that, Libby wouldn't have given the offer to sell it a moment's thought if her mother had been fit and well. Liliana, who had always been so quick-witted and articulate, was now completely silent and spent a lot of the time so quietly asleep that Libby had, on occasion, taken her pulse to see that she was still alive.

'A very rich businessman,' Libby said. 'Didn't Mr Humble use the exact same words about the prospective . . .' Rather than saying the word 'purchaser', Libby nodded again in the direction of Liliana.

'What else would you call someone with that sort of money to throw around?' asked Eddie.

The offer, which had been made anonymously for reasons Libby didn't quite understand, was considerably above the hotel's market value. Eddie was quite right, of course, Libby thought. It was a common enough phrase. She was just a little jittery.

'What does it matter who buys the place anyway?' Eddie added loudly, sinking Libby's attempt at discretion. She glanced nervously at Liliana, but could detect no flicker of interest on her mother's face.

That was true, Libby told herself. Nevertheless, she found it hard to stomach the possibility of Julia after all the trouble she'd caused!

Eddie picked up his newspaper again. 'I reckon we've got out in the nick of time with this lot in,' he said, referring to the New Labour government.

Libby wasn't as convinced as her husband that the change would be such a disaster. Mr Blair seemed such a nice, well-spoken young man, much more like a Conservative than Mr Major, if truth be told.

'Stock exchange'll drop like a stone today, mark my words,' continued Eddie. 'Property prices will be next. Just as well we're shot of it. We have exchanged contracts, haven't we?' Eddie asked, snapping the newspaper down.

'There was some last-minute legal matter,' Libby confessed. 'A technicality, Mr Humble said . . . Perhaps I'd better call him?' she volunteered, standing up and folding her napkin.

'Perhaps you had!' said Eddie angrily, making Libby more nervous than ever.

The solicitor's telephone was answered by a message. 'The office hours are nine to five . . .'

Libby looked at her watch. It was gone half past nine already.

'If you'd like to leave a message . . .'

Libby was about to speak, when she was distracted by a loud clattering, and, a moment later, Eddie was shouting for her.

When she came back into the breakfast room her mother was lying on the floor, partially covered by a white shroud of tablecloth she'd pulled down with her. As Libby tried to sit her up, brushing away cutlery and triangles of toast, and cradling her mother's head on her lap, she let out a little scream as she touched a sticky mass of something red coming from the back of her mother's head, before realizing that Liliana had landed in the jam dish.

221

'What on earth . . . ?' Libby asked her husband accusingly.

'She tried to get up,' Eddie explained.

'Are you all right, Mummy?' Liliana asked.

Her mother was staring at her. Libby had never quite believed that her brain wasn't as active as ever. Once, she was sure Liliana had winked at her, although it could of course have just been a reflex. Now, she just looked very cross.

Christopher helped Eddie get Liliana to her room, and Libby sponged the jam from her wisps of grey hair. Dr Ferry was called. He examined Liliana thoroughly and assured Libby that there were no broken bones.

'But her blood pressure is rather high,' he told Libby. 'And she does seem extremely agitated.'

'Can you give her anything?' Libby asked.

'My prescription is rest, rest and calm,' he told her. 'And no shocks or surprises.'

*   *   *

They assumed she was gaga, thought Liliana. She'd seen Eddie mouthing the word, as if her muteness meant that she was blind as well. He had always been stupid. Libby was the cleverer of the pair, but even she hadn't worked it out. Old people were only gaga when they started losing control of their mind, saying silly things, weren't they? Liliana had seen it with Ruby Farmer. First, it was the odd lapse, what they'd laughingly called a 'senior' moment, but quite quickly the erosion had become unstoppable. Liliana was determined it wouldn't happen to her, and there was a simple enough solution: she simply wouldn't speak. She'd had ninety-five years of speaking and that was enough for anyone. It didn't mean she was gaga. Quite the opposite in fact.

People had always underestimated her at their peril.

Surely they didn't think they were going to get away with selling the hotel and packing her off to a home funded by a coloured gentleman? Surely they knew that while she lived and breathed, Liliana was never going to give up the Palace Hotel? Not after everything she'd done to keep it!

It was never a good idea to underestimate her.

Rex had been the first, Liliana mused. Treating her like an underling when she married Basil, just because she was prepared to roll up her sleeves and work, unlike him and his lot lounging around. Bad enough having that decadent crowd here all the time, with Liliana having to skivvy after them. It was Reggie who'd dubbed Liliana 'Cookie', after she'd made them all a nice steak pie. Cookie! The nerve of it! Then Rex spent a fortune redecorating the Windsor Suite. Onyx and gold in the bathroom! Silk wallpaper and chandeliers from Murano! And all for him and Reggie. Money was leeching out of the place like a broken pipe, Liliana had warned her husband, and any decent person could see it was a disgrace the way Rex and Reggie carried on. If it was allowed to continue, it would ruin the lot of them.

'Your brother's not fit to be in charge,' Liliana had told Basil. 'If people knew the half of it, this whole place would come crashing down around his ears.'

'B-b-b-but n-n-n-nobody n-n-needs n-n-n-know!' Basil had remonstrated.

He'd always been far too soft for his own good.

Mr Otterway, the new young editor of the *Chronicle*, had agreed. It wasn't as if people didn't already have their suspicions, he told her, when she confided her anxieties to him. It was a matter of concern to the whole town. How could Kingshaven hope to maintain its decent reputation if it turned a blind eye to immoral, even illegal, behaviour among the upper echelons? The last thing anyone wanted was the place turning into another Brighton!

Liliana hadn't felt a shred of guilt about Rex's

223

ignominious departure. If proof were needed of how low they really were, Rex and Reggie had stolen all the cash and jewellery, including her wedding pearls, from the hotel safe on their way out.

Someone had to wield the dagger, Liliana had told her inconsolable husband. But no blood was spilled and no one had died. The Palace Hotel was simply restored to its rightful position in the community, so that life could go on as normal.

*   *   *

There was an hour before Julia was expected at the old people's home, so she decided to see whether there was anything in Life's a Beach, a surfers' shop that occupied the site where the Midland Bank had once been.

Julia flicked along the swimwear rail, pausing at a simple, fluorescent pink bikini with orange strings.

'How many bikinis can one person own?'

Julia remembered Christopher asking the question, barely glancing up from his book as she modelled the second (of only three) she had bought for their honeymoon.

Julia decided she would buy the pink bikini almost out of spite. Sonny would certainly enjoy seeing her in it, and taking her out of it, she thought, with a small shudder of pleasure.

Back on the High Street, Julia almost walked into Mr Farthing, who had been the night porter at the Palace and now drove a taxi.

'Good morning, Mrs King!' His voice was a creepy combination of unctuousness and sarcasm. He'd always been one of Granny Liliana's favourites.

'Mr Farthing.' Julia nodded at him.

'To what do we owe the pleasure?' he asked, his lips wet with the prospect of a titbit he might pass on.

'Just visiting,' she said, shortly.

'Just visiting, is it?' he said with a chuckle, as he pushed open the door of the Albion public bar.

Julia looked anxiously at her watch, wondering if there was enough time to pop in and see Sheila Silver, her friend who owned the Crystal Circle.

The window was full of baskets of polished semi-precious stones with handwritten descriptions of their healing properties. Julia fingered a small round piece of tiger eye, which looked just like a sucked boiled sweet.

'It's for confidence,' said Sheila, emerging from behind the curtain at the back of the shop.

Julia embraced her.

'Shall we do a reading?' asked Sheila, as if she sensed Julia's need for reassurance.

Behind the curtain, there was a table with a lamp on it that bathed the space in warm red light. Julia shuffled the cards and cut the stack before Sheila laid them out. She always felt a little nervous as the cards were turned, especially when the Death card appeared, and was relieved when Sheila reminded her that it simply signified an ending. It might well mean that something had was ending, something new about to begin.

The hotel, Julia told herself. It must mean the hotel.

'This line represents the physical,' Sheila continued. 'Wow!'

'What?' Julia asked.

'The World confirms what the Death card has indicated. There are new beginnings. Transformations . . .' Sheila hesitated and looked into Julia's eyes for a moment. 'Probably a lot of sex!'

Julia laughed, amazed. Then, 'Will it last?' she asked hesitantly. Did Sonny really love her or was she just his current plaything? Did she even love him?

'You're worried about being let down again?' asked Sheila.

Julia nodded.

'He'll never have another woman,' said Sheila, peering at the cards.

'. . . The Chariot reversed indicates there may be a setback, so be careful how you travel, but everything else is pointing to a future full of renewal – which is only what you deserve,' added Sheila, suddenly returning to her role as a friend. 'Everything's going to be all right!' she said, patting her hand.

Julia brushed the solitary tear from her cheek and smiled.

'Duty calls,' she said, picking up her handbag and putting down the stone that had become warm in her hand.

'Take it!' said Sheila. 'For confidence!'

There was a lightness in Julia's soul that stayed with her until she reached the three Edwardian guesthouses that now formed the Sunnyside Retirement Home. The front door was open, and a disconsolate orderly in a yellow overall was pushing a wet grey mop across the black and white tiles. The chemical citrus scent of disinfectant did not entirely mask the whiff of human decay. Julia braced herself and put on her best smile.

In the day room, one or two of the old people were so frail that their neck muscles no longer possessed the strength to hold their heads up and their backs were rounded as if they were returning to a foetal position. How strange, thought Julia, that human beings spent so much of their lives help-less. Helpless in the beginning and at the end.

All of them were women except for one man, who got to his feet to stand as Julia entered the room. His sunken face was familiar, but she could not remember who he was or in what context she had previously encountered him. Her brain ran through all the shops on the High Street, but couldn't place him in any of them. His handshake was firm, and she was wondering whether he was ever going to let go, when something on the other side of the room commanded his attention. He set off towards it, then suddenly stopped, giving his forehead a smart tap with his hand, then turned round and walked back to her.

'Forgotten my keys,' he said.

A care assistant in a bright yellow Sunny Stores uniform came in and settled the man back in his chair.

'There you go, Mr Adams, you don't need any keys here!'

'Of course!' Julia exclaimed. 'Mr Adams! He was the—'

She stopped herself just in time. Mr Adams had been the undertaker, and she was sure that was not a word the old folk would want to hear.

'It's Julia Allsop, isn't it?' asked a fat woman in an arm-chair.

'Yes,' said Julia, relieved that this one seemed *compos mentis*, if a little out of date. Julia liked hearing her maiden name again. She didn't bother to correct it.

'Rhubarb and custard,' said the fat woman.

'Really?' said Julia uncertainly. Bonkers after all.

'And raspberry drops,' said the fat woman. 'And your brother James used to like flying saucers . . . and lemon sherbets. Fizzy things . . . and Curly Wurlys . . .'

'Mrs Green?' Now Julia recognized the proprietor of Green's Confectioners. After Mummy left, their father used to take them there on Saturday mornings, allowing them to make two selections each from the tantalizing array of big glass jars. Mrs Green would swing the little white paper bags full of sweets, making twists at each corner.

Julia remembered distinctly the time when Curly Wurlys were launched and the debates she and James had about whether, since they were so long, Daddy would count them as one choice or two, and how James used to make his Curly Wurly last by bashing it against a wall, so the toffee would snap into pieces to be eaten throughout the week, instead of one long melting chocolate chewy caramel indulgence that always made Julia feel slightly sick after. She was amazed by the clarity of the memory of something so trivial that she hadn't thought about for years.

'How are you keeping?' Julia asked Mrs Green.

'I can't complain!' Mrs Green's dentures were disconcertingly white and even. 'Who'd have thought you'd grow up so slim! How old are you now?'

'I'm thirty-seven,' Julia told her, trying not to mind the back-handed compliment.

'I'm thirty-nine,' Mrs Green told her.

'Goodness!' said Julia, calculating that Mrs Green must in fact be at least ninety. The Greens lost two sons in the war, she remembered. They were always cited as an example of how to remain cheerful in adversity.

'That can't be right.' Mrs Green suddenly looked troubled.

'Lots of women stay thirty-nine for absolutely ages,' Julia told her, patting Mrs Green's soft, fat hand. 'I certainly intend to.'

The frown cleared from Mrs Green's face. 'You always were a good girl. Look who's come to see us, Mrs Burns,' she said, addressing the occupant of the next chair. 'You remember Julia Allsop?'

Julia was shocked to see how tiny Mrs Burns was now. She had been the housekeeper at the Castle in the days when Julia's grandfather lived there. She remembered her as a sturdy, no-nonsense woman standing with arms folded behind the lavish spread she had made at Christmas, watching everyone tuck in with quiet satisfaction, but never smiling.

'I can't hear a word you're saying,' said Mrs Burns.

Julia looked at her watch. Where was the photographer from the *Chronicle*?

Mr Adams was off on one of his walks again, but this time he got to the other side of the room and sat down on a free chair between two of the least able residents, one with a bib round her neck, the other asleep with her mouth open, occasionally emitting a rattling snore. Mr Adams looked from one side to the other several times, then cried, 'Help!'

The tableau was so unbearably tragic, Julia felt an awful urge to giggle.

'You know where he's coming from, don't you?' said the care assistant.

Finally, the photographer arrived, accompanied by a reporter from the *Chronicle* whose schoolboyish charm Julia knew she had to watch out for. The last time he had interviewed her, she had inadvertently revealed more than she should.

A yellow ribbon was pinned up across the front door, and the staff stood in a guard of honour outside. Julia held a pair of scissors to the ribbon while the photographer took several shots, then she snipped it in two and there was a small round of applause.

Julia already had in mind the resident she would be photographed with inside. Miss Potter, the archetypal spinster of the parish, still looked more or less as Julia remembered her in the Post Office. It occurred to Julia that perhaps women lasted better when they were without men.

Julia smiled at the camera; Miss Potter pursed her lips, determined not to.

'Can you look as if you're having a nice chat?' asked the photographer.

Miss Potter grasped Julia's arm. 'Don't let him near you!' she said in a hoarse whisper.

'Who?' Julia asked. The grip of Miss Potter's hand was like a claw.

'Dr Ferry,' said Miss Potter, her grip shaking with the effort of getting her message across.

'Look up!' said the photographer. 'Can you manage a little smile?'

The motor drive of his camera whirred.

'Murderer!' Miss Potter suddenly shouted.

Julia looked around for help. The care assistant in the yellow uniform came over.

'Are you saying naughty things again?' she asked brightly.

'Is that enough?' Julia asked the photographer, with slight desperation. Much as she wanted to be kind, there was a limit.

'Murderer!' shouted Miss Potter again.

'Perhaps we should talk outside?' Julia exchanged a smile with the reporter, who seemed as relieved as she was to get out into the fresh air. Julia couldn't wait to get back to the *Principessa* and have a nice hot shower.

'How was your visit?' asked the reporter as they walked to his car.

The row of pretty front gardens had all been concreted over to make parking spaces.

'I was very pleased to see that these good people who have looked after us all their lives were being looked after so well,' said Julia, giving the quote she had prepared, and was happy when the journalist didn't question it. 'As you know, Sunnyside is a flagship project for the Sunny Stores Charitable Trust, and Mr Patel is hoping to open many such facilities for people who have served the community,' she went on.

The reporter pointed his key at the car, which bleeped as he unlocked it.

'There are rumours that Mr Patel is looking to expand his business in other directions,' he said.

Julia tried to look mystified, but the unexpected question flustered her. 'Really?' she said, wondering how much he knew.

'People say he is about to move into the leisure market . . .' The reporter leant against his car.

'I'm sure Mr Patel will achieve great success in whatever he does,' said Julia, rather pleased with that response.

'Can I give you a lift anywhere?' the reporter asked, opening the driver door.

'No, thanks, I prefer to walk,' said Julia.

'Off the record?' he called, as she began to walk away.

'Off the record,' said Julia, turning back. 'Off the record, I think Kingshaven is in for quite a surprise!'

* * *

'One, two, three, *wheee*!'

Winston and Iris were walking over Waterloo Bridge, each holding one of John's hands, taking three steps, then swinging him up in the air.

'Again!' squealed John.

'One, two, three, *wheee*!'

''Gain!'

'Last time!'

'One, two, three!'

Winston caught the child in his arms and threw him up in the air so high that for a moment he was flying in blue sky and Iris's heart leapt with fear, then Winston caught him and put him over his shoulder like a sack of flour.

'I love this view,' said Iris, pausing in the middle of the bridge. 'I love it that all you can see is city and nobody takes any notice of you. When I first came to London, I used to stand here and think that I could be whoever I wanted to be.'

'Who did you want to be?' Winston asked.

'That was the problem!' Iris laughed ruefully. 'I never did decide.'

'You were too young,' Winston suggested.

'I would have murdered anyone who said that then,' Iris told him.

Arriving in London when she was only fourteen years old, she'd added two years to her age and everyone had

231

believed her, but underneath the defiant façade she'd been more innocent than she realized.

'Where did you live then?' Winston asked.

It was strange that there were still facts they didn't know about each other, Iris thought. When she had come to London, Winston had still been studying at Oxford.

'In a council flat in Hackney, with Vic and his brother.' Iris waved vaguely in the direction of the East End. Iris still choked when she recalled the cheeky, animated face of the Mod inviting her to climb on to his scooter, and the skull-like features of the man in a wheelchair who'd come to say goodbye to her in Italy. 'After Vic moved out, and Clive got sent to prison, I ended up on your doorstep, remember?' Iris explained, eager not to revisit the history of her relationship with Clive.

'Pizza Clive?' said Winston.

After serving his sentence, Clive had eventually made his fortune in pizza delivery, and, curiously, become a kind of Thatcherite role-model entrepreneur by confessing his past criminality. His book *Learning My Lesson* had been the business bible for a while, although his over-ambitious purchase of a chain of restaurants, and involvement in a political bribery scandal, had led to the collapse of his business in the early nineties. Now that brand of barrow-boy commerce seemed strangely out of date.

'As you say, I was young and didn't know myself . . .' said Iris.

They started walking again.

'Do you now?' he asked.

'Better than I did,' she said, not sure she wanted to spend this amazing morning soul-searching. 'When did you decide who *you* were, then?' she asked.

Winston considered his answer. 'I think I accepted I was different at an early age,' he said. 'Didn't have much choice really.' He smiled. 'But it was only at university that

I realized other things were different apart from the colour of my skin.'

'Like?'

'Like leadership. I discovered that I could take people with me. And focus. Focus is what turns talent into success. You can be a naturally brilliant sprinter, but you'll never win a race without focus.'

'Listen to you!' said Iris.

'What?' he asked.

'The New Labour guru speaks!'

To his credit, Winston didn't mind when she teased him for being pompous. He laughed, and automatically, John started laughing too.

Iris stood looking at them, wishing she had a camera to take a picture of this moment on 2 May 1997. The unseasonal summeriness of the day, and her lack of sleep, seemed to be giving everything a weird kind of brilliance, as if it really was the beginning of a new, golden, era.

'What are we doing now?' Winston asked.

'I'm happy just mooching,' Iris said.

Normally, Winston was too busy to mooch. Mooching would have to be timetabled into his diary, and that destroyed the point of it. Surely he could take the day off today?

'Shall we mooch over to greet the new Prime Minister?' Winston suggested.

'Good idea,' said Iris.

At Downing Street they were given Union Jack flags by New Labour PR people, and John looked so cute with his that Iris was sure one of the press photographers would capture this perfect example of multicultural Britain. She suddenly wondered whether, in years to come, John's generation would be known as Blair's children, just as Bruno and Fiammetta's generation had been Thatcher's children.

'You know what's strange,' Iris shouted to Winston above

the cheering, as the new Prime Minister arrived. 'I've spent most of my life fighting the Establishment, and now we are it. We *are* the bloody Establishment! Tony Blair is our generation. This is our time. We are the ones in charge. Well, you are, anyway,' she qualified.

'And your point is?' he enquired.

'I don't feel grown-up enough,' said Iris.

*   *   *

Julia watched the light outside the porthole changing from bright white to golden, then a warm rosy pink as the embers of the setting sun reflected off the water. She half hoped that Sonny would want to have dinner on the *Principessa*, so she wouldn't have to bother about getting dressed, but when he woke he was immediately restless. Julia put his moods down to caffeine addiction, because he normally settled after a cup of strong coffee, but she wouldn't have dreamt of suggesting it after all the fuss when he'd tried to quit smoking.

'Can't we just collect the boys now?' he asked. 'We could have breakfast in St Malo.'

'We're not allowed until tomorrow morning,' Julia told him. 'Apparently, Christopher is taking them out for dinner with Millicent. It's her fiftieth birthday. Can you believe it?'

'She looks older,' said Sonny. 'Why don't we go out to dinner?' he suddenly asked, making Julia wish she'd never put the idea in his head.

'But where?' she asked half-heartedly.

The prospect of a biryani at the Taj Mahal, the only sit-down option on Kingshaven High Street, didn't appeal. At the Harbour End, the choice was takeaway fish and chips, or a meal at the Ship, which was out of the question.

'How about the Castle?' Sonny suggested. 'I'd like to see what your brother's done to it.'

'They're bound to be full.'

'They'll make room for you, surely?'

He was probably right. Even if her brother wasn't keen to see her, he'd hardly be able to refuse her a table in his restaurant. She'd heard rumours that the Castle was not as fully booked as it might be. James would probably welcome the opportunity to meet a rich businessman like Sonny.

James and Fiammetta joined them at their table for coffee afterwards, and as Julia introduced her kid brother to Sonny, she thought how strange it was that though Sonny was virtually the same age as James, and had been brought up in the same town, they had never properly met. Sonny would not have been welcome at the Castle when they were growing up, not so much because of his colour, but because of money. When she and James were growing up, the Patels had been poor, but now Sonny and James could happily chat to each other about the implications of the independence of the Bank of England, leaving Julia and Fiammetta to smile at each other nervously over the petits fours.

'Mmm, these are delicious!' said Julia, allowing herself another cocoa-dusted globe of truffle 'The chocolate's so intense . . . How on earth do you manage to stay so thin?'

Julia had forged many female friendships with talk of calories or chocolate, but Fiammetta was not like other women she'd met. Perhaps because she was an artist, her thoughts were on a different plane.

'I've never been interested in food,' Fiammetta said bluntly, adding, as if she realized the words sounded brusque: 'Maybe it was growing up with a chef!'

Julia was sure Fiammetta didn't mean to embarrass her, but she'd opened a subject she'd have preferred to avoid.

'How is Bruno?' Julia asked, as nonchalantly as she could manage.

'His television series is starting next week,' said Fiammetta.

'Who's this?' Sonny's ears were almost as attuned to celebrity as they were to finance.

'Fiammetta's twin brother is a chef.'

'Bruno's a great friend of my brother's!' Sonny told them. 'They were in the same year at school.'

Julia suspected that Sonny was exaggerating, as he often did about the closeness of his connections with famous people, but if it was true that Bruno and Nikhil were friends, then perhaps that explained why Nikhil had never shown an interest in her. Not that it mattered now, she reminded herself.

'Bruno's so bloody busy with his television series, he's never at the club,' said James, wanting to underline his own association.

'How on earth did Bruno manage to get on television?' Sonny wanted to know.

'By bonking the producer!' James laughed.

Julia was sure her brother's remark was deliberately targeted. He'd always been good at needling her.

'How is the hotel going?' she asked, to pay James back, knowing that he hated the Castle being called a hotel, preferring to cast himself as lord of the manor entertaining guests for a weekend in the country.

James bristled. 'Well enough,' he said, shortly.

'You may find,' Julia couldn't resist taunting, 'that you have a bit of competition in the not too distant future . . .'

'Really?' said James.

His patronizing attitude irritated Julia so much she suddenly threw caution to the wind.

'Sonny's father is buying the Palace, and we,' Julia slid her hand over Sonny's, '. . . are going to run it!' She didn't say, 'So there!' as she would have done when they were children, but the implication was there.

The look on her brother's face was a glory to behold. The look on Sonny's was less encouraging.

In the taxi back to the harbour, her lover's anger was palpable.

'My family's business is my family's business,' he finally said, spitting out the words.

'But he's my family,' Julia tried to excuse herself, knowing she was in the wrong.

'But we agreed to keep it confidential until—'

'James won't tell,' Julia interrupted, giving Sonny a sharp nudge, because she was suddenly conscious that the taxi driver was eagerly awaiting a clue as to what they were talking about. In the rearview mirror, Sid Farthing's eyes were alert with intrigue.

Julia recalled seeing him that morning going in the Albion, and she detected a distinct sour odour in the car. Surely Sid couldn't have been drinking all day, she thought, wishing he would keep his eyes on the road.

'You haven't got your seatbelt on,' Julia pointed out, as the car hurtled round the lanes. At night, the tall hedgerows were like the walls of a tunnel.

'I hate seatbelts,' said Sonny defiantly, like a grumpy child.

Julia gripped the edge of her seat as the car swerved alarmingly, feeling as if she were on one of the theme-park rides her boys loved so much, that threw them to the brink of crashing before whipping them all back to safety.

In the mirror, Mr Farthing's eyes leered at her, enjoying her terror. She didn't know whether it would make it better or worse to ask him to slow down.

Suddenly, the taxi driver's reflection was obliterated in the blinding glare of the headlights of a car coming up fast behind them. The taxi took another corner, brakes screeching, but this time the car didn't come back down from the brink, and suddenly Julia was upside down, weightless for a moment, like the top of the Nemesis ride, where you could only scream.

Then everything crumpled into darkness.

Chapter Six

Spring 1998

One of the things Cat most liked about working in a bookshop was the high turnover of staff that meant there were always new people around. It wasn't the kind of place you'd choose to work for the money, because the pay was so bad. Usually bookshop assistants were on their way to being something else, such as writers or actors. Cat was quite relaxed about letting them fill in for each other when there were auditions, or matinée calls to attend, and so there was generally a happy atmosphere, particularly when Danny, a wannabe dancer, was working. Danny was loud, camp and very beautiful, and his presence made the shop buzz. During quiet times, he amused the rest of the staff with his impersonations of customers; at lunch time, when the shop was busy, he toned down his performance but still couldn't stop himself giving marks out of ten, under his breath, to any man who came in.

'Eight,' he muttered, as a customer approached the information desk, where he and Cat were standing.

'The crossword girl!'

A vaguely familiar voice made Cat look up from the publisher's catalogue she was reading.

'The creme-egg thief!' she replied, seeing the Irishman standing in front of the information desk. His hair was wet, and individual curls stuck to his face like upside-down question marks. 'Is it raining?' she asked, unnecessarily.

'A deluge,' he said.

His full name, she knew now, was Finn O'Hanrahan. He had a political column – 'The new columnist for the new politics' – with a photo byline in the newspaper she usually read. Sometimes he appeared as a pundit on *Newsnight*.

'I didn't know you worked round here,' he said.

'I'm the manager,' she replied, and then thought how ridiculous that sounded. Beside her, she sensed Danny rehearsing his imitation for later.

'I was at a pub quiz the other day, and I thought of you and your crosswords,' said Finn.

'You and your crosswords!' Danny was bound to pick up on that, but it was quite flattering when someone remembered little details about you. Cat was suspicious of charm. Married men were particularly good at it. Her tutor Roy had had a knack of choosing the perfect compliment to disarm her.

'I'm looking for a book,' Finn went on.

'You've come to the right place. We've got thousands,' said Danny.

Finn smiled tolerantly.

'Anything in particular?' Cat asked, trying to maintain a professional demeanour.

'The author is Michael Quinn. I'm afraid I don't have a title. He's the father of someone I'm going to lunch with. I thought I'd do some research.'

'Bruno?' asked Cat, pointing at the cookery table, where there was a stack of signed copies of *Benvenuto Bruno!*, the book Bruno had produced after the success of the television series, which had been a major Christmas bestseller.

Finn looked mystified.

'Bruno Dearchild is Michael Quinn's son,' Cat explained.

They'd all pieced together the information one Sunday brunch after the wedding weekend in Kingshaven, Cat

239

thinking it uncanny that she talked to Michael Quinn without being aware that her housemate was his son, Esther pointing out that it wasn't *so* weird since they were in Bruno's home town and it wasn't exactly a big place.

'Actually, it's Tony Quinn I'm seeing,' said Finn, adding, as Cat failed to recognize the name, 'He's a rising star in the government. According to the cuttings, he's Michael Quinn's son by Sylvia Quinn. The product of an angry young man and a fashion designer . . . perfect New Labour pedigree . . .'

'The first two books are long out of print,' Cat was scanning through the database to check, 'and I'm afraid his more recent book, *Foreigners*, appears to be too.'

It was such a shame short stories didn't sell. Cat had always thought that *Foreigners* could have been published more imaginatively as a novel. When she'd become manager of the City branch of Brooks, she'd tried to get a copy in for the staff picks table, but the order had never arrived.

'You could go to a library,' she suggested. 'Actually, I have a copy at home that I could try to find . . .'

'The lunch is tomorrow,' said Finn, sighing.

'It's a series of linked short stories about a small town that's rather like a microcosm of England,' Cat told him. 'The tone is anti-Establishment, subversive, old Labour . . .'

Finn seemed delighted with this synopsis. 'Perhaps I should take you to the lunch with me,' he suggested.

Cat couldn't work out whether he was being flirtatious or patronizing. 'I'm working tomorrow,' she said.

'The next quiz, then,' he said. 'You'll come to that?'

'Maybe,' said Cat uncertainly.

'I'll know where to find you now,' said Finn.

'He knows where to find you,' said Danny, loud enough, Cat thought, for Finn to hear as he was leaving the shop.

'Ssshush!' she scolded him.

240

'You fancy him! Do we detect a slight melting of the ice maiden?'

'He's married,' Cat told him. 'And I've had enough of married men,' she revealed, to shut him up.

'Well, well, it's always the quiet ones!' said Danny, with a look, she thought, of approval.

*   *   *

When the editor of the *Chronicle* wrote to ask Michael Quinn whether, as a renowned local writer, he would be interested in writing *A Brief History of Kingshaven* as part of the newspaper's plans to celebrate the millennium, Michael was surprised. Anyone who had read *Foreigners* would have understood that he was hardly part of the Kingshaven establishment. Yet the more he thought about it, the more the idea appealed. The history of the place from dinosaurs to D-Day had fascinated him from the time when he first arrived in the town as a schoolteacher. He had introduced the idea of local field trips for the children, standing on the ramparts of the Iron Age Fort, getting them to imagine what it must have been like to see an invading fleet of Roman ships sailing into the bay. He had always thought that Kingshaven was like a microcosm of the nation – once a proud sea-faring port, now a rather dilapidated but charming relic – and the idea of having the excuse to research it properly appealed to him.

'We're thinking along the lines of an illustrated giveaway. "Kingshaven – the first 2,000 years", that kind of thing,' said Robert Murphy when Michael went to see him at the offices of the *Echo* group in Lowhampton.

'You do know I'm neither a historian nor exactly local,' Michael warned him.

'Neither am I,' said Robert Murphy. 'But it's often useful to have an outsider's view on a place like this.'

The *Chronicle*'s editorial policy had certainly been less

reverent since the late sixties, when it had been absorbed into the *Echo* group. Michael still remembered the town's shock at the appearance of the man who'd been made editor. Mr Murphy had been a young Australian surfer. Nowadays, his springy hair was grey and cropped short, but it had once been a woolly mane of ginger.

'What brought you to these parts?' Michael asked.

'Searching for my roots?' said the editor. His voice retained the Australian inflection that made every sentence sound like an ironic question.

'Your family came from here?' Michael asked.

Robert Murphy looked surprised. As a newspaper man, he was used to asking the questions. 'I started life in a children's home just outside Lowhampton. They sent quite a few of us to Australia to be beaten up – sorry, brought up – by priests.'

'I didn't know . . .'

'Most people don't. It sounds too Victorian, but they were doing it right up to the sixties. Someone should write a book about that,' he said, almost accusingly. Then he asked, 'What brought you here, then?'

'We were trying to make a fresh start,' Michael explained. 'I'd heard it was nice down here. My brother was stationed here in the war.'

Had he, in some sense, come looking for his family too? Both his parents had been killed in one of the first air raids; his aunt had emigrated to Idaho straight after the war. Although he still thought of himself as a Northerner, he had no roots left in the North.

'Important to have a lot about the war in the book,' said Robert Murphy, looking at his watch, clearly keen to wrap the meeting up. 'Kingshaven's finest hour, and all that. Now, your fee . . .' He named a figure in excess of what Michael was expecting and added: 'You'll need access to our cuttings library. I'll ask my secretary to arrange that, and, any problems, just call . . .'

It was still pouring when Michael's bus arrived back in Kingshaven. Gusts of wind concertinaed the rain into white shapes that blew along the promenade like phantoms. He stood for a few minutes under the dripping rainshelter, as if hoping the weather might see him waiting there and stop, but it took no notice at all.

*　　*　　*

It had been raining ever since Winston left for New York, and Iris was irrationally annoyed with him for going away when the weather was so bad. Usually, the space between John waking up and going to bed didn't seem so long because she took him to the Heath, or the zoo, or to Inverness Street market in Camden to buy fruit and vegetables. They would always walk, or take the bus, because Iris was keen that John learn how to use public transport, even though he wasn't yet two years old. Winston could justify the chauffeur, his habit of flying first-class, and many other perks of his position, as efficiencies that freed up time for him to concentrate on more important things. But even though Iris knew that Winston devoted a great deal of his money and influence to improving the lives of people in Africa, she still couldn't get her head round the opulent life they led in the lovely house just off Hampstead High Street. The only way she could excuse her part in it all was that she acted as Winston's old Labour conscience, never allowing him to take any of it for granted, and she was determined that their son would not grow up thinking that these things were his due.

On Tuesday mornings, Iris took John to the mother-and-toddler group in a church hall two streets away, although Iris was considerably older than the other mothers, and considerably less willing to join in endless choruses of 'The wheels on the bus', especially the one about the mummies on the bus going 'chatter, chatter, chatter', while the daddies on the bus went 'read, read, read'. It was an indication of quite how stir crazy she was that she found herself on Saturday morning counting the days until the next meeting.

Having sole responsibility for a child was a peculiar combination of intense fascination and intense boredom; companionability and loneliness. Iris watched the rain streaming down the windows of the conservatory, wondering now how she could ever have imagined that she would be able to cope with it all on her own.

Saturday was usually Winston's day with John. The two of them would go off to Tots' Tennis or Baby Gym at a sports centre in Islington for some male bonding, and Iris would stay in bed and read, enjoying the sudden silence in the house, recharging her batteries for the equally sudden noise of them returning and the joyous impact of John jumping into her arms.

Iris looked at the floor with its debris of the morning's activity. They had done collage and she had let John win endless rounds of Hungry Hippos. They had constructed an alternative universe of Playmobil, in which Father Christmas ran a farm with two astronauts, lions, cows and penguins grazed together on the carpet, watched over by the god-like rocking horse. John rocked backwards and forwards squirming away from Iris's steadying hand. It was only ten o'clock in the morning, much too early in the day to resort to a *Thomas the Tank Engine* video.

Perhaps they should get a bus to Brent Cross Shopping Centre, which was like an indoor playground for John, with fountains to watch, different sorts of sofas to bounce on in the department store, and a table full of Brio in the Early Learning Centre? But on Saturdays it was very crowded, and the constant announcements of lost children over the public address always made Iris grip John's hand so tight he screamed with anger, or became a floppy dead weight that she had to drag along. It would be even worse in the rain,

Iris thought, with the fug of damp coats mingling with the fatty odour from McDonald's, and a film of slippery grime underfoot.

'Come on!' Iris resolved suddenly. 'Let's go for a walk.'

'It raining!' said John.

'Yes, I know, but we'll put on our macs and wellies and we might even find some puddles to splash about in.'

'Puddles!' John immediately slid down from the horse.

The paths on the Heath were small rivers, and the two of them were the only people mad enough to be out, but Iris felt refreshed by the cool wet air, as if she were a plant whose leaves had shrivelled and needed rehydrating. On the top field, as if to reward their perseverance, the rain stopped and Iris was briefly aware of the sound of traffic and birdsong. Great masses of dark cloud rushing across the sky made it feel as if the whole world was in flux. London's endless sprawl stretched as far as Iris could see in all directions. To the east, she thought she could pick out the high-rise tower where she lived with Vic and Clive when she first arrived in London. She could still remember the sensation of awe and exhaustion climbing off the back of the scooter, her knees stiff and cold after the long journey, looking up at the tower and thinking, This is it!

Iris wondered why it was that the things she imagined would solve her life never, somehow, did. When she was fourteen, to be in Swinging London was all she wished for, but her dream had quickly become to be Clive's girlfriend, and when she'd achieved that, it wasn't nearly enough, because she wanted to go to university and change the world. When she'd discovered feminism and found a career, that had been the answer, until Roman had come along. For a while, he had been everything to her, but he had reduced her to nothing. And she had thought that was it. She'd had her chances in life and she'd blown them.

The wind blew tendrils of hair across her eyes.

In her wildest imaginings, Iris could never have envisaged the gift of a loving family, Winston and John, who was so much more precious than anything before, and who made her happier that she ever hoped, or deserved, to be.

'Mummy crying,' said John, as she bent down to pick him up and point out the landmarks.

'No, silly, the rain's made my face all wet. Look,' she said. 'That's the Telecom Tower, and over there, right in the distance, are the Houses of Parliament.'

'Tony,' said John.

'Clever boy!' Iris exclaimed. How many two-year-old children knew the name of the Prime Minister, let alone made the connection with the Houses of Parliament! But when she saw where her son was looking – not at Westminster, but at the lone jogger puffing up the hill towards them – her delight turned to disappointment.

She remembered Winston saying something about bumping into her brother Anthony a couple of Saturdays before, when he had taken John out kite-flying on the Heath. Apparently, all the lunches and dinners her brother had consumed since becoming a junior minister had piled pounds on to his waistline, and the doctor had advised him to exercise regularly.

'Nice weather – for ducks!' Anthony called out.

'Where ducks?' asked John.

Anthony stopped beside them, panting clouds of steamy breath.

'What are you two doing?' he asked.

'We were fed-up with being indoors,' Iris explained.

'Winston away?'

'New York,' said Iris.

'Are you missing your daddy?' Anthony asked John in a silly voice, tickling him under the chin.

'Missing daddy,' John repeated sadly.

Iris was irritated with her brother for putting the idea into his head.

'It's difficult knowing what to do in weather like this,' she said, immediately regretting it when Anthony replied.

'Why don't you come to lunch? Marie and the kids would love to see you,' said Anthony. 'I've got to do another circuit, but I'll catch you up.'

He jogged off, leaving Iris with no alternative unless she wanted to jog after him.

'Lunch!' said John gleefully.

*　　*　　*

There had been so much rain during the past few weeks that Libby found it quite difficult to remember what a normal spring day looked like. The relentless rain cast a pall over the spirit of the place, and put the cleaners in a bad mood. Weekends were particularly gloomy. During the week, bookings weren't greatly affected, because at this time of year it was mostly small conferences of sales reps, but nobody would have dreamt of visiting Kingshaven for pleasure in this weather.

Although Libby had not been without misgivings about selling the hotel, it was only when it had fallen through that she'd realized how much she had been looking forward to her freedom. Eddie had been all for finding another purchaser quickly. The property market was soaring, and that couldn't go on for ever. Unfortunately, Mr Humble had informed them that a 'technicality' had come to light in the negotiations, which meant they wouldn't be able to sell it without Liliana's agreement. Although Libby and Eddie's name was on the lease, Mrs Liliana King was still a freeholder of the land, and any transfer would involve her signature. Power of attorney forms had been drawn up, but Liliana had ignored all requests to sign and, because she appeared to be perfectly capable of reading the document, Dr Ferry had not been helpful. Possibly that might change now that Kingshaven had a new GP. Extraordinarily, Dr

Ferry had been arrested on suspicion of killing several of the residents of the old people's home. Of course, it must be a mistake. Dr Ferry was such a caring man. But he was getting near retirement age in any case, so the young woman who'd arrived as a locum would probably end up staying.

Anyway, Liliana couldn't go on for ever.

The Palace had come to feel increasingly like a prison. Worse than that, whenever Libby escaped, for her weekly horse ride or to have her hair set at the salon on the High Street, she couldn't help noticing the hostile and suspicious glances of the inhabitants of Kingshaven, as if they actually believed the vile rumours that she had somehow been responsible for Julia's accident. It was perfectly understandable that Mr Patel should be upset, but it was a mark of how low standards had fallen in the local press that his ravings had been reported under the headline **Crash latest: Palace involved?**

*   *   *

Outside a swanky florist near Anthony's house there was a dark-green bucket of peonies, some still tightly wrapped balls of bud, others billowing open like great old-fashioned pink roses. Iris decided to buy the lot, not wanting to arrive at Anthony's empty-handed.

'Would you like them hand-tied?' the florist's assistant asked.

'How else would you tie them?' Iris asked. Then, realizing how rude that sounded, she felt she had to go along with the cellophane, and the trailing raffia bow and the lime-green tissue paper that immediately began to bleed colour when she placed the bouquet on the rainhood of John's pushchair.

The shiny red front door of Anthony's early Victorian house in Dartmouth Park was opened by Anthony's youngest child, Leonora, who had her mother's dark hair and pale skin and was at the difficult age between child and teenager.

'Your father's invited us to lunch,' Iris told her.

'He's not here.'

'Well, is your mother in?'

'Mum, are you in for Iris?'

'Iris!' said Marie, as Iris manoeuvred the dripping buggy in which John was now sleeping into the hall. 'What a lovely surprise.'

Marie was wearing a smart jersey wrap dress and much more make-up and perfume than usual, which made Iris immediately suspect that the lunch wasn't informal, as Anthony had implied, and Iris was even more annoyed with him because underneath her mac she was wearing grey tracksuit bottoms and a T-shirt that probably had glue on it.

'We bumped into Anthony on the Heath,' Iris explained, handing her the peonies. 'He invited us to lunch.'

'Flowers!' said Marie, pushing her face right into the bouquet and inhaling, as if the flowers had a gorgeous fragrance, when in fact they had no scent at all.

'We'll have to find just the right place for you,' she told the peonies.

Iris noticed that there was a vase of crimson roses on the mantelpiece of the vast high-ceilinged reception room.

'And you'll need a nice drink,' Marie continued addressing the peonies. 'I expect you'd like a drink too, Iris?'

Was it deliberate, Iris wondered, or was it simply her own sense of inadequacy that made Marie's every gesture and utterance feel like a criticism? Not only had she brought unscented flowers in the wrong colour, but she clearly gave the appearance of being an alcoholic.

'I'd love a coffee,' said Iris, adding, when she saw the pained look on Marie's face, 'but only if you're making one.'

'Iris!'

The front door banged behind him as Anthony bounded in and planted a sweaty kiss on both of Iris's cheeks.

'I was just going to make Iris some coffee,' said Marie, the look on her face speaking volumes.

'Let me do it,' Anthony told her. 'I'm sure you've got enough to do.'

The kitchen was like a show kitchen in a department store, Iris thought, with light-wood units, brushed-steel splashbacks, granite work surfaces and a floor of terracotta quarry tiles. There was a big bowl of salad leaves, and various raw ingredients laid out on the central work surface. The room smelt deliciously of baking bread. As Anthony clattered around with a cafetière, Marie pored over Bruno's cookbook and drizzled cloudy green olive oil over a huge baking tray of assorted mushrooms.

The car in the photograph on the jacket of the book was the same yellow model that Bruno and Iris had driven around Tuscany when he came to visit in the late eighties. Matching lemon trees in terracotta pots stood on either side of the entrance to the crumbling *palazzo* in the background. The television series and subsequent book had made Bruno a celebrity. Iris had her own copy of the first edition, but whenever she was browsing in a bookshop she couldn't stop herself opening one on the display and checking out the dedication that read: *For Iris, fellow traveller.*

An aromatic waft of ground coffee swirled out as Anthony broke the seal of the vacuum pack.

'Who's coming to this lunch, then?' Iris asked, sitting down on a wicker sofa in the extended area of the kitchen. A long wooden table was laid for eight. There was another enormous vase of red roses in the centre.

'Oh, you know, your average cross-section of Cool Britannia,' Anthony replied, filling the kettle.

Iris wasn't sure whether he was being ironic or not.

'An interior designer, a television producer, an advertising executive . . . Oh, and a sympathetic journalist, of course.'

'A journalist?'

'No point in hosting discreet power-broking parties if nobody gets to hear about them,' said Anthony, winking at her.

'Who drew up the guest list?' she asked. 'One of your focus groups?'

Her brother smiled at her and ignored the taunt.

'And Gianni,' Marie chipped in. 'Giorgio rang yesterday and asked if he could bring a friend. Apparently, Gianni's been poorly.'

Iris suddenly realized that Anthony's invitation was anything but spontaneous. They'd needed someone to make up the numbers, and she might well be useful handling a poorly gay man.

'I won't have the slightest idea what to say to these people,' she told Anthony.

'That'll be a first,' Marie remarked tartly.

'I mean, I'll probably say all the wrong things,' said Iris.

'Sometimes it's fun to have someone who stirs things up.' Anthony poured boiling water on to the ground coffee in the cafetière.

Clearly he had already made the calculation that on balance she was more likely to liven up the occasion than to embarrass him. All the right ingredients were in place for a perfect New Labour lunch, and she would be a piquant garnish.

In the late seventies, the guests at Anthony's lunch party would have been called 'ideologically sound' but now the label was 'politically correct'. First to arrive was a very well-groomed woman, such a busy, important person she was issuing instructions on her mobile phone even as she stood waiting for the door to be answered. Iris imagined she was the type who called herself a post-feminist, a term that seemed to mean she'd take all the things feminists fought for, like equal pay, and spend it on facials, waxes and expensive lingerie. The woman gave Iris's tracksuit the briefest glance, then swept past her to air kiss Anthony and Marie.

In the kitchen, John was proudly sitting with his cousins at the breakfast bar and refused all help eating his pasta.

Iris returned to the living room, where the first woman had been given a glass of champagne and another similarly slim and lipsticked one had arrived.

'Venetia, this is Iris. Tony's big sister,' Marie explained.

'What do you do?' the first woman, Sue, asked Iris.

'Playmobil, mostly,' said Iris, 'and occasional Scalextric.'

Sue laughed, as if she had made a joke, and looked at her expectantly for expansion, or at the very least the return of the question.

The doorbell rang again.

'I'll go,' Iris said, grabbing the opportunity to escape.

The man who was standing on the doorstep was tall and had curly brown hair that hung round his face in no particular style, as if he had better things to do than remember to get it cut. Iris estimated he was in his early thirties. He looked up from the back of the *Observer Review* he was reading and smiled at her with intelligent eyes behind square tortoiseshell glasses.

'Hello, I'm Iris.' She held out her hand.

'Goddess of the rainbow,' he said, with an Irish lilt in his voice, which she thought was a bit over the top until he beckoned her out on to the doorstep and pointed up at a bright rainbow against an almost black sky.

'Am I in the right place?'

A very camp voice at the bottom of the steps heralded the arrival of a middle-aged man with a tan as dark as wood-stain. He was holding a little white dog with a long fringe.

'Giorgio?' Iris guessed.

'And this is Gianni,' he told Iris.

The dog, the kind featured on corny greetings cards, almost too cute to be real, cocked its head to one side.

'*Ciao*, Gianni! I hear you haven't been well,' Iris said to the dog.

'*Poverino!*' said Giorgio. 'We're feeling much better now, aren't we? Say hello to . . . ?'

'Iris. Tony's sister.' Iris took the proffered paw and shook it gently, thinking, for the first time, that the lunch party might be a bit of a laugh.

'Such a lovely house,' Venetia was saying in the living room.

'Giorgio finds it a bit minimalist,' Anthony told her. 'He's suggesting black and white checkerboard tiles and fuchsia walls with candelabra . . .'

'Vermeer meets Liberace?' said Venetia.

'Perhaps you could do us on "What a difference a day makes"?' said Marie.

Iris stared at the top of her champagne glass, watching the continuous stream of pinprick bubbles surfacing through the clear gold liquid and wondering how it was possible that new little spheres of air kept appearing in the stem of the glass.

'Are we all here?' Anthony wondered out loud.

He said things that a successful middle aged family man should say, and Iris had to keep reminding herself that her brother was, after all, in his mid forties and had a proper job and that his grown-up behaviour was probably not as astonishing to anyone else as it was to her.

The original seating plan had been changed and the dog's name card removed. Leonora had adopted Gianni and was playing with him in the garden. Jack, Anthony's oldest boy, was positioning a football for John, and the middle son, Sam, was dutifully standing in the mini goal and failing to save the penalty kicks that John fired at him. It was touching to see two such big boys being so gentle with their little cousin, and John was loving every second of it.

A garlicky aroma rose from the tray of roasted field mushrooms. Anthony poured a Chianti at exactly the right temperature to combine perfectly with the earthy taste of mushroom and the yeasty bread.

'This is absolutely delicious,' said Sue.

'A recipe of Bruno's,' said Marie, adding, 'He's Tony's stepbrother.'

Iris had a certain admiration for the way her sister-in-law had managed to pursue a high-flying legal career of her own, have children, cook lunch for seven and drop names to propel the career of 'Tony' Quinn too. While giving the appearance of a loyal little wife, Marie had actually done the stuff they used to fight for, Iris thought, whereas she, a committed feminist, had ended up with no career at all and living off a rich man.

'Actually, Bruno is our half-brother,' Iris said, trying to join in, but making it sound like a correction. There was a tiny embarrassed pause.

'It was Iris who taught Bruno to cook, wasn't it?' Anthony said generously.

'You can't teach Bruno's kind of charisma,' said Venetia.

Iris was always amazed by how easy it was to feel alone at a social gathering.

There were two separate conversations going on at the table. Marie, Sue and Giorgio (who kept leaning backwards and glancing out to check on the dog, his leathery face creased with fond parental pride) were discussing whether it was a strategic mistake for Tony Blair to back the Millennium Dome; Anthony and Venetia were talking about whether it was possible to make politics fresh and interesting on television.

Iris was suddenly aware that the young Irishman sitting next to her had asked a question.

'Marie said you've been living abroad?'

'Yes. Rome.'

'What brought you back to London?'

Iris opted for the very short answer, as opposed to the very long one. 'Love,' she said.

The journalist looked intrigued. 'Of London?' he asked.

'Of Winston Allsop,' said Iris, instantly aware of everyone at the table tuning into the name.

'Iris is Winston's current partner,' Anthony explained. 'Is that the right word?'

The word Iris couldn't cope with was 'current'. For a moment, she was at a loss, fuming while Anthony collected up the starter plates and Marie carefully lifted greaseproof paper parcels from an oven tray to large shallow white bowls. Sunday lunch was clearly an operation they'd perfected.

'So, do you and Winston Allsop go back a long way?' asked the Irishman.

'He and Iris were childhood sweethearts,' Anthony replied for her.

'Not sweethearts: comrades!' Iris declared hotly.

Now Anthony was at a loss for words.

'Our passion,' Iris continued her theme, 'was civil rights and CND.'

'And then Winston grew up,' Anthony invited the others to laugh.

'If growing up means voting Tory,' Iris shot back, pleased to see her brother blush. Shame on him! 'Thatcherism wasn't just about yuppies and shoulder pads, you know,' she told the Irishman. 'It was about the Miners' Strike and Greenham Common . . .'

He listened politely, too young, she thought, and possibly too kind, to cut her off like the others, who had gone back to their former conversations, dismissing her as a ranting Leftie dinosaur.

'John enjoyed it,' Iris told Winston, when he called that evening. 'I got rather overexcited . . .' Recounting the conversation, she couldn't tell for a moment whether the silence at the end of the phone meant that Winston was cross with her or just listening. 'He was a journalist,' she admitted nervously.

'I don't think it's much of a story,' said Winston. 'Entrepreneur once voted for Margaret Thatcher shock!'

'You don't mind?'

'Iris, the last thing I'd want to do is censor you.'

Winston was *so* much more grown-up than she was. She cradled the telephone in both her hands against her cheek, wishing it was him there next to her, not just his voice.

'In any case, I think you've probably done us both a good turn . . .' Winston was saying.

'How's that?'

'We'll never be invited to one of Anthony's lunches again!' he said wickedly.

'Hadn't thought of that,' said Iris, reassurance spreading through her body like warmth. 'Come home soon,' she told him softly. 'We're missing you.'

'I'm missing you,' he told her. 'Miss kissing you . . .'

*   *   *

'He's back!' hissed Danny, with a significant glance at a customer who was leafing through a Pilates manual in the Well Being section. Danny put cappuccinos in front of Cat and a sales rep she was talking to at one of the tables in the coffee shop.

'Still here!' Danny told her, when the sales rep had finally gone. He pointed at Contemporary Fiction, where Finn was now reading a copy of *Bridget Jones's Diary*.

'We're actually closing now,' Cat informed him.

He looked up from the book, his smile part curiosity, part pleasure. It had a peculiar effect on her.

'Would you be free for a drink?' he asked.

'When?' she stalled.

'Now?'

'Is it Quiz Night?' she asked.

'No, but if you insist on the format I could ask you questions.'

Cat could feel herself blushing, and somehow that made it more difficult to say no. One drink couldn't do any harm, she thought, aware that the encounter was being closely scrutinized by Danny.

The pub near Smithfield was crowded, but they managed to squeeze behind a table next to the door.

'How was your lunch?' Cat asked Finn.

He looked mystified.

'With Tony Quinn?' she said.

'Oh, that,' he said. It had been only a few days ago, but he had obviously had several significant lunches since. 'Interesting,' he said. 'Actually, more interesting than the usual New Labour dos, which are so choreographed you never learn anything they don't want you to know. Tony Quinn's sister was there. Quite a character, and fabulously unspun . . . Another?' he asked, seeing that Cat had finished her glass of wine.

'No, thanks,' Cat said.

'Would you like to eat?'

'I'm not hungry,' said Cat, adding, 'Thanks,' because her awkwardness made her sound so rude.

'Perhaps some other time?'

'How would your wife feel about that?' Cat blurted, wishing she could have thought of some more subtle way of saying what had to be said.

'I'm sorry?' Finn looked convincingly mystified.

'Your wife, or girlfriend, or partner . . .' Cat said wearily. She'd learnt from bitter experience that unless you covered all bases the man could claim technically not to have lied.

'I'm not sure who you're talking about,' said Finn.

'The woman you were with at Roman Stone's.' Cat was embarrassed at having to spell it out. 'And child,' she added.

'You're thinking of Niamh.' Finn finally made the connection. 'She's my sister. Does that make a difference?'

Cat wished that the floor would open up and suck her down into the beer cellar. 'I don't know,' she said, furious at contriving to make a fool of herself in front of the first nice man she had met in years.

'Could I maybe call you?' he said as she picked up her bag. 'Instead of lurking round your shop.'

Cat hurriedly gave him her number; then, as she walked away down the street, she wished she hadn't because when he reviewed the encounter and realized how neurotic and idiotic she was, he was bound not to call, and yet now she would hope he would, and she would make up convoluted excuses why he had not, and jump whenever the phone rang, and dial 1471 whenever she got home, just to see if there had been any missed calls, and behave just like Bridget Jones in the book every woman of her age identified with because they had all done the same stupid things even though they were supposed to be educated, emancipated women.

She would not tell Esther about Finn, Cat promised herself as she walked up the steps to the house and put the key in the door, otherwise she'd never hear the last of it. The television was on in the living room.

'Is that you?' Esther called out.

'No,' Cat replied, assuming Esther meant Bruno.

'Can I run something past you?' Esther asked, waylaying Cat in the hall.

'Go on.'

'If You Can't Stand the Heat, Get Out of the Kitchen! – a cooking game featuring two rival television chefs getting ordinary people to do tasks, like cater a wedding, or cook a school dinner . . . combines cooking with a game show . . . and a perfect vehicle for Bruno.'

'What does he think?' Cat asked diplomatically.

'Oh, he hates it,' said Esther. 'Thinks it's cheap and

exploitative . . . But some of the most successful television is . . .'

'Where is Bruno, by the way?' said Cat.

'He's in Kingshaven, actually. One of his friends is in hospital down there, so it's nearer for him to visit.'

It sounded a poor excuse to Cat, who had never quite trusted Bruno, nor the love affair that had suddenly evolved as soon as he saw that Esther was going to make him rich. Cat wondered if his absence signalled a cooling off, but knew better than to suggest such a thing.

'That's probably him!' said Esther, leaping to pick up the phone.

'Hello? Yes, she is . . .' She handed the receiver to Cat with a face like a question mark.

'If you're not hungry, perhaps you'd like to go see a movie?' said a soft Irish voice.

The film was a romantic comedy called *Sliding Doors* about how the course of a life could turn on a single moment. Afterwards, in the crowded coffee shop next door, they both agreed that the idea was a clever one, and the performances were good, but there was something unsatisfactory about the ending. It was a very serious discussion about a light romantic comedy, as if neither of them was prepared to let the conversation veer off again into more personal territory.

'Another?' Finn asked, holding up his white china mug.

'I think I probably ought to be getting back,' Cat said.

She felt vaguely disappointed that the date seemed to have taken them backwards, not forwards, but wasn't sure how to turn it round. As they walked along the raised pavement together, talking became slightly easier now that their knees weren't touching under a small table and she wished that there was something else she could suggest doing, but she didn't want to ask him back for a coffee, and have Esther take over. Finn lived a mile or two away in Stoke Newington, he told her as she waited with him at his bus stop, so even if he were to ask her back she decided she wouldn't say yes, because somehow getting on a bus and sitting beside him on a cramped double seat would risk returning them to the stiltedness of the coffee shop. For a moment, she found herself looking at him, flustered to realize she wasn't sure whether he had asked her a question or whether the quizzical look on his face was just him thinking.

'You're not like you look,' he said.

'What do I look like, then?'

'Tall,' he replied.

From his expression, she was unable to work out whether that was supposed to be a good thing or a bad thing, but then he smiled, and she smiled back, and she felt as if something had just happened between them.

'I'd like to see you again,' he said, as a 38 bus drew up beside them.

'Me too,' said Cat quickly, not even sure that he heard her as he stepped on.

No kiss, no date, not even a wave. Cat stared at the back of the bus until she could no longer read the number, wondering why she was so bad at these things, but half an hour after she got in the phone rang again, and Esther, with a curious frown, handed her the receiver just as she had done earlier in the evening, almost like a scene from *Sliding Doors*.

'There's a play at the Donmar,' said Finn, as if he were reading down the listings for a suitable event. 'Shall I get tickets?'

All the self-help books they sold in the bookshop with tips that Danny sometimes read out loud when the shop was empty would have advised Cat to play a little hard to get, but instead she said yes immediately.

On their second date they went to a pub after the show, and caught the 38 bus together, and she didn't feel so awkward about sitting with her thigh touching his. When she got up to ring the bell for her stop, he asked if she'd like to meet the following weekend for brunch.

When they went to bed together it was still light outside. Cat had never had sex with someone for the first time during the day. Finn wasn't drunk, she didn't have to ask the condom question, and he was friendly afterwards. And really good at the bit in between.

He fell asleep with the sheet tangled round the lower half of his body as she lay very still beside him, listening to the traffic noise on Green Lanes outside. When he woke up he smiled at her, looked at his watch and reached for the phone. But he wasn't calling a wife, nor even a mate he was having a drink with, but – to Cat's blissful surprise, as she pretended not to listen – a local restaurant.

'Hope you like Lebanese,' he said with his hand over the mouthpiece. 'It's either that or pretty nasty pizza if you want it delivered. And I don't feel like getting up just yet, do you?'

*   *   *

Liliana's daughter and grandson were talking in hissing whispers, but she could hear almost every word.

'With Julia still very much on people's minds, you must think of the boys,' Libby cautioned. 'I don't really think it would be appropriate at the moment.'

'Millicent and I are two grown-up people, both divorced, who love each other . . .'

It was typical of Christopher to confuse sexual compatibility with love, thought Liliana. And why, at the age of fifty, did he feel he had to ask his mother's permission to marry his long-term mistress? The boy – Liliana still thought of her grandson as a boy – had never quite got it right in matters of the opposite sex. As a young man he'd taken so long to develop an attraction for women, she had suspected the worst, wondering whether there was something hereditary in the King men, what with Rex, and, truth be told, her own husband, Basil, who had always required the utmost patience and persistence in that department.

'I never imagined "it" would take quite as much effort,' Liliana had tentatively confided in Ruby Farmer a few months into her marriage.

In the penny dreadfuls they'd read as virgins, details were decidedly scarce, but they had both formed the impression that you were supposed to get swept away as the tidal wave of passion engulfed you. There hadn't been the slightest hint that they'd have to work so hard in the process.

'So much for lying back and thinking of England,' Ruby had concurred, with a throaty laugh.

It had been such a relief to know that she wasn't the only one, and especially gratifying when Ruby had taken longer to conceive than she had. Liliana had already had one daughter and been expecting her second before Ruby had fallen pregnant with hers.

Years later, though they'd never talked about it, Liliana suspected that they'd both suffered a pang of guilt when Christopher married Julia, remembering all too well the acute disappointment that awaited an innocent virgin, but much to everyone's surprise Julia had had a baby within a year, so it appeared that Christopher must be more competent than he looked. The mistress had done the wife a favour. If only Julia had been mature enough to see it that way, things might have continued along perfectly nicely. Turning a blind eye was often the secret of a good marriage. Nowadays, people set great store by honesty, a much overrated virtue in Liliana's opinion. Not that she condoned dishonesty. In truth, there was rarely any need for either. 'Least said, soonest mended,' as Ruby would have put it.

Ruby had been a widow, of course, when she strayed,

but the dalliance had been no less shameful. She'd been on air-raid duties when the doodlebug had come over and the soldier had been out in the street, smoking a cigarette. They'd both heard the engine cut out and known what that meant. Impulsively, she'd grabbed his hand and pulled him inside her shop and under the counter. They'd crouched there together, awaiting their fate.

Impending death had proved a powerful aphrodisiac.

'I'd never felt so close to someone,' Ruby confessed to Liliana a few weeks after the event, her eyes still bright with the memory of it. 'I thought I'd died and gone to heaven as well!'

She'd held her hands up to indicate the size of the man's thing.

'A negro?' Liliana exclaimed in disbelief, when Ruby had discreetly pointed out her lover in the street.

'Better people than me have,' Ruby told her defiantly.

'Such as?'

'Edwina Mountbatten for one, with that cabaret singer. It was in the paper.'

Not the sort of paper Liliana read. Nevertheless, instead of feeling disgust or contempt, which she was sure were the correct reactions to Ruby's admission, Liliana hadn't been able to stop thinking about it, envying, even resenting, her friend the experience that had made her as giddy as a girl.

'I hope the war goes on for ever,' Ruby had vowed dreamily.

* * *

Sometimes Julia was sure she could hear her boys telling her about tries they had scored, or goals, or moaning about school lunches. Once, she'd heard Archie saying, 'Please wake up, Mummy!' And then she'd understood. She was sleeping.

Another time, she thought she'd heard her brother James shouting, 'You must have some idea!' And a voice she didn't recognize, saying, 'There are no rules about these things.'

Now, it was Bruno's voice she could hear, talking about truffles. 'Mmmmm, smell that!' he was saying. 'Can you imagine what that's going to taste like with some lovely buttery pasta?'

Julia sniffed, but could only smell a faint whiff of cleaning fluid.

She opened her eyes.

In the corner of the small white room, a television was on and Bruno was looking out of the screen. Still dreaming, she thought, letting her eyes close again.

'Hello?' A soft voice Julia recognized, but couldn't place, was speaking to her now.

'Hello?' she responded.

'Julia?'

Julia opened her eyes again. 'Fiammetta?' she said.

'Oh my God!' said Fiammetta. 'Nurse! Doctor! Somebody! Don't go away,' she told Julia, opening the door, then calling, more loudly, 'Nurse! Doctor!'

'Where am I?' Julia asked.

'You're in hospital,' Fiammetta told her. 'You had a very bad accident.'

Then a doctor arrived and started asking her lots of questions, and Julia felt so tired she went back to sleep again. The next time she woke up, James was there with Fiammetta, and Bertie and Archie, all looking at her anxiously, their faces lifting the moment she spoke.

'I've been asleep,' she said.

'For absolutely ages,' said Archie.

It was strange to think that time had elapsed and the world had gone on without her knowing anything about it, and people knew things that she did not, and often, when she asked questions, they looked at one another, deliberating whether to tell her, as if information was a currency she wasn't yet capable of using. The only one she felt at ease with was Fiammetta because she was honest.

'Have people been coming to see me all the time?' Julia asked one day.

'Yes, all the time.'

'Sonny?'

'He died.'

'In the crash?'

'Yes. I'm so sorry.'

'What happened?'

'You were the only one wearing a seatbelt.'

'What about the other car?' Julia asked, trying to make sense of it all.

'There wasn't another car. It was just an awful accident. Mr Farthing was drunk. Three times over the limit. He's dead too.'

'How is Mr Patel?'

'Distraught.'

'Have any of the Kings come?'

'Your boys, obviously.'

'No one else?'

'No.'

'Oh.' Julia didn't know why that information should be the bit that made her cry. 'Why were you here?' she said sniffing.

'When you woke up?'

Julia nodded.

'I've been having IVF treatment, so I've been coming to the hospital quite a lot.'

'IVF. For a baby?'

'Hopefully,' said Fiammetta, looking away.

'What's going to happen to me now?' Julia asked.

'When you're a bit better, you're going to come back home with us.'

'Home,' Julia reiterated. Although she'd got her life back, it wasn't the same life as before. Everything she had been looking forward to was gone. She would have to start all over again, and she didn't know if she was strong enough.

Chapter Seven

31 December 1999

Kingshaven was famous for its fireworks. Traditionally, the carnival in August culminated with a ten-minute extravaganza fired from a barge towed out into the bay, the fountain bursts of light doubled by the mirror of water. The annual bonfire-night festivities often attracted crowds from as far away as Lowhampton. It was only fitting that the town should mark the beginning of a new millennium with a lavish display, but, as Michael trudged up the gentler of the two paths from the Harbour End, skirting the ramparts of the Iron Age Fort, he sensed that the collective anticipation was a little muffled. Rain had made the ground soft underfoot. A beacon had been lit near the triangulation point, but the damp tinder was spewing out clouds of smoke instead of crackling flames, and beneath a blanket of low cloud the misty air felt almost muggy compared with the clear, bitter bite that always seemed to characterize Guy Fawkes nights. People who had watched the scintillating brilliance of the first New Year celebrations in Sydney were asking whether it was worth anyone else bothering and the temptation to stay in to witness the global celebrations on television was strong. Looking round the ghostly faces of children waving fluorescent green sticks that some enterprising soul was selling on the promenade, Michael sensed that the people of Kingshaven were making the climb more out of a sense of duty than excitement.

Michael's work researching and writing the *Chronicle*'s illustrated book of Kingshaven's history had afforded him a better understanding of the inhabitants of the town he had lived in now for almost fifty years. Their wariness of outsiders, a trait he had always found peculiar in a long-established port, owed its origins to the cruel punishments meted out after the Civil War to citizens of a town that had remained staunchly Royalist. It was only during the Victorian era, when the railway had made it accessible and prosperous as a fashionable seaside resort, that Kingshaven had begun to open its arms to the outside world.

Suspicion had returned during the First World War, to such an extent that the Konig family, who had established their pre-eminence as hoteliers in the mid nineteenth century, had felt it necessary to anglicize their name to King. Kingshaven's much speculated-on location as one of the likely points of invasion during the Second World War had only reinforced the sense of threat. While the town had played host to some of the half a million men who had gathered along England's South Coast in preparation for the D-Day landings, it had taken its fair share of losses, and gained some unwanted arrivals.

Robert Murphy, who had been shipped off to Australia in the fifties, was exactly the age to have been the illegitimate progeny of a local girl and a serviceman, although records from the children's home he was raised in appeared to be lost.

Another embarrassing addition to the community had of course been Winston Allsop, discovered on VE night in a basket at the bottom of the beech-tree avenue that led up to the Castle. During the course of his research, Michael had discovered Winston's first ever mention in a newspaper while reading the special VE edition of the

Chronicle on microfiche in the newspaper's archive. He was looking forward to sharing it with him the next time he came down. Apparently, it was an eight-year-old girl who had originally heard the baby crying and alerted Sir John Allsop. Though the report hadn't given her name, Michael believed that this must have been Claudia, who'd been living with her refugee father in the Castle's gatehouse at that time. Michael found the idea of her place in Winston's story rather affecting. The rest of the short report had simply stated that the police were appealing to the mother to come forward.

Michael found it ironic that both Winston and Robert, whose existence their mothers had attempted to deny, should have become such public and successful figures, and he sometimes wondered whether the women had ever been tempted to lay claim to their abandoned children. Sometimes his mind meandered through a narrative of what might happen if they did, and it felt rather like the starting point of a novel.

Last to arrive on the top of the cliffs was the crowd who had been drinking all evening in the Ship, and their loudness and laughter introduced a sudden jollity to the damp atmosphere round the spitting fire. Across the town, St Mary's church bell bonged with the first chime of midnight, and a raucous cheer went up as a rocket whooshed into the air and exploded silently in a palm of orange stars. As the bang ricocheted round the bay, there was a pause, a moment of reflection almost, before an intense barrage of rockets fired up into the low cloud, a blur of explosion and colour.

As the sequence of rockets became faster and faster, the bangs were relentless, like heavy machine-gun fire pounding round the bay and reverberating through the ground. After the final ear-splitting crescendo, Michael held his breath, almost expecting the land to move under his feet, as it had done the first time he had come to the fireworks on the South Cliffs, with Iris just a little girl.

He remembered the evening as if it were yesterday. In the flickering light of the bonfire, Iris had looked so like his brother Frank, with her wild red hair and forthright blue eyes staring in amazement, that Michael had wondered whether Frank had ever stood on that exact spot, perhaps watching German planes dropping their bombs on Lowhampton, perhaps celebrating on VE night, perhaps, even, deciding to jump . . .

As the turf began to slide under them, Michael had scooped Iris up in his arms and run for his life and hers, holding her so tightly he had felt the expansion and contraction of breath inside her bony ribcage. He had leapt and stumbled until he could run no further, then stood, praying to a God he did not believe in, for the land to stay solid under his feet, with Iris's heart beating next to his, as if they were bound together by an invisible force as fundamental as gravity, as if she was what anchored him to the world.

'You're safe!' Sylvia had screamed with relief when they'd returned home.

'I was with Daddy,' Iris told her, with a six-year-old's faith in his capacities and no understanding of the danger they'd just escaped.

But Michael had been unable to silence the drumbeat of guilt inside his head.

Why hadn't he been there to save Frank?

*   *   *

Though several rows of seats above, Iris and Winston were directly behind the Blairs and the royal party and she was sure that they must be visible in the frame when the television cameras zoomed out. She was tempted to wave and shout, 'Hello, John!' in case their son was watching the television.

Annie Lennox was on the stage. Iris had always been a fan, and at one point in her life had used several bottles of peroxide trying to get her hair white blonde as hers had been. Now, by complete coincidence – perhaps they were soulmates after all – Annie had a short crop exactly like Iris's. It crossed her mind that they might meet at the party afterwards. What on earth would she say?

Winston, the one person in the world Iris felt truly at home with, had introduced her to a world of celebrity that made her feel like a complete outsider. It was crazily surreal to be sitting just behind the Queen in this giant tent with the eyes of the world watching. Iris longed to know whether there was a giddy, trembling bit of Winston, too, that wanted to scream with laughter at the ridiculousness of it all, just as they would have done if someone had told them years ago, as they sat side by side on the school bus planning virtuous lives for themselves, that at the turn of the millennium they would be sitting side by side in the VIP section of the Establishment's most grandiose folly.

'I'd like to go,' Winston had said when the invitation to the Millennium Dome had arrived.

Initially, Iris had refused. They'd never left John without one or other of them and the very thought of it made her imagine horrible scenes such as their chauffeur-driven car crashing, killing both of them, or the roof of the Dome collapsing on their heads. In any case, she'd argued, it just felt wrong not to be with their son at this unique watershed moment in time.

'He's four years old. He'll be fast asleep in bed at midnight,' Winston had argued.

Iris didn't know whether Winston was cooler about entrusting John to someone else because he had learnt to delegate responsibility in his work or whether it was simply lack of imagination. It was something she needed to become better at herself, or else she'd be in danger of becoming overprotective and that wouldn't be good for John either. It wasn't healthy to go through life fearing the worst, yet she knew she'd never forgive herself if something happened.

Her New Year's resolution should be to relax more, Iris thought, although she suspected resolving and relaxing were mutually exclusive.

'You go,' she'd told Winston.

'I'm not going on my own. It'll only be fun if you're there.'

Eventually he'd persuaded her, and they'd left John in the care of Anthony's oldest son, Jack, who was a very reliable and sensible boy, although Iris couldn't help thinking that a normal nineteen-year-old in charge of a big empty house would feel obliged to throw a party for his mates. She kept envisaging scenarios with four-year-old John wandering out into the street through the open front door, or swallowing drugs mistaking them for sweets, or suffocating under a pile of coats thrown carelessly into a dark bedroom where he was sleeping. The two times she had called on her mobile, Jack had answered the phone after only a couple of rings, giving the impression of being sober, and even put John on the line to say 'Hello, Mummy,' rapidly followed by 'Bye-bye, Mummy!' as if she had interrupted some fairly important game. She hadn't been able to detect any party noise in the background. Iris sometimes thought that the art of being a good mother was simply to hold your nerve.

Winston had insisted she'd enjoy a night out and, although she hated to admit it, he was right. After all the bad press, the Dome far exceeded her expectations. Some of the exhibition zones round the circumference were really interesting, and she was already planning to bring John to see the Human Body, with its escalator up to a giant pumping heart, that she thought he'd find even more exciting than another afternoon at Wacky Warehouse. The auditorium itself was breathtakingly impressive, like a great gold circus tent, and it *was* fun, just the two of them out together. She and Winston were a middle-aged *When Harry Met Sally,* Iris suddenly thought, who'd done it all the wrong way round. First they were friends, then they hated each other, then they had a baby, then they fell in love. Finally, at the ages of fifty-five and almost fifty, they were out together on their first date.

As the face of Big Ben with the hands approaching midnight appeared on the giant screen, Iris was shocked to realize that she hadn't thought about John for at least ten minutes. Her hand was about to go to her bag for her mobile, when Winston caught it and squeezed it gently.

'He's fine,' he mouthed.

Everyone fell silent as the clear, pure voices of two young choristers sang in the stillness, and then suddenly the moment had arrived. A group of children standing with the Queen broke from her and raced across the auditorium, grabbing the drapes on either side of the orchestral stage, causing them all to cascade to the floor one after another like a Mexican wave of gold silk. The Dome was officially open, the awesome scale of the place revealed. A huge cheer went up and, as the bongs of Big Ben were relayed, Winston took Iris in his arms and gave her a proper, lengthy passionate kiss that lasted way beyond the twelfth bong and made her feel about fifteen. Linking arms with their neighbours for the singing of 'Auld Lang Syne', her cheeks hot with delight and embarrassment, Iris wished that human beings had the capacity to freeze the sensation of a particular moment, just as a camera could capture it visually, and store it in an album, to be opened on dark days when it was harder to remember what happiness felt like.

*   *   *

A blur of orange light indicated that the fire had been lit. Kingshaven always had a beacon on important occasions.

Looking at it from across the bay, Libby remembered the time she had been asked to do the honours – the night of the Coronation in 1953. She'd been wearing a dress of yellow rayon, flammable yellow rayon, as it happened, although Eddie had immediately doused the skirt with the emergency fire bucket, and Mrs Farmer had managed to make a nice blouse out of the unscorched bodice.

'Why don't you go to the fireworks?' Libby asked her son Christopher.

Even though he probably thought it was his duty to stay and see the New Year in with them, it didn't take a very sensitive person to tell that he was itching to be with his mistress.

Bertie and Archie were with their mother at the Castle. Apparently there was a big party with lots of media types. Edwin was also there. Libby couldn't blame him. She too had enjoyed New Year's parties in her youth, although her sons would probably find that difficult to believe.

'You should be over there with the younger generation!' Libby said, waving her hand vaguely at the town.

'If you're quite s-s-s-sure?' Christopher's face lit up.

And so it was just the four of them left: Liliana, Eddie, herself and Pearl, who'd rung to ask if they'd mind her coming over, which had made Libby feel rather sorry for her sister, because she always used to have a million parties to go to.

'Do you remember our New Year parties?' Libby asked nobody in particular.

It had been a tradition. Once a year, the Kings would serve those who had served them. There had been Scottish reels and party games. Libby's thoughts returned to a particular game of Sardines the New Year that the fifties became the sixties. The end of a decade was always, somehow, more memorable.

'You loved to dance, didn't you, Mummy?' Pearl asked Liliana.

'Oyster,' barked Liliana King.

'Yes, that's right, Mummy!' Pearl exclaimed. 'I've got it now!' she told Libby and Eddie. 'Don't you remember that Mummy always used to make a delicious steak and ale pie, and her secret ingredient was oysters! That's why she keeps saying it!'

Eddie and Libby exchanged glances. It hardly seemed the most likely explanation given that Liliana said oyster at least once a day whatever the season.

'Here goes!' said Eddie, twisting the wire off a bottle of champagne as the face of Big Ben filled the television screen.

The cork flew out and he poured the foaming liquid into four waiting glasses, then handed one each to Libby and Pearl and put one down beside Liliana, who immediately picked it up and drained it.

On the television, the Queen was holding hands with the Prime Minister, who was singing 'Auld Lang Syne'.

'You're meant to cross your arms!' scoffed Pearl. 'Can't the royals get anything right these days!'

'Isn't that Winston Allsop!' Eddie pointed as the camera panned round the crowd.

'Where?' asked Libby.

The pictures had now switched to the firework display from the giant ferris wheel on the Thames.

'He's done well for himself,' said Eddie.

'Who'd have thought it?' said Libby.

'Oyster!' said Liliana, with a burp.

A loud bang much nearer home heralded the start of Kingshaven's fireworks on the other side of the bay.

'We've got the best view here,' said Eddie, opening up the French windows and putting his hand out to test the temperature of the air.

After the final bangs had echoed round the cliffs, the

ensuing silence was broken by the lonely chime of the porcelain tree clock in the hall.

'We're a bit behind the times at the Palace!' said Eddie, making the joke that one of them always made.

*　　*　　*

There had been a beacon on VE night, Liliana remembered.

From lunch time onwards the whole town had gone to the street party at the Harbour End. Ruby's fifteen-year-old daughter Jennifer certainly hadn't needed any encouragement to spend the day with Liliana's daughter Pearl. She'd dressed hurriedly in her best frock, leaving as quickly as she could in case the unusual relaxation of rules and curfews was withdrawn as unexpectedly as it had been awarded.

'You go out and enjoy yourselves!' Liliana had shooed them away.

The whole town empty; Kingshaven's High Street deserted; no one to see or hear anything unusual. It was a brief, unforeseen window of opportunity that felt like the answer to a prayer.

A kindly warmth remained in the air even after dark. A beacon had been lit on the South Cliffs and lads were scrabbling around among the tank defences on the beach for driftwood to keep the fire going through the night; the stationmaster was playing his trumpet; couples were dancing on the flat oval summit of the Iron Age Fort. You could see them from miles away and hear occasional snatches of tunes carried on the balmy breeze.

If Ruby had known that the party would go on to the early hours, she probably wouldn't have been so hasty and panicked, flooding the engine that had started hundreds of times for her, causing it to splutter and die.

In all the years Liliana had known her, through all

the trials and tribulations of marriage and death and childbirth, Liliana had never witnessed her friend crying. For a moment, seeing Ruby's head bent over the steering wheel, her shoulders heaving vigorously up and down, Liliana thought that she was attempting some strange manoeuvre to start the van, the mechanical equivalent of mouth-to-mouth resuscitation, but then Ruby sniffed loudly and wetly, and looked at her, tears streaming down both cheeks, defeated and utterly pitiful.

'What now?' she'd asked. 'What on earth's going to happen to me now?'

'Not just you,' Liliana told her. 'We're in this together.'

She'd intended the words to be supportive, but she suddenly wondered whether what they were planning was in fact a crime. Might she be charged with aiding and abetting? It certainly clarified her thinking.

'We'll walk!' Liliana decided.

'Walk to Lowhampton General Hospital? In my condition?' Ruby started shaking again.

'Just to the station!' Liliana told her gently. 'There'll be no one around. Mr Ironside's up on the hill with his trumpet. The waiting room will be warm. We can leave it there.' She glanced over her shoulder at the basket in the back of the van.

The tap of their heels echoed metallically as they set off at as brisk a pace as they could manage up the steep incline of the High Street. Liliana's heart was thumping at twice its normal speed, the fear raising her awareness, making her alert to every movement, every noise, even the slightest rustle, that might signal discovery. This was how it must have been for the airmen parachuted into Normandy behind the German lines, she thought, strangely exhilarated.

The door of the station waiting room creaked as she opened it, and inside it smelt of coal dust. Liliana deposited the basket on the bench.

'Come on!' she whispered to Ruby.

Ruby stared into the basket. 'He'll be all right, won't he?' she asked tearily. 'He will be all right?'

'Of course he will,' said Liliana.

She'd never seen a more robust newborn baby, probably because he had arrived later than Ruby had predicted, making him look more like a month old. Ruby had kept herself very trim during the pregnancy, and with an apron on, and behind the counter of a shop most of the time, nobody had noticed, or, if they had, then they'd been too polite to ask. As she was a recent widow, and a stalwart of the Festival of Flowers committee, nobody would ever have imagined there might be anything improper about a slightly plumper Mrs Farmer.

As Ruby remained staring into the basket, Liliana's heart began to beat even faster. It was extraordinary that they'd got away with it so far, but now time was running out and each second they stayed more risky.

'Come on!' she urged, grabbing the arm of Ruby's cardigan, coaxing her away.

Fear evaporated with every yard that separated them from the station, the adrenalin dispersing so rapidly that Liliana neither saw nor heard the young airman's footsteps until they turned on to the High Street, almost bumping into him.

'Good evening, ladies!' he said, his face sparkling with such a handsome smile, part curiosity, part mischief. 'Mrs King?'

Liliana glared at him. She could feel Ruby's arm clamped under hers beginning to shake again.

'Lovely evening for it!' said the man.

'For what?' asked Ruby nervously.

'The victory celebrations!' said Liliana, attempting a knowing look in the hope of indicating that Ruby might be a little the worse for wear.

'The celebrations! Hooray!' Ruby cheered belatedly.

'I expect you're on your way there?' Liliana asked the young man.

'You bet!' he said. 'What a night, eh?'

'What a night!' Ruby practically shouted.

'I think we'd better get you home!' Liliana told her.

The young man had the effrontery to wink as he stepped past them, heading up the lane past the Castle, the most direct route to the Harbour End. Liliana watched as his outline disappeared into the shadows.

'That was close,' said Ruby.

'Ssshh!' said Liliana, straining to hear the thud of boots receding until the rhythm mingled with the ephemeral snatches of music blowing over from the South Cliffs, and she wasn't sure whether she could still hear them or not. 'Come on,' she said eventually. 'Let's get you home.'

But they hadn't taken more than half a dozen steps when the warm air was rent by a howl that froze them both to the spot.

The baby would be discovered now, and speculation would begin. The young man would undoubtedly put two and two together. Liliana's thoughts raced through the possibilities. Their only chance was to quieten the baby quickly, then put him somewhere else, somewhere far away from where they'd been seen, somewhere nobody would associate with either of them.

She stood guard by the door as Ruby fed him.

'Good little thing, isn't he?' Ruby commented as the baby fell asleep and she held him on her shoulder to give him a burp. The towelling nappy pinned round the tiny baby's bottom looked very white against his brown skin.

White nappy, white sheet, and scrap of utility blanket. Liliana ran through the checklist. Nothing that would give them away.

Ruby put him back in the basket and tucked him in fondly.

'Give it to me,' Liliana said, reaching out her arm.

'Aren't we going to leave him here?' asked Ruby.

'If it's found here, that young man will remember seeing us,' Liliana said. 'I'm going to have to take it somewhere else.'

'But it's nice and warm in here,' Ruby protested.

'Give it to me!' Liliana insisted.

For a moment, Ruby looked as if she was going to refuse.

'You asked for my help,' Liliana told her icily. 'Do you want everyone to know? Because I certainly won't be able to help you then.'

'Sorry, Lil,' said Ruby meekly, handing over the basket.

*　　*　　*

'Good food and good champagne are all very well,' Julia told her brother when he'd begun to plan the Castle's millennium party. 'But what people would really pay for is reliable entertainment and babysitting for their kids, not just on the night, but the next morning, when they're nursing hangovers under their duvets.'

'I was thinking of it more as a grown-up thing,' James had countered.

'That's the whole point,' Julia persisted. 'You're allowing people the chance to be grown-up – they can eat and drink and dance and party without having to worry about the kids.'

'I'm not sure how many members of the Compton Club have kids,' James muttered, the subject of children being a slightly sore point because, as yet, he and Fiammetta had failed to conceive. Julia could see the signs that her brother was getting impatient. James was not used to waiting for things he wanted.

'The point is that those who don't have kids will probably be staying in London for the massive party,' Julia suggested tentatively. 'The ones with enough money to pay the excessive price you'll be able to charge are the age that do have kids.'

James's expression lifted at the prospect of revenue. Julia suspected his forecasts for the profitability of the place had been over-optimistic. The trouble with James was that he always thought he knew everything, and wouldn't ask for advice. He'd made the mistake of thinking that the hotel business must be a piece of cake because Julia had been successful at it, but the difference was that he never stopped to consider what other people might actually want, simply assuming that they would want exactly what he did.

Julia's theory about the New Year's party was borne out by the immediate take-up of all the rooms just days after details had been pinned up in the Compton Club and she hadn't been able to resist a slight smirk of triumph when James announced the good news.

'Perhaps you'd like to organize it all, then, since you're so bloody clever,' James had taunted her.

'I will, if you want me to,' Julia had challenged back.

'Go on, then!'

The silly thing was that whereas her brother thought of it as a bore, Julia liked nothing better than organizing things. All the time she'd been recuperating at the Castle, she'd been frustrated to see how much better it could be run, but she hadn't dared to say anything in case James decided to throw her out again. Rest and recovery had made her body strong enough to walk, but her mind was still traumatized by the crash. She hadn't been able to get into a car since the accident, let alone think about driving herself. The world beyond the Castle grounds seemed vast and terrifying. Julia didn't think she'd be able to cope out there on her own.

To her amazement, James appeared to be serious about handing the planning for New Year to her, and so, from doing nothing at all, she suddenly found herself working very hard. The billiard room was transformed into a games and dancing area for the children; the lofty entrance hall, with its curving staircases, was the perfect setting for the grown-ups' ball. On New Year's morning, there would be a treasure hunt for the children; an extended relaxed brunch would include free Bloody Marys. Her brother's obliteration of Sylvia's fussy femininity had left the Castle with a much more masculine feeling in keeping with the style of his Compton Club in Soho. The combination of cutting-edge minimalism alongside shabby antiques worked brilliantly for busy media people who wanted an exclusive place to network and party in the capital, but when people came to the country for a weekend Julia thought that they were generally looking for a more relaxed atmosphere, with comfortable armchairs as well as flat-screen televisions, abundant fluffy towels as well as internet connectivity, home-made scones as well as very dry martinis.

If the redesign of the Castle had been up to her, Julia would have improved and updated the swimming pool, rather than filling it in and recreating the walled garden, although she acknowledged that the walled garden had unexploited potential of its own. Already supplying the vegetables for the Castle kitchen, organic herbs and flowers from the garden could be used in a range of bath oils and cosmetics unique to the Castle.

'I'd build a pool house with treatment rooms,' Julia confided to her old friend and colleague from Palace days, Denise Rocco, whom she'd enlisted to help her.

A trained nurse and physiotherapist, Denise had helped Julia create the Wave Spa at the Palace, enabling the hotel to offer pamper weekends to the eighties' clientele of stressed-out, Armani-clad female executives with cash to burn, and also providing an income stream for less busy times as a health club to locals. It was one of the features of the hotel the Kings had failed to invest in after the fire, and, following rumours of Legionnaire's bacteria being found in the water supply, the sauna and jacuzzi had apparently been closed.

The new century called for a different approach. Whereas the Wave Spa had been bright turquoise and silver, with beauty assistants dressed in clinical white uniforms, the well-being centre Julia envisaged for the Castle would have a much more natural feeling: slate and wood replacing tiles and metal; solar-powered lighting instead of neon; yoga and Pilates classes instead of circuit training; colour-free organic oils and potions instead of bright white scientific emulsions.

'In my dreams!' Julia told Denise. 'Even if my brother had the funds, he's not about to let me spend them.'

'You could make a start by offering aromatherapy massages on New Year's Day. You don't need a spa centre for that, just a room with some nice music and a massage table,' Denise suggested. 'And get everyone's detox going with a fresh fruit and organic porridge option at the brunch.'

'Fantastic idea!' Julia scribbled notes, feeling happier and more fulfilled than she had for a long time.

From her experience of turning the fortunes of the Palace Hotel around, Julia knew that guests spread the word about a place if they felt that they'd been given more than they'd paid for. Money spent on little extras was an investment that paid off handsomely, whether it was a free bottle of mineral water in the bedroom, a chocolate on the pillow, or, for this special New Year, a beautifully wrapped parcel of New Resolutions including a packet of Nicorette chewing gum, a small bottle of Bach flower remedy, a cooling eye mask and a sachet of detoxifying herbal tea.

The most exciting thing about a party, as well as the terrifying bit, was that however much you planned it you could never be quite sure that everything would come together on the night. As midnight approached and Julia looked round the hall at the smiling couples dancing to mellow notes of the saxophone, she thought that she had probably got it more or less right.

Bertie and Archie were excelling themselves as childcare leaders. They had divided the children into roughly equal groups. Bertie's team was called the Millennium Bugs, and Archie had named his the Noughties. The rivalry that had always existed between the brothers, encouraged by their enthusiastic participation in cadet corps at school, added a dimension of competition Julia had not envisaged, that allowed all the different ages, from the sweetest tinies to sulkiest teenagers, to get really stuck in.

In the kitchen, there was a television for the staff, and Julia had promised triple wages. This generosity had been a major sticking point for James, who held rather old-fashioned views about staff, demanding, as their father might have done, 'Doesn't loyalty count for anything these days?'

So certain was Julia that happy and willing staff were crucial to the success of the weekend that she had been reluctantly prepared to strike the provision of fireworks from the budget in exchange. It was the one thing she still worried about. It had stopped raining outside, but the ground was damp underfoot, and even though the Castle did have a very good view of the town fireworks on the Cliffs she hoped the guests weren't going to feel cheated. Popping her head through the kitchen's IN door, to check on the arrangements for midnight, she was dismayed to see that, though the trays of fresh glasses had been prepared, none of them yet contained any champagne.

'You said to wait until you told us,' protested the chef, who had been a little defensive since Julia informed him, probably over-excitedly, that Bruno Dearchild was going to be spending New Year with them. When Bruno offered to prepare one of his spectacular desserts, the chef had been distinctly put out, but Julia could hardly have refused. A surprise appearance by a celebrity was exactly that extra-special something everyone would go home talking about.

Was this chef's revenge? Perhaps she had been too soft, Julia thought.

'For heaven's sake!' she said, exasperated. 'Please get them opened now.'

Time, that seemed to have passed rather sedately since the guests arrived, suddenly doubled its pace. Panicking a little, Julia picked up a bottle herself, breaking a nail in her haste to twist off the wire and trying to push the cork out with her thumbs.

'Need any help?' Bruno asked, behind her.

As a chef, he was never comfortable on the other side of the pass, and it was probably his natural instincts that had brought him into the kitchen at a crucial time, rather than his concern for her, Julia told herself, although she had been aware of him hovering throughout the evening.

Bruno and his girlfriend had arrived two days before. Esther was loud and self-important and got along so famously with James that Julia often caught Bruno and Fiammetta exchanging a glance. It had been gooseberry enough living with James and Fiammetta for the past months, but being with two couples disproportionately magnified Julia's discomfort. Although she was sure that Bruno had not told Esther about their affair – why should he? It was ten years ago, for heaven's sake! He'd probably had billions of girlfriends in the meantime! – she still felt that Esther saw her as competition. Esther constantly talked about how she'd once stayed at the Palace and how ghastly it was, and though she was quite amusing Julia still felt it was a bit tactless in the circumstances. Bertie and Archie were Kings after all, and while Julia was the last person to defend her former family, it didn't feel quite right for an outsider to criticize them.

Since serving the dessert – an enormous pile of profiteroles filled with zabaglione cream and drenched in dark chocolate, topped with a cluster of sparklers that made it look like a volcano – Bruno had swapped chef's whites for a black tuxedo. With the blunt ends of his untied black bow tie draped casually against the starched white dress shirt, his hair ruffled from pulling it over his head, he looked louchely glamorous, as if he was just returning from a profitable night in a casino. As he stood next to Julia, expertly twisting the corks out of champagne bottles, pouring glassfuls without it foaming over the top as hers always did, she felt the same sensation of liquefication that she had always felt when he was close to her.

As the bongs of Big Ben echoed through the house, Julia signalled for the waiters to march out with their trays amid the general cheering and shouts of Happy New Year!

For a moment, she and Bruno were alone in the kitchen.

'Happy New Year!' he said, offering her a glass and helping himself to one.

She was holding a bottle of champagne with a particularly recalcitrant cork. She put it down and took the glass from him.

'Happy New Year,' she said, unable to look directly into his eyes.

They both took a sip.

'Shouldn't you . . . ?' she began.

'Shouldn't I?' he echoed.

Finally she let her eyes meet his. God, he was beautiful, she thought. 'Shouldn't you be with the others?' she said briskly. 'We both should, really.'

'I'd rather be in the kitchen with you,' he said.

Julia looked away again. She'd never been able to tell when he was being serious and when he was teasing her. The kitchen was where they'd first made love. Was that what he was saying? Or was it just what she was thinking? A hot rash of colour crept from the bodice of her strapless black velvet dress up to her hairline. She was aware of the distant pop of fireworks and she knew that she should be ushering the guests outside to watch, but her feet felt leaden, unable to move.

Suddenly, there was a loud pop right beside them as the cork she had been struggling with eased itself out of the bottle and shot to the ceiling. Champagne foamed out over the steel preparation table and dripped to the floor, splashing on to her legs and jolting her back to reality.

The waiters were returning for refills; her children would be wondering where she was. As hostess, she had just missed the most important moment of the evening.

'You go first,' Bruno whispered.

Why was she blushing, Julia asked herself as she pushed through the OUT door of the kitchen, when absolutely nothing had happened? Not even a kiss! But perhaps the fact that they hadn't kissed, when that was what everyone did at New Year, made her even more certain that something had.

*   *   *

The original walled garden had a huge oak door with a heavy iron latch. Perhaps it had just seemed bigger to her when she was little, Fiammetta thought, as she let herself in. For the reconstruction, narrow red bricks had been custom-made with the exact dimensions of the originals. The vegetable and flower beds had been laid out according to the plan her father had returned. Now that rambling roses were beginning to trail along the walls, and the lavender bushes had started to straggle a little, it was beginning to feel again like the place she had loved as a child. Only the door was different, with its practical Yale latch that clicked behind her instead of the rusty iron one.

Inside the walls, the stillness was profound, though Fiammetta was aware of the oohs and aahs of the crowd just a few yards outside and the distant bangs and whizzes of the town fireworks. As a child she had always thought that the weather in the walled garden was different from the weather outside. As her eyes adjusted to the darkness, Fiammetta picked her way along the box-lined path to a wooden bench on the south-facing wall, stopping in her tracks each time a big rocket lit up the sky like a flare, as if someone were shining a spotlight on her. There was nothing wrong with taking a moment alone in the garden, and yet she felt guilty, knowing that James would be cross with her if he were to discover her there, and the air would be full of recrimination for failing in her duty to their guests, or to him.

Each new month that passed, Fiammetta felt that she was letting him down. Significantly, he'd stopped saying 'Don't be silly!' when she admitted this to him. His target was a child, and she had failed again and again to achieve it, even though she had done everything she was told to.

Sometimes Fiammetta was reminded of her struggle with reading when she was young, and how important it had seemed to everyone else, how impatient they were with her when she couldn't do what they wanted her to. When she had finally been diagnosed as dyslexic, everyone had been nice to her again, and helped her, and though reading had remained a struggle she had become more confident, knowing that she wasn't stupid.

She'd been hoping for a similar help when they'd been referred for testing to the fertility clinic at Lowhampton General Hospital, but no specific reason for her infertility had been found. Three cycles of IVF treatment had not worked, and she was dreading a fourth. The routine of hormone injections and implantation was horrible enough, but it was the waiting that was so soul-destroying, because the hope was always there, however much you tried to relax and think about other things, and the disappointment was crushing, however much you tried to tell yourself that it wasn't your fault. Medical intervention had separated the idea of pregnancy from sex, and the spontaneous passion she and James had shared at the beginning had disappeared with the introduction of ovulation charts. Sometimes Fiammetta felt that all aspects of her creativity had been blocked. She hadn't painted for many months now, and often found herself sitting for hours with a sketchbook staring, but not seeing anything, as if her life was on hold until she managed to conceive.

The most debilitating thing was not knowing why, and it had made her question everything, searching for causes to blame. Sometimes Fiammetta even wondered whether her body resisted because she wasn't properly committed to the idea of having a baby. There were several exceptionally cute toddlers staying over the New Year period, and though she could see James regarding their antics with watery-eyed fondness she didn't feel anything other than a headachy irritation with their squawking. Fiammetta witnessed Iris's brittle personality soften in the glow of her love for John, but even though he was completely adorable, Fiammetta had never had any maternal feelings, even when she held him in her arms for the very first time. Julia's boys, now fifteen and seventeen years old, were affable enough, but she couldn't envisage herself as the mother of gangly teenagers on the verge of being men. If James didn't manage to produce an heir, Bertie would eventually be the one to take over the Castle. He was clearly well equipped for the role and Fiammetta couldn't really see the problem with that, but she knew that James, while fond of his nephews, would have been apoplectic if she'd suggested this to him. Was her failure to conceive due to her inability to take her husband's desire for an heir sufficiently seriously? It seemed so absurdly anachronistic at the beginning of the twenty-first century.

The fireworks had ceased, Fiammetta realized. The new millennium had arrived, and perhaps it would be a new beginning for them all.

It must bode well that the party had been a success, bringing Julia, almost literally, back to life. It was so good to see her sister-in-law regaining her confidence, like a baby deer with big, blinking eyes struggling to its feet for the first time. Fiammetta had grown fond of Julia. The months she had spent nursing her at the Castle had given her own life some semblance of purpose. Their relationship was politely respectful rather than gushingly friendly, but they often sat together like a couple of companionable spinsters from a bygone era, with DVDs to watch, instead of needlepoint to stitch. It would have been invidious and disloyal for Fiammetta to confide her anxieties to Julia, but she thought she quietly understood, and sympathized, an ally rather than an adversary. Julia's friends Denise and Sheila were always talking about positive energy, and even though Fiammetta's inclination was to deride such New Age mantras both women were much happier, more sorted people than she was, so perhaps there was something in it.

Fiammetta pinched the dry fronds of a lavender stalk, and held her fingers to her nose, the sharp aromatic scent bringing her mind back to focus. It was time to stop looking inwards, she resolved, as she pushed the door of the walled garden open: time to rejoin the party.

*   *   *

'What now?' Winston asked Iris.

They were sitting in the back of the limousine, waiting for the queue of cars leaving the Dome to shift. It was going to be a long journey home because central London was closed to traffic. The Queen and the important members of the government were being ferried back along the river, but Iris wondered how they'd progress from Westminster pier. Apparently two million people had crowded on the bridges and embankments.

'What do you mean, what now?' Iris asked.

'I just feel like doing something,' said Winston, a little restlessly.

She knew what he meant. The aerial ballet show at the Dome had been terrific, but not quite the amazing spectacle she had expected. The party had been fine, but a bit official. An itch of millennium fever still remained.

'We could drive down to the coast and watch the sun come up over the sea,' Winston suggested.

'We could walk home through the crowds,' Iris said.

The Dome, which was supposed to be integral to the celebrations, hadn't quite felt like where it was at. She sensed that most of the guests would, like her, have preferred to have been outside to see the much vaunted River of Fire, and the sky ablaze with pyrotechnics.

'We could spend a delicious night at the Ritz,' Winston suggested.

'And leave John?' Iris couldn't disguise her surprise.

Winston laughed, as his idea was clearly crossed off the agenda.

'I'm sorry,' she said.

'No, I love you for it,' he said.

'For what, my neurosis?'

'For being such a good mother to our child,' said Winston.

'You didn't think I would be?' she challenged, insecurity always so near to the surface that it had escaped before she'd had a chance to think about holding it back.

'I knew you would be,' Winston soothed. 'I'd seen how you were with Fiammetta and Bruno.'

'I don't think I was as anxious with them,' Iris confessed. 'Maybe it gets worse when you're older.'

'Maybe it's different when it's your own child,' said Winston.

Iris stared out of the tinted window of the limousine, her heart thumping in her chest, knowing that this was her opportunity. The subject had come up so naturally, it almost felt as if destiny were trying to play its part.

Iris's thoughts about the baby she had given up more than thirty years ago had not receded as John grew and developed, but instead were becoming more frequent, more urgent, more inescapable. When John had spoken his first word – which, slightly disappointingly, was 'car' – Iris had wondered what her little girl's had been. When he'd made his first attempt at writing his name, she'd wondered what name her little girl had written. When he'd fallen over in the garden and cut his forehead, she'd run with him in her arms all the way to Accident and Emergency at the Royal Free Hospital, bright-red blood dripping on to her T-shirt, terrified that she was going to lose him too.

The wound hadn't been deep or serious. There was always a lot of blood with head injuries, the young triage nurse had told her. 'Is he your only child?' she'd asked, her pen poised over her notes, with the implication that Iris was an old and over-anxious mother, and Iris had longed to confound her assumptions by shouting 'No!'

Increasingly, Iris found herself staring at women the same age as her daughter would have been, wondering whether she would recognize her if their paths were to cross. It had occurred to her that her daughter might well have a child of her own. She would be closer in age to the other mothers at the toddler group. Iris might be a grandmother!

The week before Christmas, when Iris was in Waitrose in the Finchley Road, looking at the pale-pink corpses of the fresh turkeys, trying to decide what weight to buy, it had suddenly occurred to her that her daughter might have died. The horror of the thought made her choke with grief.

A man with a packet of Paxo stuffing mix in his hand had asked, 'Are you all right?'

And John had piped happily from his trolley seat, 'Mummy crying!' as if he were perfectly used to it.

*

Iris knew that it would probably be sensible to talk to someone, and that the person had to be Winston, but things were so perfect between them, so incredibly wonderful, that she lay awake at night with silent tears running down her cheeks for fear of her luck changing.

The limousine began to move on to a stretch of clear road and Iris's mind ran through arguments it had rehearsed again and again: if she told him about her daughter, then the best that could happen was that Winston would be sympathetic and help look for her. But, even if she could find her, the daughter might want to have nothing to do with Iris.

The very best that could happen was that Winston's reaction would be sympathetic, Iris would find her daughter and her daughter would forgive her. But even then, her daughter was bound to ask who her father had been, and Iris would have to tell her, and she couldn't even begin to think about the possibility of Clive getting involved.

Therefore, there was no way she was going to look for her daughter.

Therefore, there was no point in telling Winston, because the alternative scenario was that, with perfect justification, he wouldn't react sympathetically at all and he might decide to have nothing to do with her any more.

In any case, Iris argued, her daughter was probably getting on with her life and it would be selfish to intrude. The adoptive parents, whom Iris had glimpsed on their first visit to the mother and baby home, had looked like a decent couple. They arrived in a Rover and were clearly comfortably off. The woman looked nervous as she sat in the waiting room, the man beside her absently patting her knee with one hand and reading a folded newspaper with the other. Both faces had lit up when

293

the matron offered them the blanketed parcel. Then the matron had spotted Iris peering at them round the open door.

'You know you're not supposed to be down here!'

The woman had looked up, startled, but the man had smiled warmly at Iris before the door was closed in her face.

'Have we crossed the river already?' Iris asked, seeing that the car was now speeding through the deserted streets of the City.

'We went through the Blackwall tunnel,' Winston told her.

The pavements around King's Cross were crowded with people, blowing party trumpets at the tinted windows of the limousine, swigging from bottles of champagne.

'Nearly home now.' Winston patted Iris's knee, assuming that her silence was due to her preoccupation with John's safety.

She'd missed the moment, Iris realized. There wasn't enough time to begin to explain now.

Their son was fast asleep on the sofa next to Jack, who was watching the television with the sound turned down. New Year had travelled round the world to New York.

'I can have a drink now.' Jack smiled at them.

'You've abstained so far?' Iris was so delighted with him, she gave him a tight spontaneous hug. Jack, still a teenage boy, in the body of a man, stood stiffly with his arms by his side.

'Hope this compensates,' said Winston, handing over a crisp wad of twenty-pound notes, at least double what they'd agreed.

Bending over the sofa, Iris picked John up in her arms and kissed his forehead, reuniting herself with his intoxicating mixture of smells: baby shampoo; the faint, warm tang of

Huggies pull-ups; the sweetness of bribery by chocolate still on his innocent breath.

'New Year's resolution?' Winston asked.

'To be happy with what I've got,' Iris told him, and herself, very firmly.

*   *   *

Cat and Finn were on their way back to Esther's house in Islington. They usually spent nights together at Finn's flat in Stoke Newington, but it was too far to walk there, and they both felt like walking after standing for hours in the crush of people on the Embankment.

The streets and elegant Georgian squares of central London were an idiosyncratic patchwork of parties and peacefulness. On one street, they were the only people and the echo of their footsteps bounced between the buildings; then they turned a corner to find themselves outside a pub with people spilling out, drinking, dancing, snogging. Cat had lost count of the number of swigs of champagne she had been offered, or strangers she had kissed. Beyond Russell Square and Great Ormond Street Hospital the crowds thinned out a little, but as they waited to cross the Gray's Inn Road, near King's Cross, they were once again sucked into a throng of revellers with paper hats and party trumpets.

'I've never seen Londoners enjoying such craic,' Finn said.

'We like to let our hair down once every millennium or so,' Cat replied.

As someone who'd been born and brought up in the suburbs of London, she never really believed the idea that Londoners were particularly reserved, but on her recent trip to Ireland she had been surprised by how welcoming and generous people were there.

'I'm pleased we went down to the river,' she said.

After seeing the amazing celebrations relayed from Sydney that afternoon, the temptation had been to stay cosily inside, watching the global New Year on television rather than venturing out into the drizzly evening, but the spectacle of fireworks down the River Thames had been awesome. Despite all the carping in the media about the Dome and the ridiculing of the London Eye, which had just the previous day been deemed unsafe to carry passengers, there was a tremendous feeling of goodwill in the crowd, and a very un-English sense of pride.

'Something to tell one's children,' said Finn.

It was such an uncharacteristic cliché for him and she suspected that it was a clumsy attempt to lead up to the subject she'd felt he'd been teetering on since she'd flown to Ireland on Boxing Day. After introducing her to his enormous family, Finn had driven her across Ireland to join some of his old university friends in a cottage in Connemara. They'd spent clear bright winter days walking in the beautiful boggy landscape between mountain and sea, and evenings in the pub, listening to Irish music and drinking hot whisky. On the last night, they'd cooked a goose, roasting potatoes and parsnips in the fat, and put chestnuts in the oven that they'd forgotten until the blackened shells had burst, filling the room with the evocative smell of a street vendor's brazier.

Finn's friends had liked her, she thought, approved of her, even, and Cat had quickly warmed to their easy company. Though it hadn't been a test, she'd seen how important it was to Finn that they got on, the pleasure on his face as they chatted in candlelight, his laughter as they divided into teams for the game of charades she suggested. On the plane home, he'd squeezed her hand and looked at her differently, somehow, and she'd felt that their relationship had reached a new level of intimacy, and that scared her a little. Now, as they found themselves once again walking along the same raised pavement in Upper

Street as on their first date, Cat felt almost as nervous as she had then.

She finally broke the silence: 'What are you thinking?'

Finn stopped. He took both her hands in his, and for a terrible moment she thought she'd misjudged his reflective mood and he was going to say, 'Look, I'm sorry . . .'

'There's a crossword clue I need your help with,' he said.

'OK,' said Cat hesitantly.

Finn counted on his fingers. 'It's fourteen letters,' he said, 'and the clue is "I'm well. Your Mary? is the confused question." Four, three, five, two.'

'Confused means it's an anagram,' said Cat. 'Mmm, let me think.'

'And it's a question too . . .'

'A four-word question . . . Hang on . . . Oh!'

'Have you got it?'

'I think so,' said Cat.

'And the answer is . . . ?'

'Will you marry me?'

'Amazing!' he said. 'I was just about to ask you that!'

She laughed, then looked away. It was a lovely proposal, even if not quite up to the high standards of the *Telegraph*'s crossword compiler.

'I'm not sure,' she said, realizing that he was waiting for an answer.

'Oh!'

She'd never seen him looking hurt before, and she felt horrible. For a bizarre moment, Cat imagined herself relaying this conversation to Esther. As someone who'd spent the last two years trying to get Bruno to pop the question, she'd think she'd gone completely mad.

'It's just that I've always felt I was somehow owned – my parents' daughter, Esther's friend . . .' Roy's mistress, she added silently. 'But with you, I feel I'm me on my own terms. It's not that I don't love you,' Cat added quickly.

'You just don't want to be *my* wife?'

He understood!

'Would you live with me?' he asked.

She thought about it. 'Yes. But only somewhere that's mine as well as yours. I'm sorry. I've just ruined a romantic moment, haven't I?'

Finn thought for a moment, then dropped to one knee on the wet paving stone.

'Will you not marry me?' he asked her solemnly.

'Yes, I will not marry you,' she replied, laughing.

*　　*　　*

Bruno sometimes wished he smoked, because it gave you something to do in those first few moments after sex when the air was still hot with activity and the woman lying next to you expected you to say something.

'You've got a gorgeous body,' he said, running a finger lightly down Esther's back.

'You too,' she replied, her hand trailing down his leg.

Her watch snagged one of the hairs on his inner thigh, and he suddenly sat up, not wanting to be touched any more. His skin was tender, his flesh exhausted.

'Sorry,' she said.

The only thing Bruno wanted to do was fall asleep, but he knew that Esther wasn't going to let that happen, not on New Year's Eve. New Year was always a time for assessing where you were in life, and where you were going. What better excuse than the new millennium for Esther to bring the subject round to what the future held for them. Since turning thirty, her questions had been less subtle and he felt sure that they were getting almost to the point of ultimatum. He wasn't ready for that.

Esther was funny and fun, and if a bit self-obsessed, at

least she was aware of it and able to laugh at herself. At work, she was a brilliantly motivating producer. At home, she was an energetic lover. In public, they were a hot young media couple. With his skills in the kitchen and hers at work, as she was fond of joking, they made a great team. And yet . . . for Bruno, there was still 'and yet . . .'

He plumped up the pillows behind his head. The pure white Egyptian cotton was crisp with newness.

'Your cake went down well,' she said.

'Seemed to,' he said. 'There was a little bit left over. I saved it for you.'

'You're so sweet!'

He didn't feel sweet at all.

'It was quite fun,' said Esther, determined to perform a full *post mortem* of the party.

'It was all rather . . .'

'Boring?' she suggested.

'Civilized,' he said.

'I've only had a thimbleful of champagne . . .' said Esther, a wheedling note creeping into her voice.

'Do you want me to go down and get another bottle?' he asked.

'Oh, would you? That would be lovely!' Esther sat up, delighted to have got what she wanted.

Bruno pulled on a white waffle cotton robe and shoved his feet into the matching complimentary slippers – Julia's touches, he suspected. On previous visits to the Castle, it had all felt rather spartan.

As the bedroom door clicked behind him, he experienced the same elated feeling he got when leaving the house in Islington early in the morning to walk to work, or go to the gym, as if he needed physically to shake the intimacy from his limbs. For a moment, Bruno was tempted to escape now, and walk up to the ridge to watch the sun rise over the sea, his breath freezing in the cold morning air.

All the guests and staff had gone to bed. The kitchen was

so tidy and pristine, it gave no clue that a five-course meal had recently been cooked there, or that in just a few hours' time the grill would be sizzling with bacon, and chefs would be frantically scrambling eggs or sweating over pans of delicate hollandaise, as ranks of English muffins jumped out of the multi-slice toasters beside them.

There was a pannier of oranges beside the juicer and the wine fridge had been refilled with champagne for Buck's Fizz at brunch. Bruno removed a bottle. The dishwashers had only recently finished their cycle and the glasses would still be hot, but there must be glasses in the bedroom, he decided. Guessing where chef would have stored the portion of profiteroles he had saved for Esther, he opened the cold store, and found it tightly covered with cling film on the shelf between the yoghurts and a big tub of crème fraîche.

With the bowl of dessert in one hand and the bottle in the other, Bruno switched off the kitchen lights with his elbow and began to tiptoe up the stairs, remembering half-way up that Esther would need a spoon.

Back in the kitchen, he pulled several drawers before finding the one filled with teaspoons, and he was just about to turn the light out again, when the IN door opened.

The long white nightie, bare feet and startled expression made Julia look like a sleepwalking child. For a moment, Bruno tried to remember whether you were supposed to wake sleepwalkers or guide them gently back to bed.

But then she spoke. 'I heard a sound!' she said.

'I'm sorry.'

'I don't sleep very well these days . . .'

'I'm sorry,' he said again, gazing at her.

Her face was scrubbed of make-up. As if suddenly aware that the outline of her body was visible through the flimsy white cotton, Julia folded her arms across her chest.

'Well . . .' she said, with an embarrassed little smile. 'Happy New Year anyway!'

'Happy New Year!' he said.

They were about six feet away from each other. He moved towards her, bending to kiss her cheek, seeing her eyes close at the moment his lips touched her skin. There was something about the smell of her that he couldn't get enough of. He didn't know how long it was that they stood there chastely, his cheek against hers, just breathing, remembering, before she shifted position, his hands went to her waist, her arms to his shoulders, and their lips met. She tasted like some delicious forbidden fruit that he had tasted before and been warned never to taste again. Her body melted against his, the curve of her concave belly fitting against the knot of his robe, their thighs pressing against each other's, as they toppled towards the nearest table.

The first time they'd made love was in a kitchen and the connection between them had been magical then and still was, even under the bright neon lights, against a surface of brushed steel.

No one before or since had ever come close. And he never wanted it to stop.

Suddenly they both froze and drew apart, looking at each other, and then at the door.

'You absolute shit!' said Esther.

*   *   *

'What the hell was that?' James sat up in bed.

'What?' Fiammetta asked drowsily.

'Listen . . .'

She could hear raised voices downstairs. From the cadences, she couldn't quite tell whether they were shouting or laughing.

James pulled on a silk dressing gown. 'Stay here!' he warned, like a chivalrous knight venturing out to deal with a threat. There was such a ferocious look on his face, she was glad there were no swords or guns to hand.

'Be careful!' she called after him, pulling the duvet protectively right up to her chin, not quite sure whether to be afraid or to giggle.

Straining her ears, she could distinguish several voices now. A shrill female one was shouting, 'No, I won't bloody well be quiet!'

Then there was silence as James arrived on the scene, followed by footsteps on the stairs, and hysterical sobbing rushing past their bedroom door.

'Bloody hell!' James exclaimed when he came back, closing the door behind him.

'What?' asked Fiammetta.

'Your brother was bonking my sister in the kitchen.'

The way he said it made it sound like a scenario in Cluedo. Fiammetta giggled.

'Was that the noise?' she asked, surprised that Julia would cry out at such volume.

'The noise was Esther discovering them in flagrante.'

'Oh dear,' said Fiammetta. Esther was so pushy and confident, it was almost impossible to feel sorry for her, even though Fiammetta knew she probably should. 'That was a bit careless of them,' she said.

James looked shocked by her indifference. 'Careless?' he echoed. 'People have paid good money for a peaceful weekend.'

'Oh, for heaven's sake!' said Fiammetta. 'Listen to you! Don't be so bloody middle-aged.'

For a second, she wasn't sure how he was going to react to the criticism, then his face suddenly mutated from extremely cross to wickedly delighted, and then they were both laughing.

'Come back to bed,' she said, lifting the duvet for him to climb into the cocoon of warmth around her, the draught of cool air puckering the somnolent softness of her skin. 'Maybe we should have sex in the kitchen sometimes,' she whispered, rolling her body on top of his.

'How much have you had to drink?' James asked.

'We used to do it everywhere,' she went on, undeterred, feeling him responding beneath her now, tensing and relaxing.

He lifted his head to kiss each of her breasts, her neck and finally her mouth with an urgency that had nothing to do with trying to conceive, or even making love, but was simply about lust. Pure, brutal lust.

Afterwards, they lay exhausted, the duvet thrown off on to the floor, the cool morning air chilling the sweat on their bodies.

James turned on to his side, idly pulling a ringlet of her red hair straight, as if to see how long it was at full stretch.

'Fiammetta,' he said. 'Firecracker.'

'Could we make a New Year's resolution to do more of that?' she asked.

'I don't see why not.' He kissed her face.

Fiammetta's body felt as if it belonged to her for the first time in months. She let her hand trail lightly over her skin, as if she was rediscovering her breasts, her ribs, the small of her back. Then her hand went back to her breast, touching again.

She took James's hand and put his finger on her skin. 'Can you feel something?'

He made a face as if to say he didn't know what she was talking about, and then he suddenly said, 'Wait a minute,' and pressed more firmly. 'There's a hard bit,' he said. 'About the size of an acorn. Does it hurt?'

'No,' said Fiammetta. She pressed it again. It definitely didn't hurt. 'It's probably nothing,' she said.

'Better let a doctor check it out, though,' said James.

'It's probably nothing, isn't it?' Suddenly it seemed very important for him to agree.

'Probably nothing.' James yawned and rolled over, taking most of the duvet with him, and almost immediately started snoring.

Fiammetta couldn't sleep. She lay staring at the ceiling as the light outside became grey, then colourless, and the air was suddenly much colder. From time to time she would take her hand from her breast, but the lump was still there when she touched it again. She wondered which room of this house her mother had been in when she had felt the same thing, and the words of the letter her mother had written her, which she knew off by heart, would not leave her mind as fat tears slid down her cheeks, making the pillow all wet.

. . . And one day you will understand that we have experienced the same thing, and that I am close to you, even though I'm not there . . .

*   *   *

'. . . We can't go on together . . .'

Adrian King was so drunk, he could barely read the screen of the karaoke machine that Millicent Balls had rented for the millennium party at the Ship Inn, but his pelvis-pumping interpretation of 'Suspicious minds' brought raucous cheers from the crowd, and when he finally finished, in a knee slide that took him precariously close to knocking over both the microphone stand and speaker, the cry 'King, King, King!' went up.

Adrian was by far the most normal of the King children, Michael thought. Perhaps that was because he'd escaped the confines of the hotel, even if his exploration of the outside world had taken him only as far as the Harbour End. Although he was well respected as captain of the lifeboat, he was always ready to make an ass of himself, in marked contrast to his older brother Christopher, who was sitting at the table next to Michael's. In the increasingly loud and inebriated crowd, he looked as out of place as a bone-china teacup on a shelf of pint pots.

As Adrian waved the mic almost threateningly at his

brother, Christopher shook his head vehemently.

'The only song I know all the words to is "Jerusalem",' he hissed, before Millicent swooped in to the rescue, urging Adrian to pass the mic to the younger members of the lifeboat crew who were clamouring to have a go.

There was hardly room for the five of them on the small stage, and it took Michael a moment to work out why they were dressed in their yellow macs and souwesters, until he recognized the song and realized they were going to do a Full Monty.

As the crowd clapped and stamped their feet in ritualistic time to the beat, Michael glanced to his side, catching the eye of a bewildered Christopher King. Fearing that he was about to engage him in conversation, Michael decided it was time to leave. He finished his pint and waved at Millicent as he pushed open the door into the cool early-morning air.

Outside, the noise from the Ship was muffled, like the sound of a distant party. The moon had already made its transit across the sky, and the water was dark and still. In winter there were no yachts in the harbour, and without the distinctive chink-chinking sound Michael didn't think he had ever heard the place so quiet. Other than that, it wasn't much different, he thought, this new millennium. The party had been bigger than other New Years, and the hangovers would be too, but, when people had recovered, life would go on as usual. Michael wondered if there might even be a slight sense of anti-climax after all the expectation, as there had been after the much-vaunted eclipse the previous summer.

Kingshaven had not been quite in the zone of totality, but nevertheless people had bought their special sunglasses, filled buckets with water in which to look at the sun's reflection and waited with feverish anticipation to witness this unique event. A few amateur Druids, not quite dedicated enough to make their way to Cornwall, had chanted on the beach, and holidaying children had become a little more whiny than usual as their parents stood on the promenade with their cardboard glasses, shushing them and telling them not to look at the sun. But it had been a particularly grey and cloudy day, and nobody could honestly say that they witnessed anything at all apart from a slight darkening, as if it might be going to thunder, followed by a general disgruntled murmuring of 'Was that it, then?'

As Michael passed the Ship on his way back to the bookshop, the cheering was getting louder in the raunchy build-up to the final line of the song, and then amid squeals of relief and disbelief he heard the boys from the lifeboat shouting at top volume: 'You can leave your sou'wester on!'

It was beginning to get light as Michael pushed at the door of the warehouse. The dampness of winter had made the wood swell and he would have to get someone to come and shave a little off the bottom, he thought, adding it to a mental list he was compiling of things to tackle.

The smell of old books was a welcoming one, even after all these years. Michael still enjoyed the bookshop, although it was barely worth keeping open from a financial point of view. As Winston had been predicting for a while now, the internet was changing the way people shopped and even Michael could see that it made particular sense in second-hand bookselling. Browsers formed an important part of his clientele, but most customers came in looking for a particular book they remembered or needed for research. You didn't need to be a computer genius to see that being able to find what you wanted and order it in a couple of clicks from your desk at home would have obvious attractions.

'You need to get your own website,' Winston had told him, offering the services of his team of web designers, but urging him to get a move on with it. 'The most important thing is to establish a brand,' he said.

Winston had even registered several names he called URLs on Michael's behalf, but the idea of cataloguing all the stock felt a bit like homework he was putting off. One of the few signs of ageing Michael had noticed was that he seemed to need less sleep and yet he didn't seem to get any more done. He would be seventy this year. An old man, if he wasn't careful.

Instead of going upstairs to bed, Michael went into the bookshop. His New Year resolution would be to make a start on the boxes of books at the back of the shop. A padlocked door led to the storage area that had once been the yard at the back of the warehouse. Bruno's windsurf board had been joined by a miniature car with the colour, shape and marc of a miniature Ferrari, which Michael's grandson John liked to pedal along the promenade. Iris's visits with the boy were the highlight of Michael's life. John was such a bright little chap, with the determined curiosity Iris had displayed as a child, coupled, fortunately, with Winston's easy charm, which made people warm to him rather than consider him a nuisance. Beside the small tower of faded plastic buckets and spades bought by Anthony and his family over the years, there was now a sit-on yellow digger with a scoop to create major construction works in the sand, and, leaning against the stack of banana boxes containing books he had acquired in house clearances, a giant kite, which Michael moved gingerly, trying not to tangle the complicated mesh of strings and tails.

The packing tape that had been used to seal the top box was brittle with age, and the edges of the lid parted with ease. Inside, a covering layer of newspaper was dated 1979. Michael couldn't believe that the books underneath had sat there for twenty years. What changes there had been since then, he thought, pulling out a school atlas. The vast red blanket of the Soviet Union would now be a patchwork of different colours. He put the atlas down for the moment on the seat of the digger and picked up the next book, a hardback, with a torn dust jacket. Daphne W. Smythe. The name seemed familiar, he wasn't sure why. Michael opened the book to read the still-intact flap of the jacket.

'The shocking discovery of a body on the beach so shortly after the cessation of hostilities casts a pall over the coastal town of Haven Regis. On her first summer holiday for six years, Dr Winifred Smith embarks on a new investigation.'

On the back flap, the blurb proclaimed, 'More mystery from the Majestic'.

The title of the book was *The Unknown Soldier*.

Chapter Eight

January 2000

Fiammetta, when I was a little girl, I sometimes felt very sad and lonely that I didn't have a mother, and sometimes I forgot about it completely. I want you to know that if you forget about me, I will understand and I won't mind at all. And one day you will understand that we have experienced the same thing, and that I am close to you, even though I'm not there . . .

The letter that her mother had written her had stopped at that point and Fiammetta had never known why. Was it that Claudia was in such pain she couldn't continue, or was it that she knew no words could ever compensate for her absence? When Claudia wrote it, she must have been exactly the same age as Fiammetta was now.

Fiammetta had always felt the loss with a child's selfishness, and no regard for the fact that Claudia had lost her own mother. Claudia and her father had been refugees in the war. If Fiammetta had thought about it at all, she'd assumed that Claudia's mother had died at the hands of the Germans, but perhaps she'd had cancer too?

'The doctor will see you now.'

The nurse, who had taken a sample of Fiammetta's blood and accompanied her down to radiography for the mammogram, smiled at her, but Fiammetta was unable to detect whether the kindness that shone from her eyes was a good or a bad sign. James stood aside to let her go into the consultant's room first. Fiammetta wished that he could make his face a little less grim. His palpable fear was not helping.

The consultant was looking at a printout of results.

'Nikhil!' said Fiammetta.

'Mrs Allsop,' he said, shaking her hand briskly.

Very grown-up, she thought, feeling so pleased to see him that she forgot for a second why she was there.

'It's Lady Allsop, actually,' said James.

'It's Fiammetta, actually.' She smiled at Nikhil.

'I do apologize, Sir Allsop . . .' Nikhil held out his hand again.

Fiammetta could feel James's irritation in the air. Please don't correct him again, she thought, suppressing a sudden inappropriate urge to giggle.

'Please sit down,' said Nikhil, sitting down himself and waiting for them to settle.

'So?' said James.

'First of all, I think perhaps I ought to run some options past you,' Nikhil said. 'In normal circumstances, since I'm acquainted with the patient, I would pass your notes to a colleague. However, the only consultant of equal experience is on sabbatical at the moment. But if you would like me to refer you to another hospital, I would be very happy to arrange that.'

'Well, I think in the circumstances—' James began.

'No!' said Fiammetta. 'I'd like to stick with you.' She smiled at Nikhil again. 'If you are prepared to stick with me?' she asked.

'Will you excuse us for a moment while we discuss this?' James asked Nikhil, who nodded and stood up to leave.

'I don't need to discuss it,' Fiammetta told her husband. 'I have complete confidence in Nikhil as a doctor. And I know he will be honest with me.'

Now she felt that James's hostility was directed at her.

Next time, Fiammetta promised herself, she would come alone.

Any fear that Nikhil would be unnerved disappeared as soon as he returned to purely medical territory.

'I'm afraid the results of the biopsy show that the tumour is malignant,' he said, looking her straight in the eye.

'But . . .' James started on an automatic objection, then stopped as the words seemed to sink in.

'What happens next?' Fiammetta's voice sounded disconnected from her body.

'We will remove the tumour and some lymph nodes to see if the malignancy has spread,' said Nikhil. 'Do you have any questions at this point?'

'What if the malignancy has spread?' asked Fiammetta, finding it curious how quickly one learnt the language of cancer but never allowed oneself to say the word.

Nikhil hesitated.

At this point in a normal consultation, she thought it would probably be usual to fob the patient off with statistics and platitudes about crossing bridges, but she knew that Nikhil would be unable to do that to her. He knew her too well, respected her intelligence, liked her too much. That was why she had wanted to stick with him, and now she saw that she'd understood the potential difficulties better than he had. For a moment, she felt rotten for putting him in such an invidious position.

Nikhil held her eyes. 'I'm not in the business of prediction, Fiammetta, but in those circumstances, with your family history, I'd want to treat aggressively with radical surgery and chemotherapy.'

'Thank you,' she said. 'How soon?'

'I'd like to get you in tomorrow morning,' said Nikhil. 'With a view to performing the procedure in the afternoon.'

In the ten days since she had found the lump, Fiammetta had been preparing herself for the idea that she was going to die, but it was only when she heard the word 'tomorrow' that she knew for the first time it was a real possibility, a likelihood even. She'd been doing that thing of preparing for the worst, hoping to cheat fate, but now she knew that fate was stronger than she was, and it wasn't going to be fooled.

They walked down the long glass corridor towards the hospital exit in silence, and James did not speak on the way home, but stared through the windscreen, never taking his eyes off the road. The enormity of their dread seemed to fill the car, like an elephant sitting on the back seat. Finally, just as they were turning into the avenue of beech trees up to the house, he spoke.

'I'm supposed to be going to London tomorrow . . .'

'You go,' Fiammetta replied instantly. She felt he was cross with her, as if she had let him down. 'I'll be fine, honestly,' she insisted. 'Bruno can take me.'

'Are you sure?'

Fiammetta stared at the dark winter skeletons of the beech trees against the pale-yellow glow of the afternoon sky.

'Quite sure,' she said truthfully.

There were no midweek guests staying at the Castle, and Julia and Bruno were upstairs, emerging after a few minutes with the hot flush of recent sexual activity still visible on Julia's cheeks, and Bruno's long curly hair all muzzy at the back. Fiammetta hated the idea of spoiling it for them, but they both knew her so well that as soon as they saw her face they realized the news wasn't good. James shot past them upstairs without saying a word, and Bruno instinctively reached out for Julia's hand and clasped it tightly for support, a gesture that made Fiammetta feel excluded.

'I think I'll go for a walk,' she said.

'Do you want company?' her brother immediately offered.

'No, thank you,' she said.

As determined strides took her away from the house, she turned round to wave reassuringly, knowing they would both be standing at the door, watching her like anxious parents.

The ground was very cold underfoot and the air had a damp winter chill as the sunlight shrank back into a crimson disc, making a path of pink light on the pewter surface of the sea. As her footsteps pinged on the tarmac road like the regular beat of a metronome, Fiammetta was suddenly conscious that she had walked several hundred yards in a daze. The sun had gone now and darkness was falling fast. Except for the string of twinkling orange lights along the promenade, it was no longer possible to make out where the land stopped and the sea began.

Fiammetta paused for a moment, unable to find the clarity she craved but reluctant to return to the Castle just yet. As she walked down the steep hill to the Harbour End, she could see into the living rooms of the cottages, their curtains not yet drawn, where children were watching television, still in their school uniform. From one house, delicious wafts of frying onion greeted her nostrils; in another a dog barked repeatedly. As a child, she had sometimes envied her peers for their proper families and normal houses, and now she felt the same disconnection, observing the cosy little lanterns of life from outside in the cold.

It had been so long since she'd been to the Harbour End, the fishy tang of lobster pots smelt curiously nostalgic, evoking an unspecific memory of happier times. In the tall windows of the living room of her father's warehouse the lights were on.

* * *

313

Daphne W. Smythe's characterization was not her strong point, thought Michael Quinn. The novel opened with a number of guests arriving at the Majestic Hotel during the first summer after the war, each of them displaying a flaw or feature that would no doubt make them a suspect later on – the floozy with bright-red lipstick was clearly up to no good on honeymoon with her much older husband; the two antique-collecting spinsters had already given slightly different accounts of themselves to the hotelier and his elegant wife; the butcher from London had delighted the proprietors with a ration-defying gift of sausages; the insurance agent appeared to know little about insurance; the brilliantined Jack the Lad in a demob suit was the sort of person more commonly seen at the tradesmen's entrance than in the elegant hall. Only the squadron leader, who had come to lay flowers at the grave of his former wife, a Land Army girl who had met a tragic end with a combine harvester, appeared to be an upright fellow – so proper and tragic, in fact, that he was almost bound to turn out to be the villain.

In this sort of crime novel, it was always the one least likely. Michael remembered the excitement of his first Agatha Christie, when he had exhausted all the books for children in the Penny Library down the street, and the librarian had let him borrow from the adult section. The pleasure of reading it was quite different from other novels – more like getting involved in a game than being taken to a different reality.

If Michael had been reading Daphne W. Smythe's novel strictly for the pleasure of anticipating the plot, he would have been tempted to skip to the concluding pages to prove himself right, rather than ploughing all the way through, because it was quite clear that her detective, the redoubtable Dr Winifred Smith, an amateur who had apparently solved a number of mysteries at the Majestic during the pre-war years, was probably not going to enjoy the 'well-deserved rest' she had prescribed herself.

The detective was probably based to a large extent on Daphne W. Smythe herself, Michael thought. The fact that she had hardly bothered to change her name might, at the beginning of the twenty-first century, be seen as 'post-modern', but Michael felt it had probably more to do with the general paucity of imagination in the writing, which, from his own perspective, served to make the yarn utterly compelling. 'The Majestic Hotel' in the novel was clearly based on the Palace; the seaside town of Haven Regis was a barely disguised Kingshaven, and the Prince family who ran the hotel were obviously the Kings.

Daphne W. Smythe and Liliana King must have been friends, he thought, because the most flowery prose was reserved for the descriptions of the lady of the house, Lucilla Prince, 'a woman whose serenity of beauty was matched by a sweetness of nature and a manner so gracious it belied the firmness of resolve required to orchestrate the harmonious proceedings of a successful enterprise . . .' In other words, thought Michael, an iron fist in a velvet glove.

From the text, it was clear that Lucilla/Liliana had always been the one in charge, as her husband, Mr Beverley Prince/Mr Basil King, was very much in the background, a weak character, it was implied, whose refusal to criticize their headstrong daughter Perdita had encouraged the girl's already wanton tendencies. Michael smiled. Perdita, a curvaceous brunette 'with a figure and knowingness well beyond her fifteen years', was clearly based on Pearl King, a woman whose figure he himself had come to know only too well when he had been seduced by her sensual charms in the fifties, indulging in a crazy affair that could have ruined him – and would have done, he thought, if Liliana King had not decided to protect her flighty daughter's reputation from further scandal.

The first chapter of the novel ended with Lucilla Prince putting on her gloves and hat while waiting for a friend to pick her up to go out for a day's shopping. Perdita sashayed through the hotel in an immodest sundress, declaring loudly that she was going down to the beach hut. It was the perfect day for a swim in the sea.

'Be careful of the currents!' her mother, Lucilla, advised.
'Oh, do stop worrying, Mummy!' Perdita replied. 'Nothing bad could possibly happen on a beautiful sunny day like this!'

Michael looked up from the page, recalling the soft, firm texture of those lightly tanned shoulders, luscious dark curls, her violet eyes. Pearl had been a beauty in the mould of the young Elizabeth Taylor.

There was no doubt it was Pearl that his brother Frank had been referring to when he had written to Michael while he was billeted at the Palace: 'You'll never guess what the owners of this place are called. The Kings. The Kings in the Palace! How about that? And they live like it too. There are two daughters. One's a little princess all right. Some of the lads can see her playing tennis from their dormitory. When she knows we're looking, she bends over very prettily to pick up the ball!'

Michael returned to *The Unknown Soldier* and turned the page.

Chapter 2: The Body on the Beach
One of the great pleasures of a holiday at the Majestic Hotel was the custom of serving afternoon tea on the terrace. Due to the strictures of rationing the usual tier of appetizing temptations had been replaced by a single porcelain plate with an inconsequential flapjack, but, as if to compensate for this privation, the roses that clambered over the pergola were most exceptionally pink, against a cerulean blue sky. The sun was as radiant as Dr Smith had wished for, but

hardly dared expect, when she packed her trunk in the dingy hallway of her flat in Maida Vale. It was just the ticket for a relaxing sojourn.

'Begging your pardon, Dr Smith . . .'

A man's voice woke Dr Smith. Tipping the brim of her panama hat, she was surprised to see not a waiter offering to replenish her silver teapot with hot water, but the not-altogether-welcome figure of Police Constable Carr, or Sergeant Carr, as she deduced he must have become in the intervening years, from the three stripes on his blazer. Whilst her dealings with the copper had always been cordial, Dr Smith found herself disappointed to encounter him again, his very presence a shadow, like a cloud passing over the sun.

'Begging your pardon, Doctor,' he resumed. 'I could think of no one else.'

Winifred Smith sat up as he explained.

'Someone's been spotted on the beach below the chalk cliffs. The doctor's out on a visit, or so we supposes, because there's no answer at his surgery or home. Being as the hotel's recently opened its doors to visitors again, and being as you always used to holiday here at the beginning of the season, I took the liberty of telephoning, and as luck would have it Mr Prince tells me you was in the garden . . .'

'What possible service can I be to you?' interjected Dr Smith, her background as a blue stocking making Sergeant Carr's ill-educated verbiage painful listening.

'The tide's coming up too quick to get round the headland on foot, so old Pikey's going to take us in his boat.'

'Us? What possible help can I be?' asked Dr Smith in alarm, remembering the last time Carr had commandeered a boat to investigate the mystery of the poisoned oysters. Although the bay looked as calm as a millpond, it could cut up rough in seconds, and Winifred Smith was not a good sailor.

'Sounds like he might need your medical attentions,' said

the policeman. 'That is, if he isn't already beyond help,' he added ominously.

After an unnecessarily long description of the policeman and the detective's journey to the harbour, the hapless investigators finally arrived at the beach, where the tide was, as the policeman had correctly predicted, lapping round a body.

. . . He was face down in the shallows, hair fanning out like seaweed from around his head with the rise of each wave, and plastering itself back on the crown as the water receded. Dr Smith was quite sure from the angle of the man's spine that there was no point in testing for vital signs. What did come as a surprise as Sergeant Carr levered the body over was the familiarity of the face.

As Michael was turning the page to start the next chapter, a knock at the front door made him jump. Perhaps Daphne W. Smythe was not such a bad writer, he thought, with a wry smile, because he'd been so absorbed in the novel he hadn't noticed that it had become quite dark outside.

He was still smiling when he opened the door and saw his daughter standing there, and he couldn't seem to rearrange his features fast enough to react to the terrified expression on her face.

'Fiammetta? What's happened?'

'Daddy!' Her voice was a thin, desperate wail.

'What is it?'

'I've got cancer,' she whispered, as if she hardly dared to say the word.

'Oh, my darling girl,' said Michael, opening his arms tentatively, then drawing her to him and holding her head against his heart as she cried and cried like a child.

*　　*　　*

It was one of those rare evenings when Winston wasn't travelling, or at a cocktail party, or a premiere, but instead playing a variation of indoor cricket involving a frying pan and a pair of rolled-up socks that he had devised one Caribbean holiday after the suitcase containing John's toys had been put on the wrong flight. Although John had recently received a wealth of expensive Christmas presents and games, Frying Pan and Socks remained his favourite. Iris, who was stirring a big saucepan of ratatouille in the kitchen, listened contentedly to John's delighted celebration of runs and the heated discussions about madly serious rules involving sofa boundaries and mantelpiece wides that followed.

It was Winston who picked up the phone when it rang.

Iris wiped her hands on the tea towel she had over her shoulder, and went into the living room to take over, but even before she saw Winston's face she knew the news wasn't good.

'Tomorrow?' he was saying, looking at Iris over the top of John's head, his eyes indicating he'd talk to her in the kitchen. 'OK, I'm going to talk to Iris and call you back.'

They spoke in the kitchen, in low whispers, until John appeared at the door and said wearily, 'Come on, Daddy! It's your go!'

Iris crouched down to John's level. 'How would you like a little holiday by the sea?'

'Jamaica?' asked John, making them both laugh and releasing some of the tension.

'Not Jamaica: Granddad,' said Iris.

'Granddad!' John shrieked with excitement.

She told herself she must remember this unlikely moment of brightness to tell Michael.

The plan was that John would sleep in the car and be transferred into bed when they arrived, waking up in his grandfather's house the next day as if by magic. But the unexpected adventure was so thrilling for John that he remained wide awake as they drove through London's brightly lit streets and on to the M25. When he was very tired, John talked even more than usual, like a little songbird chirruping in its cage, and Iris found herself uncharacteristically impatient for him to shut up, but when he did, suddenly and decisively dropping off in the middle of a riff about fossilling with Granddad, she immediately wished that he would wake up and start again. Without his babble, there was no longer any distraction from the terror that filled the car as it slipped through the uninterrupted darkness of the M3.

Until hearing the result of the biopsy, Iris had almost managed to balance her fear with a kind of statistical logic gleaned from Winston's trawls through medical sites on the web, and yet she'd never been quite as reassured by the numbers as he appeared to be. If eighty per cent of breast lumps were benign, that surely meant that twenty per cent weren't, and so, if you had one of those, your chances of having breast cancer must be a hundred per cent. Now they knew, there was no longer any science Winston could offer to comfort her, but she had to get a grip of herself before they arrived, so that she could be strong for Fiammetta, and Bruno too, and her father, and for John as well. Iris's role was to hold the fort when everyone else went to pieces, just as it had been thirty years before, when she'd made this same journey when Claudia was dying.

Fiammetta wasn't dying, Iris told herself firmly. It was completely different this time. They were better at treating cancer these days, and if they'd discovered it early enough, the outcomes were encouraging. She must keep bright and cheerful for John, Iris told herself. And she wouldn't be alone. Winston was there.

'Thank you for coming with us,' Iris said, reaching

320

across the back of the child's seat to touch Winston's shoulder.

'That's OK,' he said. 'I have been trying to arrange a meeting with James anyway.'

One of the aspects of Winston that Iris didn't really know about until she lived with him was his single-mindedness about organization, and sometimes it still came as a shock how ruthless he could be. For her, the journey they were on was an impulsive and open-ended mercy dash. For Winston, it was compassionate leave that needed to be slotted into his schedule, and if an opportunity to tie up some business at the same time presented itself, so much the better. Iris tried not to mind. Winston's practicality and focus was probably exactly what was needed to see everyone through.

The following morning, the car took Iris to Lowhampton General Hospital, and Winston walked John up to the Castle to see Bruno and Julia.

'Where is James?' Iris asked, surprised to find Fiammetta alone in her hospital room.

'He's in London,' Fiammetta told her.

'For God's sake!'

'Don't be cross with him,' said Fiammetta. 'I don't think he knows how to feel, and, to be perfectly honest, I'd rather have you here. He's so impatient.'

'And I'm not?' said Iris impatiently.

'Not like him. There's no room for me because his impatience fills the room somehow . . . Anyway, you're never impatient with me,' Fiammetta told her. 'Not with anyone, in fact, except yourself,' she said, reaching out to hold Iris's hand.

Fiammetta seemed so grown-up and wise and yet she looked so little and fragile in the white hospital gown, her beautiful shiny auburn ringlets fanned out on the white pillow.

'At least I know what I look like bald,' she said, touching her hair, as if that was why Iris was staring at it.

There had been a time in her life, just before she met James, when Fiammetta had been so unhappy she had shaved all her hair off.

'I wasn't thinking that,' said Iris quickly. 'Is there anything I can get you?' she asked.

Fiammetta had never had a sweet tooth, and Iris didn't think she'd particularly welcome one of the Christmas boxes of Roses the shop on the ground floor was selling at half-price. She had decided against flowers because the selection at the stall in the entrance was limited to tight buds of daffodils, which looked like brown paper on sticks, and gaudy bouquets of mixed chrysanthemums, which Iris was superstitious about because in Italy they were the flowers of the dead.

'How long do I have?' Fiammetta asked.

Iris stared at her, and then suddenly realized she was referring to the time before her operation. 'I think they said they were taking you to theatre at about two,' she said, looking at her watch.

'Do you think the shop sells cameras?' Fiammetta asked. 'If not, could you get me some plain paper and a pencil or two?'

To Iris's amazement, the shop did have a couple of instant cameras, but the nearest thing to plain paper was a children's colouring pad with pages of black outlines of circus clowns and farmyards on one side, and blank on the other.

'Pig or a rainbow?' Fiammetta asked delightedly, as she turned the colouring pad upside down and began to concentrate on her task, indicating with the pencil that Iris should shift the compact mirror she was holding just slightly, so that Fiammetta could see the full reflection of her bare chest, and sketch what she saw.

The concentration on Fiammetta's face was exactly as

322

it had been when she was a little girl and Iris had taken crayons and paper to distract her in the dentist's waiting room. It made Iris wonder how it was that so many of the elements that made up a personality could be present from such a young age. When they were mapping the human genome, would they find a 'being perfectly happy to sit still and draw' gene as well as the one for breast cancer, she wondered.

'Now,' said Fiammetta, 'take a picture of me, please.' She lay back on her pillows.

'Smile!' said Iris.

'Not my face!' Fiammetta said, a little crossly.

Although Iris and Fiammetta resembled each other in colouring, Fiammetta's skin was pale and creamy, with no freckles, and her breasts were still firm and high, and showed no sign of ageing. Iris clicked the shutter as instructed: close-ups of each breast; each small surprisingly dark nipple; Fiammetta pushing her breasts up towards the camera, then suddenly covering them with her palms. Iris took another shot, before realizing that the doctor had just walked in behind her. Fiammetta looked embarrassed, as if she had been caught doing something naughty, and quickly pulled the sheet up to cover herself.

It was a peculiar medical etiquette, Iris thought, that allowed a doctor to slice into a breast with a scalpel, but not to look at its naked beauty.

'Hello.' Nikhil Patel shook Iris's hand.

She liked the way his eyes courteously engaged hers for a second, before releasing her hand. It was a simple gesture of good manners, but one that gave her confidence in him, even though he looked far too young to be a consultant.

'How are you feeling?' Nikhil asked Fiammetta.

'Fine,' said Fiammetta.

'Good,' he said. 'The nurse will get you ready for theatre, and I'll see you later.' He smiled at her.

'Thank you,' said Fiammetta.

It was a strangely polite exchange, Iris thought, given what was about to happen.

Although Fiammetta had appeared calm, almost blithe, now, as the nurse pushed a syringe of colourless fluid into the cannula in her arm, Iris saw fear in her sister's eyes, and she wanted to take her place on the bed, be there instead of her because she loved her so much, and felt so helpless, but almost as soon as the fluid had gone in, the tightness seemed to drain away from Fiammetta's limbs and she sighed. Iris let herself breathe again. And then another nurse came in and they flipped the brakes off the trolley bed and began to push it towards the door.

'Brave girl,' Iris heard herself saying as she walked beside the bed. 'You're a very brave girl . . .'

She felt Fiammetta's hand reach for hers, as if they were about to cross a busy road together, and she held it all the way down in the lift and along the corridor, right up until the double doors of the operating theatre, where she had to let go.

*   *   *

When Bruno returned from taking Fiammetta to the hospital, Julia was in the entrance hall of the Castle, sitting at an angle to the big antique desk as she scrolled through the reservations charts on the computer. As he stood behind her, she let her head drop back against his stomach, he put his hands on her shoulders, and they both pretended to study the screen, as if he wasn't really disturbing her, but when Winston walked in holding four-year-old John by the hand they jumped apart, as if they had been caught in flagrante delicto.

Winston took in the scenario with his usual cool detachment, but Bruno could tell that he was surprised to see them together, and he could almost hear the cogs of Winston's brain re-gearing for the changed circumstances.

'Is James about?' Winston asked.

'No. He's gone to London,' Julia told him.

Bruno thought he detected a flicker of anger across Winston's impassive features, and was glad because he was pretty angry about James's departure himself. Julia had tried to excuse her brother with some theory about it being James's own fear of abandonment that was making him run away, but Bruno thought he should just get over it and act like a man.

'You must be John!' said Julia, suddenly standing up, and coming round the front of the desk, conscious that neither of them had acknowledged the little boy. 'Did you walk all the way up the hill?'

'It'll be easier on the way down,' said John, clearly repeating what his father had told him. 'And we saw a rabbit.'

'Was it coming this way?' Julia asked.

John looked up at his father for guidance.

'I think it might have been,' said Winston.

'We'd better make sure that the door to our walled garden is closed, then,' said Julia.

'Why?' asked the little boy.

'Because if rabbits get in they eat all our lettuces.'

'Like Peter Rabbit?' asked John.

'Exactly like Peter Rabbit,' she told him.

Julia had a gift for talking to children, Bruno thought: she somehow got down to their level without being patronizing. Even though John didn't know who she was, he clearly felt very comfortable with her, and seeing the two of them together made Bruno feel oddly sentimental.

'Shall we go and see if we can find Peter Rabbit?' Bruno asked his nephew, offering his hand. He had a feeling that Winston had not come purely for a social visit.

'The real Peter Rabbit?' asked John, his eyes widening.

Bruno wasn't as adept at treading the line between

fantasy and lies. 'Or one of his friends?' he said, glancing at Julia, who was trying not to laugh.

The walled garden was obviously a slight disappointment to John because, in its wintry sparseness, it didn't look quite as pastel and abundant as Mr McGregor's garden in the book.

'No rabbits,' he said, after a moment or two.

'It's not really the season for lettuces,' said Bruno, looking for inspiration among the rows of suddenly boring-looking winter vegetables.

'Smells a bit,' John commented.

'That's cabbage,' said Bruno. 'But it tastes really good.'

'No, it doesn't,' said John categorically.

'It does the way I cook it.'

John looked dubious.

'Tell you what,' Bruno suddenly recalled a game Michael used to play with him when he was a child: 'see all these plants?' He pointed at the lines of root vegetables. John nodded. 'They've all got vegetables in the ground underneath. If you can guess what vegetable is under what plant, then we can have it for lunch.'

'Not cabbage,' John said.

'Of course not cabbage!' Bruno said. 'You already know which one's cabbage, so that wouldn't be a proper guess, would it?'

'OK, it's a deal,' said John, having managed to establish rules he was comfortable with. He was so like Winston, it was uncanny.

Bruno pushed a garden fork into friable soil.

'OK,' he said. 'First one. What's underneath this, do you think?'

John gave the matter some consideration. 'Aubergine?' he asked finally.

Bruno smiled to himself. It was a great answer to tease Iris with. You could take a child out of Hampstead . . .

'Very clever guess,' said Bruno. 'It's not actually

326

aubergine, but I seem to remember the plants are somehow related. Do you like aubergine?' he asked quickly, seeing the disappointment on John's face.

'Yes.'

'The thing is, aubergines don't really grow in winter in England,' Bruno explained. 'But we may have some from another country in the kitchen, so you could have them for lunch if you wanted.'

'No, thanks,' said John. 'We had them last night anyway. Can I have a clue?' he asked, still concentrating on the plant.

'Well, you can eat this vegetable various ways. You can have them mashed, or roasted, or you can even make chips out of them.'

'Potato?' guessed John.

'Let's see, shall we?'

Bruno stepped down on the fork and levered the soil, exposing several medium sized King Edwards, their skins tinged with pink.

John was speechless for a moment, and then he said, 'Can I do another one?'

They returned to the house with a zinc pail containing potatoes, parsnips and onions, and John clutching a bouquet of carrots, and leaving a trail of soil across the marble floor as he ran across to show Winston, who was going through the figures from New Year with Julia.

'Daddy! Look! I guessed them all!' John said.

'Well done,' said Winston distractedly.

'Bruno and I are going to make soup!' John announced.

After the excitement of digging and cooking and eating his lunch, John fell asleep on the big leather sofa in front of the blazing log fire, while Winston, Julia and Bruno talked over coffee as the light faded outside. The room was as warm and aromatic as Christmas, yet there was a tension that grew as hours passed without news from the hospital, and a desperation to fill any silences with conversation.

'The thing is,' said Winston, 'this place is just not viable with weekenders from London. The overheads are ridiculous . . .'

'And you can't get decent staff to work part-time,' Julia told him.

'Of course not.'

'My brother doesn't understand that. He's here at weekends, so that's all he sees.'

'It needs to work on a local level,' Winston mused. 'The trouble with James is that he's essentially metropolitan. For all he likes to think of himself as squire of the parish, he doesn't really know anything about the country.'

Julia giggled, glancing anxiously at the door in case James might suddenly appear there.

'What would you do if you were in charge?' Winston asked her.

'Well, initially, I'd try to repeat the success of the millennium party, with special weekends with the emphasis on luxury. Valentine's Day would be an obvious one. I'd have to buy in the well-being and beauty side of things, but we managed quite effectively at New Year. In the long term . . .'

As he watched Julia reeling off a set of fully thought-out plans, including a spa and holistic treatment centre, as well as a unique range of organic products, Bruno felt strangely proud of her competence, and for picking herself up after all the knocks she had taken. Just like when he saw her talking to John earlier; or sitting at the desk, looking at the computer screen; or when he watched her brushing her teeth in the mornings; or when she got into bed at night, shivering and snuggling up into him; even when she was trying so earnestly to excuse her brother's behaviour, he had the strangest feeling of desire and overwhelming fondness for her. It suddenly occurred to him now what that feeling might be, and he wanted to shout, 'I love you!' at the top of his voice, but he couldn't do that. Not with Winston there. And John sleeping. Not until they were on their own. But it was still incredibly exciting.

'The thing about a spa is that you draw in a lot of local people, not just the regular gymmers and swimmers,' Julia was saying, 'and you can offer pamper breaks, bridal packages – the wedding's held here, but the bride comes down the week before with her mum, and her bridesmaids, and they all lose a few extra pounds, have their facials, chill . . .'

I love you, thought Bruno.

'I'd also have a really good restaurant,' Julia went on, sounding like someone dreaming of a lottery win. 'There is definitely an influx of well-off people into the area. Not just second homes, but first homes too. The internet means they can work from home, they want a healthier life for their kids, the schools are good. They need somewhere to eat and they're prepared to pay London prices . . .'

I love you, thought Bruno.

'What do you say to that?' Winston was looking at him now.

Was he offering him a restaurant? Bruno tried to collect his thoughts.

There'd been a bit of a hiatus since the end of the second series of *Benvenuto Bruno!* Although it had been even more successful than the first series, he hadn't wanted to repeat the formula again and was keen for a new challenge. Though Esther had suggested all sorts of different angles, even a cookery game show called 'If You Can't Stand the Heat, Get Out of the Kitchen!', he hadn't felt properly committed to anything, least of all to her. Now that he'd treated her so badly, he'd probably never work in television again.

The idea of starting a restaurant, in a place he loved, where he could cook by day, have sex with the woman he loved – loved! – by night, and windsurf on his days off, seemed suddenly the stuff of his own lottery dream.

'I'd be up for it,' he heard himself saying.

'Seriously?' Julia asked, her eyes bright with disbelief.

Bruno remembered an afternoon, a long time ago, when he'd been working at the Palace, and Julia had been his boss, and they had been in the passionate throes of their first affair. They'd gone to pick strawberries at a local farm, stopping for tea on the way back at a thatched cottage with a garden and roses round the door.

'I'd like to live somewhere like this one day,' she'd said, looking down demurely as she pressed crumbs of cake with the pad of her forefinger. The unasked question had hung in the air. 'It would be idyllic, wouldn't it?' she'd pushed.

He'd given her some churlish response, unwilling to join in with the game of happy-ever-after. He must have been about twenty, not ready to settle down. But now, as he looked across at her beautiful face, golden in the glow of the fire, the same question seemed to be hanging in the air, and he couldn't quite tell whether it was for real, or whether they were still in the realm of fantasy.

*　　*　　*

When Cat got home Esther was in her room and she could hear her tapping away at the computer keyboard. Cat put her handbag, book and carrier bag down at the bottom of the stairs and went up to say hello.

'"*Nature lover looking for wild woman to share his tent*",' Esther read out. 'What do you reckon? I think I'd probably like camping . . .'

'You were thrown out of the Girl Guides,' Cat reminded her.

'God! So I was! I think "nature lover" means he's got a beard anyway.'

'Or he doesn't wash much.'

'Yuk!' said Esther. 'What about this? *"Down to earth landscape gardener would like to cultivate blossoming romance or dig a little deeper".*' Oh, for God's sake, I think he's trying too hard with the metaphors, don't you?'

'You might get a gardening programme out of him, though,' Cat teased.

'That's a thought . . .' said Esther. 'Unfortunately, it won't work,' she said, scrolling down the personal ad.

'Why?'

'He's vegetarian. I don't mind if someone's quietly vegetarian, but if it's so important they're prepared to use ten of their hundred-and-forty characters in the ad, then I'm out. Now, look at this. *"Knight in shining armour seeks damsel in distress!"* Hate that. He's in Wales, anyway. All the weird ones are in Wales . . . God! At this rate, I'll never find anyone!'

'Would you really go on a date with someone you found on the internet?' Cat asked.

'Everyone's doing it,' said Esther. 'Listen. *"Sorted guy seeks warm woman for quiet nights out and loud nights in . . ."* Do you think the fact he doesn't even make a stab at good-looking, or attractive, means he's hideous? I mean, "warm". I'm a bit more than "warm", aren't I?'

Cat nodded.

'He's probably desperate,' said Esther. 'The trouble is, I can't bear the ones who try too hard and I'm suspicious of the ones who don't try at all.'

'Do you think you're really ready for another relationship?' Cat asked gently. 'Bruno's stuff is still here . . .'

'But he's not coming back,' said Esther, suddenly despondent. 'He's in lurve.'

'That's a bit sudden, isn't it?'

'Apparently, they've known each other for years. They had a major affair, but she didn't want to leave her kids, so they split up. But then she got divorced and, well, anyway,

I wouldn't have him back, even if he wanted to. I'm so over him,' Esther declared emphatically, then immediately ruined the effect by bursting into tears. 'He's not having his bloody range cooker back either,' she added, as if this was the best revenge she could exact.

'How do you know all this? Did he call?' Cat asked.

'Bastard's too cowardly to call,' sniffed Esther. 'I ran into James Allsop at the Compton Club last night. He was very nice about it, actually. His wife's in hospital. We drowned our sorrows together.'

Cat thought her friend was looking a bit glassy-eyed. The mood swing from almost hysterical optimism to utter devastation was very characteristic of Esther with a hangover.

'I've got a cottage pie from M & S,' Cat offered. 'Do you want to share it?'

'I am starving,' Esther admitted.

While Esther continued to trawl the dating site, Cat put the food in the oven and sat downstairs reading one of the novels she had bought in Ireland. Finn had introduced her to the work of several young Irish writers and she was planning to run a promotion to coincide with St Patrick's Day in the bookshop, and was in touch with a number of publishers about the possibility of getting authors to come in and talk or do a reading.

'It's quite nice, just you and me, isn't it?' said Esther when they sat down together to eat, making Cat feel a bit guilty. She hadn't yet told her about their plans because it would have been a bit tactless in the circumstances, but to put it off any longer would be dishonest.

'Actually, there's something I've been wanting to tell you,' Cat began. 'Finn and I—'

'Please don't tell me you're getting married, because I couldn't stand it!' Esther butted in.

Cat smiled. 'No, we're not getting married,' she said carefully.

'You're splitting up?' Esther looked hopeful.

'Not that either. We have decided to live together and we're looking for a flat.'

'Oh,' said Esther, her lip quivering. 'But that's almost as bad as marriage.' There was something endearingly child-like about Esther's selfishness. Then she had an idea and brightened instantly, almost like a cartoon figure with a light bulb in a bubble above her head. 'Why don't you both move in here? There's enough room . . .'

'We really want to get somewhere of our own,' said Cat. 'Anyway, you don't want to live with a couple, re-member?'

Esther had been adamant about that, although it had never occurred to her that Cat might have felt the same way when she shacked up with Bruno.

'You're probably right,' said Esther thoughtfully. 'I think I might just sell up and get somewhere brand-new, with no horrid memories. Maybe somewhere modern and minimalist. All glass and steel. What do you think?'

The conversation Cat had been dreading had inevitably turned into a conversation about Esther. Which was good, Cat told herself. It had been much easier than she expected. One difficult conversation down, one to go. At the week-end, she was taking Finn to meet her parents.

* * *

James's cheek was cold when he kissed Fiammetta. He looked rough, as if he'd drunk quite a lot the previous evening.

'How are you feeling?' he asked.

'Fine,' said Fiammetta. She didn't think the anaesthetic had worn off properly yet. 'Is Iris here?'

'She was here all night, apparently. She wanted to get back for when her little boy woke up.'

'Of course,' said Fiammetta.

333

'I'm here now,' said James proudly, as if he expected praise.

On the forms they'd had to fill in when she was admitted, she'd asked Bruno who her next of kin was, and he said he thought James. But it hadn't felt right putting his name. Bruno was her next of kin and Iris too. And she wished one of them were there instead of her husband now as they waited for Nikhil to come.

'The good news is that the cancer doesn't appear to have spread to the lymph nodes,' Nikhil told them.

'And the bad?' Fiammetta wanted to know immediately.

'In a patient of your age, I would still strongly advise a course of chemotherapy. There can be unpleasant side effects, but—'

'Can I just ask . . .' James interjected. 'Can I just ask if there are implications for Fiammetta's prospects of having a child?'

'My concern is getting Fiammetta healthy again,' Nikhil told him.

'I don't want to have a child.' Fiammetta heard the words emerge from her mouth and was as stunned as the two men that she'd spoken them. Was this why she had not been able to conceive? she wondered. Had her body somehow known about the cancer?

'I think now's perhaps not the time . . .' Nikhil suggested.

'If you're cross with me for going to London . . .' James suddenly went on the offensive.

'It's nothing to do with you going to London,' Fiammetta replied.

'I really don't think—' Nikhil tried to excuse himself.

'Even if I survive this, I'm far more likely to get cancer again, aren't I?' Fiammetta asked him directly.

Nikhil said nothing, which confirmed her hypothesis.

She turned to James. 'I'm just not prepared to cause any

small person the loneliness of not having a mother. Surely you can understand that?'

'I'll give you a few moments,' said Nikhil, backing out of the room.

'You can't possibly make a decision about this now,' James said.

He was furious, but he was the one who'd started it, she thought.

'My mother died of cancer, and her mother probably did too,' Fiammetta told him.

'It's not just about you, you know,' said James.

But it was, Fiammetta thought.

'It's better that you know I won't change my mind,' she told him.

Nikhil was right, it wasn't the time to be discussing this, and yet she wasn't prepared to go along with a deception for even a second. There was so much going on in her brain, it was too complicated to add dishonesty.

'I'm tired,' she said, closing her eyes. She could feel her husband watching her, not knowing what to do. Go, just go, she thought to herself.

It had all been a dream! For one sweet second, a wave of relief washed over Fiammetta as she woke up. But then the hospital room swam into focus and she remembered where she was.

Her father was standing beside the bed, holding a bunch of hazel catkins and rosehips. The irregular outline of the twigs against the straight white lines of the ward pleased her, a little bit of wild hedgerow in a place where everything was so unnatural.

'We can't go on meeting like this,' said Michael cheerily, which made her think that he was nervous, because he didn't normally say things like that, and then he looked so anxious that he might have said the wrong thing, she wanted to tell him not to worry, she wasn't going to leave him again, not if she could help it, she reminded herself. It was strange how the sudden realization of mortality changed her perspective. What Michael had done, or hadn't done, in the past didn't seem nearly as significant now. Fiammetta had spent so much of her life angry, first with her mother for leaving her, and then with her father for lying to her, and now she felt that perhaps all that bitterness stored up inside had done her harm. It was so simple to let it go, she didn't know why she hadn't managed to do that before.

Michael put his bouquet on the bed. He had tied it with string, she noticed, not because he had the slightest idea of the current trends in floristry that favoured hessian and raffia over ribbon and polythene, but because he was of the generation that saved bits of string and kept them in a drawer. He was an old man. And she'd missed a whole chunk of his life, and he of hers.

'My mother said I would know what it was like to be her one day,' Fiammetta told him. 'And now I do . . . She must have been very frightened.'

'I think she was,' said Michael, drawing up a chair. 'She never said so. She became very cross with me, very impatient that I wouldn't cope. I suppose that was fear.'

'Really?'

Somehow Fiammetta found the thought of her mother's anger comforting. The picture she had always carried in her mind was one of tragic serenity.

'Claudia had very high standards,' Michael told her. 'She expected a great deal of people, and God help you if you didn't come up to scratch!'

It was odd to learn things after all this time. Fiammetta couldn't remember them ever talking about her mother before.

'I always thought of her as a nun in a duffel coat,' he went on.

'How come?' Fiammetta asked.

'We bumped into each other on the first Aldermaston march. She was a student at the time, wearing a duffel coat. Her white face and the dark hood reminded me of a nun, I suppose . . . And there was something almost puritanical about her,' he said. 'You're very like her, in that respect. Bruno inherited her looks.'

Fiammetta recalled how when they were children people hadn't been able to help themselves remarking on the resemblance, quickly looking away, embarrassed by their tactlessness.

'But you are more *like* her,' Michael mused. 'You inherited some of her characteristics.'

'And cancer,' said Fiammetta, her eyes inexplicably filling with tears.

Michael's hand hovered over hers, as if he wasn't sure if he had permission to touch her. Their reconciliation was still so fragile. Fiammetta wanted to be able to reassure him, but she felt so wretched suddenly, she knew she'd fall apart if she tried. Then she felt his hand clasp hers decisively, taking charge, and she was so grateful.

'It's not going to happen again,' he told her. 'They can treat cancer now. You'll get better.'

'Do you believe that?'

For the first time in years, her father's pale-blue eyes didn't shift away, or duck her glance, but looked directly into hers. 'I do,' he said.

His confidence was incredibly fortifying, and she found herself smiling at him.

'Daddy,' she said, 'there's something I want to ask you . . .'

'What's that?'

'Can I come and stay with you?' she said.

He looked as if he didn't understand.

'What's going to happen, apparently, is that I'll be discharged and then I'll have to come in for chemotherapy sessions, I think only as a day patient, but I will feel dreadful

. . . and I don't want to be at the Castle. I'd like to be at home.'

Michael waited expectantly, as if there was a punchline coming, a joke he didn't understand. Then when she had nothing to add, he started to work through the practicalities.

'Iris is staying, and John, of course. She's seeing about a temporary place for him at the nursery school this morning. She's in your room now.'

Fiammetta liked the fact that he still thought of it as her room.

'I suppose she could go in Bruno's with John,' Michael said, and then, as if he'd suddenly realized the logistics weren't what was important, he said, 'Of course you can, if that's what you want. It'll be a bit of a squash . . .'

'Like that time in the caravan,' said Fiammetta.

Her father's face brightened at the memory. 'You two loved that caravan,' he said.

It had been the long hot summer of 1976, the summer everyone remembered, the year Michael and the twins moved out of the Castle. He'd rented a caravan in the Forest Valley Park and Iris had come down from London, and they'd all crammed in together. They'd had to collect drinking water from a standpipe, and bathe in the sea, and their hair had been stiff with salt. It had been one of the best summers of her life, Fiammetta thought.

'Yes. I'm sure it can be arranged,' said Michael.

Fiammetta was relieved that it didn't seem to cross his mind to ask about James. She didn't want to have to explain something she'd only just decided herself.

Her father was smiling now, warming to the idea as he got used to it. As if he'd been lonely, all these years, almost without realizing.

*   *   *

338

The question of whether Cat's parents would like Finn was superseded in her mind by sudden doubt whether Finn would continue to like her after meeting them.

Although she was happy enough sitting reading the Sunday papers on the Tube, when it emerged into daylight at Finchley Road, and they crossed the platform to the Jubilee Line, stepping down into the smaller train, a familiar feeling of claustrophobia began to return, perversely tightening its grip as the views from the train window changed from grimy inner-city streets to the greener, more open spaces of the suburbs. Glancing at Finn, who was absorbed in an article about whether the present rise in house prices was sustainable, Cat wondered if he'd had similar misgivings about introducing her to his family. She didn't think so. With four older sisters and a younger brother, all with partners, some with children, there was so much diversity in the cramped living room of his parents' council house in north Dublin that her presence hadn't made the difference that his was going to in her parents' quiet front room. The Dublin estate had been bleak and grey, but the house warm and full of animated conversations all going on at once. All of Finn's siblings shared his curly hair and his dry sense of humour. The exotic Niamh, whom Cat had mistaken for his wife at the Stones' treasure hunt, was the editor of a woman's magazine; another worked at RTE; the younger sisters were still at college; and the boy, Donal, was in a band. They were all far too bright and busy to want to observe or interrogate Cat. She and Finn only stayed a short time for a cup of tea and a sandwich before heading off to the cottage in the west, and she was quite sure that nobody would even have mentioned her afterwards, let alone conducted the minute and prolonged post-mortem that was bound to follow Finn's visit.

The semi-detached houses with their bay windows and mock Tudor gables looked exactly the same as when she was growing up. There were few changes other than the colour and manufacturer of the saloon cars parked in the drives. Cat could almost feel her personality transforming back to the mute and embarrassed teenager she had been when she had last taken a boyfriend home.

Nigel had been the captain of the rugby team and the only boy tall enough to have the confidence to ask her out at the annual disco, organized by her school with the idea of introducing Lady Collingburn girls to suitably clever boys at the equivalent boys' schools in the area. Nigel's parents were better off than Cat's, with a neo-Georgian detached house in Stanmore. The business of establishing exactly which street it was, and how long it hadn't taken him to cycle over and what sort of car his father drove (one of the new Honda-designed Rovers, Cat seemed to remember) had at least given them something to break the ice with. In fact, her parents' enthusiasm for Nice-Boy Nigel (as Esther had dubbed him, after the umpteenth time Cat's mother had asked, 'Whatever happened to that nice boy Nigel?') had ultimately put Cat off. After the relationship petered out, she'd set her sights on slightly more dangerous types that she and Esther would meet in the smoking section of McDonald's after school and never dreamt of bringing home.

At university, Cat had been paralysed with shyness until Roy took her out to dinner, on the pretext of talking about her essay on William Blake, and told her that he was going mad with thinking about her.

When her mother's gentle probing had repeatedly drawn a blank, she had eventually given up asking 'Have you met anyone nice?' As recently as Christmas, when doing the washing-up together in the kitchen, and laughing at a round-up of the year on Radio 4, Cat's father had remarked, 'She's lesbian, you know,' about one of the presenters, leaving a question hanging in the air that Cat had declined to answer, thereby probably confirming his suspicions.

When she'd telephoned to ask if she could bring someone home for Sunday lunch and her mother had asked, carefully, 'What's their name?', the sigh of relief had been audible when Cat had replied.

'He's called Finn.'

'Finn?'

'It's an Irish name.'

'Oh,' said her mother, as Irish suspicions moved in to take the place of lesbian worries.

Now, as Cat stood in the porch, breathing the faint, familiar smell of gravy, looking at the polished letterbox and waiting for the opening of the front door, she found herself in near panic in case Finn would look at her mother and see not just a rather inhibited middle-class woman, but a vision of what Cat would be like in the future. She hadn't actually spoken much about her parents to Finn, because there was nothing very remarkable about them; yet now, she wanted to whisk him away and explain that she wasn't like them and he mustn't think that their future was going to be conservative and colourless, and that she hated the Lladro porcelain, and had only ever conspired in the collection to please her mother.

But it was too late.

'So you're planning to live together?' Cat's father took it upon himself to sum up the rather stuttering explanation Cat had given them over the apple crumble about why she was moving out of Esther's house. 'Good idea!' he added, with resolute cheerfulness. 'That's what most people seem to do these days!'

Cat stared at the row of photos on the mantelpiece.

'But you're not engaged?' repeated Cat's mother, as if she found the idea slightly difficult to grasp.

'No,' said Cat, looking down at the tablecloth.

She wanted them to know that it was her decision, not Finn's, so they wouldn't think him feckless, or

341

irresponsible, but she couldn't think of a way of telling them without making it more of an issue. For a moment she couldn't even remember what her reasons were. It seemed so ungrateful, somehow, knowing that what her mother would most have liked was to add a portrait photograph of Cat in a long white dress next to the one in a mortar-board and gown.

'Shall we have our coffee in the front room?' asked Cat's father, pushing back his chair.

'That would be grand,' said Finn, giving Cat a reassuring smile as he followed her mother out of the dining room. He seemed to be coping far better than she was, Cat thought, calculating that they need only stay another hour.

'Seems a very decent chap,' her father commented. 'You'll have to let us know when he's next on television.'

The paper Finn worked for was not one her father, or his friends, would ever read, but an appearance on *Newsnight* seemed to be proof of his credibility, and something he would be able to tell people at the golf club.

'This is Cathy in her pram . . .'

To her dismay, her mother had brought out the photo albums.

'. . . And here she is on the beach. She must be about five. She was already tall for her age, as you can see.'

Finn looked up from the album and smiled at Cat. 'You haven't changed,' he said, his voice full of affection.

The child on the windswept beach had a bob with a fringe, rather than the bob she now wore with a side parting and hair that often fell over her eyes. She didn't look very happy.

'Cathy was always well-behaved,' her mother was saying, as if she was giving her a character reference.

Finn glanced at Cat again and she rolled her eyes.

'Here she is in nineteen seventy-six,' said her mother, reading the date below the photograph.

Cat was pictured sitting on the steps of a caravan, her knees folded up to her chest, squinting at the camera.

'You had a caravan?' Finn said. 'So did we . . . We couldn't get enough of it! My dad parked it outside and all of us insisted on sleeping in it right through till winter.'

'We only had ours for one summer,' said her mother quickly. 'We found a nice guesthouse suited us better really.'

Cat winced. Everything about her family was unadventurous and boring, she thought, looking round the sterile room. And maybe she was too. Even as a teenager she'd been a good girl. Having Esther as a friend was as naughty as it got, but it was naughtiness by proxy. Cat had never smoked spliffs, or snogged boys in leather jackets at bus stops, or been threatened with expulsion from school. Why hadn't she had a teenage rebellion, Cat wondered. And why now, when she was far too old for it, did she feel like picking up one of the smooth colourless pieces of Lladro and throwing it at the beige-tiled surround to the gas-effect fire?

'I'm sorry,' Cat said, as soon as they were out of earshot.

'For what?' Finn asked.

'For putting you through all that.'

'They're very nice people,' he said. 'And you are very precious to them.'

This was true, Cat thought, and now she felt guilty for her impatience with them, her insistence that they couldn't stay for tea because they were doing something that evening, which had been a lie, and sounded like one too. And even more than the idea that Finn wouldn't like them, she hated the idea that he was going to take their side.

'It must have been difficult for you, though,' he said.

'What do you mean?' Cat asked.

'Carrying the burden of all their hopes. At least ours got spread around a bit,' he added, laughing. Then putting his arm round her shoulder he drew her into a very passionate kiss, right there, in the suburbs, where you just didn't do things like that.

*　　*　　*

'"Valentine Dinner",' Libby King read the full-page advertisement in the *Chronicle* out loud. '"To celebrate the opening of the restaurant, Castle Compton offers a spectacular champagne supper absolutely free for the first couple to book a table" . . . I don't understand why they keep calling it Castle Compton.' She looked up.

'Because it's owned by James's company,' Edwin explained. 'It's all to do with branding.'

'I thought you said Julia was in charge now,' said Libby.

'It's still the same company.'

The gossip was that James's little redhead wife had walked out on him. The Quinns had always been a bad lot, intent on insinuating themselves into Kingshaven society, then poisoning it from within. First it was Sylvia Quinn wresting Mrs Farmer's business from her hands; then that devious ginger girl Iris who'd run away with a gang of louts after helping them dig up all the flowerbeds in the Gardens; Libby didn't even want to think about Julia's lover, Bruno, who had worked at the Palace as a kitchen boy. There were even rumours that Michael Quinn and her own sister Pearl had been at it in the fifties. And now here was another one causing trouble.

'Poor James,' said Libby.

'He's in New York at the moment,' said Edwin.

'New York?'

'Looking for property. Winston Allsop is keen to expand the brand to other cities . . . Winston is the major shareholder now.'

'Winston Allsop!' said Libby. 'It really is extraordinary when you think of where he came from.'

'Oyster!' Liliana suddenly shouted.

'Clever you, Mummy,' said Libby, picking up the newspaper again so she could read out loud the menu of the Castle's Valentine Dinner. 'Half a dozen Kingshaven oysters,' she looked over the top of her reading specs at her mother, 'followed by grilled asparagus, fillet of local organically reared beef, then strawberry soup, whatever that may be, and handmade chocolates . . .' Libby put the paper down. 'Speaking of which,' she said, to no one in particular, 'we must start thinking about Mummy's celebrations.'

Liliana was going to be a hundred, and they'd have to do something special, but Libby hadn't quite decided what.

Pearl wanted to have a party. 'Mummy used to absolutely love a party!' she'd cajoled.

But wasn't that the point? In her day, Liliana had been such a brilliant hostess, it would be too tragic to see her sitting in a corner yelling 'Oyster!' at the top of her voice. Libby had to put her foot down. If Liliana were in her right mind, she would definitely not have agreed. So many of her thoughts and sentences started these days with the phrase 'If Liliana were in her right mind'.

Still, it was amazing that her mother was as fit and well as she was, Libby thought. A hundred! Would Liliana receive a telegram from the Queen? Did Buckingham Palace have a list of birthdays, Libby wondered, or was one supposed to tell someone?

*   *   *

'It really is extraordinary when you think where he came from!'

Did they know? Of course not! Nobody had ever discovered, thought Liliana, and neither she nor Ruby had ever mentioned the subject again. Indeed, Ruby had always referred to Winston as 'Sir John's piccaninny' just like the rest of town. If she'd been proud of her son's achievements she'd kept very quiet about it and the vow of silence they'd made lasted right up until the end.

'My boy will be all right, won't he, Lil?'

Nobody had heard. Apart from Dr Ferry, who was used to ignoring the ramblings of senile old ladies.

Liliana could remember VE night as clearly as if it were yesterday. Better, in fact. All the days now seemed exactly the same and she couldn't tell one from another.

The town of Kingshaven had partied all night up on the South Cliffs. Some of them, like her daughter Pearl and Ruby's daughter Jennifer, had fallen asleep on the grassy ramparts of the Iron Age Fort. Or so they'd claimed.

It was getting light when Liliana returned from her mission. In the chill grey dawn, people were beginning to drift back down into town, shivering in their summer clothes, their mouths suddenly stretching into unstoppable yawns. Everyone was up and about, so nobody questioned why Liliana would be letting herself into Mrs Farmer's shop at that hour in the morning.

Ruby was dozing on the bed, but she woke up when Liliana gave her a little shake.

'What? Oh, it's you! I thought for a moment then I was dreaming.'

'I left the basket in a hedge at the bottom of the Castle drive,' Liliana informed Ruby briskly, conscious that Jennifer would be home soon. They had to get their story straight.

'Will someone find him there?' asked Ruby anxiously.

'He was bawling his head off when I left him.'

'What's going to happen, Lil?' Ruby asked.

'It's something I have no previous experience of,' Liliana told her crisply. 'Perhaps Sir John will take him in. He's partial to waifs and strays!'

She hadn't meant it as a serious suggestion, but it turned out that she had the gift of prophesy.

'I was frit when that airman came along,' said Ruby, with a little giggle.

Liliana bristled at the poor use of grammar.

'Good evening, ladies!' Ruby mimicked his voice. 'I nearly jumped out of my skin!'

'Oh, do shush!' said Liliana.

'He knew your name,' Ruby remembered.

'I expect he was one of the boys who were billeted at the hotel,' said Liliana quickly.

'Nobody will know, will they, Lil?' Ruby asked.

'Well, they won't hear it from me,' said Liliana. 'And they won't hear it from you, will they? You will keep your mouth shut, won't you, Ruby?'

'Cross my heart and hope to die,' Ruby swore.

That wasn't quite enough for Liliana. 'Oyster?' she demanded. It was the word they'd always used to seal the most extreme oaths of secrecy.

'Utterly oyster,' Ruby agreed.

* * *

There was bunting strung across the High Street when Bruno brought Fiammetta back to Kingshaven after her last session of chemotherapy, and even though she knew it hadn't been put up to welcome her back she felt as if it was. It was strange how serious illness could make you irrational. Both her father and Iris, the two most rational people she knew, had taken to touching wood all the time, and now, with bunting flapping in the breeze, and the sun shining, Fiammetta allowed herself to think that this was a good omen, though she didn't want to say so out loud, for fear of tempting fate.

'What's going on?' she asked her brother.

'It's old Mrs King's big day,' Bruno reminded her. 'There's a service of thanksgiving at the church, and they've built a bit of a stage under the Clocktower so children can do

347

a little pageant, and she can watch the band play Happy Birthday.'

'Amazing to have lived a whole century,' said Fiammetta.

'Yes,' said Bruno, distractedly.

She could tell he was doing that thing of praying silently to a God he did't actually believe in whenever the word live, or die, was mentioned in her presence. It was uncanny how often the forbidden words did crop up. Sometimes she thought it was the effort of trying not to mention them that made them burst out at every opportunity.

Bruno's van struggled slightly on the steep incline of the High Street, and he changed down a gear. They turned left in front of the station and accelerated up the hill towards the gatehouse at the bottom of the avenue of beech trees that led up to the Castle.

'You know you're very welcome back now that you're . . .' Bruno hesitated slightly, and she knew that he was going to say 'well', but there wasn't any wood to touch, so instead he concluded 'finished with your treatment.'

'No,' said Fiammetta. 'I won't be coming back. It's still James's house. It always was his house. I was only ever squatting there,' she said, turning her head to look at the Castle as they drove past the turning and headed towards the Harbour End.

'You and James . . .' Bruno said. 'Why . . . ?'

'Because I couldn't pretend I wanted to have children, and that was what he most wanted. It wasn't fair on him. I felt he should have the chance to start with someone else and not always feel guilty if I—' Fiammetta stopped. 'Why are you smiling?' she asked her brother.

'I wasn't actually going to ask why you split up. I was going to ask why you married him!'

Fiammetta laughed. 'I wish I knew!' she said. 'I think I thought I was opting for a life without complications. And we had great sex . . .' she admitted.

'There's something about those Allsops . . .' said Bruno.

'Sex is not enough, though,' Fiammetta warned him.

'I know that,' he said, giving her a meaningful look.

'I'm very fond of Julia. And she's been through a lot . . .' said Fiammetta.

'I know. And so am I. Fond of her. Don't worry,' he said.

They'd never commented on each other's love lives, and they never would, but she felt reassured that his intentions were serious.

'Look!' he cried.

They'd reached the brow of the hill before the road began its steep descent to the Harbour End. Even though she'd seen it all her life, to Fiammetta the view was always slightly different, always a surprise. Today the grey stone of the cottages was almost white in the sunshine, and nestling beside the shimmering sea the old town was like a pearl in the vast iridescent shell of an oyster.

Fiammetta wound down her window. The breeze was fresh and tasted delicious after the disinfected air of the hospital. She tightened the knot of her silk headscarf, not because she particularly cared about people seeing her bare head, but because it was surprisingly cold with no hair.

As Bruno pulled up on the Quay to let her out, Iris and John came dashing out of the warehouse to hug her.

'I've made you a present because you won't be sicking all the time now,' John announced, with his refreshing lack of tact. He took her hand and led her upstairs to the living room.

'Be thrilled!' Iris whispered through the soft silk over Fiammetta's ear. 'Be very, very thrilled!'

'That's for me? That's fantastic!' said Fiammetta, as John proudly showed her a row of cupcakes with her name spelt out in wiggly icing, one letter for each cake.

'You're a very lucky person,' John told her.

Fiammetta was aware of Iris squirming slightly behind her.

'Why's that?' asked Fiammetta.

'Because you've got a very long name. Mine's only four letters,' John explained.

'So you don't get as many cakes as I do?'

John nodded solemnly.

'You're right, I am very lucky,' Fiammetta told him. 'But, if you like, I'll share them with you.'

'And Mummy?'

'She only has four letters too, doesn't she?'

John nodded.

'All right, she can have some of mine too.'

'It's only fair,' said John, with a shrug. 'Is it time to go yet, Mummy?'

'Quite soon,' said Iris, with a glance at her watch.

'We're going to a birthday party,' John informed Fiammetta.

'How lovely,' said Fiammetta, privately quite relieved that she would have an hour or two by herself. The anti-nausea drugs were quite effective, but she still felt horrible. John was completely adorable, but he was also very vigorous and very loud. 'Is that with one of your new friends?' she asked.

'Not *that* kind of birthday party!' said John, as if she was very stupid indeed.

'John is doing so well at his nursery school, the teacher decided that he should be the one to present Mrs Liliana King with flowers!' Iris explained, her face twisted into a grimace for Fiammetta's benefit.

'Mrs Liliana King is a hundred years old,' John informed her. 'Also called a century.'

*   *   *

Libby was pleased to see that the church was full, even if the first few rows on the other side of the aisle from the Kings' pew were taken up with residents from the old folks' home, who she felt would have been better kept at

350

the back, rather than sitting there in full view, drooling and muttering like a ghastly memento mori. When the band struck up the opening notes of 'Fight the good fight', one of Liliana's favourite hymns, Mr Adams attempted to stand and managed to push his wheelchair back into several others, creating an unfortunate domino effect that took a good five minutes to settle, rather diminishing the hymn's usual uplifting effect, even with the band soldiering on regardless.

The band had been Eddie's thought, and a very good one – far better than relying on the feeble organist – as it gave the ceremony the bit of pomp it needed.

'We are gathered here today to give thanks for the life of Liliana King,' the vicar declared from his pulpit.

Libby thought the words sounded suspiciously like the ones he normally used at the beginning of a funeral service.

'. . . And what a life it has been! Liliana, if I may call her that . . .' The vicar smiled warmly at Liliana.

'Can't hear a word, can you?' one of the old women from the home said very loudly to her neighbour.

It was difficult to tell whether Liliana was taking anything in, Libby thought, looking at her mother, who was sitting next to her in her pale-lilac dress with matching hat and veil. Liliana's eyes were open and a gracious little smile played around her lips.

'. . . Liliana was born in the year nineteen hundred, if you can believe that! There were no motor cars on the road . . .' the vicar turned his head in the direction of the schoolchildren who were sitting in the choir in their school uniform, '. . . no electricity in most houses, certainly no televisions or video games or internet . . .'

There was almost nothing worse, Libby thought, than a vicar who tried to be 'with it'. She'd specifically requested a traditional service, but she should perhaps have known that someone who last Christmas had told the story of the

351

Nativity in the form of a news bulletin (right down to a weather report about it being a frosty night for shepherds but a clear one for stargazers) wouldn't be able to resist the temptation to demonstrate his trendiness.

'Throughout her life, Liliana has been known as the Century's Daughter . . .' the vicar went on.

'I've no idea who he's talking about, have you?' the old woman from the home asked her neighbour loudly.

A ripple of giggling murmured through the choir. The headteacher glared.

The Century's Daughter was the term the *Chronicle* had used to describe Liliana, illustrating the span of her life with archive photographs of her next to photographs of iconic women of the decades, such as Mrs Pankhurst, Clara Bow, Twiggy, and Mrs Thatcher in a tank.

There was also a pull-out chart showing the changes to women's lives over the past hundred years, from getting the vote and the married women's property act to the Pill and abortions on the National Health. Libby had found it a rather distasteful and inappropriate tribute. Liliana had never availed herself of any of these so-called advancements, and yet she had been as powerful as any man Libby had ever known. Nothing the century had thrown at her – from the Great Depression to two world wars – had dented Liliana's iron resolve. In one of the national papers, Libby had read that Cecil Beaton had described another centenarian, the Queen Mother, as a marshmallow made on a welding machine, and that particular bond of sweetness and steel also fitted Liliana. Libby looked fondly down at her mother, who was still smiling, although Libby was certain that if she were in her right mind she would be as irritated by the vicar's patronizing narration as she was.

'I'm sure we'd all like to join in our final song, led by the children of Kingshaven's primary school.'

There was much shifting of chairs as the children stood up. Then their music teacher lifted the baton and they all sang in their high, tuneless voices, 'Happy birthday to you. Happy birthday to you. Happy birthday, dear Mrs King. Happy birthday to you!'

Then the band took up the tune and the congregation joined in to sing a second verse.

In her pale-lilac mist, Liliana continued to smile.

The schoolchildren left the church first, in a fairly orderly crocodile, followed by the band in their uniforms, who were going to march in front of the car that would convey Liliana to the Clocktower. With Christopher taking one arm and Eddie the other, Liliana was hoisted to her feet, having been quite clear about not sitting in the wheelchair they had hired for the occasion. She walked down the aisle, nodding from side to side, as the congregation smiled and applauded her.

The event was only mired by shouts of 'Murderer!' from batty old Miss Potter at the front of the church, who had clearly not recovered from the shock of learning that Dr Ferry had been convicted of the murder of several of her fellow residents.

It had been a blow to the whole community, and not exactly the most propitious start to the new millennium. They'd tried to keep the news from Liliana, because she had been so very fond of the doctor. With hindsight, it occurred to Libby that Ruby Farmer had passed away rather suddenly after one of Dr Ferry's visits. Who knew what his motives might have been for visiting Liliana so frequently? It really didn't bear thinking about.

*   *   *

'Happy birthday to you! Happy birthday to you! Happy birthday, Mrs King. Happy birthday to you!'

How many times did she have to listen to it, Liliana wondered. A hundred? And didn't the band know any other tunes? She was sure it was the third round of

353

'Congratulations', which had never been one of her favourites, and was 'Lily the Pink' someone's idea of a joke? Quite possibly her son-in-law's. There was little dignity in old age.

People kept talking about her as if she wasn't there – isn't she good for her age? Hasn't she kept up well? I do like her in that colour – and nobody could see that she was cold. There was quite a wind whipping up round the dais. She was beginning to regret shrugging off Libby's offer of a coat this morning – a brown one! She'd rather die than wear brown with lilac! But she hadn't known she would be sitting for hours in the cold. She'd been out in public so infrequently recently that she had forgotten how tiring it was to smile all the time. But you couldn't risk not smiling. That would always be the photo that was used.

The band seemed to have stopped at last. Thank God for that! But no, another drum roll! Surely not another speech? How many were there going to be? A hundred?

'Mummy, look!' Libby was bending down beside her. 'Look what this little boy has for you!'

She must have closed her eyes for a second. Who could blame her on the umpteenth encore of 'Congratulations'? More flowers! Where were they all going to go? The limousine was already chock-a-block with bouquets, all along the shelf at the back, like a hearse.

At least this was just a little posy. Pinks and forget-me-nots.

'Happy birthday, Mrs King!'

Liliana could hear the whirring click of cameras.

This would be the photo that appeared in the *Chronicle*: last century's old woman, this century's child. Ancient history meeting the future.

She had to make an effort to smile.

The boy's face loomed sharply into focus.

Was this someone's idea of a joke?

Brown face looking at her.

As if he knew!

Nobody knew.

Nobody even suspected.

He couldn't know. He was a baby!

And now he was a little boy.

But that wasn't right!

Liliana tried to get a grip of her thoughts. He wasn't a little boy, he was a grown man.

Blue! The child's eyes were blue, not brown. The baby's eyes had been brown, with very white whites, like a glass marble. The child had blue eyes, not brown. The skin was brown and blue eyes were staring at her.

'You're meant to say thank you when someone gives you something,' the child was saying.

The nerve of it! Didn't they teach children manners these days?

'She's very old, she can't really say anything,' Libby was telling him. 'I'll say thank you for her. Aren't they lovely, Mummy? Your favourite colours! Pink and blue . . .'

Blue, not brown.

It was so much warmer in the car, and the smell of flowers was quite overpowering.

'Thank God that's over,' Eddie was saying as they drove off.

'I don't think anyone minded, do you?' came Libby's anxious voice.

'Shouting "Not brown!" at the top of her voice. Not exactly what you'd call politically correct.' Her son-in-law guffawed. 'Made a change from oyster, though!'

Chapter Nine

11 September 2001

The warehouse felt very empty without Fiammetta. Although Michael rarely saw her during the day because he was in the bookshop and she was painting up in her room in the roof, the silence was usually companionable rather than lonely. Occasionally, he would put the closed sign up on the door and go upstairs to make a pot of tea, then carry a full and steaming mug carefully up the spiral staircase that led from the open-plan living area to the bedrooms and place it on the floor outside her door. At lunch time he took a sandwich up too, worried that Fiammetta would forget to eat and that it wouldn't be good for her. She had always been so small and delicate, and instinct told him that her body would be better able to fight the cancer if there were a little more flesh on her bones, but he had no idea whether this were true.

In the evenings, Michael had taken to cooking dinner, even though he wasn't a very good cook. Fiammetta did not talk very much during the meal, but it gave him pleasure to see her eating. He sensed that most of her brain was involved in a creative narrative, as his used to be when he was writing, leaving only a little bit to engage with other people on a superficial level. He had not asked to see what she was working on because he did not think she wanted to show it. He was tempted now, with her at the hospital, to tiptoe upstairs and have a look, but made the decision not to. Trust had taken so long to build, and was still so fragile, he would not jeopardize it, even though he suspected that seeing her work might give him pointers about what she was thinking.

Fiammetta's hair had grown back, a little paler and downier than before, and a lively brightness had returned to her eyes, but there was still a definite sense that talking about the future was taboo. Michael had not asked what she would do if she were to be discharged, and he had tried not to think about it, for fear of jinxing the results of her tests. If she were to leave and go back to London, he knew he would be very sad, because looking after her had made him feel useful – something he hadn't felt for a long time. But even that was thinking too far ahead. Fiammetta would tell him in her own time, and he would have to live with whatever she decided. The only important thing was that she was healthy again.

Since Fiammetta's diagnosis, Michael felt as if his own life had been put on hold. After Iris and John had returned to London, it had taken a little time to adjust to the absence of his grandson, who was totally delightful but very demanding. Now the weekends when they came down were like punctuation marks in the routines he and Fiammetta had established. He still went for his walk along the promenade to the New End each morning; Fiammetta tended to go for walks in the afternoons. He spent his days in the shop, reading the paper, although when customers came in and found him poring over the newsprint he'd have been pushed to say, if anyone had asked, what the news was. He had not been able to write, almost as if by not allowing himself to speculate about Fiammetta's future he had put a block on any creative capacity he possessed. Or perhaps it was just that nothing else seemed important. Or maybe, Michael sometimes thought, he was so old that his imagination extended only as far as planning what he would buy and cook for supper.

Michael paced and fidgeted, struggling to keep himself composed enough to react appropriately whether it was good news or bad. He decided to close the shop for the afternoon, unable to tolerate the potential irritation of being in the middle of dealing with a customer when Fiammetta returned. Upstairs, he did the washing-up, even though there wasn't much to do, and wiped down the surfaces; then, looking in the fridge, he decided to make macaroni cheese.

It was fortunate that he and Fiammetta both liked plain food, Michael thought, as he poured pasta into boiling water and grated the cheese. Or if she didn't she'd never said – unlike Bruno, who invariably sniffed and tasted the dishes Michael made, urging him to add a little cumin, or balsamic vinegar, or some other ingredient he didn't possess. Michael drained the pasta, layered it with the grated cheese in an ovenproof dish, scattering halved tomatoes to roast on top, then put it in the oven, breathing a sigh of satisfaction. But almost immediately, he wished he'd tried his hand at something much more complicated, because now he was waiting again, with nothing to distract him.

It was a beautiful day, but he didn't want to go out in case Fiammetta arrived back earlier than expected. Michael decided to make himself a cup of proper coffee with the coffee beans Iris brought down from London. Italy had given Iris a coffee habit that wasn't satisfied by a couple of strong cappuccinos every morning; it needed to be sated with espresso made in a little six-sided aluminium pot after every meal as well. The smell when Michael unsealed the brown-paper packet from the Algerian coffee shop in Old Compton Street brought back a flood of memories of coffee bars when he was a young man. Ground coffee still smelt like rebellion, sin, and Claudia, he thought, remembering them sitting at a table in the Expresso Bar when it first opened that very cold winter of 1961, the whoosh of the Gaggia machine making a fog of condensation on the plate-glass windows to hide their meaningful glances from the outside world. Michael smiled. Now that Fiammetta was living with him, he seemed to be allowed to have happy memories of Claudia in place of the perpetual torture of guilt and anguish. At last he was looking after their child as she would have wanted and he'd finally understood what she'd meant when she'd urged him: 'You mustn't go to pieces. You mustn't think of yourself the whole time!'

Michael took the macaroni cheese out of the oven. The tomatoes were slightly blackened, but the dish smelt good. There was some rocket Bruno had brought from the walled garden that they could have with it.

The sofa in the living area had become even lower with John using it as a trampoline, and as Michael sat down, some of his coffee slopped over the side of his mug and his teaspoon clattered to the floor. Bending to reach for it under the dilapidated seat, Michael's hand touched a hardback book. *The Unknown Soldier*, by Daphne W. Smythe.

The flap of the dust jacket marked the page where he had stopped when Fiammetta had arrived with her news, and he hadn't given the book a thought since then. He hadn't been able to think about anything much since then.

*   *   *

Iris glanced up at the clock in the kitchen when the phone rang. It must only be seven thirty in the morning in New York, she calculated, and yet Winston sounded as if he was ready for the day, whereas she had been up for four hours and hadn't done anything except take John to school and read the newspaper.

'How was he today?' Winston asked.

'Good,' Iris replied, not entirely truthfully.

Winston's business trip had coincided with the start of a

new school year and John was missing him because whenever Winston was at home he was the one who took John to school.

'Is it going to be you every day in year one?' he'd asked Iris that morning with a dramatic sigh, then dawdled so long getting dressed and brushing his teeth that she'd had to get a bit cross with him. He'd been quiet on their walk to school, and hadn't turned round to wave as his line traipsed into class as he usually did. Iris told herself it was a very good thing. John was letting go and it was great that he felt so confident so soon after the start of a new school year, but it still left her feeling a little bereft. She'd bought herself a Danish pastry from the pâtisserie on the way home, and a giant cappuccino with an extra shot of espresso, and sat on a high stool at the breakfast bar in the kitchen, reading the newspaper in an attempt to displace the vague feeling of inadequacy.

They'd decided that Iris would stay at home for the time being, since neither of them was able to stomach the idea of an au pair living in the house. It had been fine when John wasn't in full-time school, but now the hours between nine and three seemed to pass so slowly, and she felt that any talents she possessed were atrophying. Iris knew she needed to do something useful with her time and had begun to think about volunteering for one of Winston's many charities.

'There's something I want to talk to you about,' she told him now.

'Can it wait till I'm back? It's just that I have a breakfast meeting at the Marriott downtown . . .'

Winston sounded as if he was in a hurry. She pictured him in his suite at the Compton Club New York, with its huge warehouse windows looking out on to the Meat Packing district of Manhattan, mobile phone clamped between his chin and shoulder as he tied his laces and manoeuvred his arms into the sleeves of a jacket.

'OK,' she said.

'Sorry. You go ahead,' Winston said, knowing her so well that, even at a distance of three thousand miles, he could hear disappointment in her clipped tone.

'No, really. It's not important,' she assured him. 'Don't be late for your meeting. We're seeing you tomorrow anyway. John can't wait. Is there any chance you'll be back in time to take him to school?'

'I'm on the last flight out. It gets in at eight, so if we have a smooth run from the airport . . .'

'I won't tell him, just in case you can't,' Iris said.

'I'll be able to pick him up from school anyway,' Winston said, and she could tell from the warm timbre of his voice that the thought of it was making him smile.

'Any news of Fiammetta?' he asked.

'No. I thought this might be her, or Bruno.'

'I'll get off,' he said. 'I'll call you later.'

'No need if you're busy,' she told him.

'I need to say goodnight to John.'

'OK, then,' said Iris. 'Talk to you later.'

'Later,' he echoed. 'Love you!'

'Love you too!'

'And I love John. Tell him that.'

'I always do.'

'Miss you. Miss kissing you,' he said, with a certain thickness in his voice that meant he was thinking about sex.

'Go!' said Iris, laughing. 'You'll be late for your meeting.'

'I'm so lucky to have you and John,' he said.

'For heaven's sake! You're getting very American!'

'I love you.'

She imagined the words flying across miles and miles of ocean.

'I love you too,' she said quietly, realizing only then that he had put down the phone and she was speaking into space.

*   *   *

'I don't want to see you again for another year,' said Nikhil Patel, smiling across the desk at Fiammetta.

After girding herself against the worst, making herself rigid in case negative news would physically knock her off balance, Fiammetta suddenly felt as if she was floating.

'It's all clear?' she asked, trying to pin herself down, keep a grip.

'The tests we've run are all clear.'

Doctors, even Nikhil, talked in a kind of code, Fiammetta had discovered, that sounded reassuring when you were there, but became hollower when you went over it in your mind afterwards. Was it possible there were things they hadn't tested that might show different results?

'The cancer has gone?' she confirmed.

'If you have any problems at all, then get in touch, but there's no reason to think there will be.'

Nikhil stood up, walked round to her side of the desk and held out his hand.

So that was it, then. After all these months, it suddenly seemed too soon to be cast adrift, and she wasn't sure she was ready.

'Thank you for looking after me,' she said. It sounded completely inadequate, but she couldn't think of anything else.

'It's been my privilege,' he said.

She looked at his hand, then shook it with self-conscious formality, wanting instead to throw her arms round his neck and twirl as they had once when they were teenagers on the beach, round and round until they were so dizzy they crashed, breathless, to the sand.

'It feels strange saying goodbye,' she said. 'Not that I want to see you again!' she added, laughing.

She'd meant as a doctor, but from the wince that rippled across his face she realized that it hadn't sounded like that, and she was cross with herself because Nikhil always trod the line between professional distance and friendship so carefully. She wanted him to know how much she appreciated that, but she couldn't think of a way of telling him without sounding gushy and she thought that would make things even more awkward.

'Good luck!' he said.

'Yes,' said Fiammetta, turning to leave. 'Thank you.'

As she walked down the glass-sided corridor, she felt curiously deflated.

Bruno was waiting for her in the café on the ground floor, the cup of coffee in front of him still full. He leapt to his feet when he saw her, his face suspended between expectation and anxiety.

'All clear,' she mouthed, hardly daring to say the words.

'All clear!' he shouted, picking her up and twirling her round exactly as she had wanted Nikhil to, but it didn't feel right here in public when there were other people probably waiting for news of relatives too. Everyone had been so worried about her, and now she was OK, and all that fuss had been for nothing. She had prepared herself for dying, but not for living, and her brother's joy made her feel somehow fraudulent.

'I'm going to call Julia and tell her to put a bottle of Krug in the fridge!' Bruno told her.

'No, don't,' Fiammetta said. 'Not yet.'

'You said it was all clear . . .'

Fiammetta could see she'd worried him again. 'Yes, but I haven't worked out how I feel about it yet,' she tried to explain, but she could see her brother had no idea what she was talking about.

*   *   *

Cat's father was wearing a suit when he arrived at the bookshop, and she was touched that he had made a special effort on this first occasion he had visited her in her place of work, and a little guilty that she hadn't thought of inviting him to come into town and have lunch with her before. In this different setting, he seemed ill at ease and, even though he'd spent a lifetime commuting into Whitehall to work, awed looking up at the gleaming City towers as they walked along the crowded narrow pavements.

The tapas bar where she'd booked a table for lunch was in a basement and bare brick walls made it feel a bit like a cave. Cat and Danny had been there a couple of times after work, drinking fino sherry at the bar amid an ebullient crowd of traders, but at lunch time it was empty and smelt musty, like the end of a cork.

Cat regretted that she hadn't thought of buying sandwiches from M & S and sitting outside on a bench in the sunshine. It was one of those beautiful September days that arrived each year just after the end of the school holidays. Every birthday Cat could remember had been sunny and blue, with a faint edge of crispness in the air, like a barely audible warning that autumn was on its way.

'Are you looking forward to your trip?' her father asked, when they'd ordered from the long menu.

'Very much!' said Cat.

For a birthday treat, Finn had surprised her with a trip to New York, but she hadn't been able to find her passport. It was possible to get a new one quickly, she found out, but you had to present yourself in person at the Passport Office, with identification, including your birth certificate. It had been her father who'd sent the forms off for the original passport because she'd been away at university. Today, he'd volunteered to come into town with the certificate, saving her the journey.

Cat had never been to New York, and never been on a romantic weekend, except, once, to Paris with Roy, when he'd been attending a seminar at the Sorbonne, so she'd spent most of the time alone. The combination of spending long lazy days with Finn, and exploring places like Central Park, Little Italy and the Guggenheim, which she felt she knew already from books and television and movies, was so impossibly exciting she couldn't stop smiling whenever she thought about it.

'Where are you staying?' her father asked.

'At the Plaza, if you can believe it!' said Cat.

She thought it was probably the only hotel that would mean anything to her father, because he enjoyed *Plaza Suite* with Walter Matthau whenever it was on television. She was thrilled that Finn had chosen a huge, iconic New York hotel rather than somewhere small and cutting edge like the Compton Club, New York, even though Esther had informed her it was 'the only place at the moment'. The Plaza would have a certain anonymity. Cat always found the ultra-cool staff at the Compton Club in Soho slightly intimidating, and she didn't want to feel that people were judging her at breakfast.

'That'll be costing a fortune,' her father said.

'I'm trying not to think about it,' said Cat.

'He must be serious about you!'

It was such an unusually personal remark for her father to make, Cat felt herself blushing.

'We are serious about each other, Daddy,' she said quietly.

'We're very glad you've found someone,' he said.

As she tried to engage her father's eyes, she saw that there were tears waiting to fall. They were relatively old parents. Perhaps they worried what would happen to her. She hadn't realized how much seeing her settled meant to them, and she didn't know what to say now. The moment was interrupted by the waitress depositing three ceramic plates on the table.

'*Pulpo con patatas, calamares, tortilla,*' she said.

'I mustn't forget to give you this . . .' Cat's father took an envelope out of the breast pocket of his suit and put it on the table. 'But first I need to explain something.' His finger tapped the envelope repeatedly. 'I wanted to tell you, believe me. I always wanted to . . . but . . . I didn't . . . I can't blame anyone else for that now . . .'

'What?' Cat asked him, alarmed by his sudden change of demeanour.

'It's not a birth certificate,' he said.

The words seemed to echo in the empty underground space.

'What is it, then?' Cat asked him, with a tentative smile, as if he was teasing her with a riddle.

'It's an adoption certificate.'

Somehow, she knew immediately that it wasn't a joke.

'Adoption certificate?' she repeated.

'We adopted you.'

Afterwards, she thought how strange it was that she hadn't felt anything at all at that point, not anger, not even doubt.

'When?' she asked.

'You were only a couple of weeks old.'

'Why?'

'We'd been trying for years . . .'

'Not you!' she interrupted. 'Why . . . why did my . . .' She couldn't say the word mother. Mother was the anxious little woman she'd known all her life, who wasn't her mother after all. 'Why was I given up?' she finally asked.

'She was a young girl. Unmarried. The usual story . . .' said the man Cat had always suspected of having a secret. But not this one. Not this secret.

'The usual story?' Cat repeated, incredulously.

'I mean, we didn't know much about her,' he told her. 'To be honest, we didn't want to.'

'You've lied to me all my life,' Cat said quietly, stating a fact.

'It wasn't the same in those days.' He tried to reach across the table to take her hand, but she scraped her chair back from the table, unable to bear the idea of him touching her. 'I always wanted to tell you, when you were old enough,' he said.

'I'm thirty-two! How old did I have to be?'

'It was your mother. She was scared.'

'Scared of what?' Cat demanded.

'Of losing you,' he said, with a defeated shrug, as if he realized, Cat thought, that her mother's fear had just become a self-fulfilling prophesy.

'When she had her breakdown . . .'

'Her breakdown?' Cat repeated. Nothing made any sense, and yet at the same time it all made perfect sense.

'She became obsessed that you were going to be taken away,' he explained. 'Don't you remember? She wouldn't open the door, stood all day at the school gate . . .'

A long-forgotten memory flew across Cat's mind: looking out of the classroom window, seeing her mother standing in the rain, going back to her sums, praying that when she looked up again her mother would have gone, but she was still standing there.

'Was it raining when she had her breakdown?' she asked.

'It rained non-stop that autumn,' her father recalled. 'Needed to after that summer. The long hot summer . . .'

'Nineteen seventy-six?' Cat interrupted.

'It was the year we had the caravan,' he said. 'We thought we'd be a bit adventurous, try a couple of new places, but the first place we arrived, Joyce saw her . . . That was the beginning of it.'

'Saw who?'

'Your mother. Your real mother. Or, at least, that's what Joyce thought. There was a family a couple of caravans along. Funny crowd. An older man with this young woman who looked a bit odd.'

'Odd?'

'Sort of punk, I suppose you'd call it. Her hair was all

spiky. Black on top, ginger underneath. Joyce was convinced it was her. I couldn't see it.'

'Had you met my real mother?' Cat asked.

'We both caught a glimpse of her when we went to the mother-and-baby home. She looked like a nice enough girl to me . . . Well, after that, the holiday was finished as far as Joyce was concerned. We went along the coast, but she was too scared. If we could bump into them in one place, we could in another, so we came home, bought a paddling pool for you . . .'

Another memory: sitting in a bright-blue blow-up pool under the shade of the copper beech tree at the end of their suburban garden, reading *James and the Giant Peach*, and being so absorbed she didn't hear her mother calling her in for lunch, wasn't aware of her walking down the lawn, and jumped when she spoke, because she'd just got to the bit where Aunt Sponge and Aunt Spiker were being horrible to James.

'Here you are!' Her mother's voice contained a note of irritation, as if Cat had been deliberately avoiding her.

She'd been unable to see her mother's face because the sunshine was so bright behind it.

'What's that you're reading?'

'It's a story about a little boy whose parents are eaten by a giant rhinoceros . . . and then he flies to New York in a big peach.'

'Doesn't sound very suitable to me.' Her mother held out her hand to take it.

'It was a shame, really, because you loved that caravan . . .' her father was saying.

It's not about the bloody caravan, Cat wanted to shout at him. It had meant so much to him, that taste of freedom.

'Were the children about my age?' Cat suddenly asked, another memory shooting across her brain: two children playing in the rainbow spray from the standpipe at the site, and wanting so much to join in with their game, but not knowing how to ask.

Her father looked blank.

'Those children at the caravan park?' she reminded him.

'I suppose they were. It's a long time ago. I can't think what the place was called . . .'

'Kingshaven,' said Cat. 'It was called Kingshaven.'

*   *   *

Another lovely day, thought Libby King, looking up from the reservations book, her face bathed in the sunshine that was pouring in through the office window. It was often the case that the weather improved just after the guests had gone home. Not that there had been many guests this year.

Libby flipped through the advance bookings. Only the usual coach party of retired Americans who always came towards the end of September when the prices went down but the weather was still good. Otherwise the pages were blank. The only people who wanted to holiday in Kingshaven now were those with second homes. Libby couldn't think of a single guesthouse that hadn't been converted into apartments, except the Edwardian terrace that had become Mr Patel's old people's home. The Palace would eventually go one way or the other. In some respects it already felt like an old people's home, with Liliana so frail and Pearl sitting in her wheelchair.

Pearl had stepped into too hot a bath, scalding her feet very badly. How she could have forgotten to test the water was anyone's guess. Eddie guessed it was something to do with the half-empty bottle of gin he'd found on Pearl's kitchen table after the ambulance had taken her to hospital. Afterwards, she had come to stay at the Palace with them, and Libby couldn't honestly see her being able to return to her own home again. The accident seemed to have knocked the life out of her, turning her suddenly into an old lady. Although Pearl had begun to lose her youthful complexion and figure quite early on in middle age, her effervescent spirit had never faded. Sometimes, that *joie de vivre* had been embarrassing, sometimes downright shameful, but now Libby found herself missing her sister's ridiculously flirtatious antics and positively hoping to see those violet eyes light up once again with mischief. It was difficult to believe that this haunted, bloated creature with bandaged feet had once been the belle of the South Coast. Pearl had been so beautiful – a young Elizabeth Taylor, everyone had said.

Libby remembered playing tennis with her one summer during the war. It must have been close to D-Day because the hotel had been full of airmen, so Pearl would have been fifteen at most, but she'd been so much more worldly than Libby, who was four years her senior. When Pearl, a very competent tennis player, had missed the easiest of forehands, she'd bent very slowly to pick up the ball, and Libby had observed all the airmen crammed round the attic windows of the hotel watching, and heard the cheer go up, well aware that it was not her winning shot that the boys were applauding.

It was a mystery to Libby how she and her sister could be so different, since they'd both been brought up under the all-seeing blue eyes of their mother. One had always been well-behaved, the other wanton. Dutiful and beautiful, her mother used to say. There had been scandal in the King family before Pearl, of course, with the peculiar elopement of Uncle Rex, which no one was ever allowed to mention. Perhaps it was simply a case of Pearl inheriting a bad gene.

Libby looked again at the reservations book. Once the Americans had gone, there was really no point in keeping the hotel open for the winter. They would close at the end of September, she decided. Usually they waited until the clocks went back, but what would be the point? Each year the season got shorter and shorter. Sometimes when Libby bade farewell to the staff, she stood in the empty hall wondering whether she'd ever open the doors to guests again.

There was no place for hotels like the Palace in the twenty-first century. Clean sheets, a trouser press and a hairdryer were no longer enough. Now, people expected queen-size beds, free slippers and flat-screen televisions on the walls in place of a restful watercolour, and Libby was far too old to start getting involved with sushi and celebrities. It was Julia who was good at all that. You couldn't sell anything without a celebrity these days. Julia had cottoned on to that quickly, hitching herself to that television chef – who'd not so long ago been a kitchen boy at the Palace! There'd been a feature on them in the copy of *Hello!* magazine that Libby bought for Pearl, who was normally agog for all that nonsense but had barely glanced at it when Libby pointed to the headline: **BENVENUTO TO BRUNO'S NEW VENTURE!**

There was a photo-spread of the two of them dressed up in various designer outfits (how Julia would have loved that part!), lounging by the new pool, leaning over the billiard table, picking salad leaves from the walled garden. And if that wasn't bad enough, the interview had contained Julia's usual sob story about triumphing over adversity, with full details about what she called an 'eating disorder', and a recipe for profiteroles on the opposite page. There was no dignity any more.

Tradition was what the Kings had always done best – crustless cucumber sandwiches in the lounge, a proper cream tea, and a leather-bound reservations book, not a website, Libby thought. She walked into the hall. The porcelain clock that always ran a bit slow was a metaphor for them all. The Kings had never been very good at keeping up with the times.

*   *   *

In the converted warehouse, Michael flipped through the first two chapters of Daphne W. Smythe's *The Unknown Soldier* to remind himself of the plot, and was about to begin chapter three.

Dr Winifred Smith and the policeman, Sergeant Carr, had just turned over the body on the beach.

> *'But, it's the boy in the demob suit!' Dr Smith exclaimed.*
>
> *His hair, though a shade darker because of its submersion in water, was still distinctly red, and his blue eyes were open, giving his freckled face a startled expression.*
>
> *'You know him?' asked Sergeant Carr.*
>
> *'I don't know him exactly,' said Dr Smith. 'But he's staying at the hotel.'*
>
> *'A foreigner, then,' said Sergeant Carr, using the local term for visitors to Haven Regis. 'Unfamiliar with the tides. They see the sea and think it's safe for bathing . . .'*
>
> *It was clear to Dr Smith that the policeman was jumping to conclusions. 'Unusual to take a swim in a suit,' she pointed out. One of the man's shoes had come off in the water, otherwise he was fully clothed.*
>
> *The policeman scratched his head.*
>
> *'And from the way that his spine is pushing up into his brain, I'd say he'd fallen from a considerable height . . .'*
>
> *Simultaneously, the policeman and the doctor raised their eyes to look at the cliffs towering above.*
>
> *'The question is,' said Sergeant Carr. 'Did he fall, or did he jump?*

Michael Quinn suddenly stopped reading, and turned back to the previous page to the description of the young man. Red hair, blue eyes, freckled face. Then he flicked to the copyright notice. 1946. Was it a coincidence? The description fitted his brother Frank, and his brother Frank had jumped from the very cliffs the author was describing, in the year before the book was published.

Perhaps Daphne W. Smythe had read about the tragedy in the local paper, he thought. Michael had looked up the reference himself in the *Chronicle*'s microfiche archive when he was working on his *Brief History of Kingshaven*. There had been a short paragraph announcing that a body had been found, and the following week the body had been identified with his brother's name. That was all. Michael was quite sure that there hadn't been a description of Frank's colouring.

Had Daphne W. Smythe been staying in Kingshaven that summer between VE Day and VJ Day when Frank had come back? Surely Frank could not have stayed at the Palace Hotel as a guest? He didn't have the money for that.

And yet, Michael thought, it was exactly the sort of thing Frank would have done. His brother had always had a taste for the high life, taking his girlfriends to fancy restaurants, treating them to extravagant gifts he bought from a bloke in the pub with a jacket full of gold watches. Frank was a chancer. It would have been typical of him to challenge the snooty hoteliers to turn him away in his civvies, when he'd stayed there in uniform, doing his duty for the country.

But what had brought him back to Kingshaven instead of coming home?

Michael picked up the book again.

'What possible reason could that young man have to jump?' asked Dr Smith.

'An accident, then,' said Sergeant Carr. 'Lost his footing. Easy enough to slip on wet grass . . .'

'We haven't had rain for days,' Dr Smith reminded him.

Michael's reading began to speed up now, skipping quickly over the description of the recovery of the body and the policeman and the doctor's return journey to the harbour. When Dr Smith finally arrived back at the hotel, supper was in progress, and she ate a substantial meal of oysters, followed by turbot in parsley sauce (in his mind, Michael pictured her as a stout woman who enjoyed her food, although perhaps the unusually detailed description was a consequence of rationing making food so scarce it could only be savoured on the page), before sitting down in the lounge to chat about the gruesome events of the day.

Chapter Four was entitled *'Dr Smith's Suspicions are Aroused'*.

As she was not a professional detective, Dr Smith's interviewing technique was indirect, but she managed to extract an account of what each of the guests had been doing that day.

Michael galloped through the statements.

The squadron leader had been visiting the grave of his wife; the honeymooning couple had stayed in their room until mid morning, when they'd emerged to go down to the beach; the insurance agent had been suffering a migraine, but similarly left the hotel at around eleven in the hope of clearing his head with a brisk walk along the promenade; the butcher had been to the matinée at the Pier Theatre; the antique-loving spinsters had gone to value the contents of a local manor house that was coming up for auction. No one had seen the young man since breakfast, and they all appeared convincingly surprised by the news of his death. Not as shocked, however, as the young daughter of the proprietors, Miss Perdita Prince, who, on hearing the news, became utterly inconsolable.

Had Perdita seen the young man this morning, Dr Smith probed gently, perhaps down at the beach when she went for her swim?

Dr Smith had been looking out of the window of her room at the time, and noticed Perdita sauntering down the terraces of the hotel garden towards the cliff path that led down to the hotel's beach huts. Dr Smith had still been looking, a couple of minutes later, when the young man had taken exactly the same route.

Perdita stared at Dr Smith, violet eyes brimming with distress, her plump lower lip quivering.

'No,' she said eventually, as her mother, Lucilla Prince, walked into the lounge.

Pulling off her gloves and smiling with the satisfaction of a successful day's shopping, the hotel's proprietor suddenly noticed the distinctly sombre expressions of her guests.

'Whatever has happened?' she asked.

Michael turned the page to chapter five, and stared at the title: 'A Pair of Dancing Shoes'.

Dr Smith made a clandestine search of the young man's room, where she found no clues apart from the curious presence of a pair of shiny black shoes with smooth unscratched leather soles that Michael could picture exactly, not because of the particularity of the description, but because a similar pair had been returned along with Frank's shaving brush and demob clothes. Sometimes Michael had taken the shoes out of their stiff cardboard box and slid his hands into the velvety nap of the beige leather lining that had been just a sock away from his brother's skin. Occasionally he had wondered what on earth could have been going through his brother's head as he handed over a small fortune for this last purchase.

Now convinced that the book was a barely disguised

account of Frank's death, Michael galloped through Daphne W. Smythe's convoluted red herrings.

One by one, the suspects' stories unravelled as further dark secrets emerged.

The butcher's resistance to questioning turned out to be a result of anxiety about his German origins being exposed. Michael recalled that the real King family had anglicized their own name from Konig during the First World War.

It appeared that the 'fast-looking' wife of the respectable-looking 'honeymooning' gentleman was in fact a girl he'd hired for the purpose of facilitating a divorce from his wife so that he could marry someone else entirely.

The so-called insurance agent was the private detective employed to witness the 'adultery', and his unveiling provided Dr Smith with a useful foil with whom to discuss her theories – a Hastings to her Poirot – Michael thought, although for a person employed in the investigative trade the private detective was rather slow to remember the curious event he had witnessed earlier in the day: having followed his couple down to the beach, he had been hiding behind a closed beach hut, taking notes on the 'honeymooning' couple, when he had heard singing coming from inside another hut:

'Oh, soldier, soldier, won't you marry me, with your musket, fife and drum?'

'Oh, no, sweet maid, I cannot marry you, 'cos I have no shoes to put on . . .'

When Dr Smith pressed the private detective to identify the voices, he could only say that the woman's clearly belonged to someone young and well-bred, but the man's was distinctly less cultured.

The antique-dealing ladies, Minnie and Dorrie, though sweet and innocuous on the surface, were involved in a scam with the local auctioneer to declare a priceless Roman sculpture a Victorian copy and subsequently purchase it for virtually nothing. However, once their own ignominious alibi had been established, they became less cautious under questioning, revealing that they had overheard something going on during the morning before the soldier's death. The spinsters' room was next door to the Windsor Suite. According to the hotel's reservation book, the room had been unoccupied by guests, but the sound of the couple cavorting inside had carried through the open French doors and on to the balcony of the next-door room, where Minnie was performing her callisthenic exercises. After it was over, Minnie reported, discreetly leaving the type of noise she had overheard to Dr Smith's imagination, there had been some indistinct murmuring, an arrangement to meet on the cliffs.

Michael tore his eyes from the page, put the book down and got up from the sofa in a kind of daze. In his writing room, he searched his desk for the old manilla envelope in which he kept all Frank's letters to him. The letter he was looking for had been written when Frank was billeted at the Palace Hotel during the build-up to D-Day:

Dear Mike,
   Still no call to arms, so we're stuck here, twiddling our thumbs (and some other parts of our anatomy!), and I've been sampling the amenities. The posh rooms have names painted on the door. The other day, I partook of a cigarette on the balcony of the Windsor Suite . . . there's a chandelier of peacock feathers, like something out of Tsarist Russia. Long live the revolution, I say, although, 'til that day comes, it's nice to have a bit (of luxury, that is!). The beds are so soft it's like you're sinking into a cloud . . .

The message between the lines was clearly that Frank had found a girl to amuse him, and Michael had always imagined his brother with a chambermaid, someone his own class.

Pearl King could only have been fifteen then, but she had always been very advanced, very determined to get what she wanted, and very, very sexy. Had she lured Frank when he was billeted at the Palace? Was she the reason his brother had returned to Kingshaven? Surely Frank couldn't have imagined that he and Pearl could elope together? He must have known that Liliana King would never have allowed it. Had Frank killed himself because of a broken heart?

Michael could imagine his brother fancying Pearl, as any man would. But loving her?

Returning the letters to their envelope, he paused to trace a finger over his name and childhood address, written long ago in handwriting that seemed to summon Frank's presence more effectively than any photo. Michael's eyes blurred with grief, and then he went downstairs and picked up the novel again.

The sixth chapter was entitled 'The Missing Gun'.

Having extracted what information she could from the other guests, Dr Winifred Smith's attention now turned to the staff at the Majestic Hotel. None of them remembered noticing anything untoward, except a chambermaid who declared, red-faced, that while 'tidying' the squadron leader's drawers two mornings ago she had found a gun among his socks. The odd thing was that it hadn't been there when she tidied again on the morning of the soldier's death, although it had since been replaced. Finding the girl rather fanciful, Dr Smith chose to ignore this evidence. While the doctor had not performed a thorough post-mortem on the soldier, there had been no visible signs of violence, and certainly no bullet wound. In any case, a serving officer such as a squadron leader was surely entitled, even obliged, to bear arms. The missing gun, if there had indeed been a missing gun, was rapidly discounted from Dr Smith's investigations.

Michael was still as suspicious of the upright squadron leader as he had been from the beginning of the novel, and he began reading the penultimate chapter, convinced that a flaw in the squadron leader's alibi was about to be revealed. Instead, the chapter, entitled 'The Lady of the House', took the plot in a completely different direction.

Michael read with horrible fascination, the logical part of his brain telling him that this was a work of fiction, his instincts insisting that this was a plausible account of real events. The implications seemed as incredible to Michael as they did to Sergeant Carr, the hapless policeman in the book, and yet . . .

The final paragraph of *The Unknown Soldier* was most unusual.

> *The Coroner recorded an open verdict. As Sergeant Carr explained at some length to Dr Smith, conjecture and psychological insights were all very well, but what police needed to prosecute was evidence.*
> *This was not a detective novel.*

Michael read the last sentence again and again. Daphne W. Smythe was not the type of author to end her fiction with a surrealist joke and he was sure the average reader of a classic crime novel would not want an ending in which the villain not only escaped justice, but detection as well. So why had she chosen to end her book in that way?

'Daddy? Daddy?'

Michael had not heard the front door open, nor Fiammetta's light footsteps on the stairs. Immersed in the past, he had abandoned the present. He looked up into blue eyes just like Frank's looking down at him. And suddenly he remembered where she had been and what she might be about to tell him.

'They gave me the all clear!' she said.

The all clear! In his head, Michael could hear the wonderful wailing siren that used to bring an end to terror during the war, telling everyone that they'd escaped to live another day.

*   *   *

In the school playground, John's class were standing with their teacher, one or two children peeling off every few seconds when they spotted the adult who had come to pick them up. John was the tallest, and his royal-blue school sweatshirt and grey trousers made him look quite grown-up. Hanging back for a moment to observe from a distance, Iris saw that though her son was champing to be off the leash, he was making himself stand still. In repose, his face was cool and collected, like Winston's, but when he saw Iris it morphed into a smile of such high voltage she felt her own face light up as he ran towards her. She bent to hug him tight, absorbing some of his energy, inhaling his delicious smell – baby shampoo and powdered poster paint mingling with a faint sweet whiff of fart.

'What did you do today?' she asked him as they walked away from the crowd together.

'Self-portrait,' said John nonchalantly.

'Really?'

'For the calendar.'

Each year, the school produced a calendar, featuring the children's drawings of their own faces reproduced in the month of their birthdays. When John was in the Reception class, Iris had needed help to pick out his likeness, but had been pleased to see that the line he'd etched for his mouth was curved upwards in a smile.

'Anything else?' she asked.

John thought for a moment. 'Don't think so,' he said. 'Is Daddy back yet?'

'Not quite yet,' Iris told him. 'But he'll be back tomorrow and he says he's going to pick you up from school!'

'Cool!' said John.

Iris found it weird that 'cool', the word her own generation had coined as teenagers that had seemed rather sophisticated and exclusive at the time, was now so universal that everyone from five-year-olds to grandparents happily used it.

'What shall we do?' Iris asked John as they walked down the tree-lined street towards the Heath. The slight edge in the late-summer air brought a sharp memory of another September, long ago, sitting on a bench with a pram parked beside her, gazing from the infinite expanse of blue sky to the tiny sleeping face tucked in under a cellular blanket.

'Telly!' said John, snapping her back to the present.

'On a lovely afternoon like this?'

Iris wished that there were a few more choices. If they were in Kingshaven, they could play football on the beach, or make a dam of sand across the stream, or go on a treasure hunt for fossils or interesting objects people had left behind. Iris clearly remembered the joy of finding a pearl earring in the sand in front of the beach huts, and knowing she should probably hand it in to the man who issued tickets for the deckchairs from a machine like a bus conductor, but, instead, putting it in her pocket and hiding it in a ball of sock at home, occasionally taking it out and holding it on her palm, feeling the curiously human warmth of the pearl, then wrapping it up again and shoving it to the back of the drawer, the first secret she had kept.

It was too late for the zoo and too cold for a swim in the pond. As they stood waiting to cross the busy road that ran down the side of the Heath, stepping back from the kerb as a lorry thundered past, Iris wondered whether London was really a suitable place to bring up a child, then couldn't believe she'd caught herself thinking that. She'd spent her entire life trying to get away from Kingshaven. Surely it was unthinkable to consider returning now?

'Let's go and look at the view,' she suggested, taking John's hand firmly.

'Views are boring!' said John.

'Afterwards, we can go down to the playground,' she offered.

'And to Marine Ices?' John clearly sensed an opportunity for negotiation.

Iris looked at his bright little face. 'If you're very good indeed,' she said.

'Deal,' said John, putting his hand up for a high five.

*   *   *

The ramparts of the Iron Age Fort were covered in heather and wild flowers.

'Like a gorgeous carpet!' Fiammetta said to Michael as they reached the summit and turned slowly on the spot to take in the whole panorama.

It was Fiammetta who had suggested they go for a walk together, when their crying came abruptly to an end, as if there were a finite number of tears and they had cried them all.

Michael had asked her to call Iris, because he knew she was waiting for news, but she was out, probably picking John up, so she'd left a message on the answerphone. Since leaving the house, Fiammetta had barely spoken, and Michael let himself lag behind as if he was finding the climb difficult. But she waited for him, holding out her tiny hand to help pull him up the last few metres, and her grip was surprisingly strong and vigorous, a reaffirmation that she had survived. The thought was becoming easier to permit, and his relief was so profound it was all Michael, a lifelong atheist, could do to stop himself shouting 'Thank you!' up at the vast dome of blue September sky.

'May I stay a while longer?' Fiammetta asked suddenly.

Michael smiled broadly, nodding his head, as he walked away from her, across the hillocky, bumpy turf. There was sea thrift growing on the cliff edge, soft pink flowers treacherously disguising the line where land met air. The only safe way of looking over was to lie on his stomach, spreading his weight on firm ground, allowing his eyes to peep over. The tide was high and the waves were lapping against the edge of the cliff. There was no beach today. Michael stared down, as if by looking long enough into the undulating water the truth might come to him.

'What are you doing, Daddy?' There was a laugh of disbelief in Fiammetta's voice behind him.

'I'm sorry,' he said, clambering to his feet, brushing bits of grass from his trousers. 'I thought you wanted to be alone for a while.'

'You didn't answer my question,' she said, linking his arm as they walked away from the cliff edge.

'What question?'

She looked at him as if he were getting old and silly. Maybe he was. 'About me staying,' she repeated, with exaggerated patience.

'You mean with me? At the warehouse?'

She nodded.

'But of course! You don't need to ask!'

What a funny little thing she was! Impossible to know what was going on in her mind. And she'd always been like that, he thought, because Claudia had seen it.

'I know what to say to Bruno,' she'd told him, when she was trying to write letters to them in the days before she died. 'But I never know what Fiammetta is thinking.'

It was something he'd never told Fiammetta, and he wondered if he should, whether it would make sense to her now.

Maybe not right now. Not today. Today, of all days, should be about going forward, he thought, not looking back.

It was beginning to get a little chilly in the breeze.

'I've made a macaroni cheese,' Michael said suddenly.

'I was just thinking how hungry I was!' Fiammetta exclaimed.

'Ready to go back now?' he asked.

'Yes,' she said. 'Yes. I think so.'

*   *   *

It was only when the answerphone picked up the call and Cat could hear Finn's voice in the flat with her that she realized where she was. It was as if she'd been sleeping.

She picked up the receiver to interrupt his message. 'Hello?'

'You're there?' he said.

'I'm here,' she replied, looking round the living room, slightly surprised herself.

She had no memory of leaving the restaurant, but recalled standing on the bridge everyone called the wobbly bridge, though it no longer wobbled, that stretched across the river from the Tate Modern to St Paul's, and a woman with a pushchair asking her, 'Are you all right?' as she stared at the water bulging in the river below.

After that, Cat had caught a bus, and sat in the front seat upstairs, not really noticing or caring where the bus was going as frames from her life ran through her brain like a film shot by a different camera, seen from a different angle.

The image that kept returning was her father staring at her as she pretended to sleep in a dark room full of questions. She'd always known that he was trying to find the courage to tell her something, but the stories she had imagined were far more intriguing than the prosaic truth.

'I called the shop. They said you hadn't come back after lunch . . . ?' Finn was saying.

Her brain told her she should be touched at his concern, but she could feel nothing at all.

'I came home,' she said.

The flat they'd rented in Tufnell Park had a large sash window and she could see her reflection in the panes.

Cat remembered standing next to her mother once as they washed their hands in the row of basins in the public toilets in a shopping mall.

'We look so different!' she'd said to her mother's reflection in the mirror, and her mother had looked very pale. She'd put it down to the artificial light.

'You're all right?' Finn was asking.

Cat knew she should say yes, but it was too simple an answer, and yet she could not begin to tell him on the phone.

'Something has happened,' she said.

Even that was wrong. It wasn't that anything had happened. Everything was exactly as it had been, except that now she knew.

'I just wanted to make sure you were all right.'

How did he know? Had she called him? Cat couldn't think properly.

'What time is it?' she asked.

'It's four o'clock,' he said. 'Did you see the towers go down?'

Cat's brain tried to compute the sentence. Did she see the towers go down? He'd said it as if it were a completely normal question, and yet she didn't understand and it repeated in her brain like an unsolved crossword clue.

'What do you mean?' she asked, almost as if she was in one of those Alice in Wonderland dreams where everything was going along normally, then strange things started to happen and you were the only one who didn't understand.

'Don't you know what's happened?' Finn asked.

Of course she knew, but how did he know? Belatedly, she realized that he must be talking about something else.

'What?' she asked.

'Turn on the television,' he told her.

On the screen, there were pictures of people running, covering their faces, as a great dust cloud chased them up the street, like a film, but not a film. Definitely not a film.

'What's happened?' Cat asked, staring at an iconic Manhattan skyline with the twin towers of the World Trade Center gleaming in sunshine, one with clouds of smoke billowing from the top, strangely serene, like a giant candle; a small black plane hurtling out of the blue, piercing the other tower, then a burst of fire and disbelieving voices saying, 'Oh my God! Oh my God!'

A tower collapsing like a perfectly executed demolition, creating a bulging dust cloud that obliterated the blue.

'There's been a terrorist attack in New York,' Finn was telling her. 'They flew planes into both towers of the World Trade Center . . . It's Armageddon there.'

New York. They were going to New York at the weekend. The Plaza Hotel. Her passport . . . It didn't make any sense.

'Are you OK?' Finn was asking her.

'No,' she managed finally. 'No, I don't think I am.'

'I'm coming home,' Finn told her. 'Sit down and I'll be there as soon as I can.'

Was this what it felt like when the world was ending, Cat wondered, staring at the screen. Everything had changed. In just a few hours. The whole world had changed. Was this what it felt like at the beginning of World War Three?

She didn't know how long it took Finn to get back and fold her in his arms, as she sobbed uncontrollably, her whole body shaking, until the shoulder of his shirt was wet with tears and she could only snort, not breathe any more.

'I know, I know . . .' Finn tried to soothe her, but she

could tell he was alarmed by her reaction. It wasn't like her. She could almost feel him thinking it.

Would he still love her if she was different? The thought brought another flood of crying and gasping.

'It's something else . . .' she tried to tell him, thinking how insignificant her story was compared with what had happened.

'What?' he said, drawing back to look at her face.

'It's nothing . . . My father . . .'

'Your father's ill?'

'No, no . . . He was bringing my birth certificate – for my passport?'

Finn nodded, trying to understand.

'But it was my adoption certificate.'

For the first time, Cat wondered if she even had a birth certificate, or were adopted children only deemed to exist *when* they were adopted? She should have asked her father. She had left him in the restaurant. Was he still there? Or had he gone home? Had he told her mother what he was going to do? Had they talked about it? Were they waiting anxiously for her to call? Or had he not dared to go home? Perhaps he was sitting in a park somewhere, watching ducks.

'You were adopted?' Finn asked softly.

Nodding, Cat looked into his face, trying to gauge from his expression whether it made any difference to him.

Finally he spoke. 'Well, that kind of makes sense of things, doesn't it?' he said, smiling at her.

It was as if an extraordinarily complex puzzle she had been trying to solve all her life had suddenly fallen into place.

Cat took his kind, intelligent face in her hands and drew his mouth on to hers. Kissing him with every molecule of tenderness she possessed, discovering a place of tranquillity in the midst of chaos.

*   *   *

387

Michael always had the radio on when he was making tea, but it took a few moments to register what the presenter was saying, and when he did he immediately switched on the television.

He called Fiammetta down and they both watched in silence, until she asked, like a little girl, 'What do you think will happen, Daddy?'

He had experienced the exact same dread once before during the Cuban missile crisis, when the world had teetered on the brink of nuclear annihilation. They'd only recently got a television, he remembered, and, with extraordinary irony, a travelling salesman had rung their doorbell, offering to demonstrate the benefits of a home fire extinguisher, just as Kennedy's speech announcing the blockade began. Sylvia had urged Michael to come and see – there was nothing more important than safety, she'd called, echoing the salesman's spiel – and Michael had shouted back, 'We're going to need something a lot bigger than a portable fire extinguisher!'

How would this President of the United States rise to the occasion, Michael wondered? The pictures of George W. Bush receiving the news were not exactly reassuring. Apparently, he'd now been whisked away into hiding.

'What do you think will happen?' Michael asked Anthony that evening, when he rang.

'We all need to stand firm with the US,' Anthony told him, spouting the official line.

'But what does that actually mean?' Michael tried to engage him.

'They'll want to punish the people who have done this,' said Anthony. 'We'll have to zap Afghanistan, unless they hand over Bin Laden, which I doubt.'

Anthony and his New Labour peers came from a generation who had not lived through war, Michael thought. For them, 'zapping' a weak country was a privilege of the power at the disposal of a developed economy. They used the terminology of computer games, because none of them had experienced the sheer messiness of war, and all its consequences.

'The reason I was ringing,' said Anthony, clearly unwilling to get into the tedium of debating with a pacifist, 'was to see how Fiammetta got on?'

Her news was only a few hours old, Michael thought, recalling that golden moment of relief, and yet it seemed to belong to another era now.

*   *   *

'That'll be a bit of a shock to the Yanks!' said Eddie, as they watched the news for the umpteenth time. 'They've never known what it was to be attacked.'

'There was Pearl Harbor,' Libby reminded him.

'That was in Hawaii, bloody miles away!'

'Nevertheless, they did send their men.' Libby had never succumbed to her husband's anti-Americanism. She'd always found Americans very polite, and there was no getting away from the fact that their dollars had kept the Palace going over the years.

'Eventually,' Eddie grudgingly admitted.

'I expect it'll mean the coach party cancels,' Libby said gloomily. 'Nobody's going to want to fly after this, are they?'

*   *   *

The answerphone was bleeping when Iris and John arrived back. By the time they'd reached Marine Ices after a long walk over the Heath he'd been hungry, so she'd ordered a bowl of pasta to eat before his ice cream, and watched him wolfing down his supper as she stirred froth into her cappuccino. They'd caught the bus back up Haverstock Hill, arriving home much later than she'd planned.

'That's probably Daddy!' Iris told him, pressing the button to play back the message, but it wasn't Winston. It was Fiammetta.

'I've been given the all clear! Hope you're OK. Big kiss to John!'

'What's all clear?' John wanted to know.

'You know Fiammetta wasn't feeling very well . . .' Iris started to explain, conscious that she'd not given John the best explanation of what had been happening. She always tried to be honest with him, but there were times when the truth was beyond his comprehension. When Fiammetta's hair fell out, Iris hadn't wanted to say it was because she was ill, in case John was frightened that his hair would fall out if he was poorly. So she'd told him that it was because of the strong medicine Fiammetta had to take, but that had resulted in his refusal to take Calpol when he had a temperature. It was best to say as little as possible.

'Well, she's a lot better,' Iris told him.

'What about Daddy?'

It was seven o'clock, and that meant it was three o'clock in New York. Winston usually called to say goodnight from a cab on the way from his lunch appointment to his next meeting, but perhaps, since it was the last day of his trip, he'd taken a longer lunch.

'He might still be working, because it's only afternoon in New York,' Iris explained. 'Tell you what: if you have a nice bath and get all ready for bed, we'll ring Daddy to say goodnight. Deal?'

'*Blue Peter?*' John asked, looking longingly at the television.

'It's way past *Blue Peter*, and it's past your bedtime already,' Iris told him.

Iris ran John's bath and allowed him to have one boat and one dolphin in with him.

'And letters?' John asked.

'Go on, then,' said Iris, handing over the mesh bag containing an alphabet that stuck on to the side of the bath.

Carefully selecting his letters, John wrote DADY.

'That's good,' said Iris. 'In fact Daddy has two Ds.'

'There *are* two Ds!' John protested.

'You're quite right!' Iris apologized. 'I meant three Ds.'

'D-A-D-Y.' John spelt out the word.

'Tomorrow, he'll be able to give you your bath,' said Iris.

John was tired, and the steamy warmth of bathtime always made her feel relaxed too. She yawned.

'Shall we get you washed now?'

'First the dolphin has to race the ship!'

'All right, then. I'll be the dolphin, shall I?'

'No! You be the ship!'

At this time of evening, any little thing could make him kick off.

'Who do you think's going to win?' John asked, as the two plastic creatures lined up under the taps.

'The ship of course!' said Iris.

'The dolphin of course!' said John.

'Ready, steady, go!'

In a best-of-seven contest, the dolphin won.

'Best of eight?' asked John hopefully.

'You can't have best of eight,' Iris told him, then immediately regretted it, because John was far too tired for her to begin to explain the concept of odd and even. 'The dolphin's the supreme champion tonight,' she added quickly.

'Does he get a prize?'

'In the morning, he can have a strawberry on his cereal.'

'Dolphins don't eat cereal!' John scoffed.

'Well, he can have a strawberry on his fish, then!'

He laughed so much at that, she was able to lift him out

of the bath without his really noticing, and as soon as he was nestling on her lap in a big fluffy towel he curled up against her like a baby, enjoying the warmth and comfort as much as she did.

Wearing his Thunderbirds pyjamas, he got into bed without putting up too much of a fight.

'Shall we ring Daddy now?' he asked, as she kissed his forehead.

It was eight o'clock, which was four o'clock in New York time. Winston might even be on his way to the airport. The phone rang several times before clicking on to Voicemail.

'It's just us,' Iris told the machine. 'Looking forward to seeing you. Here's John.'

She handed the phone to their sleepy son.

'Goodnight, Daddy!' he said, with a yawn. 'The dolphin is supreme champion, by the way . . .'

Iris prised the phone from his little fingers.

'Goodnight, love. Have a safe flight,' she said, then blew a kiss before pushing the off button.

Iris bent to kiss John again.

'Daddy loves you,' she said, thinking that would be a nice warm thought for John to go to sleep with, but instead he opened his eyes.

'How much?' he asked.

'To infinity,' she told him.

'And beyond?'

'To infinity and beyond, and a tiny bit further,' said Iris.

Downstairs, Iris poured herself a glass of wine, and, once she was sure that John was fast asleep and wouldn't be woken up by the noise, she turned on the television. For a few seconds, she thought the report must be a drama, a remake of Orson Welles's *War of the Worlds* that she had caught halfway through. When she switched channels, ITV was showing the same pictures, and Channel 4 and

Sky . . . Iris suddenly thought that she must be the only person in the world who hadn't seen the news.

At eight forty-six, the newsreader was saying, American Airlines Flight 11 crashed into the North Tower of the World Trade Center. A film crew had been out early filming with the New York Fire Department. Hearing the noise of a plane, they'd pointed the camera upwards as the jet flew overhead.

'Holy cow!' someone could be heard saying off camera.

By the time the second plane came, the world's news cameras were trained on the building and the impact had been broadcast live.

How odd that Winston hadn't called to tell her. Iris rummaged around in her handbag. Her mobile phone was charged and switched on. There were no messages.

There was a surreal kind of beauty about the view of New York's distant skyline with plumes of smoke billowing from the towers into the huge blue sky, then the report cut suddenly to apocalyptic pictures of the South Tower collapsing.

Iris was instantly aware that nobody who was in New York could have been unaffected by this catastrophe.

Winston!

He'd been going to a breakfast meeting downtown, she remembered. But not in the World Trade Center. He would have said. They'd been there, a couple of years before. John had memorably complained that he didn't like American bacon. If Winston had been going to the Windows on the World for breakfast, he would have referred to it, and she would have said something like 'Watch out for the bacon' and they would have laughed. She was sure of it.

Iris called Winston's mobile again.

Voicemail.

'I've just heard. Please call me!'

Iris ran upstairs. John was fast asleep, an arm stretched

out behind him, his face as perfectly still as when he was a baby. She was seized with the need to hold him, but couldn't run the risk of him waking, wanting to know what was happening, why she was so scared.

Back in the living room, Iris tried to swallow her rising panic and think logically. She called again, stabbing at the keys, as if the harder she hit them the more likely she would be to get through.

Voicemail.

Everyone would be calling, she told herself. The networks were probably overloaded.

Iris's mind began to invent plausible explanations why Winston hadn't rung: he'd probably called when she and John were out at Marine Ices. He wouldn't have wanted to leave a message on the answerphone for John to hear, and so he might have called Michael instead.

She dialled her father's number, asking as soon as he picked up, 'Have you heard from Winston?' realizing before she'd even completed the sentence that Michael would certainly have called her by now if he had.

'No.'

'He's in New York . . .' The words came out like a strangled scream.

'The lines are probably down,' her father offered.

'I'm going to try the Compton Club,' said Iris, holding the handset under her chin as she frantically tore through bits of paper stuck to the fridge with magnets, until she found the number.

The slew of relief that coursed through her when the phone was answered was quickly replaced by another hit of panic when the receptionist checked the register and informed her that Winston Allsop wasn't in the building.

'Did he check out?' Iris asked, crossing her fingers. If Winston had been on his way to the airport, surely he would have escaped the disaster downtown.

'No,' the receptionist told her.

'Could you call his room?'

There was no answer from his room.

'Could someone check his room for me?' Iris asked.

'We're a little short-staffed right now.' The girl's patience was clearly wearing thin.

'I'm so sorry . . . I've only just found out . . . He hasn't—'

'I'll have someone check and call you right back.'

'No, I'll hold . . .' *He's your bloody boss*, Iris was ready to scream.

Winston was not in his room.

'I'll ask him to call you just as soon as he comes in,' the girl said.

Iris was reluctant to lose the connection, and yet she couldn't think of anything else to keep the line open. Putting down the phone, she began to cry.

Think. Think logically. And stay calm, she told herself, calling his mobile again.

Voicemail.

Every time, the same five rings, then a split second of anticipation allowing her a moment to believe that she was about to hear his voice, then the crushing disappointment of the announcement: 'The person you are calling is unable to take your call. Please leave a message.'

'I love you,' she said helplessly.

Iris stayed up all night, occasionally picking up the cordless landline to hear the dialling tone was still there, then checking the face of her mobile to see that there was still a signal. Once every five minutes, she pressed the last number recall button, and listened to the same five rings.

'The person you are calling . . .'

The images on the television were like a constantly repeating vision of hell: planes zooming into the towers; people falling through the air; crowds running before a storm of debris; rescue workers caked in ghostly white dust picking through a smoking bombsite of jagged steel that had fallen silent except for the eerie sound of mobile phones ringing unanswered.

'Mummy?'

Iris opened her eyes to find John standing right in front of her face.

The television was still on and the breakfast programme's couch couple were talking in sombre tones in front of a still picture of the second plane piercing the South Tower. Iris's waking brain rapidly returned her to the midst of the nightmare and, quickly picking up the remote, she switched the television off.

'Silly me! I must have fallen asleep on the sofa!' she said, sitting up.

'Silly you!'

'Why don't we get you some breakfast before I get dressed,' she said, her voice full of phoney brightness.

'You *are* dressed!' he said, laughing at her.

Iris was existing in two parallel narratives. In one, she had to be calm and logical, so that John wouldn't be alarmed; in the other, her brain was frantically trying to grasp a plan of action that seemed constantly to evade her. She couldn't decide whether it would be better to outline what had happened to John even though she had no answers to the questions he was bound to ask, rather than have him hear about it at school. Would he make the connection? Should she even send him to school?

Why hadn't Winston called? There was a bit of Iris that was furious with him.

'Daddy's picking me up!' John chirruped gleefully as she waved him off at the school gates.

'If he's back,' Iris qualified, but he'd already spotted one of his friends.

She stood watching the children dashing about on the tarmac until the whistle was blown and the playground suddenly fell silent. For a moment, Iris found it difficult to prise herself away from the empty space to face whatever came next. She walked home slowly, as if to tempt a phone-call by her absence, and, as she walked up the steps to the front door, she could hear ringing.

'Winston?' She snatched up the receiver.

'It's Fiammetta.'

'Oh!'

'Have you heard anything?'

'Of course I haven't!' Iris snapped, anxiety manifesting itself as crossness.

She was stranded between the need for company and impatience to keep the line free.

'What are you going to do?' Fiammetta asked.

'I don't know!' Iris's panic squealed out before she could rein it back. 'Call the office in London, I suppose,' she said, trying to think through her options. 'It's only five in the morning in New York. Maybe his secretary can check whether he was on the flight.'

'Dad says, should he ring Anthony?'

Why hadn't she thought of that? Her brother was far better placed to find out what was really happening than anyone on the emergency number they were giving out on television.

'Could he? I want to keep this line free . . . I'd better go,' said Iris.

'Hang on, Dad wants to speak to you,' Fiammetta told her.

'Iris, do you want me to come up?' Michael asked.

'No, I'll be fine,' Iris said automatically, not wanting the confusion of other people around her.

'I can take care of John, if . . .' He let her finish the thought.

She was about to refuse again, when she imagined John's disappointment if Winston wasn't there to meet him in the playground.

'I'll be on the twelve o'clock from Lowhampton, then,' Michael told her, taking advantage of her moment of ambivalence.

As Iris replaced the receiver she was suddenly gulpy that her father was coming to look after her, as she had once looked after him. Not that it was the same, she told herself, because Winston was probably fine, and any minute now she would hear the sound of his keys in the front door.

Winston's secretary, Davina, in the London office had heard nothing from him since an email sent early in the morning of the day before, asking her to cancel his afternoon appointments in London because he needed to pick his son up from school. As far as she was aware, he had had no business meetings in New York the previous day, and she couldn't think of anyone with offices downtown that he might have been going to see. She promised to check with the New York office, but it was clear from her overly patient tone that she felt Iris was being a little hysterical. All the tunnels and bridges into New York were closed and the phone networks had crashed. She was sure Winston would be in touch just as soon as he was able.

Was it disloyal to think there was anything other than a perfectly simple explanation, Iris wondered, putting down the phone, feeling almost as if she had been told off. No news was good news, she kept telling herself, and yet the fact remained that Winston had still not called, had not returned to his room at the Compton Club, and nobody knew where he was.

Iris's mind began to invent scenarios to explain the few facts she knew. Why hadn't Winston got a morning flight out of New York if he had no appointments? Should she infer from his secretary's use of the word 'business' that it was perfectly possible that he'd had a 'personal' appointment? Did he keep a mistress in downtown Manhattan? It didn't matter, she told herself, as long as he was safe. Anyway, he didn't. Why would he? And if he did, why would he have told her about the meeting he was going to? She was sure he'd said the name of a hotel. The Marriott! That was it!

She rang Davina again to ask her to find the number, but when Winston's secretary called back there was less confidence in her voice.

'There was a Marriott at the foot of the tower, but it's not a hotel Winston ever used,' she added quickly.

The silence in the Hampstead house was more dreadful each hour that passed.

'Ring, damn you! Ring! For God's sake!' Iris shouted at the phone, powerless to do anything except wait, her mind filling up with unthinkable images it was increasingly impossible to dismiss. The only way of regaining a semblance of control was by putting a time limit on it. She gave the phone until midday to ring, staring at it as if they were locked in a battle of wills. But the phone held out. Midday came and went, and one o'clock, and two o'clock. The sunshine pouring into the living room seemed to mock her with its intensity, but Iris couldn't risk going out.

Michael arrived just after three o'clock. He did not ask whether there was any news because he could see as soon as she opened the door that there was not. He clasped her to his chest, stroking her hair as the tears she had kept back all day choked out of her in great gasps until they'd all gone, and she suddenly knew what she had to do.

'If there's no word, I'm going to New York.'

All angles must be checked, all possibilities explored until . . . until . . . No! She mustn't think that.

In the whirlwind of sorting out a flight, packing, and filling the fridge with food that would be easy for her father to cook, Iris almost forgot how much she hated flying, and it was only as the plane began to taxi away from its gate that a new rush of fear threatened to overwhelm her. How mad was it to get on a plane? If it crashed John would be left without a mother or a father. Winston would be furious with her!

Except he wouldn't because . . . He might not be dead, Iris told herself, gripping the arms of her seat until her knuckles were white, because he might be wandering around New York in shock, or lying in a hospital ward in a coma, or he might have forgotten who he was and the doctors wouldn't know who to contact to authorize treatment. But even as she struggled to keep the possibilities alive, she knew that they were just fantasies, clichés from films she had seen, and as likely as a boy in a man's body, or a lover coming back to life through the sheer force of his partner's grief.

The chalky cloud of pulverized devastation had begun to settle, but an invisible but potent haze of shock lay over the city, like radiation after a nuclear explosion that would never entirely go away.

In Winston's suite at the Compton Club, his suitcase stood packed and ready to go. Inside, there was a bag from FAO Schwartz containing a Lego Firetruck, a last gift for John imbued with unintended poignancy. For Iris, there was the usual selection of gleaming hardback novels about contemporary America, which now seemed irrelevant and out of date, because in the days between Winston standing in Barnes and Noble and Iris sitting on the bed in his hotel room, both reading the same blurbs, history had changed.

The sheets on the king-size bed were crisp and clean, and Iris sniffed vainly for the scent of Winston, whimpering like an animal in distress at the smell of starched cotton. At the bottom of his suitcase she found two shirts he had worn, his dirty washing the best gift.

Iris trailed around the city, visiting each hospital, then methodically ticking the name off her list; sitting at the window counters of diners, watching the rush-hour crowds, her mind primed to focus on any tall black man who passed; glancing in every doorway, like a pilgrim in hope of witnessing something miraculous in the midst of ordinariness. Tragedy was a great leveller, she thought, as she fixed images of Winston to railings and hoardings and lampposts and mailboxes, wherever she could find space. The posters and stickers the New York office had made up for her were designed, spell-checked and laminated to last longer in rain, but they were emblems of the same hope and hopelessness as any of the handmade requests. It didn't matter whether the face in the photo belonged to someone rich, or beautiful, or young or old: each one was equal in its absence, like the names on a war memorial.

One or two of Winston's colleagues invited her for dinner, but she declined.

'Are you sure? If we can do anything – anything at all . . .'

Iris could hear the relief in their voices. They wouldn't know what to say, and she didn't want to hear their stories. It was difficult enough trying to cling on to the integrity of Winston, too soon to replace his physical presence with memories. There would come a point, she realized, as she lay in the vast bed at the Compton Club, with Winston's shirt over her face, when the dutiful and tragic partner would become the slightly embarrassing obsessive. Neither were roles she felt particularly comfortable playing. And now she felt she had known in her soul that Winston was dead long before the moment she saw the place they were calling Ground Zero; known each time she said 'I love you!' into the void of his voicemail in an attempt to turn back time and make it the last thing he heard. She'd come to New York to satisfy herself she had done everything that was expected of her and not let him down. And perhaps she had hoped to feel close to him again. But he was no longer there. And she knew that the place where she should be, where he would want her to be, was with John.

Michael and John were standing in the arrivals hall when she came through, pushing a trolley with Winston's suitcase and her own.

John's face lit up as he spotted her.

'Did you find Daddy?' he asked, rushing into her arms.

'No, I'm sorry, I didn't,' said Iris.

'Will he ever come back, do you think?'

'No. I don't think so.'

Over John's shoulder she saw her father wince at her frankness, but she was too exhausted to think of a way of making it sound acceptable.

'It's a shame, isn't it?' John said, with that terrible facility for understatement that children possess.

'Yes, it's a great shame,' Iris agreed, picking him up and burying her tears in his fleece.

Chapter Ten

Spring 2002

The human mind, in all its complexity and imagination, has a strangely simple need to say goodbye. Iris's waking brain knew that there was no possibility that Winston had survived, but some rebellious little bit of her subconscious occasionally broke rank and allowed her to dream that she heard his keys in the front door, and she woke up surfing on a great wave of relief, only to be upended by the crash of reality.

John appeared to accept that Daddy was dead. According to his teacher, he had announced his sad news to the class at circle time. It made Iris remember how very matter-of-fact the twins had been after Claudia's death. Children didn't seem to be capable of sustained grief, although that didn't mean that they were unaffected.

'Daddy was there in my sleep,' John told her one day.

'Really? What was he doing?'

'Skating.'

'You and Daddy were good at skating,' said Iris, remembering watching them on the rink in Central Park.

'Can we go skating again?' John asked brightly.

'All right, then,' said Iris, hoping that he would have forgotten by the time winter came round, knowing that the only way she'd stand up on skates would be by clinging to the edge of the rink. Occasionally she found herself

403

resenting Winston for leaving her to do everything.

Because there was no body, there could be no funeral, and for a long time Iris resisted the idea of a memorial service because Winston had been an atheist, as she was, and it would be unthinkable to say goodbye to him in church. People talked about the need for closure, but Iris wasn't even sure that closure was such a desirable thing. Those fleeting moments when she believed Winston to be back were so exquisite, she wasn't sure she wanted to let them go.

In the end, it was sheer impatience with people asking her if there was anything they could do, or staring at her anxiously, that made her resolve to do something. Winston had been a happy person, and it wasn't right to allow his memory to be buried beneath a perpetual shroud of sadness.

'I'm thinking of having a party for Winston,' she'd told Bruno first, since he was the most normal one of the family, and she thought she'd be able to gauge from his reaction if it was an appropriate or sensible idea.

'Brilliant. Will you let me cater it?' had been his instant response.

It was only when she started drawing up the guest list, thinking about the venue, deciding on the copy for the invitation, that Iris realized the function that funerals served. Even though she was organizing the event in Winston's name, for the first time in months she found herself able to string several thoughts in a row without thinking about him.

John was full of excited, impractical ideas based on his own experience of parties, such as getting a bouncy castle, or a pod in the London Eye. Not wanting to say no to all of his suggestions, Iris found herself agreeing to a magician and helium balloons for everyone to take away with them. She would have rented dodgem cars too, but she had to compromise with a real ice-cream van parked just outside the gate, which made several of the guests get out their invitations to check they'd come to the right place. The venue Iris had chosen was the Inns of Court, where Winston had started his professional life as a barrister. There was a suitable kind of gravitas about the setting, and the hall was big enough to accommodate the vast number of people if it rained, but that morning Iris had woken up to a fresh, spring day. The blossom trees were in full flower and the carefully tended lawns provided an unexpectedly tranquil setting right in the middle of London, while allowing the children to tear around in safety. With great multicoloured bunches of shiny balloons glinting in the sunlight, calypso music provided by a steel band from one of the youth centres Winston's charities supported, and waiters pouring champagne, the ambience, Iris thought as she surveyed the guests, was part society wedding, part carnival. It almost seemed a shame to break it up with speeches. She kept her own as short as possible, simply thanking everyone for coming, then handed the microphone to John, who read a short poem he had written:

'I miss you, Daddy, kicking my football in the park,
I miss you when it's dark
Sometimes I get sad at night
Then Mummy comes and it's all right.'

He smiled triumphantly at the crowd, oblivious to the tears in the grown-ups' eyes.

Anthony read a tribute from the Prime Minister, who couldn't be there because he was making a speech in the House of Commons.

David, an African student whose life had been saved from famine by Live Aid, offered thanks for Winston's life, and everyone spontaneously started clapping, which felt rather lovely. As Iris looked around the party, seeing people chatting and laughing, some even dancing to the music, she felt that the relaxed atmosphere was just right and, as people kept coming up to tell her, just what Winston would have wanted.

Was it? Iris asked herself. Was it what he would have wanted?

A part of his life had come to light that she had known nothing about, and made her doubt that she had known him very well at all. Just before Christmas, she had received an email from an American with the unlikely name of Marvin Martin. Initially, Iris had thought he was a hoaxer, a nefarious individual who had seen a way of making money from her loss, and yet there was something so utterly implausible about the story he told her she could not understand how or why he would have made it up.

A private detective from New Jersey, Marvin Martin claimed to have been approached by Winston to look for his father, whom he believed to have been one of the American military who had been stationed on the South Coast of England during the build-up to D-Day. Mr Martin had arranged to meet Winston at the Marriott Hotel at the foot of the World Trade Center on the morning of 9/11. With little to go on apart from the assumption that Winston's father was African American and of an age to serve during the war, Marvin had been reluctant to take the case. Winston had appreciated his honesty, and told him he would be in touch again if he decided to pursue it. Marvin Martin had left Winston to finish his breakfast, not expecting to hear from him again. On returning to New Jersey he had watched the terrible events of the day unfolding, he and his wife thanking God for his lucky escape. It had crossed his mind to wonder whether the suave Brit he'd met had also got out but, as he never discussed professional matters with his wife, that had been as far as it went. It was only when the two of them had come to pay their respects at Ground Zero on a Christmas shopping trip into the city that he'd seen one of Iris's posters.

Iris knew that it would have been perfectly easy for someone to find out that Winston came from a small town called Kingshaven, because it had been mentioned in the many obituaries that had appeared, but Iris was quite sure that Winston had never publicly owned up to being found in a basket. The only way that Marvin Martin could have been aware of these details was if Winston had told him.

Initially, she'd responded cautiously, half expecting to receive some extortionate demand for money, but Marvin Martin wanted nothing from her. The poster asked for information, he wrote, and as he was probably one of the last people to see Winston, he had felt obliged to tell her. He'd heard that the not knowing was worse than the knowing.

Iris wasn't sure that was true. Knowing that Winston had kept a secret from her made her doubt all the assumptions she had made about their relationship, and yet, she reminded herself, she had kept a secret from him too. How ironic that neither of them had trusted each other enough to admit their need for answers to questions that were probably best left unasked. Maybe he had been intending to tell her when he returned home? She could imagine them laughing about a character called Marvin Martin, and maybe, then, she would have told him about her daughter?

Iris tortured herself trying to remember the exact words of her last conversation with Winston.

'I'm so lucky to have you and John,' he had said, and she'd dismissed him as being 'American', a little embarrassing for her brittle Englishness.

Now it seemed obvious that he must have been thinking about family, trying to reassure her, and himself, that he was happy with what he had, as he embarked on a quest for what he had lost.

After much deliberation, Iris called the private detective, imagining him in a dingy office with a glass door with his name written on, sitting behind a desk with a gun in the top drawer, like a character from the movies. His voice was so full-on New Jersey, it made her smile.

Would it be possible, Iris asked, for him to pursue his investigations?

Marvin Martin was anxious for her not to waste her money. It was difficult enough to trace a parent when they were aware they had a child; someone who had no idea might well be impossible to find. There were no guarantees, he emphasized, and the fees he detailed were so ridiculously low, Iris now found herself fearing he was giving her special rates as a 9/11 widow, rather than trying to extort money as she'd initially suspected.

Every few weeks, Marvin emailed progress reports, and seeing his name in her Inbox had become one of the high-lights of Iris's life. There was a peculiar kind of comfort from being in touch with the last human being Winston had spoken to. She had even invited the detective to Winston's party, offering to advance him the money for a weekend in London with his wife, but he had declined, politely but firmly, citing his rule of keeping personal and professional life separate.

Sometimes, Iris wondered what she was doing. In the unlikely event of finding a black man who fitted the bill, it would be impossible to tell whether he was Winston's father without a DNA test. How would the subject be broached? It was a crazy idea. And yet, if John had a black grandfather who was still alive, she felt she had a duty to try to find him. Wasn't that what Winston had been trying to do? Wasn't that what he would have wanted?

*   *   *

There was something inescapably poignant about a mother attending her child's funeral at whatever age. The doctor judged that Liliana, though frail, was fit enough to pay her last respects to Pearl, slightly to Libby's distress, because she knew from the embarrassing struggle at her mother's centenary that they'd never get Liliana into a wheelchair. At a hundred-and-one years old, Liliana was still vain enough not to want anyone to see her as an invalid, but the aisle at St Mary's Church was too long for her to manage now, even with Christopher propping her up on one side and Eddie on the other.

'It's a pity Dr Ferry's no longer around,' Eddie remarked, with a macabre smile. 'We could have done them both at once.'

'Honestly!' Libby ticked him off, but the same thought had occurred to her, although she'd never have said it out loud.

How long could Liliana go on for? Physically, there was little sign of deterioration. Her mother still ate three meals a day and knocked back a stiff glass of gin and Dubonnet each evening. A series of strokes had robbed Pearl of her power of speech, but Liliana's silence seemed to Libby more an act of will than physical impediment, a clever way of keeping everyone on their toes trying to guess what she wanted, and remaining the centre of attention.

Was it terribly selfish to wish things were a little easier? Libby was seventy-six herself. Her youth had been taken by the war, she'd worked hard all her life, and now she wasn't being allowed to enjoy an old age. Her emotions were a constant see-saw of exasperation and guilt, wanting to shake her mother into saying something, then feeling so ashamed of her cruel thoughts that she overcompensated with kindness.

In consultation with the vicar, it had been agreed that Christopher would bring Liliana to the church before the congregation was due to arrive, and get her seated – with the wheelchair folded up out of sight in the vestry – then he could discreetly hoist her to her feet when Pearl's coffin was brought in. After the service, Liliana would remain in the church until the congregation had dispersed, then they'd push her out of the side door and into a limousine to take her to the crematorium. Pearl was being cremated because there was only room in the family plot for one more coffin, and that privilege had to be accorded to Liliana.

'Age before beauty,' as Pearl would probably have remarked in her prime.

As she stood listening to the vicar's oration, Libby was suddenly aware that the arrangements had taken so much organization, she hadn't really had a chance to think about poor Pearl. The belated realization that the lifeless body of her once vivacious sister was in the box beside her made her splutter with sudden grief. Glancing across at the pew where Pearl's former husband, Tom Snow, was standing with Pearl's children, Libby noticed that his face was wet with tears. She suspected a number of men in the congregation were similarly moved.

There had been so many times in her life when Libby had despaired of her sister because of the rumour and scandal she had brought upon the family, but, in truth, her anguish had always been tempered by a small tremor of envy. Pearl had always lived her life at a faster pace than other people, cutting a swathe through convention and relishing every delicious moment of it.

Pearl had always said she wanted the Beatles's song 'Hello Hello' to be played at her funeral. As the words of the pop song filled the church, a series of images of Pearl arriving in a room, always late, always breathless, cascaded through Libby's mind: Pearl in the New-Look frock she'd worn for the Coronation, her face almost as pink as the cerise fabric; Pearl arriving back from her tennis lesson, her eyes shining with the exertion of a vigorous game; Pearl, kitted out in floppy hat and clinging minidress, returning drunk on the night of Kingshaven's rock concert; Pearl in the ultra-violet light at Angela's wedding disco, her white underwear gleaming through her loose-woven cheesecloth smock as she slow-danced with a man half her age; Pearl on the night

410

of the D-Day commemoration ball, lying in an untidy heap on the ballroom floor with the black American veteran, their faces illuminated by a racing swirl of stars from the spinning glitterball.

Unexpected tears cascaded down Libby's desiccated cheeks as she bent for a tissue from her handbag. Along the pew, Liliana was still standing, but there were no tears on her mother's face, no trace of emotion, except perhaps the tiniest hint of a smile.

*　　*　　*

A number of mourners had gathered outside the church. While never a particularly popular figure in Kingshaven, Pearl had been an unfailing source of intrigue. As Michael Quinn approached, he sensed the looks and whispers elicited by his own presence. In the early 1950s, Pearl's affair with the hotel chauffeur had divided the town, some people feeling she should be allowed to marry the man she loved, others firmly of the view that it could never work given the difference in social status. By the time Pearl had set her sights on Michael, she had learnt a modicum of discretion, but their liaison had been widely rumoured and his appearance at her funeral was bound to confirm it.

Michael's purpose was not to mourn, though he had been saddened at the sight of Pearl in a wheelchair on the terrace, one sunny morning recently, after creeping up the steps from the beach and letting himself into the garden of the Palace Hotel. He did not think she had seen him, but it had been too risky to go any further, and so he had picked his way back down the path cautiously as several of the steps were crumbling. A couple of days later, a storm had washed the entire bottom half of the eroding cliff out to sea, and Michael had to think of another way of gaining access. He was certain that any request for a meeting would be refused. Rumour had it that Mrs Liliana

King was suffering from dementia. She hadn't been seen in public since she'd shouted a racist comment at John when he'd presented her with flowers on her hundredth birthday. The consensus of opinion was that whatever views Mrs King might hold, she would never have expressed them out loud if she'd been her usual self, and it was a shame to see a great lady letting herself down.

Michael was never sure whether the process of ageing fundamentally altered the structure of a person's brain, or whether it simply broke down the barricade of good manners that the mind constructed to protect its secrets. Sometimes he wondered whether his own determination to speak to Liliana King was a sign that he was losing it himself. What could possibly be gained from confronting a frail and senile old woman? And yet it had become a compulsion that grew more urgent as time was surely running out.

As he watched the congregation following the coffin to the hearse, and saw that Liliana was not among them, Michael suffered the same sting of disappointment as when he'd recognized that the forlorn figure sitting on the terrace of the Palace Hotel was Pearl, and not her mother. But, as the town people began to disperse, it occurred to him that if Liliana were not at the church she must be at the Palace, and he might be able to get to her while the rest of the family were out. Hurrying up through the churchyard, he noticed that the door on the side of the south transept was open.

Liliana looked up as he approached, and he could tell that she knew exactly who he was. They had spoken face to face only once, in the early sixties, but it was an occasion they both remembered. In those days, Liliana King had enjoyed a pivotal position in the town's Establishment and she had made it clear that she would destroy Michael and his family if he did not put an end to his affair with Pearl. Even though he had already been looking for a way out, he'd felt a coward for meekly succumbing to Liliana's will.

Now, their roles were reversed. He was the one with the power, but it was only a brief window of opportunity.

'I've been reading a very interesting novel,' he began.

Did the watery blue eyes twitch with concern? It was difficult to tell.

'It's all about a town rather like Kingshaven with a hotel rather like the Palace and a proprietor who could almost be you . . .'

Liliana did not look away and he wondered if she was trying to bluff him.

'It's set just after the war,' he continued quietly, almost as if he were reading a story to a child. 'A young man's body is found at the foot of a cliff. But did he fall? Or was he pushed? That's the question.'

Still no reaction.

'What the author of the novel seems to want the reader to believe is that it wasn't an accident, it was a murder, right in the midst of the God-fearing people of Haven Regis.'

Michael looked around the empty parish church with its stiff floral decorations arranged by members of the Flower Festival Committee and its colourful hassocks embroidered by the WI.

'Difficult to believe, eh?'

Liliana's chin had dropped a little and her eyes were now fixed on the carving round the foot of the pulpit.

'In the novel, the villain is a pillar of the community, completely above suspicion – the last person anyone would suspect . . .'

Now, the old woman looked up sharply and there was steel in her blue eyes.

'She probably thought the young man had it coming,' Michael whispered, in deference to his surroundings. 'Because, you see, he had been a bit of a naughty boy, first taking her to bed, and then her daughter . . .'

Liliana's expression remained completely impassive.

'The trouble was, he preferred the daughter. The daughter was young and, well, let's face it, far more attractive. That must have been hard for the grand dame to take, don't you think? Hell hath no fury and all that.'

Liliana continued to stare at the pulpit.

'Terrible thing, jealousy, isn't it?' Michael tried to goad her. 'Jealousy and shame, as well. Because he was just a working-class lad. A bit of rough, an expendable bit of rough.' Anger suddenly surged up inside him. 'It's not just a story, is it?'

He bent to put his face in front of hers, so that she had to look him in the eye. His nose was close enough to smell the stale scent of powder on her face and the cloying whiff of decay.

'A young man died in similar circumstances right here in Kingshaven just after the war. You know how I know? Because he was my brother!'

Liliana's watery blue eyes widened, and he saw that it was the first thing he'd said that had come as a surprise to her.

'Frank was my brother. He was an airman. He was billeted at the Palace. He wrote to me about you, and about Pearl . . . and . . . and you killed him!'

Fear. He was sure it was fear he could see in her eyes now. Finally, he knew why he had needed so badly to see Liliana King's face. As the policeman in Daphne W. Smythe's novel had correctly stated, there was no evidence. There would never be evidence. But it was still possible that there was a chance of finding the truth.

'You killed Frank!' Michael whispered.

The final chapter of Daphne W. Smythe's book recounted Dr Winifred Smith's conclusions about the mystery of the soldier's death: it was not Perdita but Lucilla Prince, the wife of the proprietor of the Majestic Hotel, that the antique ladies had overheard with her lover in the Windsor Suite. They had arranged to meet on the cliffs, and instead

414

of going shopping as she claimed, Lucilla had been driven by her friend to the rendezvous. Before leaving the hotel, Lucilla had taken the squadron leader's gun from his room. Up on the cliffs, she had confronted the soldier with his duplicity, before cold-bloodedly training the gun on him, forcing him over the edge.

It was the only plausible sequence of events that would explain all the anomalies, Dr Winifred Smith had explained to the policeman.

The Coroner recorded an open verdict. As Sergeant Carr explained at some length to Dr Smith, conjecture and psychological insights were all very well, but what police needed to prosecute was evidence.

This was not a detective novel.

The final paragraph had perplexed Michael for some time until it dawned on him that Daphne W. Smythe might have been offering a clue. Until then, it had never occurred to Michael to look up the Coroner's Report into Frank's death. When he eventually unearthed it in the county records office, he read with disbelief that Mrs Liliana King and Mrs Ruby Farmer numbered among the witnesses called at the inquest. They'd been out for a walk on the South Cliffs on the afternoon in question and recalled greeting the young man as their paths crossed near the Iron Age Fort. The word they both used to describe his demeanour was preoccupied.

In fifty years of living in Kingshaven, walking almost every day and in all weathers on the South Cliffs, Michael could not recall a single occasion on which he had seen either Mrs Farmer or Mrs King, but the Coroner, whose court was in Lowhampton, would have had no reason to find this evidence unusual. Nevertheless, he had recorded an open verdict, even though the balance of the facts surrounding the death seemed to point to suicide. It was why, Michael realized, when Frank's body had come home, they'd been able to bury him in consecrated ground.

In St Mary's church, Kingshaven, Michael stared at Liliana, and she stared back at him, those famous blue eyes trying to face him down, he thought, but he was going to win this time.

'You thought you'd got away with it, didn't you?' he said. 'You thought you'd got away with it, but you didn't, and now you can go to hell.'

Liliana King's lips began to quiver, her bony hands pressing down on the side of the pew as if she was trying to stand, and then with a gargantuan effort she let out a thin strangled wail.

'Oyster!'

'Granny!' Christopher King appeared at the side door behind Michael. 'Mr Quinn! Whatever's going on?'

Michael looked from the old woman to the grandson. One face stricken, the other bemused. If he attempted to explain, he realized, he would sound like an old man ranting.

One final look and then he turned away, content in the knowledge that he'd found her out. It was a kind of justice.

As Michael walked through the churchyard, his back seemed to straighten, as if a burden he had been carrying ever since his brother died had been lifted from his shoulders. When the days grew a little longer, he thought, he would go back up North and visit Frank's grave, to say goodbye to him properly, as he'd never been able to do.

*   *   *

Mrs Liliana King's choice of a suite without a sea view had never been the entirely selfless act that people had given her credit for. For others, the attraction of opalesque light on the water at sunset was irresistible, but, having spent her entire life by the sea, Liliana barely noticed the ever-changing vista of ocean, and certainly had no wish to spend her days gazing across the bay at the South Cliffs.

For Liliana, a hotel was, and had always been, what went on inside, and from her window overlooking the front door she could see all the arrivals and departures. As a child, she had crouched at the upstairs window of her family's more modest establishment, the Albion, watching the guests and making up stories that brought them to the point of their arrival in her world. Sometimes the lives she guessed were revealed as uncannily accurate; more often, the intrigues would exceed the limits of a child's imagination. Liliana had learnt to read and write at an early age, but her real education had been in observing the many lives that brushed against hers: the labels on the luggage they brought, the drift of cigar smoke and perfume, and snatches of murmured conversation, had schooled her in the complicated, duplicitous nature of human beings.

If anyone had stories to write about the crimes and misdemeanours of hotel life, it was Liliana, not that ridiculous woman Daphne W. Smythe. Truth was stranger than fiction, Liliana had told Miss Smythe on a number of occasions (and certainly more fascinating than the banal storylines Miss Smythe created, she'd thought privately).

Liliana King stared out of the window. These days, nobody came to the hotel. Sometimes she suspected that Libby had closed the place down without telling her, and sometimes she wondered if this was what it was like to be dead, looking at nothing. Sometimes she even wondered if she was dead, and it was merely her ghost hovering at the window.

How she missed having Ruby there to talk to!

Oyster!

Ruby had been there with her at the window when the young airman had returned that summer day just after the war. Ruby had spotted him first, her face draining of colour.

'What's he doing here?'

There was a swagger about Frank, and he was powerfully attractive. When Liliana had seen him sauntering up the gravel drive in his demob suit, there had been a moment, just a split second, when she had allowed herself to imagine that he was coming back for her.

Daphne W. Smythe, a guest at the time, had only seen half the story.

In those tense, expectant days before D-Day, when it had felt as if life had been put on hold, the cheeky red-headed airman was always the last to finish his breakfast, staring at Liliana as his spoon clattered into his porridge bowl. When she had asked casually, as he walked past the clock in the hall, if he'd mind giving her a hand with a lightbulb, he'd followed her up to the Windsor Suite, one step too close behind on the staircase, his groin an inch from her bottom.

The first time had been deliciously sudden and physical, mouth to mouth, skin on skin, flesh pounding into flesh.

Afterwards, he'd smoked a cigarette, blowing fragile white rings up towards the Murano chandelier suspended above the bed.

'I don't know what to call you . . .'

His accent was strange to her ears, soft and rough at the same time, like his lovemaking.

'Don't call me anything,' she'd said, exquisite sensation still tingling through her core. 'You mustn't talk to me, or even look at me.'

'Or else?' He'd propped himself up on one elbow, looking at her.

'Or else . . .'

The threat had hung in the air with the smoke and the tang of his masculinity. She'd still had her slip on, slippery oyster satin. He'd touched the small of her back, the place he'd discovered that leapt with sensation, coaxing her to climb on to him, to look at him, eyes wide open and smiling, after all those years in the dark.

Had she been jealous? Certainly not! Because she hadn't even known about Frank's seduction of Pearl until months after his death.

And it hadn't been murder, Liliana assured herself. Not at all. Her conscience was clear, as God was her witness.

Murder required an intention to kill. They'd only meant to frighten him off, which was what a filthy little blackmailer deserved.

The war had broadened people's horizons, offering them a chance to see how others lived. Some, like Frank, decided they'd like a bit of that themselves afterwards. It was much the same bloody-mindedness that had led the returning soldiers to elect a Labour government after the war instead of the country's saviour, Winston Churchill. There was no longer any respect.

If Frank had asked politely, Liliana might even have been inclined to comply with his requests, but the attempt to blackmail her in such compromising circumstances needed to be dealt with firmly.

'Your word against mine?' she'd spluttered when he'd put his proposition to her. 'I hardly think . . .'

It was rather difficult to maintain composure lying naked next to him in the Windsor Suite.

'I wasn't thinking of telling anyone about us,' Frank said, smiling down at her as if she'd just put the idea into his head. 'I'm talking about what you and your friend did with that baby.'

He'd heard the baby crying on VE night, he'd told her, but not thought anything of it, until he'd seen the notice in the *Chronicle*. Then he'd remembered bumping into her and her friend looking a bit flustered, and he'd started putting two and two together.

'And knowing that you were a naughty girl . . .' He leered at her.

'It certainly wasn't mine, if that's what you're thinking,' Liliana told him.

'If you say so.'

She'd agreed to give him the money he asked for, but only if he left the hotel immediately and never returned. They'd arranged to meet on the South Cliffs for the handover.

Borrowing the squadron leader's gun had been Ruby's idea. How else would they frighten him off for good? But when Liliana had produced it from her handbag, Frank had taken a step back. There was sea thrift growing on the cliff edge, soft pink flowers treacherously disguising the line where land met air. She could still see the look of surprise on his cheeky face. And then he'd gone.

If she had felt any remorse whatsoever about his death, it had been dispelled when Pearl's pregnancy had come to light a few months later.

'He said we would dance our way through life!' her headstrong daughter had declared in defiant defence of the surrender of her virginity. Pearl had been so beautiful, so incorrigible, so very reckless in her passions, Liliana had always felt a duty to protect her.

Now, she thought, as the funeral cars returned the rest of her family to the hotel, there was no longer any need.

*　　*　　*

The first sign of subsidence was the shattered porcelain clock in the Entrance Hall. Some sixth sense of foreboding made Libby run upstairs to her mother's room. But it was too late. Her mother had passed away peacefully in her favourite chair by the window.

After that, cracks began to appear in the garden. There were various theories as to the cause. The land around Kingshaven had always been notoriously prone to slippage; some people said that there were subterranean springs beneath the hotel that had once fed a Roman bathhouse. Christopher blamed global warming, postulating that alternate spells of freakishly dry and very wet weather may have contributed to the instability of the cliff. Climate change was the in-thing at the moment, but Libby wasn't convinced that it was any different from how it had ever been. There had always been a lot of weather in Kingshaven. It was just that people only remembered the good summers.

Whatever the reason, nobody could deny that erosion was happening, and happening fast. After the rose garden had fallen into the sea, and fissures had opened up in the lining of the swimming pool, the hotel was officially closed by the Health and Safety people. A few weeks later, Libby and Eddie were woken up by the most terrible racket, to find themselves staring not at curtains, nor window, but pure blue sky, the rear elevation of their wing having collapsed, leaving their bed teetering precariously on broken joists.

'This place has really gone downhill,' Eddie joked, as they lay there awaiting rescue, reminding Libby suddenly why she had fallen in love with him and put up with him all these years.

In the end, the choice had been made for them. There was no question any more of whether to sell the hotel, because what was left of it had been condemned.

Libby was relieved that Liliana hadn't lived to see it.

The site was under offer for a colossal sum that would comfortably provide for all the family, the deal dependent on planning permission for an estate of houses on the adjoining land, which, Libby and Eddie had been assured, would be granted because the remains of the hotel and outbuildings allowed it to be classified as a brown-field site. In any case, only one objection had been received to the planning application, irritatingly from their son Christopher with his usual bleatings about modern architecture and the environment, but Libby was quietly confident that Millicent, to whom he was now formally engaged, would talk sense into him. Christopher was all for living self-sufficiently in the Summer House, but Libby was sure that his mistress had not waited all these years for an old age spent up to her knees in horse manure.

In the meantime, Libby and Eddie were going to have their first holiday since taking over the running of the place. They'd decided on a cruise, hoping it would cater both for Eddie's need to be on water and Libby's desire for service. After fifty years of tending to other people's needs, she was looking forward to being waited on hand and foot. After that, they might just go on another one. Libby rather liked the idea of drifting round the world, stateless, with no responsibility for anything at all.

'Fifty years,' Eddie said, as they stood in the hall with their suitcases, waiting for the taxi to take them to the liner in Lowhampton.

'Almost,' said Libby. 'We took over properly on Coronation Day, our first big party. Do you remember?'

It had rained all day, but the party had gone with a swing. The lounge had been abuzz with conviviality as the decent people of Kingshaven celebrated the dawn of the New Elizabethan era. In those days they'd been ahead of the times, Libby thought proudly, with not one but two televisions for people to crowd round. And afterwards, in recognition of her new status in Kingshaven, Libby had been invited to light the beacon on the South Cliffs.

Now the carpet was threadbare; the board behind the reception desk full of keys for doors that no longer needed locking. There was already an echo of emptiness.

The hall had never felt the same since the demise of the porcelain clock in the shape of a tree. Surprisingly, for something that had been made in Germany (specially commissioned for the Palace by her great-grandparents, Beatrice and Albert, who built the original hotel), it had never been the most reliable timekeeper, always running a little slow however much money Libby had spent trying to modernize the mechanism. Nevertheless, it had been a splendidly extravagant objet d'art – Libby had recently come across the original invoice in an old file when turning out the attic – and an optimistic one, she had always thought. The tree, with its individually crafted blossom (a flower for each of Beatrice and Albert's children, she had learnt from the hand-written specification), was part of the very fabric of the King family, or the Konigs, as they'd been then. As soon as she had seen it shattered, Libby had known for certain that their time was up, though the mechanism had continued its tardy tick, even when the last fragments were being swept into a dustpan.

Libby took a last look around the hall, wondering how many people had walked through the doors. The whole world had come to the Palace, from lords and ladies to people at the other end of the scale. Some had found relaxation; others, refuge. Most were there for a good time; some, up to no good at all. The Palace had played host to soldiers and politicians, businessmen and crooks, psychics, crimewriters, and, once, a group of Elvis Presley impersonators. It was said that in Uncle Rex's time the Prince of Wales had spent the weekend with Mrs Simpson. Whether they were rock stars or royalty, Libby liked to think they'd been treated with courtesy, and gone away satisfied with the service provided.

Ordinary people were the new royalty now, or so her grandsons told her, people who appeared on so-called reality television shows elevated to absurd levels of fame and fortune. Julia and her chef knew all about that. If the Kings had held on to her, she'd probably have made the

Palace viable, but Libby doubted even Julia's miraculous powers could have stopped it falling into the sea.

*   *   *

The back of the Palace Hotel was open like a giant doll's house, Fiammetta thought, gazing up at it from the beach. She had captured the image of a palm tree keeling over when she was out early one morning taking pictures of the debris left by the storm, and since then she'd taken photographs each day from the same viewpoint with her digital camera. Running through the pictures on the laptop computer Bruno had given her for Christmas, it occurred to her that they were like frames of a time-lapse film, and she had it in mind to create an installation that would show history in reverse, the collapse of the present uncovering the past.

The council had fenced off the whole area to the east of the Clocktower and there were signs warning of the danger of landslip, but at low tide it was still possible to wade round the end of the barriers and scavenge.

A father and son with a metal detector had found the first treasure – a bronze brooch from the Roman era – and had been pictured with it in the *Chronicle*, but after some confusion about ownership of treasure trove – the position was unclear, given that the shoreline was technically property of the Crown – people had kept quiet about their finds.

Fiammetta thought that the face of the cliff was rather like one of the books on fossils her father had tried to interest her in as a child, with a cross-section of land showing the evolution of life forms suspended in the different layers of rock. Here, the remains provided clues about humanity, from bronze votive offerings and bits of mosaic to chunks of glazed Victorian sanitaryware that had been used as hardcore during the reinforcing of the terrace

424

walls. Now that the hotel building itself was collapsing, chunks of plaster in the top layer of the landslide glittered with shards of broken mirror from the bathrooms, and drops of crystal from the smashed chandeliers. One very windy day, some children playing on the beach were encircled by a flurry of old ten-pound notes, like autumn leaves, tantalizingly difficult to grasp, and worthless when caught. Rumours abounded. Perhaps the money was the proceeds of a robbery that some criminal had secreted under the floorboards? Perhaps it had been stashed by Lord Lucan, of whom there had been several unconfirmed sightings around the time of his disappearance? More gruesome was the uncovering of the bones of a number of the King family's spaniels, among them, people said, the skull of a child.

As the shutter of her camera clicked repeatedly, Fiammetta was suddenly aware of her name being called. She turned round, holding her hand up to shield her eyes from the bright sunlight, and saw the tall figure of Nikhil Patel running towards her. He was wearing a suit and his gangly gait brought back a sharp memory of another sunny day, years ago, when she had watched him running along behind her open-topped wedding car, shouting, 'Don't marry James Allsop! Marry me!'

'I've just been to see you,' Nikhil panted, his hands on his knees to get his breath back. 'But nobody was in.'

'My father's up in London with Iris. He goes up quite a bit now to be with John, since Winston . . . Did you know?'

'Bruno wrote to tell me,' said Nikhil. 'I'm so sorry. I should have—'

'It's OK,' she said. 'Nobody knew what to say.'

They both looked out to sea for a few seconds.

'The whole world's changed, hasn't it?' said Fiammetta.

'I suppose it has,' said Nikhil, with a puzzled look, as if he hadn't thought that before. He spent his life dealing

425

with individual struggles, she thought, not the big picture.

They began to amble back towards the Harbour End together.

'What brings you to Kingshaven?' Fiammetta asked him.

'An unannounced visit to the old people's home. My father likes someone to check every so often, after Dr Ferry . . .'

'And was it OK?'

Nikhil nodded. 'And how are you?' he asked.

They were walking side by side, but with a definite distance between them, as if neither of them was quite sure where the boundary lay and both were careful not to intrude on the other's space. Fiammetta wasn't quite sure whether he was asking as a doctor, or a friend, and was surprised that she had two different answers.

'I feel fine physically,' she said. 'But I'm just not sure what I should be doing, if that makes any sense. I feel as if I should be doing something amazing because I've been given a reprieve, but I still feel I'm sort of in limbo . . . Do you want to come and have a cup of tea?' she asked.

In the confines of his white hospital surgery, Nikhil's smile stopped just behind his eyes. Here, in blustery air, Fiammetta could see many layers of emotion: pleasure, compassion and something else – not the simple boyish hope she'd seen there when they were teenagers, but a much more grown-up complexity of questions and desire.

She looked away, suddenly shy, and they walked the rest of the way back to the warehouse in silence, the tension only broken with a giggle when Nikhil sank straight down to the floor with a bump when he sat on the dilapidated sofa.

Fiammetta filled the kettle.

'Are you managing to do any work?' Nikhil asked. A formal politeness had returned to his voice.

'Would you like to see?' she asked.

The sequence of abstracts she had painted since living in the warehouse was unlike anything she had made before and she had not shown the work to anyone, because she couldn't work out what she thought about it. The abstracts were propped up round the walls of her childhood bedroom. Seeing them now as someone else might see them, she was still not completely confident, and wondered whether they were even finished.

'Did you do these since . . . since we last met?'

She nodded.

'But you *are* doing something amazing!' he told her.

'Really?'

'There's a sense of progress that's very slow and careful, then it speeds up, and the colours . . .'

She looked at the paintings, seeing things she hadn't seen before. 'Perhaps they are about recovery?' she suggested.

'I love them. I'd like to have them hanging in the department!' he said.

'You can if you like,' she decided instantly.

'They must be worth a lot of money,' he said. 'But I'm sure my father, if I asked him . . .'

'No, I'd like you to have them,' Fiammetta told him. 'If you genuinely like them,' she added seriously.

'I do, but—'

'You'd be doing me a favour.' Fiammetta was quite decided about it. 'Everyone's always going on about closure. I think it would be closure for me to get rid of these now. Why don't we ask Bruno to bring them over to you in his van?'

Now that she'd had the idea, she was keen to get the pictures out and start on something new.

'If you're sure?'

'I am sure,' she said.

Nikhil smiled at her again.

In his face, Fiammetta could still see the little boy he'd been, with the anxious look of an outsider; the serious teenager, with a growth of fine black hair above his top lip; the eager young man, who had held her hand so tightly in the crowd at Live Aid; the thwarted suitor who had run along behind her wedding car; the serious doctor in the white coat, whom she had trusted to save her life. The man standing in front of her was all of those people and yet somewhere along the line he'd become really good-looking as well.

'I've missed you,' she said simply.

'And me you,' he said.

They both looked quickly back at the paintings.

'Are you doing anything later?' Nikhil asked with a slight catch in his voice.

'What do you mean?' she asked.

'I wondered if you'd like to have dinner.'

'Is that allowed?' Fiammetta asked him. 'The thing is, I want you to be my doctor, and I don't see how you can if we're going out together.'

Nikhil laughed, and she thought for one horrible, humiliating second that she'd read the message in his eyes wrongly. She'd always been hopeless at flirting.

'You can't live your life thinking that you are going to need a doctor,' he said gently.

'Does that mean you can't be my doctor?' she asked.

'Does that mean you want to go out with me?' he fired back.

They were grown-ups now, not teenagers, but it was the same question he had asked her many years ago. She was much more certain of the answer now than she had been then.

'Yes,' she said. 'Yes, I think it does!'

Chapter Eleven

September 2002

'You must remember Miranda!' said Esther.

They were having lunch to celebrate Cat's birthday on the roof terrace of the Compton Club in Soho. It was just about warm enough to sit outside and the September sun was glinting on a golden angel that Cat had never noticed before perched on the top of one of the theatres near by.

'Didn't she want to be a film star?' Cat asked, trawling back through her memories of Lady Collingburn School for Girls. She seemed to remember Miranda giving a rather virginal performance as Sally Bowles in the school's production of *Cabaret*.

'Guess who she's married to!'

Cat shook her head.

'Nice-Boy Nigel! They have four boys under ten and live in St Alban's!' said Esther, who drew inordinate pleasure from revelations gleaned from the Friends Reunited website, especially when her peers' lives had not quite lived up to expectations. The combination of showing off and *schadenfreude* was irresistible.

'You must sign up!' Esther urged.

Cat didn't think so. She could already imagine her peers' judgement as to whether her life was a success or failure. Her partner was a leading political columnist and would probably be considered a surprisingly good catch for someone so gawky and shy. Being manager of the City branch of a minor chain of bookshops was a slightly underwhelming career, and she certainly wouldn't want to reveal that she had started writing, because it was far too soon to know whether it was any good or whether she would even finish it. The birth of a child would not be a cause for wonder, when most of the people Esther rediscovered on Friends Reunited seemed to have several children already.

Cat and Finn weren't the only couple who, on that fateful day the world now knew as 9/11, had made love with unguarded, unprotected passion as if it were the last time. The midwife had told her that there was a noticeable blip in the number of babies expected around her due date. Amelie's arrival in Cat's still-reeling world had felt like an affirmation of humanity.

Cat looked across at her baby, who was now asleep in Esther's arms after being paraded round the club by her proud godmother, and suddenly saw that her little face looked exactly like the one captured in a Silver Cross pram, which she had gazed at across the dining-room table during so many Sunday lunches. Amelie must be about the same age as she was when her mother had given her up!

Amelie had arrived a week early and had weighed six and a half pounds. She was on the fiftieth centile for length. For the past three months Cat's entire life had revolved around such facts, and yet she knew none of these statistics about herself. Had she been early or late, small or big for her age? Had they even kept statistics like this in 1968? How could anyone have handed over such a precious little being to someone else?

'What?' Esther asked.

'Nothing. It's just . . . I can't understand how my mother didn't want me.' She tried to say it lightly, but her voice became thick with tears.

'Perhaps she did want you,' Esther offered gently. 'She didn't have an abortion, did she?'

'Did they have abortions then?' Cat asked, sniffing.

'The Abortion Act was 1967. It probably wasn't common, but it was possible. Maybe she was really young and her parents made her give you up.'

There were facts that Cat could probably find out, but she wasn't sure that she wanted to. She had not talked to her parents about the adoption since her father had revealed it. Initially, she hadn't wanted to talk to them at all, but when she had discovered she was pregnant a strange kind of calm had settled on her, probably because of the hormones, and she didn't feel very angry any more.

Cat and Finn had dutifully visited her parents on Boxing Day. Their relief at seeing her and their delight at the news was so touching Cat couldn't seem to think of them as people who had lied to her, only as people who had loved her very much and taken care of her as best they could.

As Finn had pointed out on the way home, her parents had lived the formative years of their life during the war, and that kind of uncertainty must have had a profound influence. A generation of British people had been paralysed by fear and it was difficult to be angry with people who were frightened.

'Maybe she was poor and couldn't afford to keep you?' Esther speculated. 'Or maybe she was just unmarried. It was different back then.'

'The swinging sixties?'

'We think that it was all peace and free love, but it wasn't,' Esther told her. 'We made a programme about it. Loads of women were forced to give up illegitimate children in the sixties. It just wasn't the same then.'

There were other possibilities that nobody ever mentioned. Maybe her mother had been raped? Maybe she'd been a criminal? All these maybes. Cat knew that the time would come when she couldn't bear the not knowing any longer.

431

'Do you ever think about looking for her?' Esther asked, tuning into her thoughts.

'Not right now,' said Cat, gazing at Amelie. What was important now was being as good a mother as she could be to her own baby. Nothing was going to distract her from that. 'What about you?' she asked, trying to divert Esther away from the subject.

'What about me?' said Esther.

'Is there anyone . . . ?'

'Would I have sat here until pudding without telling you?'

'I thought perhaps James . . .' Cat looked around the roof terrace to make sure nobody could hear.

'James is a great fuck – oh, sorry!' Esther said, putting her hands over Amelie's ears, 'but he wants a nice girl who'll provide an heir.' She pulled a face. 'Not really me, is it? Anyway, my company is my baby at the moment.'

Esther's own production company was so successful she had bought the premises in Camden where she worked, as well as a weekend place in Suffolk. She was the only one of the Lady Collingburn girls, Cat thought, who had fulfilled her breathless ambition stated on the first day, and she'd done it by her early thirties.

'You know Friends Reunited?' Esther said.

Cat nodded, determined not to be persuaded to join however much Esther tried to cajole her.

'They're launching a new thing called Genes Reunited,' Esther informed her. 'Long-lost families will be able to put up their details and get back in touch. People who've been adopted too . . . I just thought it might make it easier for you, you know, if you ever did decide you wanted to find your real mother.'

'Thanks,' said Cat, staring at Amelie, wishing she would wake up now. Her breasts were beginning to feel full.

'Just a thought,' said Esther.

When Cat didn't reply, Esther couldn't resist revealing what it was she was really getting at.

'You will let me know if you do, won't you?' she said.

'What?' asked Cat, distracted.

'Decide to look for your birth mother?'

Cat looked up at her. She hadn't known Esther for twenty years without being able to tell when there was something else on the agenda.

'It's just . . . it's just that it would make a really interesting television programme,' said Esther.

*　　*　　*

'**45 minutes from attack!**' John read the headline on the *Evening Standard* that Michael bought from a vendor outside the Tube station as they were walking back from school. 'Who's attacking now?' he asked.

Michael scanned the front page. A dossier of Intelligence had been published suggesting that Saddam Hussein had weapons of mass destruction capable of being deployed in forty-five minutes.

Michael knew that you couldn't hide the truth from a child, because they were bound to hear about it at school. Iris's policy on any tricky subject she'd have preferred John not to find out about yet, whether it was sex, drugs or terrorism, was that she'd rather answer his questions than have him learn from someone else, but on this occasion Michael didn't know what he was supposed to say.

'There's a country a long way away, where there's a bad man who has some weapons . . .' he began.

'Is he going to attack us?' John interrupted.

'I hope not,' said Michael.

They walked down the street in companionable silence. Occasionally Michael caught a glimpse of their reflection in a shop window. He was always startled to see himself looking like an old man, his shock of white hair contrasting sharply with John's black curls. He didn't feel a very different person from when he'd last lived in this area of London with Claudia. There had been fewer cars in the sixties, and fewer people on the pavements, but he had always felt invigorated by the noise and the cosmopolitan vibrancy of the city. In London, there was nothing remarkable about a white grandfather with a mixed-race grandson. The streets were teeming with all races and nationalities. There were no foreigners here, Michael thought. Sometimes he wondered how on earth he and Claudia could have decided to return to Kingshaven.

'War is not a game,' John suddenly announced.

'Quite right!' said Michael. 'Did you learn that at school?'

John looked up at him as if he was crazy. 'Mummy told me when I wanted a gun.'

Michael couldn't help laughing.

'It's not funny!' said John, outraged. 'People can die!'

'Yes, I know.' Michael held a straight face. 'Anyway, it's a long way away,' he said, trying to move them on.

'Is it the same bad man who killed Daddy?' his grandson asked, obviously remembering the long-way-away excuse. He had exactly the same tenacity that Iris had had as a child when she suspected that adults were trying to fob her off with excuses. It had driven Sylvia mad, Michael remembered.

'No. No, it's not,' Michael told him. 'But the government are trying to make us think it is so we can fight him.'

John's intelligence tried to grapple with this information.

'That's stupid!' he finally said.

'You're right. It is very stupid.' If you couldn't explain the logic to a six-year-old child, how could it be the right thing to attack a sovereign country just because it might pose a threat in the future?

'Shall I write to Tony Blair?' John asked.

'I'm afraid it's his idea,' said Michael.

'How can we stop it, then?' asked John.

A year ago, Michael thought, when John was in his superheroes phase, he might have said, 'This is a job for Thunderbirds!' But John had grown up since then, made aware, at far too early an age, of the harsh realities of life.

'In my day, we used to try to save the world by marching,' Michael told him, anxious to find a positive spin. Usually John was easily diverted by stories about when Michael was young, but now his face was sceptical. Michael tried to explain. 'The idea is that lots of people march to the Houses of Parliament together, so the government can see that people don't agree with what they're doing, then they might change their mind.'

'Can we go marching?' John's eyes were shining with the prospect of a new adventure.

'If Mummy says so,' said Michael, hoping Iris wouldn't think he was putting ideas into John's head. As a veteran of the Anti-Vietnam war protests and Greenham Common, she surely wouldn't mind this early lesson in civil disobedience.

*   *   *

The sharp September sunshine was beginning to mellow, and the angel on the top of the theatre that Iris could see across the rooftops had lost its golden gleam.

In the penthouse office in Soho Square, Iris stared at the article on page seven of the *Evening Standard* headed **Pizza pioneer dies**.

Clive, who had been Iris's first proper boyfriend and the father of her daughter, had died of a heart attack at his villa in southern Spain. The picture showing a heavy man with thinning black hair made her feel sad as she remembered how handsome he had once been, driving around swinging London in his red sports car.

All the reasons for not looking for her daughter were now gone, she thought, as her eye stopped on an article on the opposite page entitled **Long-lost relatives only a click away**. Was it a sign?

Iris's phone rang.

'Yes?'

'It's Tony,' said her brother. 'How are you?'

'We're fine, thanks. Dad's staying.'

Iris knew she should probably ask Anthony and Marie round for Sunday lunch while her father was there, but she couldn't bring herself to. They were very generous with their invitations, but she always suspected that their motives were to do with associating themselves with Winston's memory. Sometimes Iris found it extraordinary that she still felt the same suspicion towards Anthony that had developed in childhood when he used to tell on her to their mother, Sylvia. Maturity had given her a veneer of good manners, but just underneath the skin she harboured the same raw resentment as when she was a child. How could she even think of trying to contact her daughter when she wasn't mature enough to have a grown-up relationship with her own brother?

'I was wondering what your thoughts were about Mr Patel,' her brother said, interrupting her chain of thought.

Anthony never called unless he wanted something.

'Fiammetta's living with his son,' said Iris. 'You should ask her.'

'Really?' said Anthony, but Iris wasn't fooled by his disingenuous tone. The phone call was obviously an effort to gauge whether the family connection would give him the excuse to approach the businessman for a donation, as Anthony seemed to occupy some unofficial fundraising role in the Party.

'I believe he's a good man, a philanthropist . . .' Iris said neutrally.

'Deserving of an honour, then?' Anthony suggested.

'Forgive me, but doesn't that sound a tiny bit close to something that used to be called corruption? Or is that just an Old Labour concept?' Iris asked.

'I've no idea what you're talking about,' said her brother.

'You will find your funds draining away if you keep on with this ridiculous drive to war,' Iris told him. 'I've given instructions to cancel all donations to the Party for the time being.'

'You're kidding!'

Iris felt a small twitch of triumph as she imagined his smooth features going white. So much for his family connections now!

'I'm perfectly serious,' she told him. 'You can hardly expect us to support that.'

She still thought of the penthouse office and the company as Winston's, her role simply that of caretaker, but she was beginning to make her own decisions.

'I wonder if Winston would have agreed with you?' Anthony speculated.

As her brother, he still possessed the uncanny ability to touch a nerve.

'Of course he would!'

Iris was almost sure. The boy who'd sat next to her on the school bus earnestly discussing civil rights and saving the world would have agreed. The man she'd bumped into in Grosvenor Square who'd cleaned blood from her wounds in his elegant squat would. The ambitious young entrepreneur who'd voted for Margaret Thatcher in 1979 probably wouldn't, but Winston had quickly seen the error of his ways. The ethical businessman who'd been involved in Live Aid would. But there was no getting away from the fact that Winston had been very close to the New Labour leadership.

The Prime Minister had invited Iris and John to Downing Street to express his condolences personally. Winston had been an important part of the New Labour project, he'd told her, and if there was anything at all he could do to help they must contact him. The offer had given John the mistaken belief that Tony Blair was a figure rather like Santa Claus, to whom one need only send a letter for wishes to be granted.

'I'd have thought you, of all people, would approve of deposing a vile tyrant,' Anthony was saying.

'I thought the argument was disarming him, not over-throwing him,' Iris countered.

'We're trying to get the UN involved . . . You should be supporting that!'

'Only to give you cover. It's still war, *war*, Anthony! Thousands of people will die. Have you really thought about that?'

'Thinking's the easy bit,' Anthony responded. 'When you're in government you have to decide what side you're on.'

'Well, if I had any doubt at all, you've just removed it,' Iris told him, putting down the phone.

The light outside was fading now and she didn't want to miss kissing John goodnight. It frightened him to go to sleep without seeing her, in case that meant she was never coming back, like Daddy.

Iris quickly checked her emails. There was a new one from Marvin Martin with the heading *Progress? It's possible.*

Having identified the likely corps of the 3rd Army that had been stationed in Kingshaven, Marvin had come up with nothing until he'd had the idea of putting the words D-Day and Kingshaven into an internet search engine and found an advertisement for a travel company that had organized a commemorative visit to Kingshaven on the fiftieth anniversary back in 1994, and was now taking bookings for a repeat visit for the sixtieth anniversary in 2004. Assuming that a veteran who remembered a 'romantic involvement' might be more likely to return, Marvin had obtained the names and addresses of the men who had participated in 1994. Several had since died, others objected to his line of questioning, but there was one man, coincidentally of African American origin, who had replied to his queries. His fiftieth-anniversary trip had been cut short by illness, he'd told Martin, but he was intending to return for the sixtieth anniversary. The man volunteered his fond memories of the town, and in particular of a woman who looked like Ingrid Bergman.

Iris often wondered why she'd never asked Winston if he had known, or suspected, who his mother was. Perhaps she hadn't wanted to know his feelings about a woman who had abandoned her child? Now, she couldn't think of any woman in Kingshaven who looked remotely like Ingrid Bergman, but there was always the possibility that the girl had not been from the immediate locality.

Iris's hand hovered on the mouse, trying to decide whether to click Reply.

There was no guarantee that this person Marvin had unearthed was anything to do with Winston, but he fitted the profile, and that made her a little panicky. She'd never properly considered the possibility that Marvin would actually find Winston's father, and suddenly she wished she had never got involved. In her brain she could almost hear her own mother's often repeated warning, 'Be careful what you wish for . . .'

If Iris went to America to meet the old man, as Marvin was suggesting, there was still the possibility that he would be the wrong person. But would that be better or worse than if he turned out to be the right person? What if she didn't like him? What if he were a supporter of George W. Bush? What if he wasn't at all the sort of grandfather she wanted John to have?

It was getting dark outside now.

There was no need to reply straight away, Iris told herself, shutting down her computer.

Outside the office window, the city sky was almost purple, the golden angel now lit by a beam of floodlight as twinkling lights of planes travelled soundlessly across the sky.

John was already in bed when Iris got home, and his room was dark and still. Not wanting to wake him, she kissed the tip of her finger and touched it against his temple.

He stirred. 'Mummy?'

'I'm here,' Iris whispered.

He sighed contentedly and turned over, puffing up a delicious waft of a just-bathed child. 'Mummy?' he asked drowsily.

'Yes?'

'Can we go marching?' he asked.

'If you like.'

'Mummy?'

'Yes?'

'Can we save the world?'

Epilogue

15 February 2003

It was a bitterly cold day, the sort of day that felt as if the sun had been switched off, but still they came. Iris looked across the sea of people pouring into Hyde Park. Two million, the police were saying, and the police always underestimated. It was not just the usual motley crew of students and socialists, Jesus freaks and peaceniks with Peruvian knitted hats who turned up at every protest she had ever been on, but normal-looking middle-aged women, and young people of all races and creeds, and elderly men, and families, lots of families, with children walking, and children in pushchairs. The mood was not angry, but quietly determined, and they carried placards that read NOT IN MY NAME, a simple, peaceful expression of democracy that she found profoundly moving. Surely Tony Blair must see this and listen.

*   *   *

'It feels like all the people you've ever met and liked are here somewhere,' Cat said to Finn as they finally reached the rally in Hyde Park, with Amelie in the pushchair in front of them. 'And everyone you've yet to meet is here as well.'

Cat had never been on a demonstration before, and she'd

expected it to be grim, possibly even dangerous, but there was a spirit of purposeful togetherness that made her feel warm in the bitter cold.

Far away on the platform, a woman was speaking.

'That's Iris Quinn,' Finn told her. 'I met her once.'

'What's she like?' asked Cat.

Finn thought for a moment. 'Brave,' he said. 'And fun. I think you'd like her.'

The public-address system wasn't very good, and there was so much cheering that it was difficult to hear what she was saying, but Cat thought she could make out words that chimed exactly with what she was thinking.

'It feels like the kind of moment that people will look back on and say, "Where were you?" And all of us will be able to say, "We were there!"'

Acknowledgements

Many people have supported and encouraged me through the five years of writing this trilogy. I am ever grateful to the kind and jolly team at Transworld – Larry, Linda, Emma, Judith, Claire, Bill, Janine, Patsy and everyone else who works so hard on my behalf – and I am indebted to my agent Mark and his colleagues at LAW. I am very lucky to have friends like Martha, Chris, and SJ and I thank them for their generosity. But overwhelming appreciation must go to the people who have had to put up with me on a daily basis since I started on this crazily ambitious project – my loyal and lovely sister Becky, my wonderful and witty mum Kath, my funny and fabulous husband Nick and my delightful and very dear son Connor. I love you in the world!

THE TIME OF OUR LIVES
by Imogen Parker

'A heartbreaking love story and a sweeping narrative
that captivates from first page to last.
Destined to become a classic'
Kate Mosse, author of *Labyrinth*

It is 1953. At the Coronation party at the Palace Hotel,
two lives are about to change forever.

Claudia – 16, beautiful, fragile and an outsider in this
small seaside town – finds herself talking to Michael, also
a newcomer, who is struggling with a rocky marriage.
Their instant, irresistible attraction to one another will
have consequences which stretch far into the future.

Against the ever-changing backdrop of events ranging
from grey post-war austerity to technicolour rock and
roll, from Suez to the summer of love, from Bill Haley to
The Beatles, from the buttoned-up glamour of the
fifties to the rebellious freedom of the sixties, *The Time
of Our Lives* is an intesely passionate love story and a
captivating chronicle of the times.

'As addictive as a good soap opera . . . A perfect
beach read'
Sunday Times

'Divinely readable . . . I wish I'd saved it for my hols'
The Times

9780552151535

THE THINGS WE DO FOR LOVE
by Imogen Parker

Remember the time when love was the answer, even when we didn't know the question?

It is 1969 and eight-year-old Julia Allsop wants to be a princess. But a fairytale wedding doesn't guarantee happily ever after and Julia will discover that life is more complicated than dreams of love, whatever love means . . .

Nineteen-year-old would-be feminist Iris Quinn hopes to carve out a successful career, but London in the seventies is full of other temptations, and a passionate clandestine affair threatens to destroy everything she believes in.

From glass slippers to glass ceilings via Glam Rock, *Grease* and Greenham Common, the destinies of two very different women and their families interweave across two decades, as Julia and Iris's quest for fulfillment begins to uncover the corrosive power of secrets.

9780552151559